MY DEAR BRANSON

MY DEAR BRANSON

Baker Street Legacy Book One

GAIL R. DELANEY

Praise for Gail R. Delaney

I am a huge Sherlock fan so this is an interesting twist on the Sherlock Holmes story.

N. Perkins, Reader

Another winner from Suspense author Gail R. Delaney. What a novel concept - a descendant of Sherlock Holmes, MI6 agent Grayson Oliver Sherlock Holmes, finds himself on a case in Boston, where he experiences adventure and love with the beautiful Kipling Branson. Romance with the feisty Kip takes Grayson out of his solitary, heart-breaking life. The lively male-female duo combine forces to crack another case. Hurrah! I can't wait to read Book #2 in the series.

Cheryl Williams, author of "Stairway to Heaven"

I can't say enough good things about this book! From the opening line to the closing, the story sucked me in and left me wanting to know more. Even the ending, with the unresolved question marks about the future simply tantalize with so many ideas of where Ms. Delaney might take the characters of Grayson Holmes and Kipling Branson, and their story, going forward.

Esther Mitchell, author of the Guardians Inc
paranormal romantic suspense series

Art
REQUIRES HEART
#SupportArtistsNotAI
www.GailDelaney.com

To Sir Arthur Conan Doyle, who initially created the literary legend known as Sherlock Holmes, and spoiled the name Sherlock to be used by anyone ever again. I am, of course, taking a certain level of poetic license here, and mean absolutely no disrespect for the original creator.

To the Grayson in my mind. Thank you for helping me breathe life into this man. And for confirming to me, without ever knowing what you confirmed, that I hadn't gone too far in making Grayson an eloquent and well spoken man. Such people do exist in nature.

To those people in my life who unwittingly made it exceptionally easy for me to write Grayson's subtle — and sometimes not so subtle — sarcasm and, quite frankly, condescension. He said 'aloud' the things I could only think, and release through him.

To William Scarborough, Sandra Sookoo, and Lynne Connolly for letting me use them as inspiration for certain characters, both blatantly and subtly. You're all good sports.

to Niall MacDomhnaill ailias MacCuinn , who helped me make Angus "Mac" Hennessey sound Scottish and not just an American trying to sound Scottish. All spelling and word usage came directly from Niall, so no one better say it's wrong. LOL

Book Content Expectations

Due to the nature of the genre and the storyline, please be aware there are instances of terroristic violence that may feel parallel to real-world events, as well as personal danger, violence, gun violence, and abduction. The characters struggle with PTSD, grief at the loss of someone close to them, and trauma.

Though in passing, and spoken from the point of view of a non-prominent character, there are themes of ableism against the main character regarding her hearing impairment.

Baker Street Legacy

Baker Street Legacy
Storytelling Style

Baker Street Legacy is a continuous timeline, in which any given book extends the story of the book prior to it and sets up for the next book while also telling its own story. The books must be read in order to have a full understanding of the saga.

This means each book has its own story arc, but also extends the greater story arcs.

There will be cliffhangers, but as the author, I will always provide you with a payoff within the book you're reading. Each book has its own plot, it's own storyline and its own resolutions. Each book (with the exclusion of the final book in the series) will have set up for the next book. These may or may not be considered cliffhangers by some. But, be aware, they exist.

I hope you enjoy and complete the journey with us.

Baker Street Legacy
Spotify Playlist

Do you like having a soundtrack to the books you read? I've created a playlist for the Baker Street Legacy on Spotify.

You will likely notice Grayson and Kipling are inclined toward the legends of jazz along with some popular contemporary crooners. A little Frank Sinatra and Nat King Cole; a little Michael Bublé and Colbie Calliat.

I hope you enjoy.

"We have solid intelligence on the current location of Nelson Howell and his associates. He is orchestrating a splinter group in Northern Ireland so extreme the Real Irish Republican Army has separated themselves from the members of the group. Much like Al Qaeda did with ISIS. Howell is definitely involved. I need your team in Belfast by the end of the week."

Grayson Holmes nodded, writing down notes on the intel Director Jeffrey Cooper relayed by phone. "I can be back to Vauxhall in thirty minutes and begin the planning."

"Not necessary, Holmes. We'll have a full debriefing in the morning over covers and legends. Intel says he's not ready to move yet, but soon."

"Lynne should get on it as soon as possible." Grayson set down his pen. "I would feel better if I came back in and began the process. A few hours can make an exceptional difference, especially when it comes to Howell. I want him this time, Jeffrey."

"We all want him, Holmes. You forget that fact."

"I've forgotten nothing. I'll contact Angus once I'm in; we won't need Sandra until morning. It's her wedding anniversary after all."

Jeffrey sighed through the mobile connection. "Part of me regrets having rung, but truth be told, I knew damn well you'd get on to this immediately."

"Of course you did, Jeffrey," Grayson said. "We both know it's the *precise* reason you rang rather than waiting until the debriefing. We will speak in the morning."

He tapped off the call and set the mobile on the desk, already sensing Liz's presence behind him in the bedroom doorway. Grayson finished writing his notes, nudging Watson's head out of the way twice. The bossy feline undoubtedly sensed Grayson's eminent departure, and did his best to express his dissatisfaction. Grayson pocketed the phone in his breast pocket, and stood as he turned from the chair. "I'm returning to Six. Not sure when I will be back."

He nearly passed her without contact, but paused to lean in for a kiss on her cheek. Grayson knew he lacked effort, his heart not in the challenge despite his acceptance that she deserved his attempt. She neither leaned into the touch, nor pulled away, but she never shifted her brown eyes to look him in the face.

Her body was tense, her arms crossed, and she pivoted on the balls of her feet to follow him as soon as he was beyond her.

"I made us a lovely dinner—"

"I know, and I'm sorry I can't stay to properly enjoy it. Please put some on a plate for me and I'll eat it when I return." He walked through the receiving room to the hall, and opened the coat closet to retrieve his trench coat. "You know I enjoy Indian food."

"Which is why I made it," she said, her voice tinged with a sad sigh. "I'd hoped we could sit and talk, Grayson. It's been so long since we did that. You're working so much."

He shrugged on his coat and drew a brolly from the stand by the door. "You've always known what I do, Liz."

She shook her head and crossed her arms again. Defensive. Protective. "Please don't toss that argument at me again, Grayson, we met in the bloody canteen!"

"What would you have me do, Liz? Hmm?" Familiar anger stirred in his chest, but he tried to tamp it back. The anger wasn't at her, and shouldn't be directed at her. But there were days it was so hard to keep it at bay, especially when the same, tedious arguments came to the front of the discussion. "The people I investigate don't care if it's Sunday afternoon, or if my girlfriend made a lovely dinner, or if I've caught cold or my mother is ill—"

"Or if you're in mourning."

He almost shouted, almost lashed out, but he clenched his jaw and fisted his hands, looking away from her before she received the reaction she wished to inspire. She'd already told him more than once she'd rather row with him than have his silence, but she had no idea how much better the silence was for her. For them. Instead, he slammed the tip of his umbrella into the hardwood floor, dinging the pale wood.

She walked to him, her footsteps a whisper, and drew the offending umbrella from his grip to lean it against the wall. Liz laid her gentle hand on his jaw, saying his name softly until he relented and opened his eyes, focusing on her. She was lovely, truly lovely, with long and straight blond hair, flawless skin and eyes that expressed so much more than her words often did. She went up on her toes to kiss him, but he only allowed a perfunctory peck before pulling back, immediately hating himself for the tinge of hurt her eyes reflected.

"I love you, Grayson. I truly do."

"I know," he replied, then swallowed, knowing she hoped for his affirmation; words that choked him and refused to be spoken when they were less than honest.

She pressed her lips together and took a step back, crossing her arms again. "Loving you isn't enough anymore. I can't be enough for both of us."

"I know," he said again, already knowing the conversation's course.

She nodded, tears slipping free. He reached again for the brolly and picked up his keys from the hall table. "I will be leaving tomorrow for a time, I don't know how long." Liz had stopped asking long ago questions like "Where?" and "How long?" knowing he wouldn't ever be able to answer her. "I will move out once I return. Would you please care for Watson?"

"Of course, but you don't have to–"

Grayson shook his head, and offered the only comfort he believed himself capable of by laying his hand on her arm. "There's no reason for your life to be disrupted any further," he said as gently as he could, meeting her broken gaze. "I'll return to Baker Street."

She sniffed and made a small, choked laughing sound. "Of course. Baker Street."

"It's logical."

"Logical. The proper course of action." She said the words like they were poison.

Grayson reached for the door handle, and paused before opening the door to the hall. He looked back, drew in a slow, regretful breath and sighed. "I'm sorry, Liz. Truly. I'm sorry."

Liz swiped viciously at her wet cheeks, looking off and away rather than at him, and nodded. "I know you are, Grayson. I know you aren't heartless, because I fell in love with your heart. But, I can't fix what's broken."

"No, you can't," he said, admitting the truth. "No one can."

Her tears choked her words, and she finally looked at him again. "Let me know when you've returned, and I'll go to Mum's. Good-bye, Grayson. I wish you well."

He smiled, knowing it would be anything but genuine but it was the best he could manage, and opened the door. Closing it behind him felt like the end punctuated by the click of the safety lock from the inside as Liz locked it behind him.

With determined steps, Grayson Holmes walked to the lift.

Chapter One

BOSTON UNIVERSITY
BOSTON, MASSACHUSETTS
EIGHT MONTHS LATER

"My flight is scheduled for tomorrow evening. I cannot escape this cold and miserable city soon enough," Grayson groused, pacing a two-meter route in the hall outside the lecture hall of Professor Frederick Crane, otherwise known as Grayson's great uncle. "I shall never again complain about the cold of London."

Sandra's light laughter carried through his mobile. "Oh, stop kvetching, Boss. You're just annoyed you have been asked to play the part of the Infamous Holmes for your uncle's class."

"Shut up," he ordered, only partially meaning it. Then he couldn't help a chuckle when he asked, "Did you just accuse me of *kvetching?*"

Sandra laughed again. "David and I have been spending a lot of time with Mrs. Abramowicz in the flat next door. She's wonderful. And you're kvetching."

Grayson huffed and circled again. "Three weeks of dancing

around with the FBI and the CIA – tell enough, but not too much, don't show your hand – my patience has worn thin. I am hardly in the proper mood to mold impressionable young minds."

"As opposed to what?" She laughed again. "Have fun, Boss. See you on Monday."

Grayson would have cursed her, but she'd already left the call. With a frustrated sigh, he slid the phone into his breast pocket and tucked his hands behind his back, stepping to the door of the classroom.

Inside, Uncle Frederick stood at the front of the classroom with perhaps forty students in attendance, a small class due to the advanced level of study in comparative literature. Some of the students clearly paid attention, others were on mobile devices or computers. Since Grayson's visit to the class was unannounced, he could not judge the level of student interest in his presence. He extended his arm to reveal his wrist from the cuff of his jacket, and bent his arm back to check the time. The class had begun five minutes earlier, so Uncle Frederick should be coming soon to retrieve him.

The sooner he finished this particular level of torture, the better. He did not join a clandestine agency to speak publicly; though his profession with MI6 would not be mentioned; rather, his family legacy. A legacy he wished at times he could escape, like today.

Uncle Frederick's voice carried through the lecture hall but standing outside Grayson only heard the occasional word or phrase. Enough to catch his uncle's telling of fictional characters not being so fictional, and the ever-shrinking world that excluded the ability to keep secrets. Grayson took one step back to move away from the door again when movement in the lecture hall caught his attention.

A young woman, perhaps thirty – which, based on the level of the class, likely made her a postgraduate or doctorate student – stood from her chair in the third row, and edged her way past the students between her seat and the aisle. Her long, chestnut brown hair waved softly from a clip at her crown, but much of her face was hidden with her chin tipped forward and the waves forming a curtain to hide her features. She had her hand tucked beneath her hair, near her ear, as if shielding herself from some unpleasant sound. When she reached the end of the aisle, she shouldered the strap of her computer bag and draped her coat over her arm, descending the three steps to the exit level.

She looked up as she approached the door, light amber eyes catching sight of him through the small window. Grayson pushed down the handle of the door, pulling it outward into the hallway so she could exit. As she stepped into the hall, she smiled at him, but immediately her features pinched and she canted her head to the side.

His uncle's voice carried clearly now. "Until thirty years ago, it was naturally assumed the Adventures of Sherlock Holmes were fictitious, based loosely on a man admired by Sir Arthur Conan Doyle by the name of Professor Joseph Bell–"

"Thank you," she said as he shut the door.

"Certainly." He nodded, stepping back so she could proceed on her way.

She took a few steps away from him, then seemed to stumble, mumbling a dainty "dang it" under her breath.

"Do you need assistance?" he asked, already walking towards her.

She turned, color blooming in her fair cheeks. She was exceptionally soft spoken, so much so Grayson had to strain to hear her from where he stood. "No, it's just – my hearing aids are acting bizarre. I need to go change the batteries, I think."

After spending a few weeks in Boston, Grayson had become accustomed to the aggressiveness of the non-rhoticity Massachusetts accent, with an adamant hatred for the letter 'r', and noted this woman's exceptionally mild version of the common speech pattern. The accent was there, but only a refreshing hint of it.

Grayson reached her, and only at her comment did he attempt a surreptitious glance at her ears, noting the small aids no larger than the end of his thumb nestled within the curve of her outer ear.

"Are you here to see Professor Crane?" she asked.

Grayson glanced back toward the door. "In a manner of speaking, yes. I'm here to address the class–"

The door opened, and Uncle Frederick emerged, glancing up and down the hall until he saw Grayson. He stepped into the hall, the door closing behind him. "Come on in, Grayson," he called, motioning for Grayson to head back. "We're ready for you."

Grayson turned back to the young woman. "Perhaps I will see you inside–"

A massive blast ripped through the hall, catapulting Grayson and the woman forward. He slammed onto the lino, all air painfully forced from his lungs. His vision blackened, and he tried to push up and catch sight of the woman and his uncle. Uncle Frederick was to his right, face down, blood running across his cheek. Grayson tried to move, his legs weighed down, and he looked back to acknowledge the portion of wall across the back of his thighs. Sound snapped into existence again, and the screams of panic and fear overrode everything. He blinked, fighting the impending loss of conscious-ness, and caught sight of the woman a few feet further down the hall, lying on her back. He could see nothing of her face or her injuries.

Blackness slipped over his vision and his cheek hit the lino.

"What the hell were you even doing here?" demanded FBI Agent Burke DiMatto, his voice cutting through Grayson's pounding head. "Geez, this has gone from Boston Police to federal jurisdiction like that." He snapped his fingers.

"So sorry to complicate your evening," Grayson managed to say without growling. He held the cool pack to the back of his head where a chunk of wall had apparently grazed him in its flight across the hall. "Had I been aware of your prior commitments, I would have asked whomever is responsible to please allow me to leave before detonation and save you the inconvenience."

He didn't give a damn if his sarcasm angered the other agent, or not. Burke – a truly appropriate name, as far as he was concerned since he considered the man a complete birk, idiot, wanker, an ongoing plethora of terminology – DiMatto was not worth the effort of curbing his tongue. DiMatto had been in rare form since arriving at the university, even more of a tosser than usual. Grayson still swallowed the bitter taste of adrenaline at the back of his throat, and his guts were twisted. He couldn't still the too-rapid thump of his heart, even though the explosion had been three-quarters of an hour previous.

"Seriously, though, Holmes. What were you doing here?" Agent Patrick Flannery asked, his arms crossed over his chest in an effort to fend off the bitter cold.

"Whether relevant or not, I was here at the request of my uncle, Professor Frederick Crane, the teacher of this particular class," Grayson explained. He attempted to raise his head and look at Flannery, but the motion made his skull pound. "He asked me to speak to his students."

"And you just happened to be here when a damn bomb goes off," DiMatto mumbled.

"What one has to do with the other remains to be seen, though I do not consider it improbable I may have been the target. The question then arises how would someone with the intent of harming me know I was going to be here since my invitation was private. The class itself was not aware of my attendance." Grayson intentionally focused his inquiry to Flannery, who at least seemed to be a moderately decent bloke despite his unfortunate partner assignment. "How many are injured? How is my uncle?"

"The explosion killed seven students, all kids in the first couple of rows. Four additional students are critically injured, and another half dozen or so are gettin' treatment for less serious injuries. Some were near the back of the lecture hall."

"And my uncle?"

Agent Flannery flinched and shook his head. "I'm sorry, Holmes."

Grayson closed his eyes and swallowed. Frederick Crane was his great uncle on his mother's side, and in truth he had very little personal connection with the man other than the occasional visit when he and his family came to the States. Nonetheless, the idea of calling his mother with news of another family member gone made his chest ache and his throat tighten.

"Have any of the surviving students been able to provide any information?" he asked through clenched teeth, hoping to divert his own attention.

"Not really," Flannery answered. "The worst injured have been taken to Mass General already. There are only a few students left."

"What do we know thus far?"

"This isn't your investigation," DiMatto cut in. "Leave the details to us. We'll let you know–"

Grayson propelled forward off the tailgate of the ambulance, looking down his nose, chest to chest, with the arse. "Step off!" Grayson shouted, and to his satisfaction, DiMatto took a step back, but not without one hand going for his sidearm.

Typical American. Gun first, consequences later.

"Hey!" Agent Flannery yelled, shoving them both away from each other. "Christ almighty, what the hell."

"I always knew that British stiff upper lip was a crock of–"

"I said enough!" Flannery ordered again.

Grayson stepped back and turned away, rubbing his palms over his face. Only then did he note the scratches and cuts on his palms and the back of his hands, likely from debris. Behind him he heard the hushed argument between the younger and older agents, but had to focus more on regaining his control. It has been months since he'd had to tamp down the rush of rage that made him lash out, not since...

Not since the last time he faced death.

He focused on the cold biting his skin to cool his anger, closed his eyes, and pressed his hands together in front of his mouth. When the urge to chin DiMatto eased enough he could again speak, he turned to the men and opened his eyes.

"Have you considered the fact I may be intrinsically involved in this situation?" Grayson said with as much calm as he could muster. "Until we know the target, the purpose, and the instigator I would say I am very much involved in this investigation."

Agent Flannery shot an angry glance to his partner, then sighed, his breath curling in front of his face in the cold air. "We only have preliminary information. The explosive was inside the lectern stand. It was hefty, enough that if anyone had been standing there it would have torn them apart. The only thing that saved some of the kids was the distance from the lectern to the first row of seats. It looks like it was designed to kill someone in particular, not take out the room."

"So, in essence, the target was likely either Professor Frederick Crane – a tenured teacher with no known enemies, or–"

"You," Flannery finished and shrugged.

DiMatto cursed and turned on his heels, storming away. Since arriving in Boston, Grayson and Burke DiMatto had butted heads, and he had looked forward to being free of the man. That opportunity was gone, in all likelihood, for the foreseeable future.

"There was a young woman in the hallway with us," Grayson said, returning to the back of the ambulance. Someone had found his overcoat, and he picked it up to slide his arms into the sleeves. Muscles pulled across his back, and his back and leg muscles twinged in revolt when he stepped off the tailgate.

He'd had worse injuries; but that didn't lessen the immediate discomfort. And was nothing compared to the pain in his chest. Not a physical injury, but painful all the same.

Agent Flannery shook his head and looked around at the chaos of emergency vehicles and paramedics seeing to the students that remained. "She could be still here, could have gone to the hospital already. You know her name?"

"I hadn't been inclined to ask at the time." Buttoning his coat, Grayson drew in a frigid breath and squared his shoulders. He glanced toward DiMatto. "If there is no justifiable objection, I intend to look amongst those remaining. I would like to locate her if I am able."

DiMatto opened his mouth, but Agent Flannery raised his hand in a silent demand for DiMatto to shut up. "Yeah, go ahead, but if you need to be checked out more–"

"I will return," Grayson agreed.

Clenching his jaw against the painful hitch in his step, Grayson moved from emergency vehicle to emergency vehicle, momentarily pausing to listen and observe. Though it would likely be useless to question any of the victims now, he waited to hear if they might impart anything possibly useful he might wish to pursue. The first two had been seated together, possibly boyfriend and girlfriend, Steven and April, he assumed, by the way they called out for each other. The third was a young man who just kept shaking his head to each question, his eyes glazed and wide. He was too deep in shock to answer questions, and even if he could, it wasn't likely he'd remember anything. His socks were mismatched, his eyes bloodshot, and he hadn't shaved in two days; he most likely couldn't recall what class he'd attended that day or what day of the week tomorrow was.

He slowed a couple meters from the next vehicle, a moment of relief hitting him when he recognized the woman from the hallway. She sat within the ambulance on the tailgate, a blanket wrapped around her against the bitter January cold. She was relatively calm in comparison to others, her attention intent on the paunchy man treating the cuts along her cheeks. She made direct eye contact whenever he spoke. When she answered his questions, she spoke so low he had to ask her the same question twice. Behind Grayson the ambulance prepared to leave, flipping on its sirens and she visibly flinched, her hand slipping from beneath the blanket to cup over her ear.

She'd mentioned her hearing aids before the explosion, and while he had no personal idea how such mechanisms would react in the chaotic sound, he imagined it was likely unpleasant. Unseen, Grayson took a few moments to categorize other details he'd not acknowledged in the hallway. The swirling lights and otherwise dim illumination hindered his ability to see her properly. He approached from her right, staying outside her direct line of vision. It was difficult to determine much about her with the blanket bundling her, but based on her seated form and what he remembered, he anticipated her at just under five and a half feet tall, and maybe nine stones two or three. Her brown hair, tossed and tousled by the explosion, fell in heavy, damp tendrils around her shoulders, wavier now from the precipitation in the air.

"I recommend a ride to the hospital, ma'am," the EMT instructed, finishing a wrap around her wrist. "You took a hard hit, and the floor in there is concrete under the linoleum. You can't be too careful with head injuries."

"Please be sure anyone with more serious injuries is taken first," she told him, her voice barely loud enough to carry to Grayson. When the Latino man scowled, she took in a breath and sat up straighter, projecting her voice a little louder this time. "I'll be fine until an ambulance is free."

He nodded and tugged the blanket around her, his last act of ministration before moving away to the next patient.

As soon as he was away, the young woman released her trembling hand from the blanket and braced her head with her palm against her brow. She closed her eyes, taking several sharp, shallow breaths.

Kip looked up at the sound of another voice, familiar but unknown. The tone was muffled like he spoke from behind glass, the wail of sirens and vehicles overpowering everything else. Her aids had long since switched to dampening the high decibels, which in turn muffled everything except her own voice, which echoed in her ears like talking into a barrel. The man she'd spoken to in the hallway outside the lecture hall stood at the bumper of the truck to her right, wearing a long, black wool coat with a red tartan scarf wrapped around his throat and tucked into the collar.

"What?" she asked, trying to focus on his lips.

Her insides had been shaking since she shook off the black haze of hitting the ground, smothered in chaos and sound and panic. She hadn't been able to bring herself to look too far around the corner to the destruction, afraid of what she might see. She had heard the talk – at least half a dozen dead, if not more. Her stomach clenched painfully and she had to swallow hard. Lightheaded, she slid her other arm beneath the blanket to hang on to the truck so she wouldn't tip sideways.

He came away from the bumper, the shift of light from the emergency vehicles to the glow of the interior of the truck, bringing his face into focus. In the hall she'd been too intent on finding somewhere to deal with her hearing aids that she hadn't taken in most of the details. His features were angled with dominating cheekbones. A late day's dusting of auburn stubble accentuated a sharp prominent jaw line and defined mouth. Auburn hair, almost light enough to be called dark ginger, fell in chunky, thick curls across his forehead like it had been set out of control by the damp air.

"Take a deep breath," he said, his eloquent accent a challenge – British, but city or region she couldn't say other than it was a common accent – until she focused on his lips for a few words. She'd noted the accent before, but the hall had been quiet and the only interference the damn clicking in her ears. His voice was a deep baritone, almost disproportionate to his tall, lean frame. Reading the words on his lips was different than anyone she'd encountered; he spoke with his lower lip, his defined upper lip not moving much to enunciate the words. "Count to four. Release it. Count to four," he instructed, stepping in front of her but back enough she didn't need to crane her neck to see him. "It will help with the adrenaline release."

She shifted her focus from his mouth to his eyes. Kip had spent most of her life forcing herself to pay close attention to the expressions of the people she spoke with, and with that required attention to detail came the side effect of often noticing the minute details of a person's features: their mouth and the way they moved it, their own tendency to make or avoid eye contact, and the details of their eyes where she often saw just as much communication as in the words they spoke. This man's were striking; a stormy mix of greens and blues so unusual they seemed unnatural, uneven, and they had the slightest upward tilt at the outer corners. What she saw beyond the color, and the shape, was the reserve.

Kip blinked to clear her thoughts and did as he said, watching him as he watched her to make sure she did as he instructed. Three or four breaths later, she did feel less lightheaded, though her insides still twisted with tremors. All the while, he watched her. One corner of his mouth quirked when she looked at him again.

"Feeling better?"

Kip nodded and tugged the blanket tighter around her. They had said she couldn't yet wear her coat so they could examine her hand and arm more easily, to assure nothing had been broken, and despite the woolen blanket she felt exposed and chilled. The coat was likely a lost cause anyway. She only hoped her laptop, bundled in her padded briefcase, survived the hit. She couldn't afford a new one right now.

"It might take a while yet, but then you'll sleep for several hours," he told her, and again she had to focus on his mouth to put the sound with the movements.

There was too much noise, and her aids couldn't figure out where to focus the magnification, instead switching from a muffled mumble to apparently magnifying everything. She wondered if the programming had been affected by the blast and the fall. They were designed to instantly buffer loud, sudden sounds, but every tech had its limitations. Kip blinked and shook her head. She couldn't keep a thought.

"What is your name?"

She raised her head from staring at his black, polished shoes – strange shoes for this weather. "Kip. Kip Branson."

His head canted a slight degree. "Kip. Is that a nickname?"

"Short. For Kipling."

"Unusual name."

"Better than Rudyard if I were a boy," Kip said, giving her pat answer.

He chuckled a deep baritone that cut through the excess noise. "Quite right," he said with a nod, then grew serious again. "How are you?

She blinked again, the only act she could seem to focus on properly. How was she? What a bizarre question, but she tried to focus on the most obvious intent of it. "I'll be fine," she answered, avoiding the urge to nod because of the pounding behind her eyes.

"They said I banged my head pretty good, so I should be checked, but I think I'm fine. What about you?" Then she gasped. "What about Professor Crane?"

He took a step closer to her, coming more fully into the light cast from the interior of the ambulance, and there was no mistaking the strain around his eyes. She'd noted a reserve about him when they spoke in the hall, but this was more. "The paramedics and emergency staff are still cataloguing all the injured."

"Are you with the police?" she asked. A dull headache bloomed in the spot between her eyes, with a promise to get worse before it got better. Then she remembered he'd said he was there to speak to the class. A police officer wouldn't come to speak to a post-graduate comparative literature class. "I can't help notice you're not from Boston."

A quick upward tip of one corner of his mouth preceded his answer. He tugged at the lapel of his coat to reach inside, bringing out a leather bifold. He opened it and held it out for her to read, and in the dim light all she made out was the "Secret Intelligence Service" across the top. "Though this isn't representative of my purpose here at the university," he added. "It does allow me to assist in the investigation."

"Welcome to Boston," Kip said before her jumbled brain told her this might not be the best time for sarcasm.

He flipped the wallet closed, an almost indiscernible smile tugging at one corner of his lips, and extended his hand to Kip. She snaked her arm free of the blanket and took it, the warmth of the grip a contrast to the cold. He adjusted his hold to avoid the worst of her bandages while still taking her hand. "Grayson Holmes."

She arched an eyebrow. "And you think my name is unusual, Agent Holmes?"

"Agent is an American designation." As he spoke, he unwound the tartan scarf from his collar and draped it around her neck over her hair. The soft cotton was warm, and the subtle aroma of sandalwood and shave cream drifted to her through the cold air.

Kip tugged the ends of the scarf into the blanket, appreciating the gesture. "Thank you."

He didn't acknowledge the thanks, flipping up the collar of his coat in the absence of his scarf. "Might I ask, did you notice anything or anyone unusual before you left the hall?" he asked.

Kip tugged the blanket around her, avoiding with all she had the urge to glance toward the building. "No. Professor Crane began his lecture, but I had to step out."

"Because of your hearing aids…"

She realized, with a hard twist of her gut, what she thought to be shadows in the snow were actually stains of red. Kip blinked and forced her attention away from the scene. "I'm sorry, what?"

"You mentioned in the hall you were having an issue with your hearing aids," he repeated.

" I…" Kip tilted her head, her right ear buzzing as if to remind her. She slid a hand free of the blanket to twirl her cold fingers near her ear. "I thought maybe the batteries were running low or something. I was going to step out and change them."

"You thought," he repeated. "Is that not the case?"

Kip shook her head. "They're working perfectly fine now. Almost too well," she added with a wince. Her ears hurt, thumped, and she wanted to work her jaw to pop the pressure bubble she knew didn't exist. Or shouldn't. Like ascending in a plane. She almost wished they *would* conk out on her, then she'd have an excuse to shut out all the noise.

"In what way were they malfunctioning?"

Kip tucked her hand back into the blanket. "They were clicking, and I heard this low hum. Maybe a buzz. Just an unusual sound. But the clicking was annoying."

"Was it a pattern? Constant?"

Kip nodded. "A constant rhythm." She mimicked the noise, clicking her tongue in her cheek, each click a second apart.

"You were seated near the front of the hall, correct?"

"Second row, center. The acoustics are bad for me in that hall, so if I sit near the front I can see the speaker's face." She winced at the over-explanation.

Mr. Holmes nodded and tugged open the front lapel of his coat to reach for an inside pocket again. "Miss Branson, I would like to speak to you again once you are feeling better. May I?"

She nodded, taking the card he offered, glancing down at it. It confirmed his name was, indeed, Grayson Holmes, and offered a number and extension, as well as an alternative cell number, though the card said mobile. The number was Boston. She looked up at him again. "Anything I can do to help; I just don't see what else there is."

"You might be surprised." He reached into his coat again, removing a small notebook. "May I have your contact information?"

She gave it to him, and as she finished, the EMT returned, telling her she now had a ride to the hospital. Kip shifted forward to step off the back of the emergency response vehicle, and Mr. Holmes immediately offered his hands as support until she stood on the slick ground.

"Thank you," she said and reached for the scarf around her neck.

"Please." He stopped her hands with his. "I insist."

Kip nodded and stepped away with the EMT, until Mr. Holmes called out "Miss Branson."

She turned back to catch his last step as he crossed to her again. He stood close, enough she heard his voice through the chaotic din drowning her once she stepped clear of the alcove made by the vehicles, so she had to tip up her chin to see his face.

"Should there be anything you need, anything I can assist you with, don't hesitate to contact me."

She nodded her confirmation, the sirens now cutting through her head like a hot poker, and let herself be led away. A final glance back confirmed that Mr. Holmes stood in the same spot, watching her until the doors to her ambulance closed and blocked her view.

Kip glanced at the young girl who shared the ride with her, the poor thing looking frightened out of her mind, and hoping her smile did some good.

With a jerk, the ambulance pulled away from the carnage.

Chapter Two

Kip had no idea what time it was when she opened her eyes, only that the sunlight beyond her bedroom curtains was bright enough to lighten the room, even with the blinds mostly closed. She stretched, every muscle and joint screaming its protest at the movement, and rolled onto her back. The alarm clock beside her bed said 3:45, and she groaned. She hadn't made it home until 11:00 the night before, but had promptly fallen into bed, the exhaustion Grayson Holmes had warned her about already firmly set into her limbs long before the ER doctor released her and her father led her to their car.

Nearly seventeen hours of sleep, and she felt like she'd just crawled into bed. With a groan, she tossed back the blankets and sat up. It took another couple minutes to convince herself to stand. She stumbled around the foot of her bed and to the door, opening it to look into her apartment. Her father sat on her couch, watching television, and her mom was at Kip's tiny, two person kitchen table.

"Mom," she said, hoping she projected her voice enough.

Her mother looked up and smiled, waving before she signed, *"How are you feeling?"*

"Not sure yet," Kip answered, leaning her head against the doorjamb. "I'm going to shower."

Her mother nodded, and she shut the door. The doorknob clicked in her hand, letting her know it'd latched, and she mostly stumbled into the bathroom adjoined to her bedroom. It took a few minutes to remove the bandages on her hand and wrist, and she leaned over her sink to hold back her hair and examine the bruise along her hairline and the scrape on her cheek. Her aches were explained as she undressed, finding multiple bruises along her hip and side where she'd hit the pavement. Before turning on the water, she took two over-the-counter painkillers.

The shower revived her enough for her to realize she was absolutely starving. It had been well over twenty-four hours since she'd eaten anything. Even then, it had been a bagel from Dunkin' and a coffee.

She brushed out her wet hair, wincing when the teeth of her brush skimmed the lump on the side of her head, and automatically reached for the small silver case on her vanity holding her hearing aids, but stopped. The ER doctor had recommended she avoid wearing them, if possible, for at least forty-eight hours. The blast had forced pressure into her ear canals, and the aids had only made it worse, which had been why her ears hurt so badly in the aftermath. Even now, they ached.

When she left her bedroom again, her parents were in the kitchen, the tantalizing aroma of grilled cheese filling the small South End apartment. Mom turned from the stove and set a plate on the table beside a glass of milk while her dad took the opportunity to wrap her in a firm bear hug, the kind that made her gasp for breath, but the kind that made her feel five years old again and completely safe. Jack Branson was a big man, and when she was little, there hadn't been anything more wonderful than curling up in his big lap and sleeping away a Sunday afternoon.

He pushed her shoulders back so she would look at him. "How are you doing, Princess?" she read from his lips.

Kip smiled and nodded, putting as much conviction in her voice as she could muster. "I'm fine, Dad. Really. Tired, and a little sore, but I'm fine."

He shook his head, his wrinkled expression making his frown lines more prominent. "I hate where this world is heading. It's wrong when going to school in the United States might mean risking your life. You'd think this was Afghanistan or Iraq. They've said nothing on the news about what the police are doing to find whoever did this."

Her mom tapped her shoulder so she'd turn. "Come eat," and sat in the other chair. "*You received a call, an agent with the FBI. He is coming by to talk with you about what happened. I didn't realize the FBI was involved.*"

Her mom's signing was jaunty, out of practice, and Kip had to infer the parts and spots her mother missed, even though her mom's signing leaned more to Signed Exact English rather than ASL. They hadn't relied on sign language since Kip was twelve, before Kip received a decent pair of hearing aids that didn't make her head want to explode. Thankfully, technology had come a long way.

After chewing and swallowing her first bite of the grilled cheese, Kip wiped her mouth to reply. "Did he say his name?" Her mother shook her head and shrugged, which meant he might have but her mother didn't pay enough attention to remember. She loved her parents dearly, quirkiness and all. Only "quirky" would think to name their only child after their favorite author, and it could have been worse. They could have loved Fyodor Dostoyevsky or Vladimir Nabokov.

"Mr. Holmes, maybe?" she tried again. Though he wasn't strictly FBI, she wondered if he'd designate himself as such considering the situation. She had heard of the Secret Intelligence Service in the UK, but what that meant and what they did, she honestly didn't know.

Her mother did the same thing. Shake and shrug.

"When?" she asked before taking another bite.

"*Some time this afternoon.*"

"Not much afternoon left."

Her mother opened her lips to speak, but stopped and glanced toward the apartment door. "Someone is here," forgetting to sign. "Holmes. I certainly think I would have remembered that name. Your father loves Conan Doyle."

The sudden flutter in her stomach surprised her, and she ran her fingers through her damp hair, already falling in thick, untamed waves. Some moisturizer and a comb through her hair barely qualified her for receiving company.

"Good grief," she mumbled and pushed back her chair, but her mother was already at the door.

Kip stopped short when she saw two unfamiliar men standing in the hall, dressed in dark suits and equally dark overcoats speaking to her mother. One was middle aged with Italian features, a thin mustache, and gray peppering what hair he had around his temples, his bare pate exposed to the cold. The other man was probably about thirty-five, shorter but slighter of build with dark red hair and green eyes. Both shifted their attention from her mother to her when she stepped into view. Mom turned, and spoke as she signed and spelled out their names.

"Kip, this is Agent DiMatto and Agent Flannery. Agent DiMatto is the one who called earlier."

Once her mother finished, she looked to them, and immediately the hair on the back of her neck stood up and heat flashed up her throat. The look of derision absolutely clear and without the possibility of misinterpretation on Agent DiMatto's face was one Kip had seen more than once in her life, right after someone realized she was hearing impaired. She set her jaw and took a step forward, signing to her mother.

She knew how to play the game; she had plenty of practice.

"Please ask them if Grayson Holmes is part of the investigation, and if so, why isn't he with them."

Her mother arched a single eyebrow before schooling her features. She took a step back to be in a position of translation, facing both Kip and the agents. She signed as she relayed the message.

"My daughter is asking about a Grayson Holmes, and would like to know why Mr. Holmes didn't accompany you."

Agent DiMatto's nose flared and his shoulders bounced; a dismissive huff. "It hasn't been determined what part Mr. Holmes will play in this investigation, if any."

Kip allotted a quick glance to her mother to maintain the illusion, but read every word on Agent DiMatto's lips. She did her level best not to snarl her lip. He didn't answer the question.

Agent DiMatto turned fully to her mother, no longer even looking at Kip. She could still see his face, though, so she caught every word. "We're sorry to have bothered you and your daughter, Mrs. Branson. We are speaking with all witnesses to determine if they have any information of use." His dark eyes shifted to her, any attempt at even a feigned smile gone. "We won't bother you further."

Her mother relayed the information, but Kip didn't look toward her, staring only at the two agents. She signed one more question before crossing her arms. "*What do you want to know?*"

"Often witnesses see or notice things they don't realize are important," Agent Flannery said. "We are speaking with anyone there who might—"

"Again, we apologize for the intrusion," Agent DiMatto interrupted. He nodded toward Kip's mother, then turned toward his partner, speaking as he went, quite likely in whisper. "This is a waste of time. She's deaf as a—"

Anything else he said was lost when he turned his back fully on Kip and took a step down the hall.

"Geez, Burke, don't be such a jackass," Agent Flannery said after his partner, then his head jerked when he caught Kip still staring at him.

His lips twitched together and he glanced down the hall after his departing partner, then took a step toward Kip, his hand coming out of his pocket with a card scissored between his fingers. "I apologize, Ms. Branson. If you think of anything that might be of assistance…"

Kip took the card without looking down at it and slid it directly into her pocket. "I doubt it," she said aloud, and didn't feel any guilt at the flush of color that overtook the Irish agent's fair face before she shut the door.

THIS TRIP HAS TURNED INTO A PROPER MESS, GREG. I WAS NEARLY ON MY WAY HOME AFTER THREE MISERABLE WEEKS DEALING WITH THE FBI AND CIA AFFILIATES HERE IN BOSTON. I SWEAR, EVERYONE HAS THEIR BLOODY HEADS STUCK IN THE SAND OVER ISIS, BOTH SIDES OF THE POND. WE HAVE ALL SAT AROUND WITH OUR THUMBS UP OUR ARSES TRYING TO PRY INFORMATION FROM THE OTHER SIDE WITHOUT GIVING AWAY TOO MUCH ON OUR OWN.

I WAS HOURS AWAY FROM GOING HOME – HOURS – THEN LAST NIGHT, THERE WAS A BOMBING AT ONE OF THE UNIVERSITIES HERE. I WAS THERE TO SPEAK WITH A CLASS OF POST-GRADUATE ENGLISH STUDENTS AT THE REQUEST OF MY UNCLE. I DON'T KNOW IF YOU EVER MET HIM, GREG, SINCE HE'S ON MUM'S SIDE OF THE FAMILY. HE IS – OR WAS – A PROFESSOR HERE. HE DIED LAST NIGHT, AND I HAD TO CALL MUM JUST A BIT AGO TO TELL HER. THE WORST OF IT IS, I COULDN'T GIVE A REASON.

IT'S TOO SOON FOR MORE LOSS. TOO SOON, THE WOUNDS TOO RAW.

I HONESTLY BELIEVE IT WAS NO COINCIDENCE I WAS THERE, BUT WITH THAT BELIEF COMES THE QUESTION AS TO HOW WOULD SOMEONE WITH THE INTENT OF DOING ME HARM KNOW I'D EVEN BE THERE. I HADN'T DISCUSSED THE GUEST LECTURE WITH ANYONE OTHER THAN UNCLE FREDERICK. WHILE HE WAS REQUIRED TO CLEAR MY PRESENCE WITH THE UNIVERSITY, IT IS MY UNDERSTANDING THERE WAS NO HESITATION ON THEIR PART. UNFORTUNATELY, THE NAME OPENS DOORS. THERE SEEMS NO OTHER CONCLUSION AS MY UNCLE HAD NO KNOWN ENEMIES,

AND UNLESS WE DISCOVER SOME OBSCURE LINKS TO CERTAIN STUDENTS IN THE CLASS, IT ALL CIRCLES BACK TO ME.

WHICH MEANS I AM LIKELY STUCK HERE IN BOSTON UNTIL THE QUESTIONS ARE SUFFICIENTLY ANSWERED. I HAVE ALREADY SPOKEN WITH DIRECTOR COOPER, WHO HAS VERIFIED WITH DIRECTOR STANTON HERE THAT I AM TO "SET UP A SEMI-PERMANENT RESIDENCE" HERE IN THE FBI BUILDING. OF COURSE, THAT EQUATES TO REMOVAL FROM MY BAG OF THE ONE PHOTO I BROUGHT, AND PLACING IT BACK ON MY BORROWED DESK.

I DON'T EXPECT ANSWERS, BUT SOMEHOW PUTTING IT ALL DOWN IN TEXT HELPS ME SORT IT OUT. IT'S NOT AS GOOD AS TALKING OUT THE FACTS WITH YOU, GREG, BUT IT'S SOMETHING AND RIGHT NOW I'LL TAKE WHAT I CAN.

IT'S NOT BAD ENOUGH I'M FIGHTING THE REAPER ON THIS ONE, GREG; I'M FIGHTING THE AMERICANS. I TOLD YOU OF DIMATTO AND FLANNERY, AND WHILE FLANNERY SEEMS LIKE AN UPRIGHT BLOKE, DIMATTO IS AN ARSE. HE HAS MADE IT CLEAR MY PRESENCE HERE OFFENDS HIM, AND HE FIGHTS ME AT EVERY TURN, EITHER BLATANTLY OR NOT. THE IDIOT DOESN'T UNDERSTAND I'M NOT HERE TO TAKE HIS JOB; I'LL BE BACK IN LONDON AS SOON AS POSSIBLE. BESIDES, THE MAN RETIRES FROM SERVICE IN LESS THAN A FORTNIGHT.

ENOUGH OF DIMATTO AND HIS IGNORANCE.

THERE IS ONE ELEMENT OF THE SITUATION LAST NIGHT THAT STICKS IN MY MIND, THOUGH I'M NOT SURE IF IT WILL BE ANY HELP IN THE LONG RUN. A YOUNG HEARING-IMPAIRED WOMAN WAS PRESENT LAST NIGHT WHO TOLD ME HER HEARING AIDS WERE MALFUNCTIONING JUST BEFORE THE EXPLOSION. I SUSPECT HER APPARATUS WAS INADVERTENTLY RECEIVING ELECTRONIC FEEDBACK FROM THE ACTIVATED DEVICE BEFORE THE DETONATION. IT MAY BE NOTHING OF USE, BUT PERHAPS RESEARCH INTO HER PARTICULAR AIDS MIGHT GIVE US INSIGHT INTO THE BOMBS THEMSELVES WE LACK OTHERWISE.

I intend to contact Miss Branson and inquire about the details, but I felt it best to give her a day or two after the incident to find her bearings again before I discuss it further with her. She seemed clever and maintained her composure even in the chaos. This gives me hope she may recall more than the average student flustered from the experience.

Though, as you know, the impact may come later.

Her name is Kipling, first name not last, and it would seem she alternatively would have been named Rudyard had she been a male child. By her joking, I deduce she has heard commentary her entire life for the name her parents chose for her. My thoughts, as you would imagine, turned to our own particular situation, Greg.

Perhaps she would have been amused if I explained.

It's brass monkeys here, Greg. I don't think I've ever been so cold.

Until next we speak...

Ollie

With one final scan of the document, Grayson encrypted the file and applied his password before closing it entirely.

As he turned away from the computer, the raised voices of Agents DiMatto and Flannery carried through the slightly open door from the adjoined office where they both had desks, Grayson having been placed in a separate space for his interim stay. A stay with no definitive end in sight.

"You were a jackass, Burke," Agent Flannery accused, his voice loud enough to relay scorn without the likelihood of anyone in the main office space hearing them. "What the hell has been your problem lately? We interview *all* witnesses, we don't dismiss them because we think they are worthless."

"She *was* worthless. What the hell could she have told us?"

"What she *saw*, just about *anything*."

Grayson pushed back his chair, flinching at the painful tension in muscles he'd forgotten he had, and walked around his desk to the door connecting the room, opening it further with enough ease his actions didn't disturb their argument. After three steps, the hitch in his step eased. The key seemed to keep moving when possible.

Flannery and DiMatto faced off in the space in front of their desks, and as he opened the door, Agent Flannery tossed his overcoat into a lump on a nearby chair.

"Just because she is hearing impaired doesn't mean–"

"She was *deaf*–"

Grayson's nerves sparked and he stood straighter taking another step into the room.

"No, you idiot, I don't think she was. She was reading our lips, so she knows exactly what you said, and she spoke–"

"Who did you interview?" Grayson demanded, stepping fully into the room.

Agent Flannery turned on his heels to face Grayson, his hands at his hips. Agent DiMatto scowled in his direction for a moment before he looked away, dismissing Grayson's intrusion. "Nobody worth bothering with," he said, turning away to stomp to his desk.

Flannery at least had the manners to answer Grayson. "A Miss Kipling Branson. She was on your witness list."

"I know who she is," Grayson ground out. "She was the woman I inquired about last evening after the explosion. She was in the hallway with me. The question is why are *you* interviewing her?"

"Why the hell not?" DiMatto said, tossing his hand toward Grayson. "You forget your place here, Holmes."

"My *place* here is to determine what happened last night–"

DiMatto dropped into his chair like an eighteen stone deadweight. The chair creaked beneath the intrusion. "Yeah, we heard why you were there last night. The Great and Mighty Holmes," he mocked.

"Sod off," Grayson snapped back.

DiMatto jerked forward in a move to evacuate the chair, but his bulk didn't let him. Before he gained his feet, Flannery stepped into the space between Grayson and DiMatto's desk.

"Knock it off," he shouted, throwing the words in his partner's general direction before he turned to Grayson. "We were just following up on the witness list."

"We are in charge of this case, not you." DiMatto tried his old argument again.

"If you weren't such a bloody-minded–"

"Hey!" boomed a voice from the main door.

All three silenced. Grayson clamped down his jaw and sucked a hard breath in through his nose before turning to face the executive assistant director.

Carl Stanton stood in the open doorway – none of them having heard it open – with his jacket shoved back and his hands at his hips. He was a sizable black man, of a height to look Grayson in the eyes, but he had an easy three stones on Grayson, solid and formidable. The heavy gray at his temples, and intermittently otherwise in his close cut, tightly curled hair, spoke to years on the job though he only had a dozen years on most of his men.

"What the hell is going on in here?"

DiMatto tossed a pencil across his desk and Flannery kept his head down. With a jerk of his chin, Grayson turned to fully face his temporary boss. "It would seem our definition of protocol differs, sir, in reference to revisiting questions with a witness. We were… working it out."

Stanton looked between the three of them, his jaw set. "I'm sick and tired of this crap. Knock it off and get the job done, dammit. We're getting heat enough to roast a pig."

"Apologies, sir," Grayson conceded, and turned on his heels to go back to his solitary office. "I shall do my level best." He didn't care whether they read his tone as concession or derision, because he was a breath away from telling them all to piss off.

He strode through his office, grabbing his coat and new scarf as he went. While he lacked specific details for the conversation the two idiots had with Miss Branson, it had been without a doubt offensive if Flannery's opinion was one to believe. Of the two, Grayson was far more likely to side with the young man over DiMatto and his complex.

He entered Miss Branson's address into his phone as the lift descended, and by the time he reached the ground level, he knew the route the cabbie would take to reach her South End apartment. There might yet be hope of salvaging the situation.

Chapter Three

What should have been a fifteen-minute cab ride to Kipling Branson's South End flat turned into nearly twice the commute time. Grayson had contemplated instructing the cabbie to take Beacon Street route, but considered the time of day and opted for Tremont. Neither was a particularly good option for that time of day. In his three weeks in Boston, he had at least learned some of the navigation.

It was nearly six in the evening before the cab stopped along the street and Grayson made his way to the Second Empire style stretch of terraced houses someone had long ago converted to flats. Mansard roofs and dormer windows punctuated the style, with continuous cornice lines to create a cohesive line of buildings, one to the next. The jut and ebb of the brick facades, carefully preserved to maintain the history of the district, appealed to Grayson.

With his chin tucked in and his gloved hands pushed deep into his coat pockets, he doubled back half a block from where the cabbie had dropped him to the building bearing the correct address. He hit the top step as a resident left, and held the door to slip inside the warmer interior foyer. By the time he had climbed the two flights of stairs to the second floor landing he'd removed his gloves and loosened the wool scarf, reaching her door. The narrow hall-ways carried the aromas of polished wainscoting and old plaster, and for a moment, Grayson slipped back to his family's cottage, lacking only the scents of lavender, grass, and baking wafting in through the windows.

Kipling Branson's flat was at the end of the hall, likely with windows inside facing the street. As he raised his hand to knock, the door opened and a woman of advanced years, dressed in a wildly patterned anorak in jewel-tones and gold trim, bustled into the hall nearly running into him as she spoke over her shoulder to someone inside.

Grayson stepped back as she continued, oblivious to his presence. He noted, as she stepped into the hallway enough for him to see, she spoke but accompanied each word with a manual sign.

"I still don't feel right about leaving you alone, sweetheart."

"I'm fine, Mom," came Kipling's voice from inside the apartment. "I'm here, aren't I? Honest. I'm going to take it easy, I promise. I won't even leave the apartment until Monday. Maybe even Tuesday."

An elderly man, broad of shoulders and no less than Grayson's height, with thick white hair stepped into the doorway, setting his hand on the woman's – Kipling's mother – shoulder. "Come on, Mother. Our girl is fine."

Mrs. Branson sighed and nodded. "Call us if you need anything," she said and signed, but the signs were abbreviated, focusing only on the "call" part with her knuckles to her cheek, her little finger and thumb extended to mimic a phone.

Then she turned and pulled up short, gasping when she came face-to-face with Grayson. "Oh! Goodness. You gave me a fright, young man."

"My sincerest apologies," Grayson said with a dip of his head.

Kipling stepped between her mother and father to look in his direction, no doubt in response to her mother's reaction. Her eyes widened and her lips parted for a moment, and just as quickly she snapped shut her jaw and blinked away her surprise.

She looked better in the soft light of the hallway, not highlighted by the flashing red of emergency vehicles in the dim evening. Her rich brown hair, with natural strands of lighter golden brown and darker auburn, was now braided from her brow, snug to her scalp, with wisps of escaping curls at her temples and cheeks. With her hair drawn back, he noted the absence of her hearing aids, which explained perhaps her mother's inclination to sign. Here he saw more clearly the red scratched along her cheek and the shadow of a bruise, but he also noted the soft line of her features and the natural bloom of color in her youthful skin. Eyes the color of whisky, a fact he'd been unable to determine the evening before, stared at him then looked away. He'd thought they might be hazel, but they were definitely amber, a less commonly recognized color.

Mentally, he snapped shut his mind's treasure chest of useless information on lipochromes and stoma pigmentation, extending his hand to Kipling's mother.

"Grayson Holmes," he said directly to her, then glanced to Kipling. "I hope I'm not interrupting."

Mrs. Branson gasped and released the breath with an enthusiastic "Oh!" once again, and still gripping Grayson's hand, twisted enough to speak to Kipling. "This is the agent you thought was coming?"

"Yes, unfortunately," Kipling said, taking a step into the hall so she was no longer between her parents. "Your FBI counterparts came by instead."

"Unfortunate is quite the appropriate description," he said with a dip of his chin.

Mrs. Branson tilted her head and finally released his hand. "What part of England do your people hail from, Mr. Holmes?"

"Eastbourne in Sussex. It's south of London–"

"Along the coast, yes," she interjected, her tone almost whimsical. "Holmes. How interesting you should be named Holmes and be from Sussex."

Grayson jerked a lopsided smile. It was the rare occasion when he met someone with the literary knowledge to comment further than a mocking of his family name in relation to his chosen profession. In the last few years, recognition had come more readily, but only based on basic knowledge in popular media. "Yes, indeed."

She studied him quite blatantly for a moment, her chin following the trail of her study, from his feet to his hair, then smiled. She signed as she spoke, and although Grayson was not fluent in manual communication, he realized enough to know she still didn't use all the necessary gestures to fully relay everything she said. She swirled her hand in front of her face, then his, to accentuate her words.

"His very person and appearance were such as to strike the attention of the most casual observer," she recited, clearly by rote, with a cant of her eccentric head, wild hair curling around the purple knitted cap she wore. "In height he was rather over six feet, and so excessively lean that he seemed to be considerably taller. His eyes were sharp and piercing…and his thin, hawk-like nose gave his whole expression an air of alertness and decision." She skipped the section of the excerpt describing the torpor of the man in question. She smiled and extended a single finger toward his face, stopping several inches short of touching him. "His chin, too, had the prominence and squareness which mark the man of determination."

"Mom, stop," Kipling said. "I'll talk to you tomorrow." With a gentle hand on her mother's shoulder and her father's arm, she herded them down the hallway toward the stairs.

"Are you sure you don't need us to stay?" her mother asked, glancing back towards Grayson over her shoulder.

"I've got it," Kipling answered. "I doubt Mr. Holmes will stay long; after all, what would I have to offer?"

Even though she didn't look his way, Grayson felt the sting of her words, and wondered just exactly what DiMatto said in his botched interview.

As soon as her parents reached the landing and started down the stairs, Kipling turned back to him with a cursory glance before disappearing into her flat again. "Come inside," she said as she crossed the threshold.

The interior of the flat was even warmer than the hallway, and he removed his scarf entirely, folding it to a size that would fit in his pocket. She crossed the open living space to a kitchen area on the far side, basic but functional, and manipulated a thermostat on the wall. It was then he was struck with the enticing aroma of slow cooked tomatoes and seasonings and perhaps minced beef. His mouth immediately watered and he rubbed his lips together.

"My mother believes if it drops below eighty in my apartment I'll catch pneumonia," she said, turning back to him. With her arms crossed over her body, she took three steps back to him, but stopped an excess of arm's reach away. "What is it you want, Mr. Holmes?"

Her defensive stance and stern set to her delicate jaw spoke volumes, and were he one inclined to be terminated for assaulting a fellow agent, Burke DiMatto might find his chin becoming intimately acquainted with Grayson's fist. It was more than her defensive nature, it was the flush in her cheeks and her repeated pattern of looking away from him, even though she was reliant on watching him to communicate. Considering her readiness to help the night before, DiMatto had mucked up whatever repertoire they established.

Grayson took a step toward her and her gaze shifted to look at him straight on again. He dipped his chin a slight degree so as to look her in the eyes, and when he spoke, he made sure to speak clearly though it wasn't about the sound. At least, that was his suspicion.

"First, I want to apologize for the ignorant behavior of my colleagues."

"Colleague," she corrected, adjusting her arms with a shrug of one shoulder. "Agent Flannery at least had the good manners to look bothered by the other one."

"Be that as it may, and despite my as of yet defined participation in this case, they should not have contacted you without my knowledge. At least that is the way we do things where I come from." He offered a smile, hoping it would lessen her unease. "Because you and I spoke initially, it was my responsibility to follow up. I regret I wasn't able to do that before their misstep."

Her angry veneer cracked, and one side of her mouth slid up in a slow smile. "Do you always speak like that?"

Grayson arched his eyebrows. "What do you mean?"

"Like you've had a half decent education, and possibly ate a thesaurus for lunch. Since I'm not exactly used to reading such…" She swirled her hand mid-air. "…articulate language from most I talk to, and you don't use your lips like–" She stuttered to a stop and cleared her throat. "You're a challenge."

He chuckled, deciding not to comment on the use of his lips. "Considering the years I spent in university, my mother would argue my education was a bit better than half decent; however, since I've not yet eaten lunch I cannot admit to the latter."

She laughed outright, which drew another chuckle from him, but her lightheartedness lasted only a moment before the mask slipped into place again and she shook her head. "Whatever the case may be, your Agent DiMatto made it very clear there is absolutely nothing I can offer to your investigation."

Grayson let his jaw relax and drew in a breath through his mouth, huffing it out again with a drop of his shoulders. "Agent DiMatto is, by the simplest definition, an idiot, so much so his mother named him as such. I can think of a plethora of alternative terms, but considering I am in the presence of a lady, I will refrain."

"His mother named him idiot?" she asked with a cant of her head.

"Well, in England, he would be called a birk. His name is Burke."

She parted her lips in an exaggerated "Ohhhh," and ended it with a smile. "I get it." Then she shook her head and extended a hand, palm up, and shrugged again. "You took my contact information, yes, but you kind of have to. Honestly, what *can* I offer? I was in the hallway with you when it happened."

Her final words quivered and she pursed her lips, swallowing hard, moisture pooling in her eyes. She had been excessively calm the evening before, and if he had any skill at all reading people, he would bet a hundred pounds she'd held together her composure whilst in her parents' company. He was not surprised, based on his limited experience with her that she had gone this long without the reality of her survival coming to pay a visit; what surprised him wholly was his inclination to comfort her. Twice he'd consciously held back his hand from reaching out to her.

Grayson turned away enough to break the impulse, drawing in a slow breath. When he dared look to her again, he caught the end of a swipe of her fingers across her cheek. Her face was turned away from him, and despite his logical mind telling him he was a man tempting fate and had just moments before resisted the urge, Grayson took the step toward her that he needed to touch her elbow, convincing himself the contact was necessary when he couldn't speak and draw her attention again.

She darted eyes to look at him before she turned her head. When he spoke, she shifted her focus to his lips, the simple and necessary action far more disconcerting than he anticipated.

"You may be able to help in ways you don't realize, Miss Branson. This is why we talk to witnesses both at the incident when prudent, and later when they are separated from the event."

"You make it sound so clinical," she said, her focus still on his lips.

"Analysis of a situation is my job, Miss Branson." Perhaps it was good she couldn't hear the tone of his voice. "However, the most important element of any investigation can on occasion be proven to be the human one."

She shifted up her amber eyes to look at him. He acknowledged his fingertips still pressed to her elbow, but he was disinclined to remove his hand. It was with great regret he did finally clear his throat and lower his arm, taking not quite a full step back from her.

"I would like to discuss with you again the issues you experienced with your hearing aids." He pointed in the general direction of her left ear. "You aren't wearing them today."

"The doctor in the ER suggested I not use them for a day or two if possible," she explained, her voice untypically rough. "Do you need me to put them in—"

"No, not at all," he answered quickly, raising his hand to stop her before she moved away. "In fact, I'd like to examine them if I may. And if you could, provide me with their manufacturing information."

"Is this about the clicking I heard?"

"Yes, though I don't know as of yet if it is significant. I'm exploring all options."

She nodded and finally did take a step back, turning toward a door off the main entrance area. "I'll get them. Have a seat at the table if you'd like," she called out as she slipped into the next room.

He caught a glimpse of a large bed draped with a patchwork quilt in warm hues of yellow and blue, rumpled and unmade. Turning away, Grayson unbuttoned and shrugged off his coat as he moved toward the small table in her kitchen area. It was only large enough for two, possibly three, to be seated. A quick glance around the space led him to believe Kipling Branson lived alone, and likely was not in any long-term relationship. The décor of the flat was feminine but subtle, with an air toward traditional New England style. Soft colors, white trim. Some photos hung on the wall, most either her parents or female friends. Though he supposed he might be wrong about her sexual preference, he doubted it.

"I actually have the manufacturer information here," she said, speaking as she came back out of the bedroom, a silver case in one hand and a pamphlet in the other. "My father is meticulous about keeping files on everything and he taught me well." She laughed, a tinge of nervousness in the sound, and slipped into the chair beside him, setting both the document and the case in front of him. Every movement was careful, as if to avoid making any kind of excessive sound, which he found interesting since all other indications pointed to the fact she was effectively deaf without her hearing aids. "I'm pretty sure it borders on hoarding for him, though."

"Thank you."

He first opened the pamphlet and skimmed the pages. It was a basic usage and warranty document, but it did provide information on the manufacturer and some general care, maintenance, and trou-ble-shooting tips. Grayson twisted in the chair to access the inside breast pocket of his coat for his notepad, and wrote down the perti-nent information.

He honestly had no idea if the information would lead him anywhere, but it was better to have the data than not. He reached for the case, then stopped and looked to Kipling, who watched him, her hands folded on the table.

"May I?"

She nodded. "Of course."

Grayson opened the case, the two aids inside, their battery compartments open with the battery exposed. One had red printing on the portion that would sit within the right ear, based on the configuration of the molded device, the other had blue. He lifted the left and set it in his palm.

"Here, let me turn it on," she said and slid a hand beneath his to support it. Her skin was warm and soft, and he was far too aware of it. Her fingertips brushed his palm when she pinched the aid and closed the battery compartment. "There."

Then she leaned closer a few degrees and looked at his hands. He hadn't bothered to bandage his hands that morning, and she skimmed her fingertips carefully over the hash mark pattern of nicks and abrasions on the heel of his hand. He clenched his jaw to fight the tingle that shot up his arm. She looked to his other hand on the table, palm down, likely noting the similar scrapes across his knuckles. When she shifted her focus again to his face, she took her hands away, her eyes shifting quickly to him and away again. Without her contact, Grayson curled his hand around the small device. A high-pitched whine came from the aid, and he opened his hand again, looking to her.

"What?" she asked.

"Feedback?"

She nodded and tucked her hands between her knees. "Does that sometimes when I put my hands over my ears when wearing them, or try to wrap a scarf or something. Or if someone hugs me too close. I didn't know they did it outside the ear." She scowled, seeming in thought. "I thought of something earlier today, between long naps. You were right, by the way. I *slept*." Her stress on the word accompanied a smile, and he was happy to see the release of tension in her body and expression. "This wasn't the first time I've heard clicking or had other interference with the hearing aids. It's really weird, actually."

"In what way?"

He knew now to expect the funny little tug in his stomach when her gaze shifted to stare at his mouth, and even though it was far from necessary, he found he did the same in return. Her lips held a soft gloss, perhaps from a lip balm.

Dangerous…

"High end digital cameras." She paused and he focused on her eyes instead of her lips. "Whenever someone uses one and snaps the shot, I get a click. And a few months ago, I flew to Dallas and while I was in the airport they clicked like crazy. So badly I had to take the aids out entirely."

"Electronic interference of some kind, then. Perhaps security or radio waves within the airport. Sounds rather unpleasant either way."

She canted her head and shrugged, her only affirmation to his statement. Unsure what else he should be scrutinizing, he set the aid back in the case. "Thank you, Miss Branson. I–"

"You can call me Kip."

Grayson arched an eyebrow, and fought his grin. She did smile, wide and honest, her eyes sparkling. Setting her elbow on the table, she rested her chin on the heel of her hand.

"I mean, if it's not against some FBI rule or anything," she added. "Or, I guess an MI6 rule."

Grayson opened his mouth, and took a short breath, and smiled again when he answered. "There are expectations regarding propriety; however, if you insist then it's perfectly acceptable."

"Then, I insist."

Acknowledging he walked a fine personal line, and quite possibly had stepped one foot over, Grayson closed the case and pushed back his chair to stand. She stood with him, the distance only marginal between them. Grayson twisted away to retrieve his coat from the back of the chair, waiting until he faced her again before speaking.

"Thank you, Kipling, for your help."

She pulled a face, squinting up one eye. "I said you could call me *Kip*…"

Grayson smirked and pulled on his coat. "You did. I shall endeavor to remember."

She followed him to the door, and upon opening it, she leaned against it with her hand curled around the edge and her cheek resting against her knuckles. "You've restored my faith in the FBI," she said as he stepped into the hall. He turned to face her so she could continue. "Maybe your partners are unfortunate flukes."

"Either that," he said, tugging on his gloves, "or quite simply my mother raised me to behave."

She smiled wide, a slow bloom of color filling her cheeks. "Quite possibly. You seem the behaving type, Mr. Holmes."

He had to look away, focusing for a moment on the minute details of placing hands in gloves, and released a wry chuckle before meeting her gaze again. "If you insist I call you Kipling – Kip," he corrected when she feigned a frown. "Then you must call me Grayson."

"Fair enough. Grayson."

He drew in a long, slow, steadying breath through his nostrils and released it. "Thank you, again, for your assistance. If you should think of anything–"

"I'll call," she finished. "Likewise."

With a final dip of his chin, Grayson turned down the hall and walked away from Kipling's door. While it had been a substantial period since he could recall a woman stirring him to any degree, certainly none as immediately and as effectively as Kipling Branson, he was not so unfamiliar to it to believe acknowledging the attraction was without consequence.

"Bloody hell…" he mumbled as he hit the first landing.

A young woman of blended descent – a lovely mix of what he thought to be Irish or Scottish with Egyptian and Italian, based on his cursory glance – dashed up the stairs toward him, her short black hair windblown, a shimmer in her hazel eyes. She looked at him only briefly, in passing, and hurried on clearly with a destination. Grayson paused mid-staircase, one foot on the next step down, and looked over his shoulder at her retreating form.

She was one of the women pictured in Kipling's flat, only

slightly less frequently than Kipling's own parents. He felt a small bit of relief that Kipling would not be alone this evening.

He reached street level and stepped out into the frigid cold of Boston as his mobile rang. Grayson brought it out of his pocket, his hands hindered by the gloves, and paused on the top step to look at the screen. Agent Flannery.

"Holmes," he said, bringing the phone to his ear.

"Where are you, Holmes?"

"I believe you refer to it as the South End." He squinted, looking up and down the narrow street in hopes of spotting a cab. "Trying to fix what you and DiMatto mucked up with Miss Branson."

"Come back to the office," Flannery continued, not even his tone acknowledging Grayson's comment. "I need to talk to you."

"Tonight?" Grayson asked, popping out his arm to clear his watch from his coat sleeve. It was close to seven. "Bit late, isn't it?"

"It's better we talk with as few people here as possible."

Grayson sighed at Flannery's enigmatic explanation. "Fine. I'll be there as soon as I can wave down a cab."

Silence answered him, and he drew the mobile from his cheek to see the call had disconnected.

Chapter Four

"Don't you ever scare me like that again!"

Mina Russo hugged Kip with such ferocity she grunted, and at the sound, Mina pulled back, but not far. Only enough she could take Kip's face in her hands. This close, the tears in her best friend's eyes were too easy to see.

"See what happens when I go on vacation without you? I could not get back from Florida fast enough," Mina said. Kip read the words on her lips, despite the slight quiver. Her gaze shifted to the scrapes and bruises on Kip's cheek and she frowned. "Are you okay? I mean, really really…are you okay?"

Kip nodded, still gripped in Mina's hold, trying her best to keep her own raging emotions at bay. She'd been relatively stable since the explosion, but since waking she'd teetered on the edge more than once. With Mr. Holmes — Grayson — she'd nearly turned into a blubbering idiot, but had held on. It wasn't as easy with her best friend. Perhaps not having in her aids was a blessing, because if she heard the distress she saw in Mina's face, she'd probably be lost.

"I'm really really fine," she promised, then stepped back so Mina could come into her apartment. "I'm here, aren't I? No long-term damage. Some scrapes and bruises, but that's it."

"Yes, well, I'm your unofficial doctor and I'll be the judge of your scrapes and bruises."

Kip chuckled, "Yes, *Doctor* Russo."

Mina arched her eyebrows and tapped a finger in front of her own right ear. Kip shook her head. "Nothing to worry about. The ER doctor recommended I leave them out a day or two, more for comfort than anything else."

"Makes sense." Mina crossed the apartment, shucking her coat and scarf as she went, to drop onto the couch with a dramatic, visible sigh. Kip followed so she could keep up with the conversation. "When I saw the news reports, I tried to convince myself you weren't there. I just kept saying it over and over again until I heard from your parents. When they said you were in the hospital–"

"I wasn't admitted. I was checked out and released."

"Doesn't matter," Mina declared bouncing her hands off her thighs in emphasis. "The point is you had to be taken to the hospital. How dare they mess with my bestie when I'm not there to supervise!"

Kip laughed at Mina's disjointed attempt at lightening the moment, and knelt on the couch beside her friend, sitting back on her heels so she faced Mina. "How did you manage to get back so quickly?"

Mina looked at Kip to speak, already adjusting to the fact Kip was effectively deaf without her aids. Mina had been her friend since they were in elementary school, so she knew the drill. The only reason Kip had known of Mina's arrival was she hadn't yet shut the door after Grayson's departure. So when Mina explained, she made direct eye contact and slowed down her frantic rant so Kip could keep up without issue.

"I called the airline last night as soon as I heard from Mom and Dad. I flew out on the first flight this morning. What I wouldn't do for a coffee right now."

"I'll make you one."

Mina gripped her arm before she could get off the couch. "No. I'd rather you sit here for a few minutes, just until I know without a doubt you're okay."

Kip smiled and squeezed Mina's hand. "Sure thing."

Mina smiled and drew in a breath so deep it shifted her shoulders, then nodded. "Do you want to tell me about it?"

"There's not much to tell. Honestly." Kip leaned back to sit on her ankles and rested her elbow on the back of the couch, her curled knuckles against her temple. "I was just in the wrong place at the wrong time, or…I guess I was in the right place. I'd left the lecture hall just a minute or so before the bomb—" Her throat tightened, and she swallowed. "I was in the second row, and everyone in those rows died. If I'd been inside—"

Mina held up her hand. "Let's not dwell on that. You weren't, and that's what matters." She took Kip's hand and squeezed. "I'm so sorry to hear about Professor Crane. I know you liked him."

Kip pressed her lips together, another swell of emotion hitting her. She nodded and shrugged one shoulder. Her mother had turned on the news after she got up, and the local reporter had listed the names of some of those that died, including Professor Frederick Crane.

"Do they have any idea what happened?"

"Pretty obvious, isn't it? Someone bombed the lecture hall, but I have no idea why. They weren't very informative."

"They who?"

"The FBI. They were at the scene, and an agent asked me some questions. Just witness observations."

Her pulse did a funny little jump and she tried to hide her smile. Was it terrible of her to have attempted flirting with a consulting agent with the FBI while he questioned her regarding a bombing? She supposed that's what he'd be qualified as, a consulting something-or-other. It was a pathetic attempt at best, since she never quite mastered the skills of flirting. That was more Mina's area.

Mina's eyes popped wider and she let her jaw fall slack. "Holy crap!"

Kip shook her head and chuckled. "Don't get overly excited. It's not like I had anything worthwhile to offer, although Grayson had some questions about this weird thing my hearing aids did before the explosion."

"Wow." Mina shook her head, still wide eyed. "Did Agent Grayson say they'd want to talk to you again?"

"Actually, it's *Holmes*," This time she really couldn't help the grin. "Grayson is his first name. You probably passed him in the stairwell."

Mina's jaw dropped again, and Kip had a passing thought she was beginning to resemble a cartoon character. She held up her flat hand a few inches above the top of her own head. "Six foot something, thick wavy hair, gorgeous eyes, and cheekbones that could cut glass?"

Kip smirked. "I guess you did pass him."

"He was here?" Mina pointed at the floor. "He came to see you here?"

"It's not much of a story…"

"Oh, I doubt that."

The federal building was mostly dim when Grayson made it back, the majority of the lights turned off for the night, with only a few glowing from the outside for the janitorial staff or those who were there working after hours. Grayson rode the lift to his floor, and stepped out into silence. Everyone had gone home for the night.

Not everyone. He listened as he walked down the hall toward the offices he shared with Flannery and DiMatto, hearing the click of a keyboard and the shuffle of papers. He bypassed his own office to go directly to the next, pausing in the doorway. Flannery sat alone in the room at his desk, only the desk light on and not the overhead fluorescents. Stacks of case files hid part of his desk, and a file box sat on the floor at the end of the desk. The smell of old, burned coffee permeated the room and by the jerky, spastic movements of the clearly agitated agent, Grayson calculated he'd drank at least three cups since he'd left two hours earlier.

"I'm here," Grayson said, and Flannery jumped, clearly too

engrossed in whatever he read to hear Grayson's approach. "What is it you needed?"

Flannery motioned for Grayson to come further into the office. "Shut the door."

A prickle of apprehension danced up Grayson's spine as he did what Flannery asked. He crossed the room and removed his coat, draping it on the back of one of the chairs across from the desk. "Where is Agent DiMatto?"

"He left right after you did." Flannery looked up, the harsh light of the desk lamp accentuating the stress around his eyes. "He's the problem."

To say he agreed with the words of Agent Flannery would be an understatement. Burke DiMatto had been a problem since the day Grayson arrived, more so in the last few days. Were he a criminal under investigation, Grayson would suspect him of chicanery. Guilt hung on him like a wet cloak. Agent Flannery carried his own load of guilt, but Grayson had already determined within himself the man's culpability was more domestic than career related; DiMatto's source had yet to reveal itself.

"Problem…" Grayson led. "What problem?"

"Honestly, I hope to hell I'm being paranoid and it's nothing, but I've got this niggling feeling I'm not wrong." Flannery stood, and came around the desk to lean his hip on the corner, his arms crossed. "It's about the incident at the university last night. Specifically, your presence there."

Grayson drew back his shoulders and schooled his expression to give away nothing. "Go on."

"We were still here when the call came in about the bombing. *Nothing* had come through about you being there – nothing about non-university personnel, and certainly not about a member of the foreign intelligence community – it was just a report about a bombing with police already on their way. Stanton said to prepare to go, since crap like this usually feeds to us if there's even a whiff of terroristic activity."

"There was no reason for anyone to know who I was, or my affiliation, until I informed the officers on site."

Flannery nodded. "Exactly. But last night, after we talked to you, I realized something. Burke was all bent out of shape you were there, demanding to know why–"

"Yes. Please arrive at the point," Grayson cut in.

"Right. When we got the call about the bombing, Burke took the call. I was almost to the door when I heard him ask about anyone named Holmes."

The hairs on Grayson's arms bristled and he drew in a slow breath. "He inquired specifically on the name Holmes," he reiterated.

Flannery nodded. "Like I said, I don't think I even registered the question at the time. I was busy getting ready to head out. But then later, when he acted so surprised you were there, it didn't feel right. The more I thought about it, the more I realized why."

"Was he told at the time of his asking that I was present?"

"I don't think so," Flannery said with a sharp jerk of his head. "Whatever they said, he didn't like it. Like he didn't hear what he expected. On the way to the campus, we got the call you had identified yourself to the authorities. I was surprised, but…Burke didn't seem to be. He tried to act surprised, but he's a lousy actor."

Grayson drew in a long, deep breath and walked to the office window. He tucked his hands behind his back and looked out on the city. Everything glistened with moisture, lights stretched and reflected in the street and on the buildings.

"You thinking what I'm thinking?"

"Perhaps," Grayson answered, tipping his head enough to see Flannery's silhouette in the poor light of the desk lamp. "However, perhaps we should first assure you and I have come to the same conclusion."

"I don't know if I want to put a name on it yet," Flannery said, tapping his knuckles on the desk. "Specifically, who knew you were going to be at BU?"

Grayson sucked in a breath and turned to face Agent Flannery, putting his back to the city. "Within Boston, only my uncle and family, and the individuals at the university he needed to notify of my presence on campus."

"And outside of Boston?"

"My team members in London and my family. Specifically my mother and father; whether they told my sisters I don't know."

"Crane was your uncle, on your mother's side?" The sentence began as a statement, ended as a question. "I'm sorry, by the way. It's gotta be tough to lose a family member in a situation like this."

"I pray you never know the reality of it," Grayson said, thinking *twice*. "Yes. Frederick Crane was my maternal grandfather's brother."

"I guess your mother is the American, huh?"

Grayson's arched eyebrow was his only means of countering Agent Flannery's statement. Agent Flannery shrugged a single shoulder. "They gave us a basic dossier before you arrived. We were told you technically hold dual citizenship, and the whole family history thing."

Grayson nodded. "Understandable." His acceptance of the fact didn't imply he appreciated the sharing of information. "Based on the current data, do you conclude it is of concern that your partner apparently knew I would be at the university at the time of the attack?"

Agent Flannery huffed and crossed his arms over his chest. "Damn it. Yeah…it's definitely of concern. But right now we have no proof, just my interpretation of his actions."

"Then I suggest this matter go no further than you and I until such a time as we have concrete evidence." He stepped forward and extended his hand to Patrick Flannery. "Agreed?"

He hesitated, the unease of the situation clearly playing across his features, then took Grayson's hand in a firm grip. "Agreed. It's one hell of a rotten situation, but I agree."

Grayson did his best not to let his opinion manifest in his expression. Instead, he cleared his throat again. "You have managed to capture the essence of the situation quite eloquently."

Agent Flannery chuckled, a strange and humorless sound. "You know, Holmes, sometimes when you get rollin' I swear you could be calling every one of us a bunch of idiots and we'd be none the wiser."

Choosing not to address the obvious, Grayson asked, "Was his lack of reaction your first point of concern?"

Flannery pulled a face and settled against the edge of the desk. "I've worked with Burke for three years, and in the last six months I've seen a change in him. His attitude is crap, especially since you showed up."

"Clearly…"

Flannery chuckled. "Yeah, but it didn't start with you. It started before that, but this…this is beyond a piss poor attitude and checking out before he actually retires."

Grayson walked away from Agent Flannery, lifting his coat from the back of his chair. "It's clear you have a decision to make, Agent Flannery. What do you intend to do?"

Flannery huffed as he stood as well. "I don't want to burn the guy on his way out the door, but we can't let this go. I guess I do what we are trained to do. I investigate."

"With which I am happy to help should your superiors allow the outside assistance; however, you must see I cannot be involved with bringing the actual accusation to light." When he saw the counterargument in Flannery's face, Grayson raised a hand to stop him. "As you pointed out, your partner has issues with my presence here, with the added frustration on all sides that my stay has been extended. Were I to be a part of the revelation, he would argue the validity as my wish to undermine him. That isn't the case, but it would slow the wheels of progress in this. No, Agent Flannery, the final accusation of wrongdoing – should it come to that ultimately – must come from you, and you alone, as his partner. Not only would the validity be questioned when coming from someone else, but the fact I am not a member of your intelligence community will only add to the questionability of my accusation."

Flannery huffed and set his hands at his hips. "Damn it. I know you're right."

Grayson pulled on his coat and buttoned the front, flipping his scarf around his neck. He had a passing thought that Kipling had not offered to return the scarf he'd given her, nor had he asked. "I do commit to assisting in all ways possible," he reiterated. "Clearly, this is personal for me as well."

Agent Flannery came around the side of the desk, hand extended, and Grayson took it before putting on his glove. The shake was firm, honest. "Thank you, Holmes. I know we've butted heads a few times, but you're a good guy."

"Of course." With one last nod, Grayson turned and left the office, hearing the squeak of Flannery's chair again as he moved down the hall.

In the lift, he sighed and leaned against the side of the car as it descended. There was no good end to this folly. Grayson had no interest in being involved in the downfall of an intelligence agent's career; however, he had even less interest in living in Boston as a target.

Either way, nothing would end well.

Chapter Five

Kip slipped into Marsh Chapel on the grounds of the university, mingling with the rest of the sizeable crowd in attendance for the memorial service for Professor Crane. The pews were already nearly full with university staff and many she recognized as students, though she couldn't place a name to any of them. That fact dug at her. She wasn't inclined to make dozens of friends, and focused almost solely on her studies rather than socializing, and for some she wouldn't ever have a chance.

Some students still bore the signs of injury from the explosion, with bandages, bruises, and in some cases casts and stitches. She nodded to some who made eye contact with her across the space of the chapel, but didn't move forward to join them. She carried her own bruises and marks, but Kip couldn't deny her feeling of guilt for having stepped out of the room just moments before the explosion. If she hadn't…the thought of it made her throat tighten and her eyes burn.

If she hadn't, the combined memorial for the students who died to be held the next day might have included her.

She selected a pew three from the back, noting the position of the wall-mounted speakers. Kip didn't want to be right beside them, but she had no chance of sitting close enough to the front to hear any speakers directly. Conscious choice about seating was automatic, always had been. She slid into the pew and sat along the aisle, setting her purse beside her. The wood was hard, but warm, the interior of the chapel well heated despite the cold air coming in from outside. Soft organ music played below the hum of conversation, and Kip drew in a slow breath through her nose. The pleasant aroma of polished wood mingled with the heady combination from the plethora of floral arrangements along the front of the pulpit. Kip folded her hands in her lap and closed her eyes, drawing in another breath to release through her lips.

"Kipling?"

Kip startled, gasping. She raised her head to see Grayson Holmes standing at the end of the pew immediately in front of her, his hand resting on the rich colored wood. His dark suit was completely appropriate for the style of dress for everyone else: dark and somber.

"Hello," Kip finally said, her surprise settling. "I—Well, I started to say I'm surprised to see you here, but I suppose if you were there—" She stumbled over the words, not knowing how to categorize anything about what happened. "—to see Professor Crane, you must have known him."

He glanced down at his own hand resting on the pew, his knuckles white with his grip on the ornate pew end, then looked to her again. A veil of calm hid more behind his eyes. "Actually, Frederick Crane is family," he said, his voice heavy, and Kip's chest immediately tightened. "He was my uncle. Great uncle," he clarified.

Kip stood, her still stiff and sore muscles protesting at the sudden movement and instinctively laid her hand over his, the thought of restraint only hitting her once she made contact. "Oh, Grayson. I'm so sorry." Her chest squeezed her lungs and she had to swallow before speaking. "I'm sorry," she said again, not knowing what else to say.

What people did, whether consciously or subconsciously, often spoke more to Kip than words ever did. She'd learned to rely on the subtle cues as heavily as the words she sometimes either did or didn't hear. Tension practically vibrated through Grayson's body, and the grip he held on the pew beneath her hand was tight. Despite the calm in his expression, his eyes stormed and he eventually looked away from her, down to the single point of contact — hand on hand.

Kip moved to withdraw, but he reacted quicker than she could pull away and turned his hand beneath hers, wrapping his long fingers around her hand, palm to palm. He covered their joined hands with his other, sandwiching hers between his. Grayson drew in a long, slow breath that expanded his chest and made his shoulders draw up, releasing it just as slowly before he raised his chin and looked at her again.

"Thank you, Kipling," he said, the small tick at the corner of his lips not even remotely passing as a smile. "Your compassion for a stranger is appreciated."

She squeezed her fingers, his grip responding in kind, and tried to offer a smile, stepping slightly closer. "You're not a stranger," she insisted, and acknowledged the bloom of warmth in her stomach when he made eye contact. "You never know; we might just end up friends."

The melody of the hymn played on the massive, built in organ at the front of the chapel changed, indicating it was time to settle for the service. Kip looked past Grayson to a group of mourners near the front of the chapel as they filed into the first two pews from the altar.

"You should probably join your family," she said, but lilted the word to be a question.

Grayson turned his head to look over his shoulder, and swallowed. "My company is neither welcomed nor missed," he said as he shifted his focus back to her again. "Nor can I blame them, as it's quite possible my presence in Boston brought about their pain."

Heartache tightened around Kip's lungs and she curled her lips together, fighting back the sudden wave of sadness his words carried. What could she say? It wasn't his fault? She wasn't an expert on the reality of being an intelligence agent, but she didn't have to reach too far into her imagination to realize his profession brought with it life altering risks.

"You're welcome to sit with me."

To encourage him to join her, Kip released his hand so she could sidestep further into the pew, retrieving her purse to make room at the end for him to sit. The simple act of bending to retrieve the purse sent pulses of pain along her spine and into her shoulders. As she tried to right herself, Grayson laid his hand on her arm and offered just enough support she managed to straighten and settled again. He sat beside her, hands now linked in his lap, and faced forward as everyone in attendance took their seats.

Click! Click! Click! Click!

Kip stood in the darkness, raw cold prickling her cheeks and curling her breath. She squinted, trying to see anything; only the faint glimmer around her implied limited light reflection off polished linoleum. "Hello?" she called out, but heard nothing. Not even her own voice. She felt the projection in her throat, felt the rasp, but the silence was smothering.

All but the clicking.

Click! Click! Click! Click!

She spun around, arm out away from her seeking anything.

Click! Click! Click! Click!

Panic rose in her throat, bitter and burning. Kip stumbled forward, hunched with her hands ahead of her. The constant, echoing click was the only sound, each pulse a painful jab through her head. Click! Click! Click! Click!

The darkness exploded in heat and fire, and the impact hit her back, throwing her forward into the darkness. Her hands hit hard, cold ground, pain shooting up her arms, and her head bounced off the unforgiving floor. All the air in her lungs gushed out, leaving her dazed, dancing at the edge of consciousness.

Click! Click! Click! Click!

Fire surrounded her, singeing her skin, heating the air she tried to suck in to stave off unconsciousness. Kip pushed herself up onto her hands and knees, squinting against the flames, trying to see anything beyond. She sat back on her heels, and raised her hands. Blood soaked her skin, saturated the sleeves of her coat, and dripped from her fingertips.

Kip's scream tore through her.

Kip jerked awake, her Macbook sliding off her legs to thump on the living room floor. She gasped for breath, her skin damp with sweat, scrambling to anchor herself in reality. With shaking hands, she pushed her loose hair off her face and leaned over to retrieve the computer, thankful the fall wasn't too bad. The computer had survived the explosion, but it would be just her luck if she killed it from a short drop off the couch. Her screen lit up with the partial page she'd been working on in her word processing program. After her breathing steadied and her heart stopped trying to jump out of her chest, she slumped into the couch cushions and laid her hand across her forehead.

She looked at the television, muted, and huffed at the sitcom rerun. The clock on her DVD player said 1:49. The noontime news had been on last she remembered, with follow up reports on the university attack and coverage of Professor Crane's memorial service the previous day and the student memorial that morning. That was when she'd turned off the sound, and by avoiding the screen she didn't have to know what they said. Seeing the photos and names of those who'd died tore at her and made her heart hurt.

Any other Thursday and she would be at work right now with plans for her comparative literature lecture tonight, but Beatrice insisted she take a few days off after learning Kip had been hurt. Had it really been a week since the explosion? Sometimes it felt like she'd just woken up. Most of her bruises had faded to mottled greens and yellows, and the scrapes on her face were healing well thanks to some special ointment Mina had given her, so since she was relatively presentable, Kip almost preferred to be at Dog-Eared Pages than sitting home alone in her apartment. She couldn't focus on her paper, and Mina was on duty for another few hours, so she couldn't even call her best friend for distraction.

With a groan to the empty apartment, Kip rolled off the couch and went to the kitchen. She wanted a large Dunkin', but ironically didn't have the energy to bundle up and walk the block and a half to the nearest Dunkin' Donuts, so a cup of tea would have to do. Sleep had been shallow the last couple of nights, and she never woke feeling rested. She was frazzled, jittery, and unfocused. As she set the pot on the burner, a knock at her door made her jump.

Kip banged the pot down on her burner in frustration. "Geez Louise," she mumbled. "Get a grip, Kip."

Pushing her fingers through her hair in a futile attempt at looking somewhat kempt after her unplanned nap, Kip went to the door and looked through the peephole. All she saw was a highly teased and sprayed poof of blond hair. She slid the chain lock and twisted the deadbolt before opening the door. In the hall stood a woman with perfectly styled hair and immaculate make up, dressed in a sharp power suit beneath her long coat, a microphone in hand. Behind her was a twenty-something guy holding a camera.

"Miss Kipling Branson?" the woman asked as soon as Kip opened the door.

"Yes." Kip squinted, recognizing her as Ellen Kennedy, a special interest reporter on one of the Boston television stations. Immediately, her gut twisted.

Kip's recognition was confirmed when she introduced herself and gave her station call sign. "I'm sorry to surprise you like this, but we are following up on some of the students who were hurt in the bomb attack a week ago today. Do you have a few minutes and can we talk?"

Kip shook her head as soon as Ms. Kennedy stated her intent, and didn't stop until she had a chance to speak. "No, I'd rather not."

She moved to shut her door, but Ms. Kennedy set her hand against the wood. "We want to show the city the positive side, the faces of those who survived. Don't you want—"

"No," she said again. "There *is* no positive side." The quick catch in her throat didn't surprise Kip, but it made her mad. She was too tired, too sore, and too fresh off her nightmare to talk.

She doubted she'd ever be ready to talk. Especially not with a reporter with a camera in her face.

"Oh, I understand this must be exceptionally upsetting for you.

Of course, we can also see the marks left behind from your ordeal and we understand you had stepped out of the classroom just minutes before the explosion. Have you thought about what might have happened if you hadn't–"

"You mean have I considered the fact I could be dead?" Kip snapped, taking a step forward so Kennedy had to step back. She had to clench her jaw and swallow hard before she could speak. "Constantly."

Miss Kennedy opened her mouth to say something, but Kip didn't hear it. She slammed the door and removed her hearing aids as she walked, leaving them on the table while she went to the cupboard for a mug. If she couldn't hear them, they weren't there. None of them were there. She slammed the mug down on the counter, only feeling the vibration through her hand, and hunched her shoulders trying to fight back the tears.

You are fine.

She repeated the words in her head again and again.

You are fine. You are here, you are alive, and you are fine.

It took another five minutes before she felt convinced, and by then steam curled from the teakettle. She poured the water over her teabag and added honey before retrieving her hearing aids and going back to the living room couch. Her stomach rumbled, but she didn't want to eat yet. Didn't want to bother. There were plenty of leftovers from her mother, including enough American Chop Suey to feed a small army. Kip curled her legs up with her on the couch and draped an afghan across her lap, taking a glance at the television. It had moved on to a talk show, but she had no interest. Setting her mug on the end table, she drew her laptop back into her lap. The university campus had been shut down for the remainder of the week, and since she wasn't working, she wanted to use the valuable time to catch up on her paper.

An alert on her mail icon at the bottom of the screen said she had four new emails. What were a few more minutes of procrastination? She opened the program with a sigh.

One email was a reminder her cell phone bill was due soon, one from Professor Phelps rescheduling their guidance meeting until the

next Monday, one pitching a "new drug" to "enhance male performance" – which she chuckled at before deleting without even
opening – and the last was from Grayson Holmes.

FROM: GRAYSON HOLMES <GOSHOLMES@IC.FBI.GOV>

SUBJECT: FOLLOW-UP TO OUR DISCUSSION

GOOD DAY, KIPLING

*FORGIVE MY FORWARDNESS, BUT I WISHED TO THANK YOU AGAIN FOR
YOUR KINDNESS YESTERDAY AT MY UNCLE'S MEMORIAL SERVICE. WHILE
I CANNOT CONVINCINGLY SAY I WAS CLOSE TO UNCLE FREDERICK, HIS
DEATH HAS BEEN DIFFICULT FOR THE FAMILY. HE WAS MY MOTHER'S
UNCLE, AND SHE WAS UNABLE TO MAKE IT FOR THE SERVICES.*

I DIGRESS…SUFFICED TO SAY, YOUR COMPANY WAS APPRECIATED.

*I OBSERVED YOU SEEM TO STILL HAVE DISCOMFORT FROM YOUR
INJURIES. HOW ARE YOU RECOVERING? IF THERE IS ANYTHING YOU
NEED THAT I MAY BE ABLE TO ASSIST YOU WITH, PLEASE LET ME KNOW.*

*AND FINALLY, ON A MORE IMPERSONAL NOTE: THANK YOU AGAIN FOR
YOUR WILLINGNESS TO SPEAK WITH ME THIS SATURDAY PAST. YOUR
CONTRIBUTION IS WORTHWHILE AND APPRECIATED.*

*IF AT ANY POINT YOU RECALL A DETAIL YOU THINK MAY BE RELEVANT,
NO MATTER HOW MINUSCULE IT MAY SEEM TO YOU, PLEASE CONTACT ME
DIRECTLY; EVEN IF YOU ARE UNSURE OF THE RELEVANCE.*

*I WOULD LIKE TO REITERATE, IF THERE IS ANY ASSISTANCE I MAY
PROVIDE, I AM AT YOUR SERVICE.*

RESPECTFULLY,

GRAYSON HOLMES

Kip smiled at the completely unintended innuendo – which, if she didn't find him appealing, she probably wouldn't have read as such – and hit reply.

You don't need to thank me for yesterday. I'm glad I could help, and your company was appreciated just as much.

Thank you for checking on me. I'm fine. Nearly all the bruises and scrapes are gone now, thanks to a best friend who is a doctor with a tendency to hover. I am still sore and stiff, but it's less each day. Another couple of days and no one will be the wiser.

Do you have advice on how to keep away nosy reporters?

Kip

P.S...I need a large Dunkin' Dark with an extra shot. JK :)

Not expecting to hear back from him since the email was obligatory at best, Kip took a sip of her tea, set down the mug, and toggled her screen to her dissertation. Her topic wasn't exactly mainstream, which made for an interesting paper but limited her reference options. Today she challenged herself to dig up some more obscure analysis papers on *The Island of Doctor Moreau.*

Three solid knocks at the door connecting his office to the office of Agents Flannery and DiMatto drew his attention from the spread of files on his desk. Agent Flannery stood in the open doorway. Grayson sat up and motioned for Flannery to enter, surmising by the tense expression he had no positive news.

"It has begun," he stated as Flannery crossed the office.

Agent Flannery dropped with a heavy grunt into the chair on the other side of Grayson's desk, bringing one leg up to rest his ankle on the other knee. "Yeah. Director Stanton knows about my concerns and has agreed to begin an internal, covert investigation. Sounds like he probably had some similar ideas, because he didn't try to convince me otherwise. If it turns out to be nothing, he doesn't want to smear Burke's 'good name' if he doesn't have to, ya know?"

"I understand the sentiment, yes, though I can't say I entirely agree."

Flannery jutted up one eyebrow and tilted his head in an offhanded show of agreement. "Yeah, well, it still sucks. Thanks, by the way. For your backup on this."

"I committed my assistance," Grayson reminded, tapping the end of his pen against the stack of files. "I couldn't begin the inquisition, but my silence would have been far more detrimental once the facts were brought to light. It is my hope we will now be capable of moving forward to a solution."

"Speaking of…Stanton is having all files connected to the university incident brought down to us – from the police, forensics, everything. We dig in fresh tomorrow, I guess."

Grayson nodded, the pop of an email icon on his desktop monitor catching his peripheral attention. "So it would seem. Has there been any progress that you are aware of regarding research into the hearing aid manufacturer or model information provided by Miss Branson?"

"Ah, yeah. Hang on." Agent Flannery sat up and gained his feet, heading toward the connected office.

As Flannery departed, Grayson clicked his mouse cursor on the mail icon, opening the program. Various official notifications displayed as both read and unread in the inbox view, but the most recent came from Kipling, responding to his earlier email.

Hiding the involuntary hitch of his smile, he glanced toward the open door before opening the email.

"Here we go," Flannery said, coming back through the door with a thin stack of papers in his hand, stapled at one corner. "Not sure there is anything worth anything here. But, you might see something I don't."

He reached the desk and handed Grayson the papers before sitting down again. Grayson skimmed the first page and looked at the second. The document was detailed, but some of it repeated the information he'd gathered from her manufacturer's pamphlet regarding specifications and capabilities. He actually found the full spectrum of services and options for the hearing aids to be quite impressive. If chosen as an optional application, the user could actually use a Bluetooth connection via the aids in conjunction with any Bluetooth enabled device such as MP3 players or Smartphones with the program. The user could have a conversation with someone without needing to hold their phone, as long as it was within a certain vicinity and the wearer could hear much clearer than with the phone in hand. This particular brand of hearing aids offered "smart" technology that switched programs in different surroundings, including restaurants and concerts, to better help the wearer; and the devices were programmed to instantly buffer exceptionally loud noises like sirens.

"What?" Flannery asked.

Grayson looked up. "Though I don't yet see anything specific to what we are currently investigating, I have the thought that the IC here and the JIC could benefit from access to some of the technology found in these advanced devices. They are quite remarkable."

Flannery snorted a laugh. "We're always the last to know." He pushed himself out of the chair again. "I haven't had lunch yet. Gonna head to Faneuil Hall. You want anything? I'm thinking Ned Devine's, but if you want something different..."

"No, thank you," Grayson answered. "But perhaps you can answer a question for me."

"Yeah, sure."

"What is a *Dunkin'*?" He stressed the unfamiliar word.

Flannery laughed. "Like someone said 'I sure could use a Dunkin'?"

Grayson read the screen again. "Yes, precisely."

"You need to learn the lingo of The City, Holmes," he said, starting back across the office to his door, speaking over his shoulder. "Just means they want a coffee from Dunkin' Donuts, the very lifeblood of Boston." His voice grew louder as he crossed the threshold into his office.

"Dunkin' Donuts," Grayson repeated, and nodded. He'd seen several of the coffee shops all over the city; an overabundance in truth.

"Yep," carried Flannery's voice from the other space.

Grayson stared at Kipling's email for a few moments, reading over again what she'd said. It didn't surprise him she had been visited by the media. As in London, the media were bloodthirsty sharks; that fact didn't seem to change between countries, only changing in the extent they would go for what they felt to be newsworthy events.

He opened a search engine and typed 'Dunkin Donuts South End locations'.

"Honestly, Mom, you don't need to come over. I have so much leftovers from earlier this week I'm good until at least Saturday. I'm working on my paper, and I'm taking it easy. I promise."

"You can't blame me for worrying, Kip," came her mother's strained voice through the aid connection.

Kip had set the phone down on the couch beside her so she could continue surfing social media. It wasn't dissertation writing, but the distraction was good for her brain.

"I don't, Mom. It's not like that. I'm just tired, and if you came you'd just be sitting here watching me be tired. If I need anything I promise I will call, and you can make Dad go out in the cold to get it for me," she teased, and her mother giggled. "Why don't you plan on coming Sunday? I'll be out of leftovers by then."

"Alright, Kip. We'll be over on Sunday. I'll make a lasagna."

"Sounds great. I'm going by Mina's in the afternoon, but I'll be home by probably five."

"We'll be there by six. We want to talk to you about our cruise, too. We don't think we're going to go, not with everything going on with you."

"Mom," Kip cut in. "Stop it. Your cruise is in a month, and you're exaggerating a bit. By then this week will be long forgotten. It's your last chance to catch this cruise before my graduation."

Her mother sighed heavy and long. "We'll talk on Sunday."

"Okay. But you're going."

"We love you, sweetheart. Call if you need anything."

"Love you, too, Mom. I will."

Kip waited for her mother to hang up rather than reaching to disconnect the call herself. The broken line would reset the hearing aids without her going for the phone. She scrolled down her account wall, stopping on the occasional friend's post, but not seeing much to catch her eye. There were some funny joke memes, and she shared the ones on grammar or with literature references, knowing at least a few would get them. But, since she only had a handful of friends, there wasn't much to see. Kip sighed and toggled back to her paper. Quizzes to determine which classic literature writer she was most like didn't get her paper written any faster.

The phone rang again; her generic ringtone, and she glanced over to see if it was someone she wanted to bother answering for. It said Unknown, but the number itself seemed familiar, though she couldn't place it. She reached out and tapped the green answer button.

"Hello?"

"Hello, Kipling. It's Grayson." He paused a beat. "Holmes."

"I'm glad you clarified," she said, with a grin. "I know so many Graysons with a British accent, I can't tell you apart."

He chuckled, a low rumble that carried through the connection, the sound comforting to Kip. "I shall remember to always fully identify myself in the future."

"Yes, please do," she teased, smiling at the amusement in his voice. "Is there something you needed?"

"It's what you require, Kipling," he said. "Advice. If this reporter continues to be bothersome, feel free to tell her you have been advised not to speak of the investigation and she may direct all her inquiries to me or to the FBI public relations office."

Kip set her laptop on the couch beside her and drew her legs up onto the cushion, wrapping her arms around her knees with her head resting on the back of the couch. "Wow. That's a bit above the call of duty, isn't it?"

"Not at all. You are, without question, part of an active investigation and as such, it is your prerogative not to speak of it to anyone other than official representatives."

"Well, thank you. I don't know if she'll be back, but if she does come back, I'll give her your card."

"Please do."

A knock at her apartment door interrupted him, and she

laughed. "Gee, maybe that's her." She unfolded her legs and tossed off the afghan, padding across the floor in her stocking feet. The knock came again. "Hang on," she called out.

Before opening the door, she slipped the chain so she could use it as a buffer if she needed to. She peeked out, but instead of big blond hair, she saw a beanie. "Who is it?" she called through the door.

"Uh, you're named Branson?" came an adolescent male voice.

Kip scowled. "Yes…"

"I've got a delivery."

"I didn't order anything. What are you delivering?" she asked with skepticism.

"Look, lady, your coffee is getting cold. It's all paid, even the tip, so all you gotta do is take it."

"Coffee?"

"You did say you needed one, did you?" Grayson said, and she swore she could hear the grin in his voice.

Kip slid the chain lock free again and yanked the door open with enough force to make her hair puff back from her face. A teenage boy wearing a Dunkin' Donuts uniform, holding out a large to go cup and a brown bag to her. Staring at him, she reached for the coffee, and as soon as she had it, he tossed a casual salute and jogged back down the hall to the stairs. Kip looked down at the cup.

"Kipling?" Grayson said, and she blinked, shaking her head.

"You sent me a coffee?"

"You did say you needed one, correct? And I did put myself at your disposal."

"Wow, you mean business."

Grayson laughed. "I'm pleased to be of assistance. Have a good day, Kipling."

Chapter Six

What I wouldn't do for some immediate and personal advice, Greg.

Details have come to light to cause me exceptional concern. Agent Patrick Flannery requested a private meeting, during which he relayed to me observations that make me believe not only was the bombing that killed Uncle Frederick one intended to kill me, but that quite possibly his partner Agent DiMatto played a role in the bombing. He described Agent DiMatto's reactions when he heard of the bombing — prior to them being aware of my presence — at which time DiMatto specifically asked of my whereabouts.

When the FBI was officially informed of my presence at the bombing, Agent Flannery stated Agent DiMatto attempted to act surprised, but having been his partner for some time, Agent Flannery was not one to be deceived.

This leads us both to believe Agent DiMatto was not only aware of the impending bombing, but my presence at the

UNIVERSITY. SINCE VERY FEW PEOPLE KNEW — LIMITED ONLY TO MY TEAM, FAMILY, AND THE ADMINISTRATION OF THE UNIVERSITY — AGENT DIMATTO'S KNOWLEDGE OF THE FACT HAS SENT UP SEVERAL RED FLAGS.

AGENT FLANNERY AND I HAVE BEGUN A COVERT INVESTIGATION INTO AGENT DIMATTO. DIRECTOR STANTON HERE HAS REQUESTED WE KEEP IT CLANDESTINE UNTIL SUCH A TIME WE HAVE PROOF WORTH PURSUING AS AGENT DIMATTO IS SCHEDULED TO STEP DOWN FROM SERVICE WITHIN THE FORTNIGHT. THEY DO NOT WISH TO SOIL THE REPUTATION OF A LONGSTANDING AGENT IF IT ISN'T JUSTIFIED. IN THE MEANTIME, I AM WATCHING MY BACK. WE HAVE NO LEADS ON THE IDENTITY OF THE POSSIBLE BOMBER.

UNCLE FREDERICK'S MEMORIAL SERVICE WAS THIS WEEK, AND HE HAS BEEN CREMATED AS REQUESTED BY HIS FAMILY. IT WAS DIFFICULT TO BE THERE, GREG. I MUST READILY ADMIT MY EMOTIONS RUN FAR TOO CLOSE TO THE SURFACE IN MATTERS SUCH AS THIS, AND I HAVE FOUND MYSELF STRUGGLING ONCE AGAIN WITH MY ANGER. I THOUGHT I HAD REGAINED MY CONTROL, BUT THIS INCIDENT HAS BROUGHT IT TO THE FOREFRONT AGAIN. RIGHTFULLY SO, THE CRANE SIDE OF THE FAMILY HOLDS ME AT LEAST PARTIALLY RESPONSIBLE FOR UNCLE FREDERICK'S DEATH.

DESPITE MY EXPLANATION OF THE ABOVE SITUATION, IT IS NOT THAT WHICH I WOULD APPRECIATE YOUR ADVICE.

MISS KIPLING BRANSON.

SINCE I LAST WROTE, I WENT TO SEE KIPLING AFTER THE ABOVE-MENTIONED AGENT DIMATTO ACTED THE PART OF A BOORISH ARSE AS PART OF THE 'INVESTIGATION'. I WENT IN HOPES OF SMOOTHING THE WATERS, SO TO SPEAK, AND SPEAK WITH HER ABOUT THE INCIDENT.

I SAW KIPLING AGAIN ON WEDNESDAY AT UNCLE FREDERICK'S MEMO-RIAL SERVICE. SHE WAS COMPASSIONATE WHEN SHE LEARNED OF OUR

FAMILIAL CONNECTION, AND HER ACTIONS AND WORDS WERE − I MUST ADMIT − THE MEANS BY WHICH I SURVIVED THE SERVICE.

I ALSO SPOKE WITH KIPLING THIS THURSDAY PAST. WHILE ONLY BRIEFLY, THE CONVERSATION WAS PLEASANT.

HERE IS WHERE I MUST ADMIT I AM…ENTHRALLED BY KIPLING.

I'M QUITE SURE IF I WERE ABLE TO SEE YOUR FACE UPON LEARNING SUCH NEWS, I WOULD SEE COMPLETE SHOCK AND QUITE POSSIBLY AMUSEMENT.

IT IS MY SUSPICION SHE MAY BE EQUALLY INCLINED.

DAMN IT ALL, GREG. WHO AM I TO EVEN CONSIDER SUCH A POSSIBIL-ITY? YOU, MORE THAN ANYONE ELSE, HAVE ON MORE THAN ONE OCCA-SION POINTED OUT MY SHORTCOMINGS. IT'S QUITE LIKELY SHE IS SIMPLY A FRIENDLY WOMAN, THOUGH I AM NOT OFTEN INCLINED TO QUESTION MY INSTINCTS WHEN IT COMES TO PEOPLE.

UNLESS SOME OTHER REASON SHOULD MANIFEST THAT REQUIRES I INITIATE CONTACT AGAIN, IT'S QUITE LIKELY I MAY NOT HAVE REASON TO SPEAK TO HER AGAIN IN THE NEAR FUTURE. I AM NOT SURE IF THAT MAY NOT BE FOR THE BEST.

I YEARN FOR YOUR ADVICE ON THIS MATTER, GREG. I'VE NO DOUBT IT WOULD BE WITHOUT PRICE.

UNTIL NEXT WE SPEAK…

OLLIE

Grayson read the epistle again, considered editing out some of the most honest portions, then password-locked the file, saved, and closed the document. If he couldn't be honest in a correspondence intended for Greg, of all people, he had no hope of honesty with anyone. Including himself.

The writing complete, he left his laptop on the edge of the table while he took up his bowl of porridge. The residential hotel he currently called "home" was sufficiently warm, but the howling wind outside his windows gave him a deep chill and a desire for something more fortifying than toast and jam. He had learned since coming to Boston he never had a true concept of frigid. London was wet, and it dropped cold enough for scarves, long coats, and wool caps, but Boston was a different climate entirely. More than once he'd stepped outside and swore his nose had immediately frozen closed, or the air in his lungs iced over.

He'd made the mistake once of deciding the short walk to Center Plaza from his South Boston hotel was easily manageable, a distance he would have covered without a moment of hesitation in London. By the time he'd arrived in his office, his toes hovered between complete numbness and outright pain, especially as they warmed. Until the weather changed, or until he went home, he took a cab. And on days like today, a weekend where he had no particular place to be, he enjoyed his hot porridge and equally hot tea.

As he scraped the last spoonful of warm cereal from the bowl, his mobile vibrated on the table a second before the "You are my Sunshine" melody played. Grayson smiled and slid his thumb across the screen before bringing it to his ear. "Have you been waiting all day to call?"

His mother's light laughter carried through the phone from thousands of miles away, and he chuckled with her. "Yes, I have, in fact. It is rude to tease a mother for missing her only boy."

"Not teasing," he defended, then sighed. "The truth of it is I'm pleased you called. How are you, Mum?"

Annalise Holmes made a tutting sound in her cheeks, a sound he recognized on a soul level from his childhood when she soothed away bad dreams and skinned knees. "Oh, sweetheart, I'm just fine. My heart is a bit heavy, of course, but it's my worry for you that weighs on me much more."

"Don't worry for me, Mum. I am fine. What did you do today?" he asked, hoping to divert his mother's concerning thoughts.

"Your sisters have been here all day, and I said it rather felt like Christmas again, except you weren't here."

The tinge of sadness in his mother's voice tugged at Grayson. His director had informed him just before Christmas of the need for him to leave for Boston, so the time spent with his family had extended no further than the day after Christmas. He hardly felt he'd seen them at all. Holiday celebrations went on for several days in the Holmes family, and the cottage was always full to bursting with extended family.

Her own sigh filled the silence. "No dwelling on such things. You'll be home soon enough."

"I hope so, Mum."

"We did call for another reason. Shirl has news."

"Oh?" He sat straighter and set his elbow on the table to support the phone. "What news?" He already knew, and had been waiting for the announcement since Christmas, but he wouldn't steal his sister's – or his mother's – thunder.

"Hold on, sweetheart. She wants to tell you herself."

The rustle of his mother handing off the phone precluded his little sister coming on the line.

"Grayson?"

"Who else would it be, silly girl?"

She laughed, but he heard more than the lighthearted giggle in her tone. Shirley was breathless, and he easily heard the smile that had to be spread across her young face. "Could have been Watson."

"Watson has not stirred from the center of the bed since I left it this morning. I fear he has grown far too accustomed to having his own way here, and will be an insufferable kitty when we return."

"Hasn't he always been?"

"Truer words…now, tell me your news."

She squealed. Literally squealed. "Daniel and I are getting married!"

"No, no, completely unacceptable," he cut in, doing his best to sound stern. "I've yet to complete my thorough background check of this man. Far too many things I don't like. You can't trust a man with so many library late fees."

"Grayson, stop," she argued, the breathless joy still in her voice.

"I will not. I simply can't–"

"Grayson!"

He smiled at her exasperation, a sound he'd loved inspiring since she and Johanna were five and he was twelve. Johanna was too level-headed and analytical to tease, so he made up for it with Shirl. "Absolutely not. *Because...*" he dragged out, "If I were to allow you to marry, I would be required to admit you are old enough to do so, and that is something I am entirely unprepared to do."

She laughed. "Tell me you're happy for me?"

Grayson bowed his head and closed his eyes, smiling as he imagined her clutching the phone to her cheek with both hands, wide-eyed, waiting for him to answer.

"Of course, I'm happy for you, dear heart."

They spoke a minute more before he was then passed briefly to Johanna, then his father, and finally back to his mother who spoke for nearly half an hour, filling him in on every bit of information she could come up with; everything from the state of the community to the weather. He knew reaching out was his mother's way of confirming all her loved ones were well – especially after another loss to the family – and in truth, he didn't mind in the least. After a long goodbye, he disconnected. He didn't manage to set down the phone before it vibrated in his hand, and he chuckled, swiping his thumb to answer without looking.

"What could you have possibly forgotten to tell me?"

"Grayson?"

Her soft, a bit too tentative, slightly strained voice skittered over his skin, igniting his nerves, and he sat up straighter. "Kipling."

"I'm sorry to call you on a Saturday–"

"What's wrong?"

"Nothing. I–" she said quickly. Behind her voice, he heard conversation and the jingle of a bell, the kind designed to hang at a shop door to signal someone entering or exiting.

Grayson stood, grabbing his bowl, talking as he walked to the sink. "Tell me."

She cleared her throat. "Hang on." Then to someone else, she said, "Rach, I'm stepping out back for a second. Be right back."

While he waited for her to speak again, he went to his bedroom and pulled his coat from his closet. Watson lifted his gray-striped head, blinked slowly, and then stretched out again over Grayson's coverlet. The click of a door closing preceded her momentary silence. The slight, soft sound of her breathing only served to make him hold his breath in anticipation. She blew out a long breath, a slight whistle indicating to him she had pursed her lips.

It was all Grayson could do to keep his tone level. He shifted the grip on his phone from one hand to the other, keeping it to his ear so he could finish putting on his coat. "Kipling, what's wrong?"

"I'm sorry. I'm trying very hard not to run screaming from the store." She spoke softly, possibly trying to keep anyone from hearing. "The clicking in my hearing aids started again."

"When?"

"A few minutes ago, but it's not constant. I swear I jumped three feet in the air when it started, Grayson."

"I'm quite sure. How long has it been since you heard it last?"

"Maybe five minutes? I called you as soon as it stopped so I could use the phone."

"Where are you?"

"Berkeley Street. I work at a bookstore. Dog-Eared Pages."

"I will be there as soon as possible." He started to take the phone from his ear, then stopped. "Kipling…"

"Yes?"

"I'm very glad you called."

"Just get here quick so I can stop freaking out," she said on a wry laugh.

He disconnected the call, and whipped his scarf around his neck, heading toward the door, dialing as he went. It rang twice before he heard, "Flannery."

"I require immediate assistance and an IT specialist. Meet me as soon as possible at a bookstore called Dog-Eared Pages on Berkeley

Street," Grayson said without greeting. He reached the lift and pressed the call button. "We need electronic frequency scanners."

"Hello to you, too," Flannery mocked. "What the hell is going on?"

Grayson paused when the lift door opened, checking first that the car was empty before stepping inside. "I received a call from Kipling Branson. I realize your interview with her was unproductive, but did you read my statement?"

"Yeah. She said she heard some kind of interference with her hearing aids."

"She is hearing it again."

"Jeezum," he hissed. "Do we need the bomb squad?"

"Not likely as the clicking seems intermittent and the bookstore still stands. It is my suspicion the interference isn't from an explosive device, but if we can determine what kind of electronics is affecting her aids it might help us in the investigation."

"Got it. It'll be thirty before I get there."

Grayson reached the lobby and motioned toward the clerk at the door that he required a cab. "I expect to be there within fifteen. And Flannery...I would prefer your partner not be aware of the situation."

He didn't wait for Flannery's response before disconnecting the call. The concierge in the lobby door opening the door as he approached and he could move directly to the cab at the curb. Although mid-day, the frigid air bit into every bit of exposed skin. He slid into the back of the cab.

"Berkeley Street. Quickly."

The clicking was nearly enough to drive Kip to insanity. It took all she had not to flinch every few seconds, and sometimes she couldn't help it. Every click affected her nerves like the tap of a trigger being pulled on a gun. Her body braced each time for the deafening explosion that had knocked her to the ground days before. If she thought about it too much, she broke out in a cold sweat and her heart jumped to her throat.

"Is there something wrong?" her customer asked, taking her change from Kip.

Kip closed her fist to hide the tremble and forced on a smile. "Headache. Thank you for asking."

The middle-aged woman smiled and took the bag of books Kip held out to her. The little fifteen-hundred square foot bookstore was packed, with Saturday afternoons being a prime retail day for them.

For the moment, there was a pause in customers at the register and Kip busied herself with shifting around some of the countertop point-of-sale items. It took at least a minute for her to realize – with a long breath she felt like she'd been holding for ten minutes – the clicking had stopped. In a strange counterintuitive effect, the relief dragged at her limbs and made her suddenly exhausted.

The shop door jangled, and she habitually glanced toward the front of the building in time to see Grayson tug off his gloves and rake long fingers through his damp hair. Light snow fell outside, just enough to leave wet spots of melting snow on his shoulders, and whatever he thought he might accomplish by trying to push back his hair only managed to wave it worse into thick curls.

Damn sexy.

Heat infused her from toes to hairline, and she turned to Rachel, their high schooler. "Rach, take over the register for a bit."

Rachel nodded, the chain connecting her lower lip ring to her ear cuff jingling against her cheek. She was a sweet girl, but her dark red, almost black spiked hair, and black lipstick startled some. "'kay."

Kip came around the end of the wooden counter and walked with as much nonchalance as she could muster, bracing for the clicking to begin again at any moment. Grayson had paused at a display of classics they'd just obtained from an estate in Cambridge. He shifted his gloves to one hand and touched the cover of one of the books, a smile just barely curving his lips.

Kip stepped beside him, close enough to see the title he

admired, and had to smile herself. "*The Hound of the Baskervilles*. It's a first edition."

He glanced at her and withdrew his hand. Kip thought she might see a hint of embarrassment at being caught admiring the century old tome. "I know," he said with a lopsided grin. "1902. Illustrated by Sydney Paget."

Kip arched an eyebrow. "A man who knows his antiquities. Talk like that is considered a form of seduction for a bibliophile."

The words were out of her lips before her better sense could slap them shut, but when he turned his head enough to focus his unique eyes on her, she lost the ability to say much else.

"I cannot claim any exceptional knowledge," he finally said after what was probably no more than a second or two, but her pounding pulse made it feel much longer. He spoke low, beneath the sound in the shop, and she instinctively looked to his mouth. "My father has this edition in his library."

"Too late," she managed to say after swallowing. "The damage is done."

Grayson looked down at the gloves in his hand and sucked in a sharp breath, letting it out on a strange chuckle, the corner of his lip nearest her ticking up in a grin that slipped away just as quickly. "In light of that, it may seem inappropriate to ask if there is somewhere we may speak with privacy, but I assure you..." He raised his head and leveled his gaze on her again, and Kip had a hard time remembering how to breathe. "My inquiry is honorable."

"Good lord," Kip said on an exhale, not sure if her whisper was a curse or a benediction. An antiquarian with the gift of eloquence; add in those eyes and he was a triple threat. "I can't offer much," she managed to answer. "I don't want to upset Beatrice if I don't have to. She owns the shop." It was easier to keep talking than risk doing something foolish like another pathetic attempt at flirting. *Flirting?* Since when did she even attempt flirting? She sucked at it. Kip glanced around. "Um, follow me."

She led him to the far back corner of the small shop, tucked behind the parallel aisles of seven-foot high, double sided bookshelves, where they displayed the travel and tourism books alongside the self-help section. As she expected, the corner was empty. Kip walked to the corner and turned, putting her back to the shelves to face him again.

"I can't hide back here for long," she explained.

"Understandable. I assume you aren't hearing anything unusual at the moment?"

Kip shook her head. "It stopped again just before you arrived."

"Agent Flannery is on his way here with a technical team. It is my hope they will be able to determine the source of the interference."

Kip didn't even try to hide her grimace at the name. "Great. One of my two favorite agents."

A squeal sliced through her head and Kip cried out before she could temper her reaction. She hunched forward, scrambling to yank the aids from her ears. Grayson gripped her elbows, steadying her, her forehead against his chest. The squeal died but went immediately to the dreaded clicking as she pulled them from her ears. Her heart pounded so hard it made her dizzy and she raised her head, looking up at Grayson.

The world had gone silent. No idle conversation between customers. No crack of old spines as books were opened and thumbed through; only the thumping of her own heartbeat deep in her ears.

Deep lines dug between his eyes and his lips formed a tight, strained line. Kip held up shaking hands, palms up, the aids in the center. Holding his gaze on her, Grayson released one arm to fold his hand over hers, holding it for a moment before he squeezed and then took the aid from her palm.

"We'll work this out," she read on his lips.

Kip nodded. "Just figure it out before I have a heart attack, okay?"

He smiled and nodded. Kip blinked, the heater vent in the floor beneath their feet kicked up a puff of dust along with the gust of hot air in her face. Grayson released her arms and she took a step back as he glanced over his shoulder. When he turned back to her, he waited until she looked up at him before he spoke.

"I need to speak with your employer."

Happy to escape the hot air blowing in her face, Kip nodded and led him again to the front of the store, spotting Agent Flannery standing near the door, another man with him dressed in an equally nondescript suit and coat. She headed toward the door toward the back office and tried to figure out as she walked just what she'd tell Beatrice Solomon about the two FBI and one MI6 agents following her.

Chapter Seven

Kip's head had to be splitting apart. There just had to be a crack in her skull from the middle of her forehead all the way to the top of her spine, because that was the only thing that could justify her headache. Her ears hurt deep, even though she had finally relented and removed her aids, and the pain continued to the back of her skull down her neck, exacerbated by the tension in her shoulders from constantly bracing for the next wave. Beatrice had been a doll to let her take the last half hour of her shift in the back room, with the lights turned down and lying on the couch. She could have gone home, but Grayson's cohorts weren't finished and she wanted to find out what they learned.

The office door opened, letting in a slice of light, and Grayson's tall, lean form filled the space. He left the door ajar and crossed the room, and Kip moved to sit up, but groaned instead.

He crossed the room quickly, his hand out, motioning her to lie back down. She obliged and sank back into the pillows. Grayson came to the side of the couch and crouched, not quite sitting on the edge, so she saw his face in the light from the door. It accentuated the angles of his features and the mad ruffle of his wavy hair. He'd taken off his coat shortly after Agent Flannery arrived, and it was draped over her feet. She hoped he didn't mind she'd confiscated it, but the office had a draft. Having only seen him in either his long coat or his dark suit that screamed "Secret Agent Man", she liked him in his dark sweater with a blue, thin-striped shirt beneath, folded at the ends of his sleeves to be shoved up near his elbows.

He pointed toward his lips. "Can you see me sufficiently?"

She nodded, but picked up her aids from where she'd rested them on her chest, since moving to place them elsewhere was too much effort. "I can, but I'll put them back in."

He touched her hand with his fingertips. "Are you sure? It isn't necessary for my sake," she read on his lips.

"I'm sure." She did take a deep breath, and released it, before sliding the aids into place and closing the battery cases so they chimed into activity and the noisy world snapped back into existence. Thankfully, there was no interference and no clicking. She looked to Grayson with a nod and thumbs up. "All good."

"How are you feeling?" he asked.

"Wicked headache," she answered, rubbing her fingers across her forehead. "It happens sometimes when I have too much input. That make sense?"

"Perfect sense."

"Did you figure it out?"

He smiled, one corner of his mouth bowing upward a beat before the other. "After much cursing and moaning on the part of Agent Hailey, we believe we found the source of the interference."

"First, just tell me…no bomb, right?"

"No bombs or explosives of any kind," he answered, the smile carrying in his voice. "However, determining the source might, as I suspected it would, assist with the remainder of the investigation. Every detail counts."

"What was it, then?"

He raised his eyebrows, his lips parting for a moment before he answered, as if the answer was amusing. "The building's heating system."

"What?" She started to sit up, but the rush to the front of her forehead, and Grayson's hand on her shoulder, put her right back down again.

His hand lingered on her shoulder long enough for Kip to forget her headache for a moment and focus on the weight of his touch through her cardigan. She wanted to look at the point of contact, to assure herself his hand was there and not just the phantom of it, but she was afraid if he still touched her and she looked, he'd take away his hand. Instead, she looked at him in the dim light, and her heart did a funny skip.

She was falling, even though she was lying down.

He withdrew, his fingers skimming her arm a moment longer before he linked his hands together, resting on his knees. He did shift sideways enough his hip came against the side of the couch for support.

"Yes, the heating system," he repeated. "There is a singular central heating boiler in the basement beneath the shop that heats all the other shops and the flats above us. It would seem the individual thermostats in each area communicate wirelessly with the heating boiler, sending a signal when each zone requires heat. What you heard was the interception of that signal. I suspect when it was most intense was the times when the shop's system kicked on, just as it did shortly after I arrived."

Kip scowled and shook her head against the throw pillows. "But, why all of a sudden? I mean, it's not like that system just went in this week."

"That question I cannot answer," he said with a shrug. "Perhaps there is a recent malfunction in your devices that has inadvertently attuned them to the frequency."

Kip shook her head again. A cold sweat skimmed her skin and her lungs restricted. It had been days since the explosion, and the physical signs on her face and body were all but gone, but every time the damn beeping went off she'd been back there all over again. She braced herself now for the stupid things to go off any second. Now, to know the only reason she were alive was a fluke, a malfunction, made her stomach twist. "So, just out of the blue the universe decided to screw around with my hearing aids so I don't get blown up?" She couldn't look at him, embarrassed by her tears, and stared at the dark ceiling.

The touch of his knuckles against her cheek made her breath catch, and she turned her head toward him, a tear escaping to slide down her temple to the point of contact between his skin to hers. Kip blinked, clearing her vision already compromised in the darkness.

"If that is the case," he said soft enough that she took the words more from his lips than what she heard, "then I am eternally grateful to the universe."

Three knocks made Kip startle and look toward the door, and Grayson draw back his hand. But he remained in his place beside the couch. Agent Flannery pushed the door further open and cleared his throat. "We're wrapping up."

"I'll be there shortly."

Grayson rose to stand, bracing his hand on the side of the couch. His fingers brushed her side, and Kip entertained the thought for a moment that the contact might have been deliberate. Once he stood at his full height, he looked down at her, the light from the store spreading across the floor to put him in the spotlight.

"I'll be right back. I want to assure you reach home safely."

Kip nodded and swallowed, watching him leave with the other agent. He had to come back; he'd left his coat draped across her legs. Squinting against the light, and the painful pulse behind her eyes, Kip sat up and swung her legs off the couch, drawing his coat into her lap. Before she thought better of it, she lifted the dark wool to her nose and inhaled. It smelled just like the scarf she still had at home, and had forgotten to give back to him. Fresh, clean, with layers of sandalwood. Nothing overpowering, but it stirred her senses and she thought perhaps even eased the headache a slight degree.

Either that, or the painkillers she'd taken half an hour before had finally kicked in.

By the time he came back into the office, she actually felt human. Though her ears still ached deep down to the drum, the headache had eased and she no longer squinted against the light from the main shop. When he returned, Beatrice walked with him, Kip's coat on her arm and a worried mother look on her face.

"How're you feeling, Kippie," she asked.

"Better. Thank you." Kip set aside Grayson's coat and braced her hands on either side of her knees to leverage herself off the old, sunken couch.

Grayson held out a hand.

She looked up at him for a moment before steeling her breath and setting her hand in his. With a gentle tug, he brought her to her feet, and squeezed her fingers before he let go. Kip took her coat, and before she could shrug it on, Grayson had it and held it for her. His fingers brushed her collarbones as he settled it on her shoulders. She couldn't remember ever being so aware of another person, but every touch – no matter how innocuous – felt monumental.

While Kip buttoned her coat, Grayson stepped around her to extend his hand to Beatrice. "Thank you, Mrs. Solomon, for being so gracious today in allowing us to investigate."

"Of course," Beatrice declared, waving off Grayson's words. "Why wouldn't I? I haven't managed to wrap my brain around it all yet, but I'll do what I can to help."

"Your attitude is much appreciated."

Beatrice reached for Kip's hand and squeezed. "You've frightened us all quite enough this week, Kippie. Now go home and rest. I'll see you on Tuesday."

Kip nodded, realizing with the movement her headache wasn't fully gone. "I will. I promise. Thank you so much for everything."

"Of course, Kippie. How are you getting home?" she asked as Kip took a step.

"Walk, as usual," Kip answered. "I can make it four blocks."

"I'll see to it she makes it home, Mrs. Solomon."

Beatrice smiled. "You do that, Mr. Holmes." Then she grinned wider. "Holmes. How funny. Did you say you were consulting on this?"

Grayson smiled, but it looked born more of discomfort than amusement. "Yes." He picked up his coat from the couch. "Thank you once again."

She continued talking as if he hadn't spoken. "I remember a few years back – oh, goodness, could have been twenty years or so. I can't remember things like that anymore – there was this whole group of literary scholars who came out with the 'revelation' Sherlock Holmes was a real man after all. I don't suppose you're old enough to remember all that, are you, Mr. Holmes?"

"On the contrary," he answered as he picked up his coat. "Thank you for your hospitality," he reiterated, and Beatrice nodded with a wide grin.

He pulled on his coat and buttoned it with one hand, curling his other around her elbow to lead her toward the door. The store was dim now, the "CLOSED" sign turned out to the street. It was only six, but winter in Boston already had the streetlights on and the sky dark. Thankfully, the weather had warmed to about forty, and the earlier flurry hadn't amounted to anything more than a wetting of the street. It would be February in a few days, but winter in Boston meant radical changes from one day to the next, from bitter cold to shirtsleeve weather all within the same week.

Grayson paused on the sidewalk, looking up and down each street specifically at the street sign designations. "You live this way, correct?" he asked, pointing to their right.

Kip nodded, realizing if anything the cool night air was doing wonders for her headache. "I'm impressed. It usually takes people months to get acquainted with the streets in Southie."

Grayson canted his head, a slight tug at the corners of his lips the only indication of another self-conscious grin. "Yes, well, I have a strong sense of direction." He pushed his hands into his coat pocket and looked down, his breath curling around his nose as he exhaled. She was about ready to ask him what was wrong when he lifted his head and looked to her again. "Are you hungry, Kipling?"

She smiled, warmth infusing her. "Yes. There's an amazing diner around the corner from my apartment building. They're one of the few in South Boston open on a Saturday night."

This time, the tick of his lips turned into a slow smile that creased his cheeks. He tilted his head in the direction of her building, and she stepped to his side. When they reached the corner, and the light changed to let them cross, his hand wrapped around hers, and he held it until they reached the diner five blocks away.

"This sandwich is absolutely obscene."

Kip chuckled, dipping the corner of her grilled cheese into her bowl of tomato soup. "I warned you they were big."

"This is beyond *big*," he argued. He stared at the three-inch thick turkey club sandwich and a pile of fries, his hands on the table on either side, palm up. "How does one manage to bite into something so obscene?"

"Ummm…carefully?" she offered with a grin before biting off the soup-drenched sandwich corner.

Kip smiled wider. Conversation was easy with Grayson; then again, so was flirting. Or, at least she equated the tendency of her tongue to spill out thinly veiled innuendo without asking her brain for permission to flirting. She kept her chin down, feigning interest in the crust of her sandwich, but watched from the corner of her eye as he maneuvered and finagled the sandwich until he managed a bite.

Once he managed to chew, swallow, and wipe his mouth, he sighed. "Certainly a challenge, but worth it. This is quite delicious."

"Nothing can beat a good diner. If you have room, they have great pie."

"Mmmm, I do love a pie, though Mum's would be difficult to improve on." He reached for the malt vinegar at the end of the table and drizzled it over his fries.

Kip sat back in the red and white vinyl booth seat and crossed her legs beneath the table. "Tell me about her."

He looked up from his next attempt at picking up the turkey club sandwich. "My mum?"

"Your family. You." As soon as the words left her mouth, once again without proper permission, heat bloomed in her cheeks and she looked away, reaching for her Coke. "You don't have to."

"Why wouldn't I want to?"

The rougher hint in his voice made her glance to him again, and he watched her with those intense eyes.

"Because it's none of my business."

His lips parted, just for a moment, before he spoke again and she wondered if he was mulling over how to respond, and she braced herself for an affirmation that was, indeed, none of her business.

"My mother," he began, picking up one of the fries, "went to university to be a teacher. Science. She's quite brilliant," he added with a whimsical smile. "Also quite extraordinary and a beautifully free spirit. She is the perfect counterpart for my father, who is an engineer and is every part the stereotype. He grounds her and she helps him fly."

Kip smiled on a sigh. "They sound wonderful."

"I wouldn't have agreed in my foolish youth, but I know now they are exemplary." He licked his lips from the fry and sipped at his water. "She is also American."

Kip realized her eyebrows bounced up in surprise faster than she could restrain her response. Grayson chuckled and added, "She was born and raised in Hampstead, New Hampshire a couple hours north of here, and attended New York University, who sent her to study in London for a year. While there, she met my father. They didn't marry until after she graduated, but once he proposed, they were wed within weeks."

Kip smiled. "Oh, that's a lovely story."

"I am the oldest, and have twin sisters," he continued. "Shirley and Johanna."

"Identical?"

He chuckled. "Hardly. They are like night and day, in both appearance and personality. Shirl is very much our mother's daughter and Jo her father's child."

"What about you? Who do you take after?"

His smile was strange, sincere but something more. Like the

answer was a question. "By what I have been told, I take strongly after my great-grandfather, but having never known him, I can't say for sure. I suppose, considering my mother's lightness of being and my father's analytical approach to life, I consider myself most like him and wish I were more like her."

His words, or maybe it was the way his eyes looked when he spoke of his parents, made Kip's chest squeeze a little tighter around her heart, and her vision blur. She blinked and sniffed, sitting forward again to focus her attention on her dinner.

"I don't know, Grayson Holmes. You don't strike me as the uptight and analytical sort. Observant, maybe, but that must be a job requirement, yeah?"

"Perhaps it is the company I keep that defines me."

He didn't look at her when he made the statement, but his tone made it seem he almost asked a question, and not of her. Not having his answer, she tried a different angle.

"You told Mom you grew up in Sussex. It's beautiful there. I visited once when I was in high school. I took this organized tour throughout the UK."

"What type of tour? Tours go through the Cotswolds every weekend, but I don't imagine a teenager taking an 'area of outstanding natural beauty' tour through southern England."

She smiled and tilted her head. "It was a themed tour." His raised eyebrow was now his common way of asking her to elaborate, and she liked it. "It was like a literary tour. Taking us to all these places made famous in books or by authors."

He looked down, intent again on the remains of the first half of his sandwich. "Now I understand."

"I bet you do," she said, teasing. "They took us to this cottage with a plaque on the outside declaring it was where Sherlock Holmes retired when he gave up being a consulting detective. I'd heard the theory Beatrice mentioned, that Sherlock was real, and I wonder now if that was the cottage in truth."

"Not likely," he answered, tapping a fry on the side of his plate to free it of excess vinegar, but tossed it back in the pile without eating it. Instead, he picked up the last bit of the sandwich half he'd been working on. "Sherlock Holmes was a very private man, by my understanding, and isn't likely to have declared far and wide where he settled in his final years."

"With a name like Holmes, you must have heard all the jokes, hmm?"

"Yes," was his simple answer before he popped the last of the sandwich half into his mouth. He brushed his hands together and chewed, speaking only after he swallowed. "If I intend to save any room for this amazing pie, I must stop now."

"We can share," she offered, then cleared her throat. "If you want."

When he looked at her again, it was with the same intense warmth he'd turned on her before that made her skin flush. "Sounds perfect."

The waitress came with take home containers, filled their drinks again, and took the order for one slice of apple pie à la mode, warm. When alone again, with a clear table, Kip folded her arms on top and rested her chin on her wrist.

"Now, tell me more about you."

"I'm far from interesting—"

"Liar," she cut off, and winked when he looked surprised. "You work for MI6 on loan to the FBI in Boston; how is that not interesting?"

"Perspective, I suppose."

"Did you always want to be an agent?"

"In one form or another," he answered, making her smile when he matched her pose so they looked at each other across the table with only a few inches between them. "Though technically I'm not an agent. I'm what is termed an officer. I handle or supervise a team of agents."

Kip made an "impressed" face, and followed with a wide smile. "Pardon me. So, did you always want to be in intelligence?"

"I knew as a child I wanted to be a police officer or detective inspector like—" He cut himself short, and huffed, shifting to rub at the corner of his eye. "As I grew up, and the world changed into this dark place, I decided I wanted or needed to be more. My cousin

Greg and I attended Cambridge together, and we joined MI6 together as well."

"I didn't think MI6 would dare recruit anyone from Cambridge."

Grayson arched an eyebrow, this time more in surprise than inquiry.

"Yes, I know my history," she said. "The Cambridge Five. Upper crust British students recruited by the Soviet Union during World War II and joined MI6 to accomplish it. Not usually covered in basic level history classes, but…" She shrugged. "I'm a reader."

"Well done." He sighed softly. "I would imagine by the time Greg and I attended Cambridge, the agency's screening methods were a bit more detailed beyond the social standing of your family name."

"That's awesome. I don't have siblings *or* cousins. My mother was an only child, my father was an only child, and I'm an only child. I think I envy you."

"We often envy what we don't know," he said cryptically.

The waitress came back with the pie, and although Grayson declared it the best he'd had in the States, it still fell to the shadow of Annalise Holmes' masterful creations. He demanded quid pro quo on the questions and answers, and she gave him the basics. An only child, as she'd already told him. Both her parents were literary professors, thus the embarrassment of her name was born of their love of Rudyard Kipling, and her in-born love of all things literary. So much so that she was a student of literature herself, and in her final semester before earning her doctorate in literature.

"What would you like to do once you've finished?" he asked, cutting away one-third of the pie's curled crust with the side of his fork.

"What else can you do with a degree like that?" she said with a chuckle, scooping up some of the remaining warm apple filling coated with melted ice cream and half of the remaining crust. "Teach."

"Here? In Boston?"

She shrugged. "I don't know. I'm open to anything."

"Would you leave Boston?"

"It would depend on the opportunity. I've traveled all over the world, and love so many of the places I've visited."

"What of your parents?"

Kipling laughed. "They are out of Massachusetts more than they are here. Since they retired, they do a *lot* of traveling."

He reached for the last bit of crust.

"That's the best part, hmmm?" she said as he scooped it up. "I love the crust."

He had a way of capturing her when he looked at her at times, like his eyes held her in place. He stared at her for several beats of her heart, and she swore she could see a battle stirring behind his eyes. Then, the battle won − or lost − Grayson held out his fork to her, offering the last bite. Her heart skipped and sped up, and holding his gaze, Kip leaned in and slid her lips along the fork, taking away the last bite. She hummed in appreciation and licked the flakes from her lips.

"Thank you."

"You're quite welcome," he said with a rough scrape to his voice as the waitress returned with the check. Sliding free of the booth, Grayson took his wallet from his pocket and left some bills on the table.

"Hang on, that's too much for your portion." Kip reached for her purse, but Grayson laid his hand on the table over the money he'd set down.

"I insist." Then he offered his hand to her and helped her from the booth. "Is your headache improved?" he asked as he helped her with her coat.

"Pretty much, yes. I needed to be away from the interference, I guess. I'll call my audiologist on Monday about having the aids looked at. Honestly, I'm not sure I could go another day like today."

"I have requested Agent Hailey provide me the frequency of the signal. Once I have it, I will pass it on in the hope that your doctor can possibly use it to repair the issue."

"Thanks. That'd be great."

He held the door for her and she brushed past him onto the

sidewalk. They walked out of the diner and turned together toward the street that led to her apartment. Grayson said nothing as they walked, and this time he didn't take her hand when they crossed at the corner, his hands shoved deep in his coat pockets. Each time they passed under a light, Kip looked to him and the tension around his eyes and mouth made her stomach knot. At her building, she unlocked the door and he followed her inside, but stopped at the bottom of the stairs leading up to her floor.

"Kipling," he said, curling his hand around her lower arm to stop her.

She turned, standing on the bottom step so she was eye level with him. "What?"

When he raised his chin to look at her, her skin chilled and she had the distinct feeling she wouldn't like what he was about to say. He looked down again and slid his hand along her coat sleeve until he reached her hand, and wrapped his cool fingers around hers. Then he huffed and cleared his throat.

"Spill it," she said. "I think whatever it is you've been trying to get the nerve up to say it all evening."

Grayson raised his chin and smiled, but it was hesitant and incomplete. "You are quite perceptive, Kipling."

"And you are quite lucky," she said, smiling when that eyebrow twitched. "You are the *only* person I let get away with calling me Kipling."

He chuckled once, and smiled briefly, but it slid away again. "As one not inclined to speak of sentiment and such, I find this is quite possibly one of the most difficult conversations I've had in a long time."

"If we were together, I'd think I was being dumped."

"How apropos," he said a bit softer. "Kipling…"

She turned her hand in his and linked their fingers. "You don't have to say it." He looked down at their joined hands, then raised his head and focused on her again, making her insides flutter. Which made the conversation sting all the more. "I'm no expert on agency rules, whether it be the FBI or MI6, but I've read enough romance novels and watched enough television shows to guess there's some kind of stipulation saying we shouldn't have eaten dinner together, let alone anything else. And..." She bounced their joined hands. "You probably shouldn't even hold my hand."

His hold relaxed, but she tightened hers, and didn't let him pull away. Not yet.

"As I said. Quite perceptive." The weight of his voice was tangible, and despite the conversation, she couldn't help the hitch in her breath when his gaze settled on her mouth. "However, my hesitation is not due to any agency obligations, whether it be the FBI here or the SIS. There is nothing regarding your involvement in this investigation that would prevent us from seeing one another should we wish to. My trepidation is rooted elsewhere."

Embarrassment burned hot beneath the surface of her skin, crawling up from the collar of her coat all the way to her hairline. She swallowed and looked away, unable to look him in the eye anymore. She tried to chuckle it off, quirking a strained smile. "Hey, no worries," she said, still averting her eyes. "I'm a big girl. You don't need to say anything else."

He shifted his stance to bring himself into her line of vision again, waiting until she gave in to the urge to look him in the eyes. When she did, he shook his head, a slow easing to the left and right. "I fear I am handling this poorly, and for that I beg your forgiveness, Kipling. This situation is..." he trailed off, smiling. The kind of smile that made her coat smothering in the warmth of the foyer. "... unique for me."

Grayson laid his other hand over hers, sandwiching her fingers between both his palms, and rubbed his skin across hers. Kipling found it hard to breathe, tensing her arm to keep the tremble in her stomach from traveling to her fingers. He stared at their joined hands for a few moments before meeting her eyes. "Kipling, that night at the university I was in preparation for leaving Boston. Were it not for what happened, I would have already been gone."

Kip cleared her throat and looked up the empty staircase, taking a moment to try to find a regular heartbeat before she looked to him again. "How long are you here now?"

"I do not know," he answered, shaking his head again. "I have been ordered by my director to remain in Boston until the perpetrator is in custody, or until it is determined my presence at the attack was coincidental and my continued assistance is no longer warranted."

"That sounds so clinical." She tried to smile again. "I love your eloquence, but sometimes it makes it worse."

"I am sorry—"

"Don't be. It's okay." Kip shook her head. "I understand." She shifted on the balls of her feet, nervousness and disappointment making her antsy. "The heart of the matter is when this is over, one way or another, you go back to London."

He didn't answer right away, and in the hesitation, she knew the answer already. Grayson nodded, his unusually colored eyes shifting to study her face with the same effect on her as a touch. A caress that didn't exist. Kip pressed her lips together and swallowed, nodding.

"I tell you what," she managed to say, avoiding his direct stare as she said it. "I'm going to give you an easy out."

"An easy out?" he asked with a scowl and cant of his head.

"Yeah." She drew in a fortifying breath before looking him in the eyes again. "Tell me this was one-sided, all on me being a foolish American entranced by your accent and great hair and sexy cheekbones…"

She rattled off the characteristics with a toss of her hand in an attempt to convince herself it would make the whole conversation easier. It didn't.

"Tell me you see this sort of thing all the time. You feel nothing more than the obligatory concern for another human being as required by your job title, and I will be so mortified and so embarrassed I'll hope not to see you again."

His expression saddened and his eyes shifted left and right, his gaze skimming her face. She thought the way his eyes felt like a touch was torture, but it was nothing compared to him raising one hand to skim her hairline with the tips of his fingers. He slid his thumb across her cheek where only the slightest pink marks remained from her fall, then brought the same thumb to her lips.

All the old clichés came to mind. Weak in the knees. Heart pounding like a caged bird. Breath shallow and rapid. Dizzied by his touch. She had to fist her free hand to keep from sliding it inside his coat to see if his heart beat as hard as hers.

Was this how Jane Eyre felt when Mr. Rochester touched her?

Elizabeth Bennett and Mr. Darcy?

"I cannot and will not lie to you," was Grayson's answer. He stared at her mouth, where his thumb drew at her lower lip. "My conscience tells me it is unfair to pursue whatever might be between us when I might very well be on a plane to Heathrow within twenty-four hours."

"So what you're saying is you're trying to be a gentleman and spare my tender heart?" she asked, her voice barely coming as a raspy whisper.

"Your heart. And mine." His touch firmed just enough to urge her to tip up her chin, her heart jumping when she swore he moved an inch closer. "This…scenario…is entirely foreign to me to such an extreme I have no personal intuition regarding the proper way it should be handled. I do know I have let myself tempt fate this far, but I have reached my limits. I have no more restraint."

"You're making it really hard to be mature about this," Kip whispered, loving the feel of his thumb still on her lip.

He smiled, slow and heated. "As are you, Kipling."

She sucked in a fortifying breath and shook her head, breaking the contact, her hair falling around her face. "I know I should wish you the best of luck, but part of me—" She hated the crack in her voice. How could she be so upset over losing something she never had?

Grayson raised her hand to his lips, and pressed a kiss to her fingers before meeting her eyes. "I must go."

She nodded, but couldn't find anything to say. Didn't know if she could speak if she had the words. One more kiss to her knuckles, and he released her, walking to the door. He paused, the door open with the cold night air swirling into the foyer, looked to her for several pounding beats of her heart, then slipped through the door.

And was gone.

Chapter Eight

Watson jumped onto the low table where Grayson had spread out the various files on the university case, and without pause, strolled across the laptop keyboard and into Grayson's lap. With a bump of his head on Grayson's chin, he effectively blocked Grayson's view of the screen.

"Can I help you?" Grayson said with a chuckle, rubbing Watson's head. "I'm a bit busy here baring my soul. Or at least attempting to. Do you mind?"

Watson bumped his chin again before stretching across Grayson's lap, partially on the laptop keyboard. The cat had been uncharacteristically affectionate since the night before when Grayson returned from seeing Kipling home, even going so far as to sleep on Grayson's pillow; something Watson had never done, and Grayson preferred he not repeat. It was one thing to share a corner of the bed with the moggy beast, another thing entirely to share his pillow.

"I'm busy," he scolded, and lifted the cat off his lap to the cushion beside him, then slid the laptop closer to type again.

Not to be dissuaded, Watson scooted under Grayson's arm and again stretched across the keyboard. Grayson sighed and let his hands drop to the cushion on either side of his legs, staring down at the possessed tabby. Watson was a roommate and sometimes served as Grayson's sounding board and silent council, but affection usually only occurred when the cat was hungry or bored.

He seemed neither at the moment unless irritating Grayson was his means of curing his boredom.

Grayson sighed and laid his hand on Watson's back, the cat twitching at the contact but his rumbled purr vibrated against Grayson's palm. He never considered himself a "cat" person, or a pet person at all, but three years before his mother had discovered a mongrel litter of kittens in their tool shed and had aggressively volunteered Grayson and his sisters to each take one of the grey and black tabbies. Grayson learned fairly quickly if he were to have a pet, the independent cat was probably his best option, and while he could have left Watson with his parents or a sister while he traveled to Boston, he ultimately decided he preferred the pest's company over none at all. Skirting the requirements of pet transportation between the UK and the US had been troublesome but being a member of the Royal Majesty's Secret Service held some benefits and some clout.

The cat's name had been Shirl's idea, carrying on the family tradition of mocking the family tradition.

"I suppose you'd offer just as valid advice as Greg," Grayson said to the cat, rubbing his fingertips between the cat's ears. "What do you think I should do about Kipling?"

Watson raised his head and looked at Grayson, blinking slowly over his green eyes. Grayson saw neither an answer nor any interest beyond Grayson's petting. He chuckled and shook his head. "You're no help."

His mobile toned and vibrated across the stack of files, and Grayson once again set Watson on the couch cushion so he could reach forward and retrieve the device. The screen displayed Flannery's name, and Grayson sighed before answering.

"Holmes," he said, leaning forward with his elbows resting on his knees.

"I just got the preliminary report back from the tech team. You said you wanted the frequency range on that thermostat setting, right?"

"Yes." Grayson shuffled through the files, finding a pencil and his notebook. "Go ahead."

Flannery rattled off a frequency code, and Grayson repeated it back to be sure. "Yeah, you got it," Flannery confirmed. "What did you need it for?"

Grayson tossed down his pencil. "I intend to provide it to Miss Branson. Perhaps having the exact frequency will assist her audiologist in making adjustments to her hearing devices so she won't continue to have the issues she had yesterday."

"You two seemed awful chummy yesterday."

"You would do well to focus on the investigation," Grayson cut off, realizing too late he probably made the assumption worse by defending himself too quickly. "This is a courtesy only."

"Yeah. Okay," Flannery said. "Look, I gotta go. The wife wants to take the kids candlepin bowling, get 'em out of the house for a while."

"Thank you for the information."

"Yeah, sure, chief."

Then the line clicked off and Grayson set the mobile on the table again, staring at the image of his sisters he used as his phone wallpaper, Shirl with her blond waves and big smile, Jo with her darker, shorter hair and reserved eyes. Suddenly he missed his family a great deal.

Perhaps more because he wished their counsel. Anyone's counsel other than unanswered ramblings and a brooding cat.

Though, he doubted he would require much imagination to assume what advice each of his family members would provide. As always, an even division amongst the Holmeses. His father and Jo would be on the side of reserve, his mother and Shirl on the side of surrender to the plans of the universe. They would also likely be ecstatic over Grayson's particular predicament, having long since said he required a good shaking up when it came to such things.

Greg would be the tipping vote. Unfortunately, Grayson could not easily discern the advice his cousin would offer, not exactly. Greg had always been the ladies' man between them, never without companionship on a Friday or Saturday evening, though none of his female companions stayed long past a few weeks, many claiming a sense of secondary importance to the demands of his job. Perhaps the longest association Grayson could recall had been Esther, and she and Greg had gone so far as to share a flat for nearly six months; hardly comparable to the two semi-permanent relationships Grayson had had since his sojourn into adulthood, with only a smattering of dates between.

None since Liz, either because he hadn't felt so inclined, or because his heart had been too broken to think of companionship beyond Watson and his family. Liz didn't break it, but she had been inadequate to heal it either.

There had never been a woman who affected him like Kipling Branson and in a completely unexpected and utterly indefinable manner. Even as he attempted to convince her – and himself – that they should have been nothing more than acquaintances, he had been unable to resist the necessity of touching her. It hadn't been a wish, a desire; it had most definitely been a necessity.

What could it be about this woman to awaken – create – such a compulsive need?

Walking away the previous evening had been an exacting task, considering his strongest desire had been to taste her lips to see if they tasted of the apple pie they shared.

He stared at the phone and the information scribbled in his awkward hand and raked his fingers through his hair. Watson lay beside him, content now to bathe by licking at his short hair and ignoring Grayson's struggle.

With a growl deep in his throat, Grayson snatched up the mobile and opened his contacts, clicking on her name. Her profile held only a silhouette image generic to the phone, and he had a passing wish to replace it with an image of her before he left Boston entirely. Shaking off the thought, he dialed.

She picked up on the third ring. "Grayson?"

He smiled; pleased she had to have programmed his number into her mobile. "Hello, Kipling." When she didn't say anything immediately, he cleared his throat. "I've been provided the exact frequency on which the heating boiler transmits, and thought it might possibly be helpful when you visit your doctor."

"Of course," she said, softer than before, and he heard some shuffling. "Mina, could you hand me that notepad? Thanks. Go ahead. I'll write it down."

He provided it and waited until he heard the tap of her setting down her pen.

"I hope it is of assistance," he said.

"I don't know. I'm calling Doctor Seshadri first thing tomorrow to explain. Thank you, Grayson."

Grayson closed his eyes and rubbed his eyelids with his thumb and index finger, a knot of dread in his stomach at the reserved tone in her voice. Not that he didn't outright deserve it. He'd been a prat to entertain the draw between them only to tell her he was wrong to do so, and then walk away.

"How are you feeling today?" he asked. "Better?"

"Yes. I needed to get away from the shop yesterday, and," she paused, a sigh carrying in her voice. "I felt better after we ate. The fresh air did me good."

"Good." He winced, hating his sudden loss of the ability to string together a decent sentence. Grayson cleared his throat. "I know you have company, so I won't keep you."

"Thank you," she said again, more strain in her voice. "I appreciate your thoughtfulness."

"Of course."

"Goodbye, Grayson."

"Goodbye, Kipling–" but the line was already disconnected.

Grayson tossed the mobile on the table, making Watson jump. "Bloody hell," he cursed and flopped back into the couch cushions.

Kip tapped the red disconnect button on her phone screen and stared at the image as it changed to her standard wallpaper, a photo of Fenway Stadium at night. She let out a long breath and sat forward, resting her forehead in her open hand.

"Was that the agent you told me about? Grayson?" Mina asked, crossing from the kitchen in her condo to where Kip sat in the breakfast nook. Kip nodded as her best friend sat, sliding a cup of tea toward Kip. She didn't have the energy to correct the "agent" designation. "Why did he call? Something happen?"

Kip snorted, surprised by the hot tears prickling at the back of her eyes. "Funny way to put it. Something most definitely did *not* happen."

Mina scowled, stirring honey into her cup. "Okay, you've been off since you got here, and you look exhausted. Are you sleeping? Tell me what's going on."

Kip groaned, long and dramatic, and dropped her head onto her folded arms. "I don't even know where to begin," she moaned to the tabletop, her voice echoing back to her.

When Mina didn't say anything, Kip finally raised her head and set her temple against her hand, propping herself up. She was tired, a bone-weary tired. She hadn't slept well the night before, and it was one of a series of restless nights. She hadn't slept solidly since the day after the explosion and she'd slept all day, just like Grayson told her she would. She found her best friend staring at her, just…waiting.

"Grayson Holmes," Kip finally said. "He is what's the matter."

Mina's scowl went from curious to concerned. "Kip, did he do something inappropriate?"

Kip couldn't help it. She laughed, laughed until tears ran down her cheeks and her side hurt, and until the tears turned their course to the heaviness that had sat in her chest since he'd left her. Mina left the table only long enough to come back with a box of tissues, setting it in front of Kip. She refused to let the tears remain, refused to cry over something that had effectively never existed, so after one solid jagged sob, she sucked in a breath and made them stop. Under control again, Kip pulled her feet up into the kitchen chair and hugged her knees to her chest.

"To answer your question, no, he hasn't done anything inappropriate. And therein lies the problem."

"I don't get it…"

Kip sniffed and rubbed her cheek against her knees. Then she told her best friend the entirety of the day before, from the way Grayson came as soon as she called, to the way she'd flirted before she even considered the act, to the many times he touched her in simple, small ways that made her skin sing, and yet he had appeared to agonize over every moment. How he watched out for her, took care of her, never made her feel her hearing was a detriment, and never once made her feel she put him out for calling on a Saturday. She told Mina about his family, and how he spoke of his mother with a reverence and endearing love that had made Kip's heart ache with the loveliness of it.

And she ended with their farewell in the foyer.

"I swear, Mina, if he *had* actually kissed me I think I would have–" She huffed out a breath. "Well, it would have been embarrassing, whatever I did. Do you remember that amazing *non*-kiss from *Pride and Prejudice*? The one with Kiera Knightley and Matthew McFadyen? When they're standing in that gazebo, and the rain is pouring down, and for all their arguing you're holding your breath waiting for him to kiss her?"

Mina hummed in appreciation. "Oh, and the way he kept staring at her lips like he wanted to lean in *so* bad."

"That's how I felt, Mina." Kip unfolded her legs and stood, walking toward the kitchen counter. "I told him if I said it was one sided, if it were just me romanticizing everything, I'd be mortified but I'd be okay with it." She turned again and looked at Mina. "He wouldn't. He said it would be a lie, and he wouldn't lie about how he felt."

Mina pressed her lips together and her eyes glistened. "Damn, Kip, that's beautiful."

Kip turned on the balls of her feet and groaned out loud, shaking her fists. "It's like someone slipped into my brain and found the one man absolutely perfect for me! He's attractive, he's educated, he's eloquent, and he knows his book antiquities–"

"Good lord, how did you not jump him in the back room of the bookstore?"

Mina's jibe made her laugh, and some of the tension eased away like it always did after some time with her best friend. She turned again to face Mina and crossed her arms, smiling. "I tell you, I was hard-pressed not to. In fact, I pretty much told him as much."

Mina's jaw dropped. "You did not!"

"Yep, I did." She went back to the chair and sat again, taking a sip of her now lukewarm tea. "So, there you have it. The whole sordid affair. Or, non-affair."

"I don't get why he is holding back. What's the big deal if it's not some regulation or something?"

"Yeah…there's one detail I've left out." Mina's eyebrow jumped up, and for a moment it reminded her of Grayson. "Grayson isn't FBI, technically."

"Technically…" Mina led.

"He's MI6. He's helping until the investigation is done, or they decide he no longer needs to be a part of it."

"MI6?" Mina practically shouted. "That's like the British CIA, right? He's British?"

"English, yes. When this is done–"

"He goes back," Mina finished.

"And my life sucks…"

Kip usually wouldn't walk the twelve blocks from Mina's condo to her apartment, but she wanted the exercise and needed the fresh air and it wasn't nearly as cold as it had been. By halfway home, she regretted her choice because the sun went down and the temperature dropped. Four blocks left to her house and her lips were numb and the tip of her nose stung. She tucked Grayson's tartan scarf around her chin and neck to fend off the chill.

Her breath curled in front of her face as she rounded the last corner leading to her street. Two more blocks and she'd be back inside, warm, and she might get feeling back in her toes. As she passed the end of an alley between a thrift store and a Greek pizzeria, a thundering crash echoed off the brick building walls, and Kip screamed.

"Sorry, ma'am," came a voice down the alley. "Didn't mean ta scare ya."

Kip pressed her hand to her chest, able to feel her heart pounding viciously through the thick padding of her coat, and tried to breathe normal. She squinted and looked down the alley, realizing one of the staff stood beside an old maroon Dumpster.

"Hey, you okay?" he asked, walking toward her, half a smoked cigarette hanging out of his lips. "Oh, hey, Kip."

She blinked, feeling lightheaded, finally bringing Nick Manos, the owner's son, into focus. Kip tried to talk, but nothing would come from her throat. Nick came toward her, holding one hand out toward her.

"Kip, you okay?"

She nodded, finally finding her voice enough to say "Yeah. I'm fine. I'm-I'm fine."

"You sure?"

She nodded more vigorously and started down the sidewalk again. "G-goodnight, Nick."

By the time she reached her apartment, her chest pounded, her pulse raced, she couldn't catch her breath, and her vision was out of focus. Her hand shook so violently it took her half a dozen tries to get her key into the door lock and the door open. Kip stumbled into her apartment, yanking off her smothering coat, and fell to her knees on her kitchen floor, sudden and choking sobs tearing their way out of her throat. Kip curled over her legs, arms wrapped around her body, fighting for control.

"I'm fine," she hissed out to the empty apartment. "I'm fine. I'm fine. I'm here and I'm fine."

Chapter Nine

"What the hell is all that?"

Grayson turned from the wall of his office now covered with photos, printouts, and long strands of thread tied to push pins. He stepped down from his short ladder and turned to Agent Flannery. "It's a data map."

"Looks like an art project my five year old put on the fridge." The agent set his hands on his hips and scanned the display. "How long have you been here doing this?"

Grayson rubbed at the corner of his eye by his nose, trying not to think about just how long he'd been awake. "It was about two am when I got here. I'd done all I could at the hotel, and there was no wall of sufficient size."

"That, and I'm pretty sure you'd lose your security deposit." Flannery walked forward, still studying the map. "You're connecting the dots."

"Precisely. I've reached a point where a visualization of the data seems prudent. This investigation lacks any viable data, so I am starting at the beginning. Considering our attempt to keep your partner separate from the actual research, it has been a challenge."

"Soon my *former* partner," Flannery corrected.

"I do suppose, regardless of the reason, you will be free of him soon. Where is he? I haven't heard him, and since he has a tendency toward the loud and annoying – especially when he believes his volume might disturb me – I'm quite sure he has yet to show up this morning."

Flannery looked over his shoulder toward the connected office. "Yeah, I haven't seen him either. Who the hell knows these days?"

Grayson crossed to his desk to pick up the last photo he needed to complete the existing map. "I'm compiling correlative data between all students in the class – both those there that night, and those absent – and anyone connected to them that may have explosives knowledge and a possible grudge. Finding nothing worth pursuing, I then expanded to faculty, staff, contractors, associates, family connections…" He rolled his hand with each level, encompassing the wall.

"Any connections?" Flannery asked, looking over his shoulder at Grayson. He squinted back at the data map. "Did you figure out anything?"

"There are a precious few connections that have narrowed down possible avenues of investigation to three." Grayson moved around Flannery to stand between him and the wall, placing the final image in its position. A loose thread hung from a tack, waiting for assignment, and Grayson pinched it between his fingers to wrap around the tack holding the photo. He pointed at the threads connecting various clusters of photos and notes.

The data map was cumbersome, and likely appeared to be little more than chaos to Agent Flannery, but the links served a purpose: to illustrate to others in the best way possible the three-dimensional labyrinth in Grayson's mind. In his reality, he stood in the center of a fully graphed Cartesian coordinate map, able to mentally turn and track each fiber no matter how substantial or ethereal. Unfortunately, even now, the connections were weak. A single fact or bit of evidence, one way or another, could either break a thread or strengthen it.

"These are the common connections. They overlap, here…" He pointed. "Here…and here. Now, we need to find how *those* elements connect. Whom. Sadly, even those threads I've found are weak and unlikely to actually produce answers."

"No theories?"

"It is a capital mistake to theorize before one has data," Grayson said, shaking his head as the familiar quote was out of his mind and lips before he could hold in check the impulse.

"Have you looked for connections to you in any way?"

Grayson sighed. Agent Flannery's question evoked the claw of frustration that had dug at him since the afternoon prior. There was nothing, *nothing* connecting any student or person connected with the university back to him other than the ambiguous fact the students attended a class his great-uncle taught. The likelihood of that being the instigation seemed so far beyond probability he hadn't bothered to calculate the chances.

"I have found none save for those thinnest threads that lead nowhere and are easily broken, like a spider web."

Flannery chuckled and shook his head. "You could have just said you didn't find any."

Grayson scowled and looked at the other agent. "Didn't I?"

"Yeah, sure. Okay. So, now what?"

"Deduction. We keep looking. We keep searching for the tiny bits of data that reveal the truth."

Flannery smirked and crossed his arms. "Did you just seriously say deduction?"

"Yes. It's accurate. Deduction is the inference of particular instances and conclusions by referencing general laws and principles. We take what we know, and we determine what we don't."

"Yeah, but seriously. *Deduction.*"

Grayson scowled and shook his head. "I fail to see your point."

Flannery chuckled. "Never mind."

Grayson turned away from Flannery, knowing he schooled his expression sufficiently to convince the other man he was "clueless" to the reference. If Agent Flannery wished to play the numpty, Grayson was willing to oblige and help him along.

"So, what do you need from me?"

Before he could answer, the office door flew open and Section

Chief Stanton stepped in. "We've got a lead," he snapped out without preamble. "Kinda."

"What?" Grayson demanded.

"He's one cocky son of a bitch." Stanton crossed the room and held out a color print out of a photographed piece of paper. "Local branch of a credit union in Beacon Hill was robbed at gunpoint twenty minutes ago. But get this: he only asked for the available cash in the cashier's drawer, and handed her this before he left."

Grayson took the piece of paper and turned it so he could read. Two distinct phrases, printed in an elaborate, yet computer generated, font, in large letters so the words took up the top two-thirds of the paper.

The game is afoot.

There is nothing new under the sun. It has all been done before.

Beneath the quotes was a headline clipping from the Boston Globe.

PROFESSOR, STUDENTS KILLED IN EXPLOSION AT BOSTON UNIVERSITY, MANY INJURED
NO SUSPECT KNOWN

Grayson raised his head and looked to Director Stanton, whose flushed cheeks and set jaw spoke of his anger. "This clarifies, then, the intended target."

"How do we know?" Flannery asked, taking the paper from Grayson. He tapped it with the back of his fingers, the paper snapping. "I mean, this guy could just be trying to take blame for the explosion. Looking for credit when it's not him at all. That happens all the time."

"Except for the literary references," Grayson pointed out, and Flannery looked at him with arched eyebrows. "The game is afoot,"

Grayson repeated. "One of the most infamous lines of dialogue from *The Adventures of Sherlock Holmes*. The second reference is also from *A Study in Scarlet*, though a paraphrase from Ecclesiastes. Since my identity was withheld from all media reports, the person who left this love note is aware of who I am, and my presence at the lecture hall."

"Geez, full of yourself much?" Flannery asked with a mocking laugh. Grayson turned a slow, non-amused glare on him, and Flannery cleared his throat. "So, what…we've got a wackjob on our hands. An obsessed Sherlock Holmes fan, or something?"

"A *wackjob*, as you put it, or a fan; either way they have personal knowledge on me. There are several angles of this revelation that trouble me."

"Well, I guess you're not getting out of Boston any time soon," Stanton said, taking back the paper. "I'll send a message to Director Cooper and apprise him of the situation."

Grayson never contemplated the ability to feel so many warring emotions at the same time, alongside his disappointment at not returning to London and his indignation that someone would dare threaten him via the Holmes name was his sudden and undeniable pleasure at the realization he would be in Boston for at least a few days longer. His conscience immediately reminded him all this still meant he would be leaving eventually, but as he had often done before, he shut the mental door on his inner dialogue.

"I assume the thief was not captured," Grayson asked.

"No," Stanton confirmed. "He took the cash in hand, not in a bag, so the cashier couldn't slip in a tracking device or ink bomb. The stack of bills only equaled a few thousand dollars and he pocketed the cash. He was in and out in less than two minutes, and most of the other employees and customers in the bank didn't even realize they were being robbed. He was apparently very polite."

"Was he American?" Grayson asked.

Flannery snorted a laugh. "Probably not. A polite bank robber has to be British."

Stanton shot Flannery a look, glaring at him while he answered Grayson. "He didn't wear a mask, but the cashier described him as white based on what she could see. Some unshaved facial hair, like a day or two growth. Dark brown. Less than six feet and average build. That's all she could say since he was in full winter wear, beanie, scarf over half his face, and gloves included. Winter in Boston makes it easy to be in disguise, I guess, without drawing attention."

"CCTV?"

"We're working on getting the files now. Whether intentional or not, the guy robbed a local bank, which means the robbery doesn't fall under FBI jurisdiction. We received the report as a courtesy since robbers sometimes escalate, and once they hit a national reserve institution the case is ours. The message caught my attention, and I made some calls. We should have the video by the end of the day."

"Intriguing…" Grayson said.

"In what way?" Stanton asked.

"Isn't it obvious?" Grayson asked, raising his head to look at the director, then to Flannery.

Their expectant stares answered his question.

"Clearly it's not," he said and sighed before continuing. "The intent of this robbery was not for the money, it was to send this message. They only took what was in the drawer to avoid the tracking device or ink pouch. It allowed them to get in and out quickly. And by robbing a small local branch, it delayed the FBI's involvement long enough to blur the trail."

"So, first they try to kill you – whoever they are – then they hatch a plan to wave and say hello?" Flannery said, making a derisive, dismissing snort. "I don't know if this bastard qualifies as an idiot or a criminal genius."

Grayson nodded. "The truth remains to be seen."

Kip woke on the kitchen floor to complete darkness and an imbalance in the noises around her. She pushed herself up and raised her head enough to see the time on the microwave display.

3:47

A quick touch to her ears helped her determine both aids were still in place, but the lack of input said the batteries had died in the night at some point. Weary to the bone, she got to her knees and used a kitchen chair for leverage to gain her feet. She stumbled through her apartment to her bedroom and collapsed on the bed, still fully dressed, but too drained to bother for pajamas. The best she could manage was setting her dead aids on the bedside table so she at least had the peace of silence.

Despite the exhaustion that dragged at her bones, she never fell fully back asleep, spending the rest of the morning hours tossing and turning, jerking awake each time her body tried to find the rest it needed. She hadn't slept more than two hours at a stretch since Saturday night, the sound of incessant clicking, explosions, and sirens filling her dreams when she did find sleep.

When the sun rose and the clock told Kip it was late enough to call her audiologist, she forced herself from bed and to the shower. She was bounced from receptionist to technician, and finally to Doctor Seshadri when she called, and she explained to each in turn what was wrong.

"How quickly can you be here?" Doctor Seshadri asked after Kip's third explanation.

Kip sat on the edge of her bed and hunched forward, one hand supporting her head at her brow while the other held her phone. She couldn't muster enough focus to look at the screen while talking and was thankful the Bluetooth interface didn't require she actually hold up her arm.

"Um, probably an hour and a half," she said, knowing she mumbled. "I need..." She forced her eyes open. "I need some coffee, and then to get across the city." With a groan, she remembered she also needed to go to the university campus later in the morning.

She hadn't been there since the explosion.

"Get here whenever you can, and we'll take care of this. See you soon, Kip."

By the time Kip reached Doctor Seshadri's office building in Cambridge she felt at least mostly human. She'd gotten an extra shot in her Dunkin' that morning, and the caffeine revived her senses. She only had to wait for ten minutes for the receptionist to send her back to Doctor Seshadri's office, and the middle-aged Indian woman met her with a hug rather than a handshake.

"I'm so pleased you are okay," she said, releasing Kip. "I watched all the news reports – who can help but to watch? – but I didn't realize you had been there."

"I suppose that type of information is kept moderately confidential," Kip said, sitting in the chair across the desk from Doctor Seshadri's chair. "The media gave the names of those who died, but not…" She trailed off, not sure anymore how to categorize herself. "Doesn't mean people don't know. I've been visited once by Ellen Kennedy looking for a story. The survivor's angle."

"I assume you didn't speak with her?

"No," Kip said, shaking her head. "Definitely not."

"Either way, I'm happy you are fine. You are, aren't you?"

Kip nodded and shrugged. "I'm here, right? I'm fine."

"Well, it's just like the witnesses said," Agent Flannery said, then sighed and motioned toward the video screen playing out the robbery from that morning. "Scarf. Beanie. Gloves. Hell, he's practically covered from head to toe. There isn't enough of him visible for even our best face recognition programs to work."

Grayson drew in a slow, metered breath before answering, fighting the urge to shake his head.

"Be that as it may, we can still garner useful information from the surveillance video. Though black and white, it's ascertainable the man is Caucasian. He's just shy of six feet tall, and probably eleven stones six." He paused and ran the calculation in his head, knowing once he spoke that Flannery and Stanton wouldn't understand. "About one hundred sixty pounds."

"That describes half the male population of the city," Stanton said. "We can get on correlating your list, Holmes, with the description. Might give us something."

"There is more. His gait is uneven and he holds his arm against his side as if either recently injured, or perhaps habit from an old injury. If he is our bomb maker, the injury may be an old hazard of the trade."

"I didn't catch that. You're right," Flannery said, leaning forward to bring his nose closer to the screen.

"He does not walk with authority or self-confidence, nor does he carry his frame like a man sure of his mission. This may imply he is a man easily manipulated." Grayson tapped his finger on the large computer screen where they viewed the CCTV recording of the morning's burglary, the details falling into place in his mind like a cascading puzzle. "This man is not the planner. He may possess knowledge to build a bomb and access to the university, but I suspect he is being guided to do what he has done. We need to find *him*, yes, but we need to find the man pulling the puppet's strings."

"Damn it," Stanton cursed.

Grayson braced his hands on the edge of the desk and pushed away, thinking a far worse explicative. "Now I understand why I could find no common threads between myself and anyone known to be on the campus or connected to anyone involved with the university. I probably would have had more luck finding a connection between myself and a florist in Boise, Idaho." He turned back to face his American peers. "If whomever is truly behind this is as clever as I suspect, they would have intentionally found someone of no consequence, with no knowledge not directly fed to him, and someone with no connections to find."

"Fat lot of good this did, then."

Grayson canted his head. "No, actually, this has done a great deal. I know now where *not* to look, and sometimes, that is the best place to begin any search." Grayson chuckled before adding, "It is of the highest importance in the art of detection to be able to recognize, out of a number of facts, which are incidental and which are vital. Otherwise, your energy and attention must be dissipated instead of being concentrated." He looked to Stanton and Flannery. "If our criminal can quote Sherlock Holmes, then so shall I."

Kip hadn't been to the campus since the explosion, not needing to since her final semester consisted mostly of research and the occasional visitation with a professor. Her only lecture class had been comparative literature, and the future of that class was still in question. There was talk of canceling it outright and freezing the grades of the students who survived the bombing. Those in good standing would receive their graduation credits. The decision was forthcoming. She'd been scheduled for a meeting with Professor Phelps the week before, but it had been rescheduled until the campus was reopened.

She hadn't wanted to go back, didn't know how she would take possibly seeing the destruction in the light of day. Some details of that evening were lost to her, moments and conversations, and some she remembered with vivid clarity – the shine of lights off the iced snow banks, the smell of scorched wood and carpet in the air, the soothing tone of Grayson's voice when he calmed her – but even the dull memories she wanted to avoid.

Nothing prepared her for the twisting of her stomach when she rounded the concourse and the lecture hall building came into view, along with the caution tape blocking the steps leading to the lobby and hall beyond. Workers moved back and forth, carrying equipment and building materials, and the noises of equipment cut through her head. Kip diverted her eyes and turned down the path away from the center, taking the long way to the fine arts building.

Doctor Phelps began their discussion with asking her how she was, and she knew she answered, but it was non-committal. Her heart had been racing since she stepped off the T near the school, and it hadn't stopped. To the point she felt lightheaded and detached.

Flashes of the night before haunted her, and she clenched her jaw, refusing to give in to the panic boiling in her chest. She was alive, she was fine, she was lucky, and she needed to get over it.

"You have a wonderful beginning, Kipling," Doctor Phelps told her, settling behind his desk, her dissertation printout in his hands.

The use of her full name grated on her, but she couldn't bring herself to say anything. Only one person could say it without her neck twitching.

"Thank you," she said, halfhearted.

"I will tell you, I've never had a literature student write a dissertation on time and space referencing *The Time Machine* and *The Island of Doctor Moreau*. Usually, the topics are stuffy analysis of water imagery in the works of Virginia Woolf or Wordsworth and visions of nature."

Kip tried to smile. "My parents told me much the same thing, so I tried to be interesting."

"You have succeeded. I've made copious notes on the pages, so if you have questions on any part, just let me know."

"Thank you, Doctor Phelps." Kip reached for the pages he offered, and stared at the words, the red marks blurring into nonsense.

"We're all very upset over what happened, but I imagine it is doubly difficult for you."

Kip raised her head to look at him. He was well into his seventies, and a long-standing feature at the university, and Kip had always enjoyed his classes as she progressed through her years, but right now speaking casually with him was the last thing she wanted. Or needed.

She didn't know what she needed.

"I'm here, right? So I'm fine," she answered.

He tilted his head, making a dismissive humming sound. "Don't attempt to convince yourself of that too much, Kipling. You might begin to believe it."

Kip stood and shoved the paper into her bag, extending her hand to Doctor Phelps. "Thank you, again," she said. "I'll have more pages for you in a couple of weeks."

He stood and took her hand, but held it for a moment longer than needed. "Take care of yourself, Kipling."

She nodded, pulled her hand free, and turned to go. It added four blocks to her walk, but she left the campus from the opposite side of the lecture hall to avoid passing by it again. Kip felt wrong, though she didn't know how. Just wrong. Ready to fly apart.

The psychology classes she'd taken came back to haunt her, telling her this was some sort of post-trauma breakdown. But what was there for her to deal with? She hadn't died. She hadn't been seriously injured. She'd walked away.

All because her hearing aids had annoyed her.

Kip stumbled and sank onto a cold bench bolted down along the sidewalk near a bus stop, sucking in deep breaths of raw air. Her guts twisted and quivered like she was being frozen from the inside. Kip clenched her hands together and folded forward over her lap, rocking to try to calm the chaos threatening to blow her apart.

In her coat pocket, her phone vibrated, the distant melody of Mina's ringtone barely carrying through the heavy layers of wool. Fumbling, Kip managed to bring the phone free and slid her thumb across the screen to answer, waiting for the second needed for the phone to connect to her aids. She took the moment to suck in a breath, hoping she would sound sane.

"H-hey…" she forced out.

"Hey! What's up? Where are you?"

Kip cupped her hands around her ears, trying to diminish the whistle of wind coming down through the tall buildings so she could hear Mina through her aids. She covered them too much and they whined, so she turned her back to the wind.

"I'm at the university," she said but had to pause before she spoke again. "I'm just on my way home."

A train of fire trucks and emergency vehicles came screaming down the city street. Kip flinched, her hearing aids instantly compensating for the overwhelming noise by dulling the wail. As soon as they passed, Kip blinked and took a shaky breath.

"Kip honey, you okay?"

Kip closed her eyes and pressed her lips together, swallowing hard in a desperate attempt to calm her rioting emotions, but all she managed to do was strangle a sob tearing at her throat. She sucked in a hard breath, staring down at the phone screen with Mina's smiling face, her contact photo.

"No. No, I don't think I am okay." She choked again trying to draw in breath through the thick lump in her throat. "I don't think I'm okay at all, Mina."

"Kip, honey, what's wrong?" Mina asked again.

"I don't know," Kip whispered, shaking her head. She looked up, staring at the historical buildings around the campus. Everything blurred, the tears on her cheeks immediately chilling. "I don't know," she choked out again.

"Tell me what's going on," Mina demanded, her best friend voice tempered by her 'I'm a doctor, tell me the truth' tone.

"I can't catch my breath," she said, trying to fill her chest but feeling like an elephant pressed on her ribs. "My heart is pounding. I can't-I can't stop shaking. I feel like I'm choking. Like I'm drowning."

"I'm coming to get you."

"No!" Kip blurted, then clamped her jaw closed when the people nearby waiting for the bus shot a concerned glance at her. "No, I-I can get home. I need to go home."

People walked past her, not glancing at the crazy woman having a meltdown. The wail of a police cruiser cut through the city sounds and Kip jumped. Pain sliced through her chest as her heart tried to break free. She stumbled off the bench and began to run.

Chapter Ten

The cabbie let Grayson off outside Kipling's building, and he handed the man two twenties, knowing it more than covered the fare, but not caring. Considering the route Grayson had requested he take to the address, which the cabbie did without anything more than an odd look in his rear view mirror, he deserved the extra payment.

Once the cab pulled away, Grayson stepped to the edge of the sidewalk and looked up. Kipling's flat was on the second floor from street level, third row of windows up from the street. Drawn curtains filtered the light from inside the flat, flickering perhaps because the source was the TV.

She was still awake. If he had seen no sign of life, if the flat windows were dark, he would have gone home.

He snapped his arm out straight, and bent his elbow to draw his watch clear of his sleeve and looked at the time. It wasn't quite nine, but his day had run long.

Had he been given the option, he would have been here hours before when he first heard Kipling's non-message. Grayson had been in a meeting with Stanton and Flannery, avoiding DiMatto, and had left his mobile in his office. When he returned, he saw the notification of a voice message from Kipling and had immediately opened the program. The message had been several seconds long, but through it, Kipling had said nothing at all. He had been unsure whether the call had been unintentional, or whether she had sat on the line saying nothing. Either way, his nerves had been on edge since then; his unease heightened when none of his subsequent calls went answered. Grayson had even tried a text, but again without response.

Considering the conclusion that he was, indeed, the likely target of the university attack, Grayson's instincts pushed him to check on her. Despite his sense of urgency, he'd worked a theme once he left the FBI building, requesting the cabbie stop at a twenty-four hour convenience store, a chemist shop, and a grocery. When Grayson noted no double sightings, either of faces or vehicles, he felt it safe to proceed to the South End flat.

He crossed the icy sidewalk and ascended the brick constructed steps to the foyer entrance, and on a chance, tried the door. It opened, so someone had been careless when they came home or departed. Once inside he tugged hard on the door to assure it latched before he started up the stairs. Tonight he found no comfort in the smells of the hallway that had reminded him of home during his first visit.

Grayson hesitated again at her door, taking his time to tug off his gloves. This was quite possibly the most selfish action he had ever taken.

Just as quickly as the thought occurred to him, he knew it was a lie he told himself. Only one other act eclipsed this, and it was that which would haunt him until his death.

Taking a short breath, Grayson lifted his head and raised his knuckles to the door, knocking three times. He heard movement inside, then the slide and click as the locks were disengaged.

"You got here fast—" began the exotic woman Grayson recognized from Kipling's photographs, and the stairwell the first time he'd been here. She stopped short, staring at him. "You're not Mom and Dad."

"No, I can safely say I am not."

She shook her head and blinked several times. "You're Grayson, right?" He nodded, but she continued before he could add anything. "I thought you were Kip's mom and dad. I called them to come." Her eyebrows pulled together and she tilted her head, pointing over her shoulder with her thumb. "Did–did Kip call you?"

"In a manner, yes." Every nerve came to life and Grayson's gut twisted. "Is there something wrong?"

"She's a wreck." The woman shook her head and glanced back into the apartment. "I gave her a sedative a bit ago, but I can't seem to help otherwise."

"A sedative–" Grayson snapped his attention to the woman.

"I'm a doctor," she offered, then extended her hand. "Mina Russo. Kip is my best friend."

Grayson took the extended hand, trying to read the expression on the woman's face. Surprise, yes, but also apprehension, and concern. Possibly fear. But not terror; fear for Kipling. He recalled Kipling's mention in an email about her best mate being a doctor; considering the ratio of photographs in the flat of Kipling and this woman, she had to be the particular friend.

"Please. Tell me what's wrong," Grayson begged.

Mina looked back into the flat, lips pressed tightly together, then stepped into the hall so he had to take a step back and pulled the door behind her, leaving it open a few inches. She crossed her arms and rubbed her lips together, her eyes vividly bright with restrained tears.

"I called her at lunch." She sucked in a breath. "At first she tried to sound like she was okay, but I could tell she wasn't. She told me she couldn't breathe, her heart was pounding; she was in a full-blown panic attack. She just hung up on me. I came here as soon as I could."

Grayson closed his eyes and released a pained breath, swallowing before he could look at her again. She swiped at her damp cheeks. "She's not okay. She's...lost in a nightmare. I'm not a psychologist, but I'm pretty sure this is some form of PTSD."

"Let me see her." He set his hand against the door to push it open, but she stepped into his path.

"I thought you weren't going to come here anymore," she accused.

"I wasn't," he admitted, then shook his head. "I should have come hours ago, but I allowed my foolish commitment to avoiding the inevitable to keep me away until now."

Mina pressed her lips together and sniffed, nodding, then pushed open the door and preceded him into the flat. The space was lit only in the kitchen, and the light from the receiving room was the flickering of the television screen, volume off. Kipling sat on her couch, knees drawn and hugged to her chest, her eyes on the screen, the light playing off the wet streaking her cheeks.

"She's just sitting there, watching," Mina explained. "With the sound off. It was off when I got here. I don't think she could take the sounds anymore. She's just…reading their lips."

"What is she watching?"

Mina shrugged and shook her head. "Whatever comes on. It doesn't matter. She's just staring at the screen, crying, shaking."

Grayson had his coat and suit jacket off before she shut the door behind him, and tossed them on the back of a kitchen chair on his way to the parlor. Kipling never looked up, never acknowledged the conversation he'd just had with Mina. She was lost in her own thoughts, oblivious to them. If he didn't clearly see her aids nestled in her ears, he would have assumed she was in her silent world; the fact she wore them spoke of a much worse state of mind.

The realization was a punch to his chest; a delayed response to the trauma and shock she'd tamped down after surviving the explosion. He'd thought then she was too calm but thought over time that it was simply her nature. He realized, with a wrench to his heart, that he didn't know her well enough to know she had been struggling for control. He'd suspected and then ignored his suspicions.

In his profession, ignoring suspicions could cost lives.

Grayson sat on the couch cushion beside her and lowered himself down, one hand on the back of the furniture, the other he set gently on her knee. Darkness shadowed her eyes, and he wondered if she had slept much since he saw her last.

"Kipling," he said as calmly as possible.

She jumped, turning shining eyes to look up at him. "Grayson…" she said, surprise tipping up her voice.

He settled beside her and moved his hand from the back cushion to smooth her hair from her face. Her skin was clammy and cold, her eyes too bright. "Yes, sweetheart."

She spoke slower than usual, softer than usual, likely a side effect of the sedative Mina had given her. Her gaze shifted from his eyes to his mouth, then his chest, and back again. A shuttered breath made her tremble. "I can't stop crying," she said, slow tears rolling from her eyes. "I don't know why…"

"I know," he said, rubbing her knee through the soft fabric of her flannel pyjamas. "Maybe you should try to sleep. Rest will help you find your balance again."

She shook her head and looked back at the television. "I can't sleep." Her voice faded away to almost nothing.

Grayson glanced toward Mina, who stood at the edge of the light from the kitchen, arms crossed over her body, watching Kipling with her own grief in her twisted expression. "I don't think she's been sleeping," Mina whispered, but Grayson doubted Kipling would actually hear her. She was too lost.

Mina turned away, going back into the small kitchen and Grayson heard the click and clatter of dishes as she tried to move about without making much noise. It was elementally obvious she felt lost, not knowing what to do for her friend. Doctor or not, the wound of heartache and fear was not one easily treated.

A fact Grayson knew all too well.

"I was going to call you," she admitted and shook her head. She pushed her fingers into her loose hair, drawing it back from her forehead. "I wanted to ask you a question, but I…" She trailed off.

"What did you want to ask me, Kipling?" he urged, brushing his knuckles across her cheek to draw her attention.

She didn't look away from the television, but tilted her head into his touch, shifting to create her own caress. Grayson looked toward the television. Some sort of game show, with bright lights and elaborate sets, played on the screen. "Why did they do it?" she asked, but her question had nothing to do with the missing letters in the puzzle. She looked at him again. "Why did they kill?"

To get to me…

The answer lodged in his throat.

Grayson shook his head and drew her hand from her hair, bringing it to his lips to kiss her knuckles, her fingers cold. "I honestly don't know yet, Kipling. But I swear, I am going to find out and I am going to bring them to justice for what they've done."

She stared at him, amber eyes wide, then nodded. "I know you will." Kipling blinked and tears fell from her lashes. "Grayson, I–"

She didn't finish, her gaze shifting away from his eyes to his mouth, but her eyes had no focus. Grayson smoothed her hair and ran his thumb along her slick cheek. He hoped perhaps the touch would bring her back from the darkness she slipped deeper and deeper into.

"I don't know why…" Kipling said, her thoughts still broken.

"What don't you know, Kipling?"

She turned to him again. The lost distance in her eyes made his heart hurt. "Why I'm alive when others died."

Grayson's throat constricted and he pressed his lips together to quell the choking ache. He touched her forehead, running his fingers along her brow, focusing on the touch to ground him. Grayson shook his head and somehow found the control to answer.

Even if there was no answer at all.

"I don't know," he answered honestly, "but, as much as my heart breaks for those lost, I cannot be anything but glad you are here."

She sucked in a cry, tears freely slicking her skin, and shook her head. A vicious sob jerked through her and she tried to take in a hard breath. Grayson folded her in his arms, pressing his eyes closed to hold back his own sorrow, and she curled into his chest, weeping. Grayson rocked her, holding on as tight to her as she did him, her fingers curled into the front of his shirt. He didn't try to quiet her, or soothe her, because this moment had been long overdue, and she deserved nothing less than to be free of the poison that had been simmering for days.

She shook with the viciousness of her crying, but Grayson didn't release her, holding her to ease his own heartache as much as hers. Kipling wept until there was nothing left, and eventually, the tension in her body eased and she relaxed in his embrace. With a long, shaky breath, she slipped into sleep, and Grayson closed his eyes, thankful she must have found some peace.

He waited for several more minutes, wanting to be sure Kipling truly was asleep. He pressed a long kiss to her hair, then with careful ease, he slid his arms beneath her and stood, lifting her to his chest. Mina looked up from where she sat at the table as he passed through to Kipling's bedroom, and although he saw the question in her eyes, she didn't stop him.

The bed was a shamble, torn apart, a clear indicator that whatever time she had spent in it had been restless and troubled. Grayson set his knee on the mattress and set her down, supporting her head until he could rest it on her pillow. She hummed, a low sound in her chest, and inhaled deeply but didn't awaken. With as much care as possible, Grayson drew her sheet and quilt over her and paused to study her in the cast of light coming from the main room of the flat. Even in sleep, he still saw tension between her eyes, and her lips turned down in a slight frown.

Hoping he wouldn't wake her in doing so, he fumbled in the dim light to slip the hearing aids from each ear, remembering she had said they would feedback if covered and he didn't want anything to disturb her sleep. She moaned softly but didn't awaken.

Grayson leaned down and pressed a kiss to her forehead before he reluctantly left her to sleep. He only partially closed the door, wanting to be able to hear her if she awoke. Mina had made two cups of tea while he'd been in the bedroom, and she set one in front of the empty chair while she took her seat in the other. Grayson sat and picked up the tea, taking a sip.

"Thank you," he said, glancing at Mina through the steam rising from the cup.

"Thank *you*," Mina said, stressing the word. "I didn't know what else to do. I think–" She pressed her lips together and drew a breath in through her nose. "I think she needed you, which, I'm not sure I get since you two really barely know each other. Right?"

Grayson stared down at his tea, the steam rolling up to moisten and warm his face. "I am hardly one to explain such things," Grayson admitted, taking another sip. "I am in no better a place than you to understand how Kipling can mean so much to me so quickly, but if she feels the same, I am blessed."

Mina sat back in her chair and folded her hands in her lap, staring at him for several moments as he drank his tea. He saw the thoughts churning behind her strained eyes, and waited for her to speak, knowing it would begin with a question.

The fact it wasn't surprised him.

"She told me you didn't feel right about seeing her when you might be leaving at the drop of a hat."

Grayson pinched the bridge of his nose, rubbing at the inner corners of his eyes with his fingertips. "As I said, I cannot explain the ferocity of my feelings. I only know they exist."

"That's a pretty hefty statement, Mr. Holmes."

Grayson smiled, knowing it held no humor, and held his attention on the cup in front of him. "It is not something I would ever say lightly, I assure you. Nonetheless, it is the absolute truth." He took another drink of the tea, hoping it would give him the wherewithal to make it through the night. He set down the cup and looked at the woman seated across from him.

Mina glared at him with her arms crossed. "I don't know how she's going to feel about you being here once she wakes up, and right now I'm happy you're here because she's at least sleeping, but I'll tell you this…I may not look Irish, and my hair isn't red, but I've got enough of my grandmother in me that if you hurt her, you're going to have an Irish devil to deal with."

Before he could offer any promise for the protection of Kipling's heart, a muffled cry came from Kipling's bedroom just as the intercom system mounted by the door buzzed, a light connected to the unit flashing at the same time. Both Grayson and Mina gained their feet, and he went directly to the bedroom while Mina went to the door.

Kipling was on her back, one arm cast out perpendicular to her side, the other over her head resting on the pillow. She had already kicked away the blankets. Grayson sat on the bed edge at her side, facing the headboard, and leaned over her, setting his hand on the mattress on the other side of her hip. With his other hand, he smoothed her hair, shushing her despite logically knowing she wouldn't hear him. She turned into his touch, her cheek pressing to his palm, and she drew in a long, deep breath, releasing it as her body relaxed.

An intrinsic part of his training had included handling post-trauma episodes with witnesses and survivors of terrorist acts, but as an investigating agent, he was most often removed from such personal contact to never see the ramifications of such events. He was at a loss as to what to do for her, beyond comforting her, and at that he felt painfully inadequate and doubted he even had the right. Hadn't he told her two days before something as intimate as this had only one course…an end?

"What good does it do to save the world, when I have no one to save it for?" Grayson asked the empty room. He ran his thumb along her cheek where only a slight pinking of her skin remained from the abrasions she'd suffered.

The outside had healed.

The inside took longer.

At least in that he had intimate knowledge.

From the main flat he heard the door open, and additional voices he recognized as Mr. and Mrs. Branson, Kipling's parents, and recalled the fact he'd pushed aside earlier in his need to see Kipling. Her parents had come at Mina's bidding.

Kipling shifted and rolled onto her side toward him, curling around his hip and she laid her cheek against his lower thigh, her arm draped across his lap. She made a noise in her sleep but didn't awaken. Grayson sighed and stroked his hand up and down her back. The bedroom door eased open, and Grayson looked over his shoulder. Mina stood in the doorway, the kitchen light behind her, and he saw Kipling's parents waiting.

"Grayson," Mina said simply.

"I'll be there momentarily."

Mina left the door open, and Grayson had no doubt it was for the benefit of Kipling's parents. Were he the father of a beautiful woman like Kipling, he would likely not be so calm about a man being in her bedroom.

Reluctant to leave her, Grayson eased her arm from his lap and carefully edged off the bed. He drew the blankets over her again, and kissed her temple, before leaving the bedroom. Mr. and Mrs. Branson stood waiting in the kitchen, with Mina at the stove again, putting on the kettle.

"Mr. Branson," Grayson said, walking forward, his hand extended to the man. "I regret meeting you once again under such conditions."

Mr. Branson took his hand, but the grip was possibly excessively firm and his expression was credulous. "I would agree, Mr. Holmes."

"Would either of you like to tell me what's going on?" Mrs. Branson demanded, looking between Grayson and Mina. "What is wrong with our daughter?"

"Perhaps once Mina has made the tea," Grayson said, trying to smile. "I have no intention of leaving until morning, and I don't believe I am incorrect in assuming that is the intent of each of us, so we have all night to discuss…" He paused, not sure how to define the exact situation. "Our mutual affection and concern for Kipling."

"I'll get a couple of folding chairs," Mina said, disappearing into the parlor.

It was going to be a long night.

Chapter Eleven

Grayson balanced the formed cardboard cup tray in his left hand while he jingled the set of keys Mina had left with him in his right, finding the correct one to unlock Kipling's flat door. Managing the lock, he pocketed the keys and turned the knob as quietly as he could, easing open the door.

Only to realize his attempt at quiet so as to not wake Kipling too soon was unnecessary, and he made no attempt at hiding his smile when he found her standing in her kitchen – barefoot and dressed in her flannel pyjamas and Red Sox tee shirt, with hair slightly tousled from sleep – reading the note Mina had left for her.

She looked up, amber eyes wide.

"Good morning," Grayson said, closing the door behind him. The fact her attention didn't shift to his lips to read what he said, he assumed she had placed her hearing aids in when she awoke and before coming into the kitchen. And in that moment, he also realized the true folly in his attempt at stealth. Had she actually been asleep, no amount of noise would have woken her without her hearing aids. He silently chastised himself for forgetting such a simple reality.

He set the drink tray and brown paper bag on the table and

unbuttoned his coat to take it off again. Kipling had told him the first time he was here that her mother liked the heat high, and he saw no exaggeration in her statement. The flat was nearly too warm, even in just his shirtsleeves.

She still said nothing, her stare shifting from Grayson to the takeaway tray, and back to him. Grayson took the white large cup and bag from the tray.

"I do hope I've done this correctly. Mina wrote it down for me, very specifically, so as to hopefully prevent an error. I have a..." He made a point of setting down the items and taking from his trouser pocket the piece of paper Mina had provided. "...large Dunkin' Midnight regular – which I've learned constitutes two creams and two sugars," he added with a glance at her. Still staring, wide-eyed. "...with full cream and, quote 'the yellow packet' artificial sweetener. And since she wasn't sure if you wanted savory or sweet, I have both an *everything* bagel, lightly toasted, with *veggie* cream cheese as well as half a dozen *Munchkins*, with an even balance of glazed chocolate cake and blueberry."

Kipling still looked dazed, staring at him and the note with a deep V-line digging in between her eyes. Grayson set down the note and took the two steps to her, laying his palms against her cheeks. She tipped back her head to look up at him, her eyes shifting and her lips slightly parted.

"Kipling," he said softer. "Are you going to say good morning?"

She inhaled slowly through her nose, then blinked, and seemed for the first time since he'd come through the door to be fully aware. And in a blink, her distant look changed to one of shock. "Oh, God..." She groaned. "It wasn't a dream."

"I wish it were." He took his hand from her cheek to brush back her hair. "For your sake."

She still held Mina's note in her hand and lifted it away from her side to look at it past Grayson's arm. "Mina came last night." She scowled. "I barely...I barely remember, but I remember her being here."

"Yes," he affirmed, his chest aching with each word she said. She truly had been lost.

Kipling raised her chin again and looked at him, still within the hold of his hands. "I thought I dreamed you. I thought the dream was so real I could smell your cologne when I woke up."

"I assure you, I am here." Grayson gave in to his need to be nearer to her by pressing a kiss to the center of her forehead.

Her eyes popped wide and she gasped, stumbling back from his hold. A step or two away from him, she covered her face and groaned, turning away. "Oh, God…"

"Kipling–" He reached for her again, but she dodged clear, shaking her head.

"No, don't." She threw her arm back, palm to him, to stop him from getting closer. When he stopped, she covered her face and hunched forward, her auburn hair falling around her head. She mumbled into her hands, but he couldn't understand her.

"Kipling." He took another step toward her. "Darling, I can't understand."

She twisted away and took another step back, facing him with tears glistening in her eyes. "Please, Grayson," she begged. "Please, I can't stand how pathetic I was…just…please go before I die of embarrassment."

"Pathetic?" he repeated. "No, Kipling."

"I lost it!" she cried out, shaking her head until her hair tumbled over her shoulders. "I was a–" She didn't finish the thought. "How pitiful am I to…*break*…like that? For no reason! I've no right–"

Grayson ignored her plea to stay back and reached her in two long strides. "You have *every* right," he said sternly, gripping her shoulders so she couldn't move away from him. "Kipling, what happened to you was terrifying."

"But I'm fine!" she shouted, trying to pull away. "I'm fine! Who am I to fall apart over–"

"Surviving?" he demanded. Unbidden, the familiar choke tightened around his throat, and he swallowed hard. She stilled in his hold, staring wide, shining eyes at him. "Kipling," he said softer, knowing his voice could not hold out much more. Grayson loosened his hold on her upper arms and slid his hands to her shoulders until he touched the side of her throat with his thumbs, feeling the rapid pounding of her pulse. He closed his eyes, and touched his forehead to hers, inhaling before he could speak again. "Surviving isn't a crime, because the ones who survive have to relive it again, and again."

"I didn't want it to change me," she said softly.

Grayson opened his eyes and drew back only far enough he could look into her face. "You can't help that, Kipling. It did change you."

She studied him, he saw the questions forming behind her eyes, and his breath caught behind his ribs when she slid her arm between them and laid her palm on his chest. Her gaze slipped down to focus on his lips, and he wondered if she felt the upbeat in his heart rate. "I thought I dreamed you beside me while I slept."

"I was there." Her gaze came back to his eyes. "I held you until you fell asleep, then I laid you in your bed."

"You stayed here all night?"

Grayson nodded, smoothing his thumbs over her warm skin. "I couldn't leave you."

"Mina was here, too?"

He nodded, then reluctantly added, because he suspected how she might react, "Your parents were here for a time."

Kipling groaned and let her head fall forward until her forehead rested on his lapel. Grayson chuckled and kissed her hair. "They were here because they care, as we all do."

Kip raised her head, and he gave in more to temptation by taking his hand from her shoulder so he could touch her cheek and smooth his thumb near her lip.

"I thought…I thought after Saturday I wouldn't hear from you for—" She shrugged. "I wasn't sure I'd hear from you at all. Why did you come? Mina didn't call you, did she?"

Grayson shook his head. "No, You did…of a sort." He paused to press his lips together, then smiled, though it was more of contriteness than amusement. "You called and left me a voicemail, but you didn't speak. When you didn't respond when I tried to reach you, I grew concerned, and came to check on you."

"And instead, you found a basket case—"

"No," he said with a shake of his head. "I found who I needed, more than anyone else."

"You can't keep saying things like that to me, and then tell me we can't…" she trailed off, her voice a rough whisper, looking down and away from him.

Grayson swallowed, a feeble and useless attempt at calming his pounding heart. He touched her chin with his thumb so she would look up to him. "Then I will not mention the latter again."

"But it doesn't change anything. We haven't solved anything, have we? You are still going back to London *whenever*, and I'm still going to be here in Boston."

Grayson smiled when his response came to mind, accepting not for the first time how engrained the words and antics of his ancestor had become to his life, true or not. "My great-grandfather was once quoted as saying that nothing clears up a case so much as stating it to another person."

Her lips quirked into a small, slow smile and she tipped up her chin. "Well, if we're quoting, Richard Bach asked can miles truly separate you from friends? If you want to be with someone you love, aren't you already there?" Even though she kept her voice level, a slow color crept up her throat to her cheeks.

Grayson hummed in appreciation, and added, "Francois del a Rouchefoucauld said 'Absence diminishes small love and increases great ones, as the wind blows out a candle and blows up the bonfire'."

"There you go again," she said with a heavy breath. "Foreplay for a bibliophile."

Grayson groaned but grinned. With a reluctant sigh, Grayson said, "As much as the idea of verbal foreplay appeals to me to no end, I must go. For now. I must return to my hotel, wash and shave, and report to the Bureau."

"Tonight?" she asked.

"I cannot say. I am resolved to find answers."

Kipling nodded, tapping her fingertips on his chest. "I know."

Grayson knew he tempted fate, but he'd decided some time during the night he didn't much care. He slid his hands up her neck to lay his palms along her jaw and leaned down to kiss her cheek. His honest intent was to give as much as he dared, but realized in a hard thump of his heart, he had dared too much. Her breath hitched, warming his skin, and Grayson closed his eyes, holding his lips to her cheek, unable to withdraw. Kipling slid her hand from its place over his heart to his shoulder, her fingertips skimming his throat at the open collar of his shirt. She tipped her head back a degree and turned into his cheek, her lips brushing the corner of his.

He was lost.

Each shift, each touch, was careful…hesitant, for at least on his part, to give in too quickly would be to lose whatever barely existing control he had remaining. Grayson slid his cheek along hers until his parted lips held over hers, her breath mingling with his, rapid and warm. She trembled in his hold. He rolled his tongue forward, tentatively seeking until he moved past her lips and tasted her soft moan. They sealed the kiss, the cautious exploration immediately shifting to an intensity that snapped through him. Grayson released her jaw to wrap his arms around her, pulling her firm against him and her arms raised to circle his neck and shoulders.

Her tongue met his, and he tasted peppermint. His only thought was to be closer. Hold her closer. He needed her. Desperately.

Only when her shoulders hit something solid, did Grayson realize they had moved together toward the bedroom and she had come in contact with the wall beside her door. He braced his palm against the jamb and broke the seal of their lips, yet only enough that he could press his face to the curve of her throat, her hair falling around him like a curtain, her breath rapid against his ear.

"Kipling," was all he could manage to say, the name carried on a rough groan.

She responded with a hum, her fingers pressed into his hair. With one more tempting kiss to her throat, Grayson raised his head and looked down at her. Flushed cheeks, shining eyes, and glistening lips tempted him beyond reason.

"Kissing is like drinking salt water," she said with a wicked, teasing grin. "You drink, and your thirst increases."

Grayson chuckled despite the heated demand of his body to

return to the kiss. His hand rested at her hip and had slipped beneath the hem of her tee shirt so he felt the soft heat of her stomach. The sensation more than he could deny, he drew back his hand and touched her face.

"I've heard it said anticipation is the greatest aphrodisiac," he told her, watching the trail his fingers traced along her lips. "I don't believe that to be true. Now, knowing what I must leave is the greatest incentive to return."

Her eyes fluttered, and she smiled, shifting closer to him until he knew there could be no doubt in her mind how desperately he wanted to stay. "You'd better go."

Grayson nodded and, with reluctance born of his soul, stepped back. He took her hand as he walked so she followed him back to the table where he lifted his coat from the chair where he'd discarded it.

"Are you returning to work today?"

Kipling huffed, blowing upward so the hair at her brow shifted. "Yes, later this morning. We open at eleven."

He let go of her hand to draw on his suit jacket, buttoning it. "Did you see your audiologist?"

"Yeah, yesterday. She said she fixed it. Shouldn't happen again." Kipling shrugged, tapping a hand on her leg. "I guess we'll see today when the heat kicks on, right?"

Before putting on his coat, he reached into the pocket and retrieved Mina's keys, holding them up for her to see before he set them on the table to be returned to Ms. Russo by Kipling. With his overcoat on and buttoned, Grayson paused and studied her. She truly was the most beautiful woman he had ever known, with rumpled hair and her pyjamas, rosy cheeks, and shining lips from their kiss. Unable, or quite possibly unwilling, to deny his need to touch her, Grayson reached for her again and pulled her to him for another kiss.

"I want to hear from you later," he said to the space between them with his forehead resting on hers. "I have no idea how today will go—"

"I know," she assured. "I understand."

"I will speak with you later."

She nodded. "Okay."

He released her and regretted it immediately, but with as much resolve as he could muster, he picked up his gloves from the table. "Drink your regular," he teased, with a wink, saying it as if it were a proper name. With his hand on the doorknob, he paused to look at her again. "Be safe."

"Go on," she said, opening the door for him. "Get out before I forget you work for the better good."

He took one last quick kiss, which served more to torture his soul than release his desire, just as the Chinese proverb Kipling had quoted implied, and walked away toward the stairs. The voice of regulation shouted in the back of his mind that his actions could cost him more than he may be willing to give up, but a much louder voice told reason to sod off.

"We narrowed it down from the list you gave me to a few that come close to matching the physical description we've got," Agent Flannery announced, walking into Grayson's office.

Grayson didn't look up, instead reaching for a piece of paper he had printed out and left waiting on his desk blotter. "As do I. Three names: Isaac Sheldon, Charles Malcolm, and Edward Smith."

Flannery paused, looking down at his list. "Yeah, I've got those, but we've got another half dozen more—"

"Don't bother. These are the three we need to focus on. Each has no less than two connections, although the connection to Smith has four degrees of separation so he isn't my top choice. Begin with Sheldon."

Flannery raised his arm and looked at his watch. "It's not even nine. How long have you been here? Were you here all night again?"

Grayson stood and straightened his jacket. "No, but I would say

I gained clarity over the dark hours. That and I am attempting to acquire a taste for your coffee." He ticked his chin toward the white takeaway cup with a pink and orange logo on his desk. After purchasing one for Kipling, the smell had tantalized him sufficiently enough that he obtained an acclaimed "regular" for himself on the way to the office.

"Can't live in Boston and not drink Dunkin'," Flannery said with a grin and jump of his shoulders in a quiet laugh.

"No more than I suppose one can live in London and not drink tea, hmmm?" Grayson slapped down his laptop, which he'd had open on his desk beside his desktop computer. He headed for the door, re-buttoning his suit jacket as he walked. "I would like to discuss some theories with Director Stanton."

"Yeah, sure." Flannery waited for Grayson to pass him through the door, and fell into step behind him, folding the paper he carried. "Did you really figure it out because of that map thing you put on the wall?"

"Amongst other means," Grayson answered.

"Huh."

Grayson stopped and turned a few degrees toward Flannery. "Is there a problem?"

"No problem," Flannery said, holding up his hands, the paper held between two fingers of his left. "It's just that we heard all this hype about you before you got here. The amazing Grayson Holmes. The real-life legend, all that. Then you got here, and you seemed to be treading water like the rest of us. Now, boom…you hand me stuff more precise than even the computer algorithm program came up with after working on it for twenty-four hours."

Grayson turned away, walking again toward Stanton's office. "I cannot build bricks without clay."

They reached Stanton's doorway as Flannery speculated, "So if you'd had all the information right away, you might have solved it by now and be on your way back to merry England."

The reality made his chest thump and he managed to recover from the hitch in his step before Flannery noticed. "I cannot know for sure what the outcome may have been, as some of the intrinsic data was derived from events and sources only obtained in the last few days."

"The hearing aids thing."

"Amongst other pieces of information, yes. Confirmation I was the intended mark allowed me to shift focus, and sweep away everything no longer pertinent."

"Are you two going to come in here, or are you going to stand in my doorway and chitchat all morning?" Stanton demanded.

"Apologies, sir," Grayson said and led the way into the room.

"Shut the door, sit down, and tell me what you've got. I've already approved the request for a subpoena and forwarded it for submission. Now, tell me what I'm going to say when they ask why."

Chapter Twelve

"Your father and I have been talking, and think maybe you should get out of the city for a bit," Kip's mother offered, looking from Kip's father to Kip.

Kip shook her head and used the side of her fork to split a chunk of her mother's savory Yankee pot roast. She'd come home from work to the smell of beef and potatoes and gravy permeating her apartment.

"I can't do that, Mom. Not with work and school."

"You can come back as you need to."

"I have no car, remember? I don't need one in the city, and I'm not going to make you or Dad drive me back and forth from Chelsea several times a day." She slid the meat off her fork and chewed, though it practically melted in her mouth. "And it could be several times a day," she added once she'd chewed for an appropriately polite period of time.

"Then perhaps you could stay with Mina?"

Kip paused, the next forkful of food half way to her mouth, then set it down to balance on the edge of her plate. "Mina is still in the city. What is this really about?" She canted her head. "Mom, I'm not going to have a mental breakdown if I'm home alone. Yesterday was just…bad, and won't happen again."

"Princess, we worry," her dad said, and sighed. "You don't know what it does to a parent's heart to get a phone call like the one Mina made to us."

Kip pressed her lips together and took a steadying breath before she reached across the small table to take a hand of each parent. "I know, and I'm sorry for last night. But, I'm fine."

She immediately regretted the words.

"Okay, maybe I'm not *fine*," she corrected before either could say anything. "But…I'm better. I promise. The world breaks everyone, and afterward, some are strong at the broken places. Right?"

"I hardly think quoting Hemingway is going to make us feel any better," her mother said with an exasperated huff and roll of her eyes. But she smiled and squeezed Kip's hand before letting her go back to eating.

She gave her mother five minutes before bringing up the next topic, and was surprised when it actually took seven.

"Now, about Mr. Holmes…"

Kip chuckled and set down her fork again, sitting back in her chair. "What about him?"

Her mother stared at her wide-eyed. "I would think that's obvious, dear. We arrive here well past one in the morning to find this man we don't know from Adam coming out of your *bedroom*."

"He was only checking on me–"

"So Mina said."

"And would Mina ever lie about such a thing?"

Her mother pressed her lips together and scowled. "The point still stands, Kipling Marie Branson."

Oh, boy. This was serious. Not even her mother used her full name unless it was serious.

"How well do you know this man to have him in your apartment in the middle of the night?"

"Mom, he was here because he…" She sighed, actually enjoying the pleasant flush of heat spreading up her throat to her cheeks. "Because he was worried about a friend."

"Friend? You two are friends?" her mother asked, indignant.

Kip stole a glance at her father, whose silence had not gone unnoticed. She answered, but watched for his reaction. "We are becoming friends, yes. Quickly, but we are becoming friends."

"What kind of friends?"

She looked away from her father to meet her mother's question straight on. Being an only child of the type of parents she had, they had the kind of relationship her friends both envied and thanked the heavens they didn't have with their parents. Honesty ruled, even if someone didn't like it.

"Good friends, Mom," Kip answered. "The kind of friends who stay all night to assure the other is okay and be an absolute gentleman about it. I would have done the same for him if I thought for a moment I could help."

"But, you just met him! How do you know he can be trusted to be here alone with you?"

Kip almost chuckled but managed to suppress it. "Mom, you left me here alone with him just days ago. Have you forgotten?"

"No! But that was different–"

"And besides," Kip continued, probably enjoying a little too much the rise she got out of her mother. "If the British Monarchy and the U.S. government trust his service, who am I to question?"

"And that's another thing," Jane Branson said, wagging her finger at Kip. "He's only here temporarily. He told us so. As soon as he completes his investigation into the university attack, he's most likely returning to London."

Her lightheartedness slipped a degree or twelve. "I know."

"You're vesting a great deal of yourself into a relationship that will soon be from thirty-two-hundred miles away."

"And you are putting a great deal of weight on a relationship that has barely begun, Mom. I just met him."

"And yet, when your heart was breaking you called him."

"I don't even remember calling him–" she blurted, realizing too late her confession probably offered no assurance.

Her mother scowled deeper and sat back, pushing her plate away. "Well, at least that coincides with what he told us last night."

Kip's warm flush turned cold, and she stared wide-eyed for several moments. "What…what did he tell you last night?"

"Despite all my years teaching literature, and despite the fact I consider myself to have a passing grip on the English language, I doubt I could relay his intent nearly as eloquently as he did. Honestly, he had me quite enthralled." Her mom finished with a dramatic shake of her head.

"Okay, tell me the gist of what he said."

"Well–"

Her father interrupted, and where Grayson was eloquent her father brought it down to the basics. "He's falling in love with you."

Kip stared, wide-eyed, once again, absolutely unable to form enough of a thought to respond. Her mother gasped and tapped her father's arm. "Jack! He said no such thing!"

"Close enough," he said, stirring a hunk of carrot through his gravy. "You've read enough Tennyson, Browning, and Shakespeare to cut through all the pretty words and get what he meant. He loves our girl." He pointed toward Kip with the tip of his gravy-dripping fork.

"He can't love me," Kip argued, shaking her head. "Not yet. Is that possible?"

"He might not know that's what it is yet, Princess," her father said around the potato in his cheek. "Sounded to me like he was trying to figure it out."

Perhaps as a universal means to free her of the conversation, or possibly to provide her father with more fuel for his argument, Kip's phone went off with the theme of the James Bond films, a tone she had loaded on a whim and a lark during one of the many quiet moments at work that day. Kip cleared her throat and stood, taking steps toward her bedroom.

"Excuse me."

"Tell Grayson we said cheerio," her father said as she stood.

"Cheerio means goodbye, Dad," she said over her shoulder as she headed for her bedroom.

Her parents were deep in hushed conversation by the time Kip closed the bedroom door and clicked on the call. She waited the couple of seconds it took for her phone and hearing aids to link up and the Bluetooth to engage before she said, "Hello."

"I wondered if I'd called at a bad time. Were you having a kip?"

Kip chuckled. "I think that's your job."

Grayson's deep, rolling laughter filled her ears and Kip smiled, chuckling. "Fair enough. That is a turn of phrase I shall have to be more aware of in the future."

Kip looked at the time on the face of her phone. "It's almost eight. Are you still at the office?"

"Leaving now." He sighed, and she heard the sound of traffic and city noise around him. "I apologize I haven't had a chance to call before now; we accomplished a great deal today, but there is more to be done."

"I would ask, but since I know you probably can't talk about it, have you eaten?"

"Bit of a sandwich a few hours ago. We truly have been straight out today. I intend to go home, try to make amends with a gray-haired tabby who is quite likely put out with me and may very well have expressed his displeasure throughout the suite, and see what my refrigerator may yield."

Kip pulled her lower lip through her teeth and looked toward her closed bedroom door. The sounds of her parents cleaning up the dishes carried through the wood.

"Kipling…" Grayson led. "Are you still there?"

"Yeah." She closed her eyes, simultaneously attempting to convince herself to jump in with both feet and be cautious at the same time. "If you'd like, I can bring you dinner." She winced, waiting.

The sound of a car door closing preceded the silencing of the city sounds. "Residence Stay, Congress Street," he said away from the phone. When he spoke again, it was directly to her. "I would like that very much, Kipling."

Her entire life, the sound of her full first name was enough to make her skin crawl; yet, when spoken from the lips of Grayson Holmes, it was an endearment. "Okay," she said, after taking a slow, calming breath. "Residence Stay, Congress Street. Yeah?"

"Yes. I'm on the top floor. Off the lift, to the left, last door on your right."

"Okay." She closed her eyes, knowing she had to come up with a better response. "I'll see you soon."

"I look forward to it. More than you know."

She disconnected, and once the aids were back in full ambient use, headed for the bedroom door. Her mother was just wrapping the leftover pot roast, and her father wiped down the table.

"I assumed you were done, honey," her mother said, opening her refrigerator door. "How is Mr. Holmes?"

"Fine," she said, stepping behind one of the chairs to set her hands on the back. "He said it's been a long day. He sounded exhausted."

"Oh, well, that's to be expected I suppose. Is he coming over?" Her mother looked at Kip over her shoulder. "Do you need your parents to clear out?"

Kip blushed and smiled. "No, he's not. He's heading home for some rest. Like I said, long day." It was the truth, but a niggle of guilt still dug at her.

"Speaking of long days," her dad said, coming around to put his arm across her shoulder. "You should get some sleep. Whether your friend is coming or not, we're clearing out. Right, Mother?"

Mom's response was a slightly irritated hum. "If you say so, dear. We'll call in the morning."

Kip hugged them, kissed her father's cheek, and waited at the front window until she saw them get in their Subaru and pull away from the curb before she went back to the kitchen and took the leftovers back out again.

The hotel was beautiful; a restored brick building in the historical district of the seaport with a view of the harbor. Kip walked into the lobby atrium and looked around, lips parted. It was gorgeous, modern but accentuating the old structure beneath. Brick and wood and subway tiles made the lobby tactile and warm.

The attendant at the front desk looked up, but when she walked past she must have convinced him she knew where she was going because he said nothing. Maybe the bag she carried had him assuming she was delivering food. By the time the elevator arrived, her heart raced, but with a pleasant excitement that left a permanent smile on her lips.

She followed his instructions: left off the elevator, last door on the right. Taking a deep breath, she released it through pursed lips and knocked.

"Coming!" carried Grayson's voice from beyond the door, followed by "Watson, get out of the way…"

She grinned. *Watson?*

The door opened, and for a second she thought her heart might have actually stopped. She'd seen him mostly in suits, which he wore amazingly well, but something about him in a light and smooth weave, cream-colored sweater, jeans, and bare feet made her stomach do a funny, pleasant flip. His hair was still damp from the shower he must have taken when he got home, and the usual waves were darker with the dampness and more like chunky curls, falling haphazardly over his brow. She had a passing curiosity of what those thick curls would feel like between her fingers.

"Hello," he said but did a funny hop and sidestep. Then pushed open the door, and in the same movement, bent and swooped up a gray tabby, bundling the cat to his side. "Foolish cat," he mumbled. "Been trying to kill me for leaving him alone too much. Come in."

Kip rubbed the cat's head as she passed. "He's a cutie. Watson?"

Grayson shut the door and tossed the cat onto a nearby bench as she set down the thermal bag of food to take off her coat. "Yes," he said with an embarrassed laugh. "My sister's idea of a joke. Can't have a Holmes without a Watson."

"That's adorable."

Grayson stepped behind her to help her off with the heavy coat, and once her arms were free, he threw the coat on the same bench – the cat barely jumping free in time – and slid his arm around her to turn her into his embrace. His other hand braced the back of her head and he kissed her, so perfectly, so deeply, her stomach fluttered and her knees threatened to give out beneath her. He was the only thing keeping her upright. Kip's arms hung useless at her side for several seconds before her body and mind connected enough through the kiss's delirium for her to raise them and return his touch. She moaned, unable to help the sound, and it seemed to spur him on, his tongue sliding along hers.

His damp hair slid through her fingers, and she held on as he tipped her back. Still holding the kiss, he drew her back up, easing his way out of the kiss until he slid his cheek along hers and held her, each breathing hard.

"I apologize," he said near her ear, his voice so intense it practically vibrated through her. "I didn't intend to be so vehement in my *welcome*." His chuckle rumbled through the words. "But once I saw you, kissing you was the only thing I could think to do."

He drew back to look at her and Kip smiled, shaking her head. "No worries. Trust me, if you always want to say hello like that, I'm good with it."

Grayson smiled, the kind of smile that changed his entire face and wrinkled the corner of his eyes. He released her, but only enough to take her hand in one and pick up the bag off the bench with the other, scolding away his cat who had taken a great interest in the contents. Grayson led her toward a corner of the large suite designed as a kitchen area with stainless steel appliances and a granite counter, fully equipped with a full-size refrigerator, microwave, stove and cooktop, and dishwasher. All carefully configured along one wall to conserve space. A tall bar served as a table with two chairs.

"This is a great space," she said, looking up to the twelve-foot post-and-beam ceilings. The outer walls of the suite were brick, the interior plaster, accentuated with wood and chrome. Just like downstairs, a beautiful mix of old and new.

"You can thank your FBI," he said, lifting the bag to his nose before he set it on the high counter. He inhaled and hummed in appreciation. "This smells amazing. What is it?"

"Sit and I'll get it out for you." He pulled out one of the two side-by-side stool chairs and sat with his hands together on the flat surface. "Dishes?" He pointed, grinning wide. As he watched she pulled out the large storage container and popped it open, releasing more of the savory smells. The roast had still been hot when her mother packaged it, so even now it was warm. "A special treat for someone from 'away'. That's what we call anyone not from New England."

"Being from England doesn't count?"

Kip shook her head, dishing out the food. "Definitely not. This is a New England classic. Yankee pot roast. Go too far west in the U.S., and they won't even know what you're talking about if you ask for it."

She filled his plate with thick brown gravy-coated chunks of tender roast, sliced carrots, and chopped potatoes. While the plate warmed in the microwave, she unwrapped the crescent rolls and set out the butter she'd brought.

"I didn't know if you'd have any. You made it sound like your pantry was pretty wanting."

"Butter I do have," he said, grinning as he watched her move around the tiny kitchen space. "However, I had nothing left to put it on as I ate the last of the bread yesterday."

"Do you have any wine?"

"I do." He hopped down from the chair and retrieved a bottle of pinot noir and two glasses, pouring them out as she set the plate back where he had sat. "You aren't having any?"

"I ate before you called. I cannot take credit for the meal, might as well get that out there now. Mom made it. But…" She winked. "I am a decent cook. I promise."

"It wouldn't be proper eating without you."

"It's okay." She reached again into the thermal bag and drew out a take-out container from the diner around the corner from her apartment. "I brought pie for each of us for dessert. I did not, however, bring ice cream."

Grayson stilled, his smile relaxing, but not fading away. He stood, staring at her, and Kip rubbed her lips together at the sudden sense of self-consciousness. He took the step needed to reach her and touched her cheek. His gaze followed the line his fingers took along her jaw to her hairline.

"What's wrong?" she asked.

The smile slanted up again, and the look in his eyes spread a blossom of warmth from the center of her chest. "Nothing," he said finally, the shake of his head almost indiscernible. He reached for her hand and closed it between both of his, holding it to his chest. Rubbing her knuckles, he studied their joined hands for a moment before raising his head. "Kipling, I want you to know something. I–" The smile widened, making her smile more. "I don't know who I am when I'm with you."

Kip canted her head. "Is that a good or bad thing?"

"It's good. It's amazing. It makes me wonder who I've been for the last thirty-four years, and the last several months quite specifically."

"I don't understand. You seem the same to me."

"Because I changed, possibly the moment I met you. This…" He squeezed her hand and brought it to his lips. "Something as simple as this is…not who I am. Who I have been."

"Grayson, I still don't understand."

He moved closer so her hand was caught between their bodies, and if he leaned in just a little, he could kiss her again. She tipped up her chin, hoping he would. "Do you remember asking me who I was more like, my mother or my father?" She nodded. "I told you I feared I was more my father, but wished I was more my mother."

Kip nodded again. "You said he grounded her, and she helped him fly." She blinked, sudden tears blurring her vision at the memory of how his words had touched her.

"Kipling Branson, you have made me fly."

Chapter Thirteen

"Watson, hmmm?" Kip said softly, rubbing the head of Grayson's cat. The tabby crawled into her lap, rubbing along her chest as he bumped her chin with his head. "I bet you could tell me all sorts of juicy stories, couldn't you?"

Watson purred, and circled in her lap, doubling back to bump her again. Kip looked up as Grayson crossed the space to them, having been loading the dishwasher, and she smiled at the happy smirk on his face.

Watson jumped from her lap to the back of the couch behind her and rubbed along her hair. Kip laughed and leaned forward so the cat couldn't reach her. So, he curled up on the cushion.

"He's so affectionate," she said when Grayson reached them.

Grayson chuckled and sat beside her, draping his arm along the back behind her, scooting his cat out of the way. "It would seem I am not the only one affected by your presence. Watson has not been so *affectionate* as in the last few days. For three years, we have cohabitated, mostly on the premise I exist as his slave."

Kip drew her feet up onto the couch, tucking herself against his side so she could be close but look up to him. "You're all talk," she said, tilting her chin at him in mock defiance. "You love that cat, or you wouldn't have schlepped him across the Atlantic to be here in Boston with you."

Grayson raised that single questioning eyebrow, an expression that made her smile wider. "Schlepped?"

She pressed her lips together and nodded. "Schlepped."

Grayson rubbed at the inner corner of his eye and laughed. "And here I believed it was because I didn't want to expose a hapless pet-sitter, or worse a family member, to Watson's attitude and mood shifts."

Watson chose that moment to stroll along the back of the couch, stepping both in the space around Grayson's arm and on his arm, pausing along the way to rub his head against Kip's hair and bump against Grayson's temple. Grayson made a show of grousing and moving out of the way, but Kip saw the sparkle in his eyes.

Once Watson moved on, Grayson looked down at her and she melted a little inside. He leaned to her and kissed her forehead. "How are you?" he asked, the seriousness slipping back into his eyes.

"Do you mean am I on the edge of a mental breakdown?"

"No," he countered with a small chuckle. "But I do worry."

Kip sighed and pushed her hair back from her face. "I realized earlier tonight my catchphrase has been 'I'm fine' since that night. I've been saying it automatically, maybe to convince myself as much as anyone else." She laid her hand against his chest, loving the feel of his heartbeat and the firmness of his body hidden by the sweater. "I'm not *fine*, but I'm better." Kip looked him in the eyes again. "Definitely better."

"Good." He nodded, offering a small, lopsided smile.

She shifted in closer and rested her head against his arm. "Can I ask you something?"

"Of course," he answered easily.

"You say you aren't the same anymore. I can't imagine you any other way. So, how are you different?"

He hummed, laced with a single muffled chuckle, and looked away. Color spread up his cheeks, and Kip tried not to smile too much at the fact he blushed. "For one," he began, looking down on her again, "you inspire me to speak about matters of the heart, an occurrence I've adamantly avoided in the past. I find the words are past my lips before I properly consider the ramifications."

"And here I thought you enjoyed our verbal foreplay." She lifted her head off his arm to face him better.

His uneasy grin warmed into a sexy one, and his gaze shifted to stare at her lips. "Oh, I enjoy it. Exceedingly so."

"What else," she asked, loving the play in his eyes as he watched her lips, and wondering if this was how he felt when she did the same.

He cleared his throat and bent the arm behind her so his fingers could slide through her hair, and she was glad she'd not bothered to clip it back or braid it like usual. The simple touch did wonderful things to her insides. "Perhaps, as embarrassing as it may be on my part, that explanation would be best illustrated by confessing the reason for the end of my last relationship."

"We're at the exchanging war stories stage," she said, hoping to put him at ease. "You tell me yours and I'll tell you mine."

When he began, his focus remained not on her face but on his own hand drawing locks of her hair. He combed his fingers through until her hair fell to her shoulder again, then stroked his thumb along her brow, and repeated. "Her name was Liz, and our relationship ended several months ago. We were together for about a year before we ended it."

"Did you love her?"

"No," he answered immediately, punctuating with a sharp, single shake of his head. "Liz was a good woman, kind and lovely. There was no fault in her and we were very compatible. She works for Six, not in any field capacity, but she is a part of the culture." He sighed, looking regretful for what he said. "I enjoyed her company to put it as gentlemanly as I am able, but regardless of the many things about Liz that made her appealing, I must readily admit the downfall of the relationship truly was mine. I was an arse, in the simplest of terms." He finally brought his gaze back to her, and the desire – because there was no other word for it – in his eyes made her flush.

"I would not lie to her and say I loved her when I didn't, and I was not enough for her otherwise."

"Enough?"

"I felt no inspiration to be anything more than I was and felt little true desire to attempt to mend the situation by forcing a need for physical affection I didn't possess. I tried, on occasion, to make a focused effort to give her as much as I was honestly capable, but it was a concerted effort each time."

Kip shook her head. "I can't imagine…"

"Therein lies the change." His smile bordered on self-deprecation. "Not only have you inspired the loosening of my tongue, and an undeniable desire for your affection, but you have shone a blinding light on my past shortcomings."

The confusion had to be evident in her expression because he smiled and nodded. "I cannot recall any moment when I looked at Liz, as truly lovely as she was, and as deserving as she was for something better than I offered, and experienced an undeniable and overwhelming need to kiss her." He chuckled as he slid his free hand along her thigh from knee to hip, and drew her closer to him. "I cannot – to fall back upon the use of a worn cliché – keep my hands off you, Kipling."

"I don't mind, trust me," she said, finding her voice caught in her throat much more than usual. She tilted her head, studying his face. "The first time I saw you, in the middle of all that chaos, I saw the reserve in your eyes. Then when you came to my apartment, and Saturday at the bookstore, you seemed to weigh out every word you said. There was always a hesitation before you touched me, even if it was meaningless."

His lips turned up. "In majority, because the urge was unfamiliar and I did not – and still don't – know how to be this person you've inspired. Each time I judged my actions to all possible outcomes and no matter, it seems I always chose you." The smile quirked. "You are quite possibly the most observant person I have ever met outside of the service. Have you ever considered a career in the Royal Majesty's Secret Service?"

"Are you offering?"

He chuckled, and she loved the way his chest rumbled with it. "Were it in my power." He drew a breath through his nose, focusing on his hand as he rhythmically rubbed her leg. "Your observation was quite accurate, Kipling. I have been undeniably drawn to you from that first night, although I didn't fully acknowledge it until the day after the attack when I was at your flat and saw your strength and your vulnerability." He lifted his gaze and looked at her. "I wanted very much, even then, to…" His touch on her leg firmed, and his hand in her hair cupped the back of her head.

She didn't let him finish before she pushed up and pressed her lips to his, the kiss instantly overwhelming. There was no slow build, not even a pause before every part of her demanded every part of him. Grayson gripped her hips, and as she rose over him, holding his face in her hands, he pulled her over his lap to straddle his hips. Her insides fluttered, warmed, and liquefied and she shifted over him, relishing in the deep, aroused groan that vibrated against her mouth.

In one smooth, powerful move Grayson lifted them both off the couch and flipped her onto her back, moving over her, their lips barely parting for more than a second. His glorious weight pushed her down, electrifying every nerve. She was no blushing virgin, but never had she felt so alive and so desperate.

He kissed her until she couldn't think, and he kissed her more, the press of his hand on her stomach and hips made her breath hitch and her blood heat. Grayson moved to her throat, nipping at her skin, and she panted his name, holding on to his shoulders as he rocked against her. She curled her fingers into his hair, the buried dampness in the thickness cool on her skin, a sweet contrast to the flush of her skin.

Her hearing aids whined several times in protest when he leaned too close or pressed too far to the side of her throat, but she didn't care. She wanted to hear him, hear the way he sounded when he wanted her, far more than she wanted relief from the momentary feedback.

It wasn't until Grayson groaned again, this time in absolute and obvious frustration, and dragged himself down her body before he moved off the couch did she realize someone knocked at his suite door.

"Bloody hell," he said, practically on a growl, stumbling more than walking toward the door.

Kip flopped back on the cushion and draped her arm over her eyes, fighting to control her breathing again and possibly bring her pounding heart to a normal rhythm. She swore her body tingled and ached at the same time, and yet, the flush on her skin was more from mortification. She had never been so…wanton with a man. Wanton, was that even the right word?

She ran the definition through her head: shameless, unchaste, immodest. Yep, that about covered it.

The knock came again, firmer and more demanding. "Boss!" a deep male voice called from the hallway.

Grayson stopped short an arm's length from the door, his hand extended toward the knob. His arm dropped, and his chin tilted to his chest. Kip sat up, a prickling heat flushing over her when she realized whoever was at the door was far more than hotel staff or someone else randomly interrupting.

"Grayson," came a woman's voice, high and cheerful, with a slightly more pronounced British accent than Grayson. "Let us in, we're freezing. I need to get off these trainers. My toes've gone numb."

"Just a moment," he called, loud enough they'd hear. He looked back to Kipling, appearing apologetic. "I'm sorry," he mouthed.

"What's the matter," came a third female voice, hers a completely new accent with long vowels. "Did we interrupt you gettin' it off?"

Grayson lunged at the door and yanked it open. "Lynne, honestly," he snapped.

A woman led the group into the suite, laughing robustly. She was perhaps in her early forties, with thick brown hair falling in chaotic curly waves just past her shoulders, and red-painted lips tucked together in a mischievous smirk. "Never been honest a day in my life," she said, turning once she cleared the doorway so her back was to Kip, clearly still oblivious to the second person in the room.

Grayson shoved the door wide to let in the next two. A petite woman, barely tall enough to come mid-chest on Grayson, blew in with a wide, dimpled smile and short, dark hair flying a bit wild from her head. Behind her was a mountain of a man, easily six-foot-five and two hundred pounds of muscle with silver hair and a silver-and-white mustache and beard.

"What the hell are you doing here?" Grayson demanded, shutting the door just before Watson bolted through it. "Jeffrey said nothing of you coming."

The big man laughed. "Spose he just wanted us tae help—" He stopped short the moment his light blue gaze snagged Kip. His mouth hung open, and his eyebrows — only slightly darker than his hair — arched high enough to wrinkle his forehead.

Kip swallowed and stood as the other two members of the descending crowd realized the man had stopped, and the two ladies followed his gaze. They might as well have turned on an interrogation spotlight. All three stared now, varying expressions of surprise on their faces. Then the first woman, the one Kip thought was Lynne, burst out again in laughter, her head tipped back. Grayson cleared his throat and shouldered his way between the big man and the tiny woman. He motioned for Kip to join him, and she took an uneasy step forward. When she was closer, he held out his arm and took her hand.

"Not entirely how I ever expect to make introductions," he said to her, his smile intending to put her at ease. He cleared his throat again and pointed at each person in turn. "This is my team. The brute there is Angus Hennessey, affectionately called Mac. A story for another time." The big man dipped his head in a nod. "Beside him, Sandra Sookoo." The petite woman smiled and waved a hand. "And the loud-mouthed, brassy one is Lynne Connolly."

"What? I'm loud-mouthed because I was right?" Lynne demanded, but the spark in her dark eyes made the accusation a tease.

"Stop it," Grayson ordered again. "She hardly needs your mouth, Lynne."

"I'd be safe to say she prefers yours over mine," she mumbled with a quirk of her perfectly formed eyebrow.

Grayson muttered a curse, possibly the first Kip had ever heard him use. His grip tightened on her hand. "Do *try* to behave, Lynne."

"That's no' likely," Angus said with a laugh. "Nae oor Lynne."

Sandra came forward, extending her hand, and Kip took it with her free one. "Don't mind them. They get grumpy when they're cold and peckish. And tired." She winked. "Maybe if they'd shut up, Grayson might be able to tell us your name."

"Kipling," Grayson said. "Kipling Branson."

Sandra gasped, her eyes brightening. "What a beautiful name! Are you named after–"

"Rudyard Kipling, yes," Kip said.

Sandra looked at Grayson, her two hands still folded around Kip's. "Oh, Grayson, she's just lovely."

Across the room, Grayson's phone chimed on the desk and annoyance flittered across his expression. "Yes, she is," he confirmed, gave Kip's hand a quick squeeze, then released it to cross the room to the phone. He snatched up the phone and answered. "Holmes," he snapped.

Kip tried to pay attention to his conversation, but Sandra's tug on her hand forced her attention away. "You'll have to forgive us, Kipling. Honestly, the last thing any of us expected when we got here was to find Grayson–"

"Getting a bit of how's your father–" Lynne cut in.

Kip looked at the woman. Though she hadn't heard the phrase before, the woman's wink and smirk said it all.

"*Entertaining*," Sandra stressed, shooting an admonishing glare at the other woman.

"Is that what the kids are callin' it these days?" Lynne asked.

Angus laughed with a deep and rumbling sound that seemed to come from his toes. Kip smiled when she realized the big man was holding Watson to his chest, rubbing the cat's head, and Watson was drinking in the attention. Lynne tossed off Sandra's correction, unbuttoning her dark grey, long coat.

"Don't bother," Grayson said, sliding the phone in his pocket as he crossed back to them. "It would seem you lot will be getting a tour of the FBI building tonight."

"Is there something wrong?" Kip asked.

Grayson reached her side, hesitating to speak, his jaw working as he seemed to think of what to say. He brought his hands in front of him, palms together, like a prayer. "No, not at all. It seems Director Stanton just learned of the arrival of three additional Six agents and would like to be formally introduced." Grayson took her hand and took a step back from the group, bringing her with him. "You," he said, pointing to the three newcomers. "Stay here. I will be right back." Then he drew her away and led her down a short, doorless hall leading to the bedroom. The hall opened to the bedroom space, with a bed on their left, a bureau against the wall across from it, and a bathroom en suite to their right.

Grayson tugged her around the corner until they were just out of view of anyone who might walk past the end of the hallway. Voices and laughter carried from the living space.

He brought up his hand to touch her face. There was something so simple, so natural, about the touch. "I'm so sorry about that. I had no idea they were coming to the States." He smiled wider. "Your skin is hot, flushed."

"Gee, I wonder why…"

He stared at her lips for three solid beats of her heart, then leaned in halfway, stopped again, and finally finished the contact by pressing his lips to hers. In comparison, the kiss was far more chaste than any they'd shared, but it stirred her all the same. Too soon, he drew back, stroking her cheek with his thumb.

"I must return to the Bureau. Allow me a few minutes to change, and I will escort you home."

"You don't need to," she said, shaking her head only slightly so she didn't pull away from his touch. "I can get home."

"I do not doubt your ability; however, my faith does not lie with the other residents of the city." He smiled, a quick tip of his lips. "I will see you home and leave from there."

He dropped his hand and took a step backward before turning to head for the attached bath, also doorless. She had only caught a glimpse of the bed and such beyond but did note the entry was without a door. She held her spot, but when he reached behind his neck and gripped the collar of his sweater to pull it over his head – briefly exposing the lean definition of his back – she was sorely tempted to follow. A pang of jealousy made her lip curl when Watson scurried around the corner and into the bath after his owner/slave.

Then she heard his voice carry from the bathroom, but with the distance and architecture between them, all she knew was he spoke and nothing made sense. She leaned toward the doorway, not daring to take a step, clearing her throat so he heard her before she spoke.

"I'm sorry. I can't understand..." she called.

She gasped, startled, when he rushed from the bathroom having already changed from his jeans to suit pants, in the process of pulling on a white shirt as he walked. She might have had the pleasure of seeing his bare torso had he not apparently put on a white tee shirt beneath the button-down. A suit jacket and tie draped over his arm, and he tossed it on the foot of the bed.

Watson followed, hopping up onto the white duvet. He apparently had enough sense not to lie on Grayson's suit and pranced past it to flop near the pillows.

"I apologize," he said, seemingly unfazed. "I said I wish I could make solid plans; however–"

"No, don't apologize," she said, leaning her shoulder against the wall. "I understand."

He sat on the foot of the bed to put on his shoes, looking at her as he did. With the last shoe on and tied, he sat up and shook his head, setting one hand on his knee. "I find I do not like that phrase, and I like it less each time you are required to say it."

"Required?"

With both shoes on and laced, he stood to finish buttoning his shirt. Damn, but watching him dress did as much for her as she thought watching him undress might. He moved quickly, his actions clearly stating his need to get to the Bureau building. With his shirt buttoned, he tucked it in, finished buckling his belt, and picked up the tie from the bed.

"Yes, required."

"Why would you not like me to understand?"

It was only then that he actually slowed down, mid-way through knotting his tie. Grayson paused, silk Windsor knot already set, stared at her, then adjusted the tie to his throat. Grayson pulled on the jacket as he walked to her, his black shoes clicking on the hard-wood floor.

By the time he reached her, the smile of moments before was gone and seriousness pinched at the corners of his eyes. Kip turned to tuck her hands behind her and lean fully against the wall when he stepped in front of her. She tilted her head, studying his face, a worm of worry curling in her stomach. She had gotten very good at reading as much in someone's expression as their words, and he hated what he had to say.

"In light of how very close I was tonight to making love to you–" His words bloomed heat in her cheeks again, but she managed to only blink and hold his gaze. "I feel quite the bastard now for leaving, and it vexes me that rather than remaining here with you, you are *required* to *understand* why I must leave."

"But, I do understand, Grayson."

"If you don't come out soon, I'm sendin' Mac in," Lynne's voice carried from the main room.

His expression tensed, his eyes pinching at the outer corners, and his lips tightened. "Lynne severely lacks in manners," he said through a tight jaw.

Kip smiled and laid her palms against his cheeks, smoothing away the tense lines with her thumbs until he relaxed. His gaze shifted from her eyes to her lips, and back again. He looked down and away, releasing a hard breath, and abruptly took her face in his hands and kissed her. When he let her go, he only moved back enough that she could see his face but didn't drop his hands. "You mesmerize me, you beautiful woman."

She grinned and reached high to push some of his hair away from his forehead. When left to its own devices, his hair apparently had a tendency to wave and curl even more than she'd seen already. She probably hadn't helped by indulging in the wish to feel the thick waves between her fingers.

Reading her smile, Grayson huffed. "Yes, I fear there is no taming it. A curse in my family. The only cure is practically shaving it off."

"Don't you dare." She shook her head. "Mmmm, I wouldn't call it a curse. I call it damn sexy."

He arched his eyebrows, looking surprised, and Kip kissed him quickly before stepping free of his arms. "Come on, Mr. Holmes. You have a job to do. The sooner you're done, the sooner we can finish what we started. "

He smirked, adjusted his tie one more time, and followed her back to the sitting room. The moment they stepped clear of the hall, the three members of his team looked away, doing a surprisingly poor job of hiding their eavesdropping.

"For spies, they are pretty obvious," she said to the side.

Grayson laughed, retrieving their coats when she went to the couch to slip on her shoes. He spoke to the others, each paying close attention, but she didn't catch any of what he said since his back was to her and he spoke softly. She rubbed Watson's head before standing. Grayson opened the suite door and preceded everyone into the hall, locking the door behind them. Once he locked the door, he took her hand and they walked together to the elevator where the others waited. Sandra's blatant glance at their joined hands made Kip's cheeks heat again, but she saw only a pleased expression in Sandra's smile. Angus did his best not to notice, and Lynne looked positively smug.

"Honestly, Grayson, you don't need to take me home. Just go and do what needs to be done," Kip insisted in the car.

"She seems perfectly capable—" Lynne began, but Grayson shot her a look.

He had said they were his team, and even though they teased him without mercy, Kip saw the underlying respect and she wondered if he was not a part of the team, but the head of the team.

Kip tugged his hand to wrap around her and he had to bend a bit to be closer to her, and she toed up to speak near his ear. "I'm a woman, full grown," she said with a grin, and the slow curl of his smile told her she'd gotten the desired effect.

"I don't like it," he said, turning so she saw his face and he could mouth the words and the others wouldn't hear. "But I cannot argue with just how much of a woman you are, Kipling. I concede, but text me when you reach your flat so I know you are safe."

She leaned up and pressed a kiss to his cheek. "Deal."

Angus cleared his throat, and Kip glanced at him. His fair, freckled cheeks were crimson and he was doing his level best not to notice the exchange between her and Grayson. Kip smiled. Despite their means of introduction, she had a strong suspicion she would like these three people.

Once in the atrium, the night clerk went outside to get them taxis. The other three MI6 agents moved away toward the door, speaking in hushed tones. The only one blatant enough to glance back at them was Sandra, but she did so with a wide, genuine smile that popped deep dimples in her cheeks, and a wink. Grayson slowed their steps to lengthen the distance, and Kip turned toward Grayson, intending to say something outrageously flirty, when her left hearing aid snapped and clicked. Just once. She jumped and gasped, her heart jumping to her throat.

Grayson's steadying grip on her elbow pulled her closer to him. "What is it? What's wrong?"

Kip shook her head and released a slow breath to try to calm her irrationally short breath. "Nothing. My aid just did something weird."

Grayson raised his gloved hand, hovering it near her ear with deep lines digging into his brow. "Like at the university and the shop? I thought your doctor fixed them."

"She did," she said, shaking her head. "It was just the one click. Probably just a–" The aid clicked again, and she jumped. Again. She grit her teeth and closed her eyes. "Damn it."

"Tell me."

She opened her eyes again, still clenching her jaw. "Do you remember me telling you they react sometimes to things like digital cameras and weird electronics?"

Grayson nodded, still scowling.

"Like that."

He looked around the empty lobby, no one but the inn's staff was around that late in the evening. Then he looked up at the high ceilings, squinting. "Perhaps they have a security camera."

"It's probably something just that simple, but I didn't hear it when I arrived." She shrugged. "Then again, I didn't hang out in the lobby."

"Ye a'right, Boss?" Angus called.

Grayson looked up and shook his head. "I'll explain en route."

The clerk came back through the glass doors, holding them so Angus, Sandra, and Lynne could move past him to the outside. "I have your taxis, Mr. Holmes," the clerk called.

One final click made her flinch before they left the lobby, and she managed that time only to tighten her hold on Grayson's hand as an outward show of the pounding of her heart. She hated she'd allowed something that would have been an annoyance a couple of weeks before to become something able to steal her breath and make her break out in a panicked sweat.

It had grown colder since she'd arrived, and it had been cold enough then to chill the tip of her nose. The wind whipped between the buildings, making her aids whistle.

Grayson pointed toward the first cab and motioned for his team to get in, walking Kip to the second. The driver hopped out and came around the back of the vehicle with a wide and eager smile. "Good evening," he said jovially, opening the back passenger door for Kip.

"I'll take care of her," Grayson said, with a smile and a nod to the driver. He pushed back his coat to access his back pocket, and brought out his billfold, removing a bill. Kip opened her mouth to protest, but Grayson shook his head and smiled, giving the bill to the driver.

In apparent understanding, the driver went back around to get back in, leaving Grayson standing in the open door space with Kip. The wind quickly stole the feeling in her face, making her lips feel thick and her cheeks tingle. Grayson stood with his back to the open door so she was caught between his body and the warmth of the car interior. His company was infinitely more appealing than the warm car.

"I'll text when I get home," she said, repeating his request. She grinned up at him, feeling naughty. "I suppose you're too British to kiss me goodbye in front of your team?"

For several beats of her heart, she regretted teasing when he said nothing at all. He stared down at her, only the slightest shift in his gaze as he studied her. She drew in a breath, ready to repeal her challenge, but her words were forgotten when he dipped his head and pressed his lips to hers. It wasn't a passionate kiss, not like they'd shared upstairs, but it still made her blood warm and her heart palpitate.

When he drew back, Kip knew she probably grinned like a fool, but she didn't care once his own lips tipped up. "I would be too much the fool if I ignored an opportunity," he said and tapped the end of her nose with his gloved hand. "Go on home. I'll speak with you tomorrow."

She started to slide into the cab, then stopped and looked up at him again. "Good luck with the third degree. I get the distinct impression those three aren't going to let you off easy."

Grayson looked to the cab still parked in front of them and sighed. "Once again, your observation skills are keen."

She chuckled and sat in the back seat, waving through the window once Grayson shut the door. He approached the waiting cab while they pulled away.

Lynne and Sandra were already in the cab when Grayson reached it, Mac standing outside the closed back passenger door with a wide grin curling his mustache.

"Shut up," Grayson said, marching past him to the front passenger door of the cab, and opening the door.

"I never opened ma moo'," Mac said, chuckling.

"Good. Keep it that way," Grayson turned enough to partially face the big man who towered a good four inches over Grayson even without the heavy-heeled boots he wore. "I can do without–" He stopped short and looked down. Dancing across his chest was a red dot, circling in a jerky, unsteady pattern over his heart.

In a blur, Mac whipped out his thick arm and knocked Grayson down onto the cold pavement, shouting "Sniper!" at the same time.

The window glass behind Grayson's back a second before shattered and rained down on them. A woman screamed from somewhere nearby battled with the pings of a second bullet ricocheting off the brick face of the building with sharp clarity. The back passenger door of the cab opened and both Lynne and Sandra lunged out, hitting the ground beside Mac and Grayson.

The angle of the shot put the shooter on the other side of the street and either on the roof or from a high window. Grayson curled up enough to squint at the suspected point of fire, but the darkness of the light with the contrast of the street lamps made it impossible to make out anything.

"In America less than a month, and you've made some powerful enemies," Lynne said from her position against the car. She smirked at him and winked. "Your totty have an old boyfriend with a sharp shot?"

Grayson ignored Lynne's commentary, scanning the visible area for the dancing red dot, and saw no sign. He looked into the cab, meeting the wide-eyed, terror-struck gaze of the cabbie who had spread himself across his front seat. "Are you all right?" he asked. The man only stared, the whites of his eyes stark against the contrast of his skin. "Are you all right?" Grayson demanded again, louder, and the cabbie nodded but said nothing more.

In the distance, the wail of approaching sirens echoed off the high buildings. Bracing his hand on the pavement, Grayson pushed himself up and sat back against the open cab door, brushing tiny bits of shattered auto glass off his shoulder and out of his hair. He offered Sandra his hand to bring her to her feet, and Mac did the same for Lynne until the four of them stood together shoulder-to-shoulder.

"All joking aside," Lynne said, brushing at her coat. "I would say this confirms your suspicions someone wishes you harm, Grayson."

"That much had already been validated, but this certainly erases all doubt," Grayson confirmed, taking his mobile from his pocket, checking first it wasn't damaged from his impact with the frozen pavement. He tapped in his security code, and opened his contacts, preparing to call Director Stanton.

"Jeezo, jist as weel she wis oota here," Mac said. "So, she kens whit ye are? Aye?"

Grayson paused with his thumb over the contact icon. "Yes, she does," he answered. "The circumstances under which we met required honesty from the start; of course, at the time I hadn't any inclination she might be more to me than…" His words trailed off even as his thoughts sped up. He turned to his left to face Sandra. "I need you to do something for me."

Sandra tilted her head, her smile acceptance of whatever he would ask before he asked it. "What do you need?"

Kip unlocked her apartment door and shrugged off her coat, draping on the back of the chair nearest the door. She'd been wide awake the whole time at Grayson's, and most of the way home, but as her mother would say she was "hit with the tired stick" a few blocks from home. It hit her hard and fast, and she hoped it meant she would sleep.

She was halfway to her bedroom door when she realized she'd

left her phone in her coat pocket, and went back for it. In her room, she toed off her shoes as she typed a text.

> I'm home. Safe and sound

Kip didn't expect a response, at least not right away. His debriefing – or whatever he'd call what was going on – would keep him busy, she was sure, but she'd done as she promised. She dropped the phone on the bed and went into the bathroom, shucking her clothes and pulling out her aids as she went. The warm shower relaxed her, and by the time she went back into the bedroom dressed in her favorite flannel pajamas and tee shirt, she was ready to climb into the bed and try to sleep.

She picked up the phone and looked at the screen.

> Please let me know when I might call. I need to speak with you.

> Kipling...have you gone to bed already?

The two messages were five minutes apart. Kip went back into the bathroom and retrieved her aids, turning them on as she placed them back in her ears. As soon as they chimed on, she tapped on his name and the phone icon, initiating the call. It only rang twice before he answered.

"Kipling..."

The way he said her name sent a pleasant rush along the back of her neck as if the word was his greeting, an endearment. Kip closed her eyes, imagining him safe and sound and with her.

"Kipling, are you there?"

"Yes," she said, sucking in a deep breath. "Sorry. I texted I was home and then took a shower, or I would have called sooner. Is there something wrong?"

"I'm afraid so."

In a heartbeat, her relaxed lethargy disappeared. Replaced by a cold chill that shot up her spine to the base of her skull. "What? What is it?"

"I fear I am unsure how to explain without causing you excessive worry–"

"You can start just by *saying* it, Grayson."

"Right. Yes. Kipling, any moment now Sandra is going to knock on your flat door. I need you to let her in immediately. She is going to stay with you tonight, and we will work out further details tomorrow."

"Why does Sandra need to stay with me?"

"To protect you."

"Protect me? Grayson, what–"

"Shortly after you left me tonight, an attempt was made on my life. This is what we suspect to be the second attempt, the first being–"

"The explosion at the university." The realization came to her like a snap near her ear. "Oh, God. Grayson, are you okay?"

"Yes, I'm fine. I'm perfectly fine, thanks to Mac's quick response and massive arm," he finished with a chuckle.

"I'd rather you not joke."

"I'm sorry. I truly am, Kipling, but with this second attempt I cannot take the risk you meeting harm for your association with me. If they were waiting for my departure from the hotel, they saw you, and there can be no doubt in their mind your importance to me."

Her chest hurt, and she set the phone on the bed beside her to keep from squeezing it until it dug into her hand. "I'm sorry," she managed to whisper.

"Whatever for?"

"For causing you more concern than you need."

"Kipling," he said on a sigh. "Don't think that for a moment. This is hardly the first time someone has wished to see me dead, and I rather doubt it will be the last. Your involvement is my guilt to bear."

Kip laughed, more out of nervousness than humor. "You admit someone is trying to kill you with as much concern as hearing you're out of tea."

"Oh, no. Being out of tea would be much more serious."

Kip did laugh, even though fear sat in the middle of her chest like a kettleball. The laugh turned into a choking lump in her throat. Kip pressed her lips together and covered her mouth with her hand, trying to stifle her tears. She sniffed, louder than she intended, and managed to ask, "So, is this what it's like to-to be with you?" The words felt assumptive, but she didn't know how else to ask.

"Is it too much?"

"No." The answer came out before she made the mistake of thinking whether it was the right answer, or not. Which meant it had to be right. "I can't promise I'm not going to worry, though. Or ask too many questions. Is that okay?"

"I'd rather have your questions, than silence." There was that heavy voice again, wrapping around her.

Four solid knocks at the apartment door made Kip gasp and jump, and before Grayson could ask what was wrong, she told him, "I think Sandra is here."

"Stay with me until you are sure."

Kip snatched up the phone, knowing it wouldn't maintain the connection as far as the apartment door, and jogged through the kitchen just as Sandra knocked again, calling out "Kipling? It's Sandra. Are you awake?"

"Coming," Kip assured, and peeked through the peephole, just seeing the top of Sandra's head. "It's Sandra," she said to Grayson as she opened the door and motioned the woman into the apartment.

"Did Grayson reach you?" she asked.

Kip nodded and held up her finger. "She's here."

"I feel better knowing you aren't alone."

"Are you with Mac and Lynne, then?"

Sandra scowled, looking perplexed, looking down at the phone in Kip's hand.

"Yes. I've stepped out of a meeting with Director Stanton to speak with you."

"I worry about you."

"That means a great deal to me, Kipling. More than I can say." He cleared his throat.

"Grayson, I–" She stuttered, the words catching in her throat. She stared at Sandra, feeling suddenly self-conscious. "I miss you. Call me whenever you can, even if it's two in the morning. Promise me."

"I promise. Goodbye, Kipling."

"Goodbye," she whispered and waited until he ended the call. As soon as her aids re-engaged for ambient sound, Kip tapped her cheek and smiled at Sandra, already understanding the woman's confusion. "The phone routes through my hearing aids."

Sandra pulled a face and shuddered. "Bit too much like a Cybus ear pod for my liking."

Kip laughed, immediately feeling better in the woman's company. Of course, she shouldn't be surprised Sandra was a Doctor Who fan. It was probably a prerequisite to maintain your British citizenship. "Not quite," she said, shaking her head. "No worries. I'm not going to turn into a Cyberman."

Sandra smiled wider. "Oh, we are going to get on brilliantly." In a blink, Sandra's smile slipped and deep lines dug in between her eyes. She took a step toward Kip and laid her hand on Kip's arm. "Are you doing okay, pet? This must be an awful lot to accept."

Kip swallowed and nodded, trying to convince herself as much as Sandra. "Considering how we met – you could say I was literally swept off my feet–" She tried a chuckle but failed miserably. "I probably shouldn't be so surprised. But, until now, the fact Grayson is an intelligence agent seemed…I don't know…separate from *him*. I don't suppose that makes sense."

"Grayson isn't an agent, you know."

Kip wrinkled her nose and shook her head. "Right. He did tell me. I guess I don't understand the difference."

"When he told you we are his team, he didn't mean a team he's *on*. He meant a team he *runs*. Where he leads, we follow. Where he says go, we ask how quickly we need to be there." Before Kip could process that detail, Sandra smiled, and Kip wondered if anyone could possibly *not* smile when she grinned. "It makes perfect sense, by the way. Not that I've been on your side, but my husband said something similar after I told him who and what I was. I suppose you are at an advantage."

"How is that?" Exhaustion hitting her again, Kip sank into one of her kitchen chairs, motioning for Sandra to join her.

She did, unbuttoning her coat as she sat to slide it off her shoulders. "When David and I met, I told him I was an antiques dealer and my name was Jane Snow. He didn't know my real name for three months." A sadness that looked completely foreign in Sandra's bright eyes stole her smile. "I will always remember the look on his face when I told him, and will regret it forever. He looked betrayed, and didn't speak to me for three weeks." Then she sighed with a bounce of her shoulders, and the smile was back. "But he forgave me. That was twelve years ago."

"Why did you give David a fake name and story?" Kip drew one foot up into the chair to rest her cheek against her raised knee.

"I was playing a legend," Sandra explained. "I'm not entirely sure I should be telling you all this, but since you know the high points already…might as well. When we work on an investigation, those of us in the field use legends. Names. Histories. Jobs to suit the situation. I was in Chaguanas trailing–" She stopped short, the grin popping her dimples. "Well, that part doesn't matter. But I met David completely unintentionally. I was in Trinidad for three weeks and started seeing him to help establish my legend. By the time I went back to London…" She sighed, a dreamy sound. "I asked to have him vetted."

"Vetted?"

Sandra scrunched up half her face as if she'd tasted something unpleasant. "It's how we decide who we can and can't tell who we are. We usually only do it when we're serious about someone. Can't just tell everyone about your secret identity, can you?"

"Am I–would I be *vetted*?"

Sandra shrugged. "As a formality, maybe. The genie is out of the bottle." She stood with a huff. "So, where am I bunking? The couch?"

Kip stood slower than Sandra, her thoughts churning with too many questions. So many she couldn't categorize them or put them all into complete thoughts. "Yeah. I'll get you some extra pillows."

By the time Kip came back to the living room with two pillows hugged to her chest, one question had taken form. "Sandra, how does David handle it?"

Sandra had sat on the couch and taken off her shoes. She looked up at Kip, her smile more reserved than before. "He hates it. Hates every single second of it. But he loves me more than he hates my job."

Kip nodded and handed the woman the pillows. With a wish for a good night and sweet dreams from Sandra, she went to her room but held no hope for a restful night.

Chapter Fourteen

"What's up with your hair?"

Grayson didn't bother looking away from the preliminary report of the shooting. Two bullets had been retrieved, two casings had been found on the roof of the building across the street and down the block from the FBI building. Marks in the snow and ice on the roof showed footprints and indicators of where the gunman rested his rifle. The casings were in forensics, hoping for possible partial prints or DNA, and the forensic team took photos and cold molds before the imprints disappeared. Thus far, nothing of use. The shooter was long gone before police arrived.

"Seriously, what's up with your hair?"

Grayson shot a glare at Agent Flannery. "Two assassination attempts on American soil of a member of the British Secret Intelligence Service, and you're concerned with the state of my hair?"

Flannery shrugged. "Concerned? No. Curious? Hell, yeah."

Grayson fought the urge to raise a hand and shove it through his hair. The thick waves were often a challenge to tame, even on the best of days, and Kipling's fingers had done little to help the matter. Even cut shorter, the waves could be persistent when left to their own nature. Add to it the light snowfall that had begun while they waited with the police, and he now looked like a pre-pubescent schoolboy who didn't know how to comb his hair. He tried very hard not to think about the tactile sensation of Kipling's touch, and the accompanying kiss.

"You contacted me at nearly eleven in the evening, a point in time at which I was not anticipating a return to the office. My apologies if my hair doesn't pass inspection."

Flannery laughed, dropping into a chair across from Grayson. "Easy, chief. It's all good."

Flannery sighed, tapped his joined hands on the table, and looked down the table to where Lynne and Mac sat side by side, Mac on his custom build computer while Lynne reviewed all the evidence and data they had recovered since the bombing, including all information from the bank robbery intended to mock Grayson and possibly draw him out.

"Do we know the whereabouts of Agent DiMatto this evening at the time of the shooting?" Grayson asked, glancing at Flannery with his head still tilted down. "I seem to recall his absence from the office at the time of the robbery."

Flannery cleared his throat and leaned back, swinging one arm over the back of the chair. "We haven't gotten ahold of Burke yet. No answer at home or on his cell."

"Hmmm." Grayson focused on the report. "Interesting."

"There's no way he was the bank robber," Flannery argued. "You saw the video. There is no way that was Burke. And sure, he can shoot, but not at sniper level like this."

"That does not exclude the possibility of his involvement."

"No, I guess it doesn't."

"Perhaps it is time surveillance is applied to one of your own." Grayson still didn't look up from the report, deciding it was best to allow Flannery to consider the option without the pressure of direct address.

"We put surveillance on him after I talked to the director."

Grayson did look up then. "And? Yet you do not know his whereabouts?"

"If your people put a tracker on you, wouldn't you know how to shake them if you wanted to?"

Grayson conceded with a single nod. "Point taken. And of course, if he has avoided your surveillance team, he is likely now aware there are suspicions held against him."

Flannery's non-verbal response was a jerked tilt of his head and a grimace. He looked down the table again. "Quite the menagerie you've got on your *team*."

Grayson glanced to Mac and Lynne to see Mac taking a massive bite of some paper-wrapped hamburger with cheese and sliced tomatoes. Giving in to Mac's complaining, someone had gone out for food; not an easy task at one in the morning. American fast food was far from preferred, but Grayson was under the impression Mac would eat anything if it stayed still long enough.

"Don't underestimate them," Grayson said, acknowledging his pride as he watched their diligence. "My people represent some of the best in the JIC." When Flannery said nothing, Grayson looked sideways at him and saw the man's incredulous look. Grayson sighed. "Angus Hennessy is a computer genius. He can hack into and disassemble any computer system in existence. There is no fire-wall he has failed to get through when he wished it. He can build anything electronic, practically from bailing twine and paperclips, earning him the name Mac."

"Like a Mac computer?" Flannery asked, his bunched brow saying to Grayson he didn't believe Grayson's claim.

"No, like *MacGyver*."

Flannery chuckled a short snort, and nodded. "Oh, right. Got it."

Grayson looked back at his team. Mac pinched half a dozen chips between his fingers, shoving them in his mouth. Lynne sat beside him and Grayson caught the soft look she gave the big man and the small smile curving her lips. Mac seemed to, as well, and held out the paper bucket holding the chips, offering her one. She shook her head, but he held it out further, and she conceded to take a single chip. Mac grinned and set the package between them to share.

"Lynne Connolly can be anyone, anywhere, for any reason. The only character she cannot play is a man, and given the right opportunity, I wouldn't be surprised if she managed it. She is fluent in seven languages, including vulgarity, and could kill you with two fingers without leaving a mark. And Sandra…" He couldn't help his smile when he thought of Sandra. He had bargained and begged to have her on his team. "Sandra Sookoo will create any legend seamlessly for Lynne to assume, with details right down to which knee you skinned in primary school should the detail be required. Her imagination is matched only by her skill. I've told her that were she not in her current profession, she would make a gifted novelist."

"I saw her at your hotel before we came back here. She's cute–"

"And you're married." Grayson then added, "So is Sandra, and there is no force on earth that would dissuade her heart from David."

Flannery snorted and crossed his arms over his chest, shifting again in his chair. He was like a primary school student, unable to sit still for long. Likely a result of the multiple cups of coffee he'd consumed since their return to the Bureau building.

"Where did she end up?"

"She is taking care of someone for me."

"Taking care of someone," Flannery repeated. "What? Your cat?"

"No." For this, Grayson sat up fully and looked the man in the eyes. "Kipling Branson. She left in a taxi from the hotel not two minutes before the shooting occurred. I must assume I am or have been watched, and thus until we have this would-be assassin in custody, I want her protected."

Flannery made a sound somewhere between a laugh and an exclamation, nodding his head. He pointed a finger at Grayson. "I thought something was going on between you two."

Grayson tossed his pencil onto the table and lifted his hands in mock surrender. "You have ferreted me out, Agent Flannery."

"Don't be such a smug ass," Flannery countered, though his smirk belied his protest. "She was at your suite, huh? How long has this been going on?"

"Long enough for her to be at my suite for dinner."

"Is that how you pick up your women, Holmes? Literally *pick them up* when they get blown over?"

Grayson pushed back his chair and stood. "I fail to see your humor."

When he stood, so did Lynne and Mac, and Mac slapped shut his computer, tucking it under his arm. Grayson snapped out his arm to reveal his watch beneath his sleeve. Nearly four. Three hours until sunrise. He could sleep for two.

"We are returning to the university at first light."

"For what?" Flannery called after him.

Grayson stopped mid-stride and turned on the balls of his feet to face back the way he came. "When last there, the area was chaos. I need to observe in the light of day and in the oppressed calm that exists there now."

"Forensics already looked over the whole area."

"The world is full of obvious things which nobody ever observes. They *looked*, but did they observe." It wasn't a question, nor did he expect an answer. If Flannery offered one, Grayson was too far away to hear it.

Were Grayson a believer in the supernatural, he would believe the oppressive cold that blanketed the grounds of the devastated lecture hall might be from something more than the bitter chill of a North-eastern winter. The air was thin, the sky gray, and gravity sat heavy on his shoulders as he walked the iced walkway and stepped into the building. Every breath hurt, prickling in his lungs, and frost clouds curled in front of his face.

Yellow strips of cautionary tape marked off areas where it wasn't safe to walk, for fear of injury from the remaining portions of the buildings. Heavy equipment and tools filled the lobby and spilled into the common, indicating the school had already begun the process of repairing and rebuilding. The hall was one of the original to the school, and a city like Boston held firm to its history.

"Jeez min, it's Baltic oot here," Mac groused. "How come you're no' a block of ice, Boss?"

"Warm porridge every morning," Grayson gave back, pulling open the door to the lobby of the lecture building.

"I'd say his new bird helps." Lynne's smile carried in her tone.

They had been relentless, Lynne and Mac, each in their own way. Mac had tried to whittle information from him. And Lynne… not a subtle bone existed in her body. Grayson supposed he should be thankful Sandra wasn't there to add to their efforts.

He paused in what remained of a hallway, the air just as cold inside as outside. The lino was littered with building debris. His footsteps echoed in the hallway. He stopped, closed his eyes for a moment to still his thoughts, then opened them and did a slow rotation, scanning left and right, ceiling to floor. Nothing of use caught his attention, and he moved to the hole blasted in the wall leading into the lecture hall. His team followed.

He wished his team was complete; Greg had been the explosives expert. He could taste the type of accelerants used, and could judge velocity and determine source at a glance. His knowledge would have been priceless.

The front of the hall was also cordoned off by yellow tape around the charred, destroyed space where the lectern had stood; the point of origin for the blast. The bodies had been taken away long ago, but Grayson swore he smelled death hanging in the hair. It stuck in his throat and made his chest ache. He could never go too long without the smell of ash and death burning his senses. A lifetime wouldn't be long enough. He pushed his hands into his pockets to hide his clenched fists.

After more than a year, the smell still made him sick.

"I don't think I'll ever be able to clear that smell from my memory," Lynne said, walking gingerly across the damaged floor, speaking the words Grayson thought.

He didn't have to tell them what to do. They all knew what to do.

Grayson walked toward the burned, twisted remains of what had been a wood and metal lectern, studying the pattern of burn away from the stand and the impact scars on the walls. Mac started up the steps to the back of the room for a wider view, and Lynne went left to note different elements of the scene. Grayson crouched behind the lectern, staring at the black interior.

He stood, keeping his hands at his side to avoid touching the charred remains, not because he would affect evidence, but to try to stay separate from the death tainting what remained. Grayson looked up and to the back of the lecture hall, the spot he would have stood had he made it into the room that evening. He realized – with a hard pinch to his heart – he was quite possibly alive because he had paused to speak with Kipling. Had he not, it was likely he would have perished along with his uncle and the other students.

Grayson squinted and tried to focus on the wall along the back of the room. Mounted to the wall, hanging at a slight angle, was a digital video camera.

"Mac," he barked, drawing the big man's attention. When Mac looked up, Grayson pointed to the spot on the wall. "Determine if the recordings are internal or routed elsewhere."

Grayson took the steps leading to the back of the room as Mac climbed onto one of the desks in the back. With his height he was able to hoist himself almost eye level with the camera. Grayson watched, hands tucked in his coat pockets, as Mac did a cursory examination of the camera that was at least twelve to fifteen year old technology. With a sharp nod, Mac jumped down, the impact of his boots on the lino echoed in the hollow space. Mac slapped his hands together, nodding.

"No' that I'm haddin oot much hope o anything guid. Looks like a basic bit o kit tae me. Mebbes hooked up wi' something ootiside. Could just be on a loop that gets rid every couple o hours."

"Brilliant," Grayson said, taking his phone from his pocket. Using his teeth, he tugged his fingers free of his glove and tapped in his security code, dialing Agent Flannery.

"Yeah, Flannery."

"There are security cameras in the school. Do we have the recordings?"

"Of the lecture and the explosion? Yeah, but none of our suspects were there that day. We already figured they set the bombs way before…" Flannery trailed off, and Grayson nodded.

"Yes, precisely. We know when construction was done on the building, at least a time period. Get them."

"On it."

Before Grayson could disconnect, he heard Flannery call out his name, likely sensing he assumed the call was over. He brought the mobile back to his ear. "Yes"

"We found Burke." The weight of his voice made Grayson pause in his descent to the front of the hall. He stopped short, waiting. "In an alley off Thomson Place, running behind the building the shots came from. Shot in the back of the head, execution style."

"Bloody hell," Grayson cursed.

Sunlight ended at a forty-five-degree angle from the corner of the multi-story brick building just a few doors down and across the street from the extended stay suites Grayson had inhabited for the last few weeks. Police officers stood at the end of the alley, keeping away curious eyes, and yellow caution tape marked the area as off-limits. Grayson approached Agent Flannery, who stood on the outside of one strip, Lynne and Mac walking behind him. His breath curled in front of his face, despite the bright sun.

Grayson nodded to Flannery in greeting, noting the grim expression on the man's face. Flannery held up the tape for Grayson and the others to duck under, Mac having to practically fold himself in half to clear it.

"You didn't have to come back," Flannery said, falling into step with Grayson as they turned into the dark alley. "Forensics will be finishing up soon, then we're taking him out of here."

"Which is precisely why I came," Grayson said, taking in the details of the narrow alleyway. "There are details here that will be lost once the scene is disturbed."

"I didn't realize you were trained in forensics."

"I am trained in science," he said.

"Yeah, well, I took chemistry and biology in college, too. Doesn't mean I want to see what there is to see down here."

"You have yet to understand him, have you," Lynne said, her tone not asking a question. Grayson gave her a look, which she promptly ignored. "Under your nose this whole time. How pathetic."

"Lynne…" Grayson scolded.

"I saw that data map craft project he did on the wall, sure. But what's that got to do with my partner's brains blown out in an alley."

"Nothing," Grayson said, attempting to divert the conversation. He stopped mid-stride to turn enough to face Flannery. Despite the circumstances and suspicions, the man had just lost his partner. If Grayson had any common understanding on this, he knew at least once the men had relied on each other for their lives. Death was still a wound. "Nothing at all; however, if I can help in any way, I am glad to."

Flannery looked from Grayson to Lynne, then proceeded down the alley without saying anything further. Approximately thirty feet into the alley were two people wearing latex gloves and special slips over their shoes. FBI on their jackets indicated they were there working the scene on behalf of the Bureau. They seemed to be finishing up as one draped a tarp over a hunched form while the other finished packing up their kits.

"You good?" Flannery asked when one turned to face them.

"We've done all we can. From here, answers will come in the lab and the autopsy," the man answered, looking curiously at Grayson.

"He's gonna take a look."

With a nod, the forensic specialist walked past them to the end of the alley, the second – a woman – followed carrying some of the kit. Mac and Lynne hung back, standing with Flannery while Grayson crouched beside the lump in the alley. Agent Flannery had told him it was an execution-style killing, so he was not surprised to see Agent DiMatto's body positioned on his knees, hands behind his back, face down in the red-stained snow.

The entry wound in the back of his head implied a close-range shot. Moving gingerly, trying not to disturb the body any more than necessary, Grayson leaned his stance and hunched to see DiMatto's face, which was turned only slightly in Grayson's direction; likely knocked that way when he fell forward. The small but prominent exit wound had destroyed most of his left eye and the bridge of his nose.

"May I have a pair of gloves?" he asked, pivoting on the balls of his feet.

Flannery turned and jogged to the end of the alley, speaking with one of the crime scene investigators, and promptly came back with two latex gloves he handed to Grayson. Once on, Grayson gingerly made a cursory examination of the wound, making a guess the weapon had been likely a 9mm. He pressed his finger to the flesh of DiMatto's cheek, feeling no give; but that did little to establish a timeline since he was likely killed during the night, and with the frigid, far below-freezing weather, any determination of rigor was impossible until possibly after toxicology and autopsy tests were complete.

The light was poor for examination, but the shadow of DiMatto's jaw looked wrong to Grayson. Granted, he had fallen forward into a metal bin, but the jaw looked dislocated, and an impact at that proximity wouldn't have been sufficient to dislocate his jaw. Grayson pressed his fingertips to the tip of the mandible, confirming the jaw was definitely out of place.

"Could you please call back your forensic team," Grayson said, squinting to try to see more clearly.

"Allan," Flannery shouted, his voice echoing off the cold bricks. "Come on back. You need the photographer?" he asked of Grayson. When Grayson nodded, he yelled again. "Bring Kelly." He took a step toward Grayson. "What you got?"

"Not sure yet, but I want it documented."

The FBI forensic team returned, and Grayson waited while

Kelly retrieved her camera. He waited until she was ready before he pressed on the lower jaw. Rigor and cold made the body resistant. "Retractor?" he asked, and Allan dug into his kit for the tool. Grayson winced as he slid the retractor between DiMatto's teeth. With enough pressure the bone popped and the jaw released.

"Do you have a small torch?" he asked Allan. "A small pen light. Flashlight."

Allan nodded and took from his kit a small LED light, handing it to Grayson. Holding the jaw open with his left hand, he shined the light around the opening. Deep in the mouth, likely so deep DiMatto choked on it before his death, was a folded piece of paper.

"Pinchers," he said, holding out his hand, palm up.

Someone, likely Allan, slapped a tool into his hand. Long, skinny pinchers he used to slide between DiMatto's teeth to retrieve the tip of the paper. All the while, Kelly continued to take pictures. With the folded paper free, Grayson released the jaw and stood

Pink tinted the corners where they had dug into DiMatto's soft palate and oropharynx. Kelly came to his side, taking photos as he unfolded each angle. The writing was upside down when he finished opening the note, and he rotated it to read the words written in careful, yet heavy and masculine handwriting.

"What does it say, Grayson," Lynne asked.

"I must take the view, Your Grace, that when a man embarks upon a crime, he is morally guilty of any other crime which may spring from it," he read, his blood-chilling more with each word, because with each word a terrifying reality crept into his mind.

"What the hell is that?" Flannery asked.

"It's a quote," Grayson said. "A quote the perpetrator of this murder would know I, before anyone else, would immediately and undeniably recognize."

"A quote from what?"

"Who, more precisely." Grayson took from Allan an evidence bag and dropped the note inside. "Sherlock Holmes. One of the lesser-recognized short stories titled *The Adventure of the Priory School*." He looked to Flannery, pain darting down the sides of his neck from the force of gritting his teeth. He forced a hard breath out through his nostrils before managing to say, "Whoever this bastard is, they want to bloody well make sure *I* know they know who I am, and this is intended for me. I have no doubt, in time, a distinct significance in the words themselves will come to light." Grayson snapped off the gloves, tossing them into a hazmat bag left by the forensics specialist.

Grayson turned and marched from the alley, back into the sunlight, his heart lodged at the base of his throat.

Chapter Fifteen

When you have eliminated the impossible, whatever remains, however improbable, must be the truth. Correct? What if I have neither the possible nor the impossible? The probable, or the improbable? I have theory and conjecture, concepts only, and nothing on which to base any viable hypothesis.

With the scads of data we gathered — names, connections, motives — I was only able to give name to three possible leads for my would-be assassin; but even then, those connections were of gossamer thread. I have never experienced a situation in which my conclusions were so weak, so without substance.

But it is this utter lack of connection that concerns me the most, Greg. I have suspected for some time that the trigger man in this is not the mind behind the game, and if this mind has manipulated the situation so much so as to completely hide his identity, I have no doubt he has been equally cunning and thoughtful in his execution of the plan — pardon the pun.

He plays a vicious and deadly game, and I am his pawn.

The first attempt on my life failed to remove me from the game, but whoever this did harm to my family. That act alone earns him my revenge. The second act was equally a failure, but he came far too close to possibly harming Kipling and I cannot allow this to continue. My life to risk is entirely different than the life of others, especially those for which I must accept are a reason to live.

Nothing clears a case so much as stating it to another person. Even as I type this, a thought occurs to me. What if the intent of this individual is not to kill at all? But to continue the game? Surely, had he intended my death at the university, the explosion would have been grander so as to leave no room for question. He has no qualms with killing, that is clear, so why hold back? Why not murder an entire room to accomplish a single goal?

The shots at the hotel were precise but ill-timed. Had he fired when Kipling was still present, I would have been closer to his location and an easier shot. One might argue he was not in position at the time, but one could count the passage of time from her leaving to the first bullet in seconds. The window of opportunity and preparation was short. For someone whom we believe to be so well trained, the implementation was sloppy.

Unless fully intended to be so.

The message at the robbery was just that. A message. A calling out, perhaps. Until that point, with our data so weak, neither myself nor any other investigator had clearly determined I stood as any sort of target. Until then, I could have been a coincidental victim.

COINCIDENCE IS THE WORD WE USE WHEN WE CANNOT SEE THE LEVERS AND PULLEYS, AS EMMA BULL SAID.

NO, THAT ROBBERY WAS INCONSEQUENTIAL IN THE GRAND SCHEME, BUT IT SERVED A VERY DISTINCT PURPOSE. IT MADE SURE I KNEW MY PLACE IN THE GAME AND ASSURED MY CONTINUED STAY IN BOSTON.

WE NOW HAVE THE ADDED ELEMENT OF THE DEATH OF AGENT BURKE DIMATTO. SINCE THE BOMBING, AGENT FLANNERY AND MYSELF HAVE HAD JUSTIFIABLE DOUBTS IN THE MAN'S LOYALTY AND WHAT WOULD APPEAR GROUNDED BELIEF IN HIS INVOLVEMENT. UPON INVESTIGATION OF THE AREA SURROUNDING THE BUILDING WHERE THE SHOOTER WAS LOCATED, AGENT DIMATTO WAS FOUND MURDERED IN AN ALLEY. WITH CLEAR PREJUDICE. THE MAN WAS ON HIS KNEES, SHOT IN THE BACK OF HIS HEAD WITH WHAT I CURRENTLY SUSPECT TO BE A 9MM BASED ON THE SIZE OF THE EXIT WOUND. IT'S TOO SMALL FOR A .45, AND ANYTHING SMALLER WOULDN'T HAVE MADE IT THROUGH THE SKULL. WE AWAIT NOW THE RESULTS OF THE OFFICIAL AUTOPSY TO DETERMINE IF THERE IS FURTHER EVIDENCE OF ANY USE.

I EXAMINED THE BODY AT THE SCENE AND DISCOVERED A NOTE. A NOTE THAT ERASES ANY POSSIBILITY IT WAS MEANT FOR ANYONE OTHER THAN MYSELF.

"I MUST TAKE THE VIEW, YOUR GRACE, THAT WHEN A MAN EMBARKS UPON A CRIME, HE IS MORALLY GUILTY OF ANY OTHER CRIME WHICH MAY SPRING FROM IT."

WHAT IS THE GAME THIS MURDERER PLAYS? IT IS TWICE NOW HE HAS USED LITERARY REFERENCES TO SHERLOCK, QUITE SPECIFICALLY. WHAT IS THE PURPOSE? IS THIS A MADMAN OR A GENIUS?

I HAVE SEQUESTERED MYSELF FROM KIPLING, UNWILLING TO UNWIT-TINGLY PUT HER IN HARM'S WAY BY BEING WITH ME, AND CURRENTLY, SANDRA HAS CONCEDED TO STAY WITH HER. I FIND AFTER SUCH A VERY SHORT TIME IN HER COMPANY, I MISS HER INTENSELY. I MISS HER WIT,

HER SMILE, HER HUMOUR. AND CONTRARY TO EVERYTHING I'VE EVER BELIEVED OF MYSELF AND MY NATURE, I MISS HER TOUCH.

I AM CONFLICTED. CLEARLY, IT IS A NECESSITY TO FIND THE PERSON BEHIND THESE ATTEMPTS AND RESOLVE THE DANGER PERMANENTLY. BY DOING SO, I CAN FEEL AS SECURE AS IS POSSIBLE FOR SOMEONE IN OUR LINE OF WORK THAT MY LIFE IS NOT IN DANGER. NOR THE LIVES OF THOSE I CARE ABOUT. BUT IN THAT RESOLUTION COMES A MORE PERMANENT OUTCOME WITH MY DEPARTURE FROM BOSTON...AND FROM KIPLING.

HOW STRANGE IT IS THAT JUST MINUTES BEFORE THE EXPLOSION AT THE UNIVERSITY, MOMENTS BEFORE I LAY EYES ON KIPLING FOR THE FIRST TIME IN WHAT I CONSIDERED A PASSING AND TRIVIAL EXCHANGE, I HAD LONGED FOR AND EAGERLY ANTICIPATED RETURNING TO LONDON.

NOW, I DREAD IT.

I FEEL LIKE A MAN BOUND, ALLOWED ONLY TO OBSERVE AND POSTULATE, BUT NOT ACT. AS A VISITOR HERE, I AM RESTRICTED TO THOSE TASKS THAT CAN BE COMPLETED HERE WITHIN THE CONFINES OF THE FBI BUILDING. MAC, LYNNE, AND I HAVE SCOURED REPORTS, ANALYSED BACKGROUNDS, AND FORMULATED IDEAS. WE HAVE OFFERED PLANS OF ACTION, BUT IN THE END, WE MUST SIT ON OUR HANDS AND WAIT FOR THE ACTION TO PRODUCE A CONSEQUENCE. MAC HAS BEEN WORKING WITH THE VIDEO FILES FROM THE UNIVERSITY, BOTH FROM THE CAMERA WITHIN THE LECTURE HALL AND THE SECURITY CAMERAS OUTSIDE THE ROOM, BUT IT IS SLOW GOING. AS OF YET, THERE HAS BEEN NOTHING OF WORTH.

AGENT FLANNERY HAS TAKEN A TASK FORCE TO ALLSTON-BRIGHTON IN SEARCH OF CHARLES MALCOLM, WHOM WE HAVE BEEN HOLDING UNDER SURVEILLANCE ALONG WITH ISAAC SHELDON AND EDWARD SMITH. OF THE THREE MEN I HYPOTHESISED AS POSSIBLE SUSPECTS, MALCOLM HAS THE MOST EXTENSIVE BACKGROUND IN WEAPONS TRAINING AND SHARP-SHOOTING. HE IS A FORMER, DISGRUNTLED, AND DISHONOURABLY

"He's here, Holmes."

Grayson stood, closing his laptop. "Has he been processed?"

"Doin' it now. He'll be taken to interrogation in the next twenty minutes. I figured you'd want to be there."

Irritation dug at Grayson anew. He could be there, but he could not question the man supposedly intent on ending his life. "I will retrieve Lynne and Mac, and we will be along shortly."

"I called the AV lab on my way up. They'll meet us there." Grayson nodded his thanks, walking to the door. "The other one still with your girlfriend?" Flannery asked as Grayson passed him into the hallway. Flannery fell into step with him.

"If I am to assume by *the other one* you mean Sandra, and by the rather juvenile term of *girlfriend*, I assume you mean Kipling, then yes, Sandra is with Kipling until this is resolved."

"You're wicked touchy when it comes to her. You know that, right?"

"I tend to be wicked touchy, as you put it, when someone I care about is placed in harm's way. If Malcolm is the perpetrator of these attacks, he has already killed a family member and several innocent people in his pursuit of me. It stops, and it stops now."

"Got it, chief." Flannery chuckled. "You're the only guy I've ever met who needs twenty words to say what it takes others three. Hell, maybe even one."

They reached the end of the hall, and Grayson pressed the call button for the lift. The interrogation rooms were two levels below them. He tucked his hands behind his back and twisted enough to acknowledge Flannery even though his thoughts slipped back with ease to Kipling, who had commented more than once on his verbose nature. However, her opinion was far more appealing.

His mobile vibrated in his shirt pocket, saving him from formulating an unnecessary response to Flannery's observation. He hid his smile, his chin dipped down, as he read the text. It had been forty-one hours since he'd placed Kipling in a cab, having no idea what was about to occur and how things would change. Her brief texts, although sometimes it took him an hour or more to read them or respond, helped ease the strain of the days even if only for a few moments.

> Why did the baby strawberry cry?

> Because his mom and dad were in a jam.

Grayson read the text again and chuckled, but wondered the intent behind the text. It was certainly random. A scrolling series of dots on the screen indicated she was typing again. The lift arrived and the door opened, and he followed Flannery inside, waiting to see what she had to say.

"Must be an interesting text," Flannery said as the doors closed.

"I'm interested," Grayson replied, not looking up. "So, I suppose you are correct.

> Why shouldn't you write with a broken pencil?

> Because there's no point.

> What was Beethoven's favorite food?

> BaNaNaNaaaaaa
>
> What is the longest word in the dictionary?
>
> Smiles, because there's a mile between
> each s.
>
> Are you smiling yet?

Grayson laughed, garnering him a mocking glance from Flannery. He cleared his throat and quelled the chuckle, tapping his thumb on the screen to respond.

> Yes, I am most definitely smiling.
>
> So much so I fear I draw too much attention. But, you have brought sunshine to an otherwise unpleasant day. Thank you

> Good. That was the goal. A shipment of books came in today, and I found this silly one-liner joke book.
>
> Sandra said you wouldn't laugh. She says you have no sense of humor. I don't know who this Grayson Holmes is she keeps talking about, but he's no one I know. <3

The lift stopped again before he had a chance to respond, and he reluctantly pocketed the phone again. Flannery chuckled, shaking his head as he led the way down the hall. They reached the observation room first, and Flannery opened the door, holding it for Grayson to enter. Mac already stood at the window, thick arms crossed over his chest, feet set wide apart, a deep scowl on his face. Lynne stood beside him, twisting at the waist enough to see Grayson, and she nodded in greeting. Grayson took a stance beside Mac so he could watch the proceedings, and crossed one arm over his torso, bracing the elbow of the other against it. He worked the pad of his thumb across his lip. Thinking. Watching.

Malcolm sat at the metal table, his hands cuffed through a ring on the tabletop with a chain long enough he could bring the cup of water by his left hand to his lips if he wanted. By the level of water in the clear cup, he had not, a passive-aggressive stance against the FBI questioning. Beside him sat a man dressed in a well-tailored, dark suit with dark blond hair, carefully groomed, and a perfectly trimmed mustache and beard. Pockmarks scarred his cheeks, but disappeared beneath the facial hair, making Grayson suspect the marks were the reason for the growth. The only assumption was the man was Malcolm's lawyer.

Across from them sat an agent Grayson recalled as Stuart Donovan, and in front of Donovan an open file folder.

"We confiscated from your property, amongst a long laundry list of weapons one Barrett M98 sniper rifle and one .22 LR Rimfire pistol. Both guns are being compared to forensic evidence gathered at the shooting two days ago outside the Residence Suite." Donovan looked up from this folder, leveling a calm, unwavering glare on Malcolm. "You're facing attempted murder charges for the shots fired at four international intelligence agents, and murder charges in the deal of FBI Agent Burke DiMatto."

"You have no justifiable cause for your illegal search and seizure," the lawyer said, his accent ringing strangely off, as if a practiced or learned Bostonian accent versus natural. It was subtle, but Grayson heard the variation.

Malcolm sat silent, hands folded, an overconfident smirk tilting the corners of his mouth. Donovan kept asking questions, and the lawyer kept denying answers. All Malcolm did was shift his position into something more casual, relaxed.

"He is convinced we have no evidence to directly link him to the university bomb and the shooting. Or to DiMatto's death," Grayson said aloud, not so much to anyone standing with him, but to speak the evidence. "His lawyer will press the issue, hang on to that detail."

It usually helped him think; from the oral to the visual aspect of his data maps. He and Greg had worked out many investigations simply by talking out the facts.

Oh, to do that now...

"He's not saying anything because he is overconfident."

"We *don't* have anything specific, just the dots – your mind mojo, or whatever – and an arsenal of weaponry that just happens to include the kinds of weapons we pegged at the scene. His background points in the right direction, and so does his record. But that's it. If he doesn't break, we lose him, " Flannery said. "And if he *is* our man, and walks out of here, you've still got a target on your back."

"Then we find a weak spot. Find what will make him crack. We just need a threat, a slip, anything."

"Where? How? What?"

Grayson dropped his hand and shook his head. "As much as it pains me to say so, I do not know."

"Someone write this down," Lynne blurted from the other side of Mac. She leaned forward to look around the big man's chest to look at Grayson with wide, mocking eyes. "Grayson Holmes admitting he doesn't know something."

"As always, Lynne, you are infinitely hilarious."

Mac barked a laugh, then cleared his throat, his expression sliding from mirth to stern seriousness. "Jist gies three minutes wi' him, Boss. I'll–"

"Three minutes?" Lynne interrupted, raising an elegant eyebrow with a teasing smirk touching her lips.

Mac looked down at Lynne, a slow smile tipping his mustache. "Aye nae bother tae the Big Yin, Macushal Twa minutes wid crack it."

"What if I prefer more like thirty?"

"Good God," Grayson snarled, overpowering whatever flirty comeback Mac had to offer, and turned his back to them to march across the room. "Could we possibly *focus* on the problem at hand with as much enthusiasm as the two of you put into *not* shagging each other?"

"They always like this?" Flannery asked, stepping away from the window.

Grayson shot an angry glare to his contrite-looking team. "Unfortunately." Without a word of order, they both quit the room, returning to whatever task they had been working on prior to Malcolm's arrival.

Once they were gone, Grayson focused his attention on Flannery. "If they weren't so bloody good at their jobs, I'd have pulled their commissions years ago. They'll get the job done. How long will you hold him?"

"We can hold him up to forty-eight hours unless his lawyer can manage to get him out sooner."

"Forty-eight hours longer than I want to wait to resume my life."

Chapter Sixteen

"I appreciate your assistance in this," Grayson said to the hotel manager on the other end of his call. "I apologize now for any ungentlemanly behavior on Watson's part. I fear he has been nettled by my extended absence."

"Not a problem at all, Mr. Holmes. We'll assure he's been taken care of," the man said with a possible snicker behind his words.

If it meant Grayson could continue his focus on the investigation without worrying about his cat, he would allow them their amusement.

"Thank you." He set the phone in its cradle and sighed, rubbing his brow.

Since Tuesday evening upon his return to the Bureau, he had been back to his suite a total of six hours in three days. Long enough to see to Watson, shower, shave, and change into a clean suit, and return again to the office. Sleep had only occurred in short one to three hour spurts on the couch in his office, and once with his head rested on his desk when he could fight the exhaustion no longer. It was Friday, and hours were ticking away for them to take legal action against Malcolm before they exceeded the maximum legal holding period without formal charges being filed. Malcolm's lawyer was utilizing every feasible channel in an attempt to free the suspected failed assassin; once free, Grayson feared he would lose the trail to determine the true mastermind behind this man, or Malcolm would disappear, or both.

FBI Chief of Staff Suarez had informed Executive Assistant Director Stanton that if they couldn't find evidence to hold Malcolm by 6:00 that evening, he was to be let go. With deep, extensive surveillance, but freed nonetheless.

The race was on.

He had not seen Kipling since Tuesday evening, and since then had only managed one brief telephone call and sporadic messages via text. There had been moments, when his fatigue was at its greatest and his tolerance at its lowest, when he'd questioned whether the moments with her had been real or a manifestation of his imagination. It always happened that at his lowest mental moments, at his weakest physical moments, she would somehow know to send him a message and lift his spirits.

Data files of the CCTV at the university had been downloaded to the Bureau network, and Mac had been scouring the records for any record of Malcolm, Sheldon, or even Smith in the hall at any time with no results. The camera was set on a timer based on class schedules; however, they had learned the schedules were not accurate. There were times the camera recorded an entire lecture, times the camera cut in late or ended somewhere during the lecture, or recorded an empty room. Unfortunately, no moment could be ignored. Every minute had to be reviewed.

They had also downloaded and now reviewed all cameras within the vicinity of the lecture hall, including the hallway outside the room and the lobby to the building.

Waiting.

It's all he'd done. Or so it felt.

He pushed back from his desk, and with a groan born from his chest, forced himself to his feet. Perhaps a short ten-minute walk would clear his head. Despite his good English upbringing, he found himself solidly addicted to the coffee of the city: Dunkin' Donuts. Two or three trips to the corner a day kept him functioning, and he fully intended to lay the blame at Kipling's feet.

The idea made him smile.

His phone vibrated in his pocket, and he considered leaving it there, but in the middle of an investigation he couldn't leave any contact ignored. Grayson drew the phone from his pocket as he left his office, turning toward the lifts. Rather than a number on the screen, he saw a text message, and he smiled.

> Don't need to respond. I thought you might like a thought for the day. I was doing some reading, and when I saw this, I thought of you.
>
> "One can know a man from his laugh, and if you like a man's laugh before you know anything of him, you may confidently say he is a good man."
>
> You probably know, but it's Dostoyevsky.
>
> You should know I love your laugh...

Grayson stopped in the hall, swiped his thumb across the phone, and unlocked it, tapping on the text. Instead of typing a response, he tapped the icon to call her.

It rang three times before she answered.

"Hey!" she said, breathless. "I didn't expect you to call."

"Your text was perfectly timed. I have a few moments."

"How are you?" she asked.

"Tired," he answered honestly. He reached the lift and hit the call button with his thumb. "Progress here has been slow. How have you been getting on with Sandra?"

Kipling laughed, and the tension through his shoulders eased as he released a slow breath. She held an amazing power over him, and he had no doubt she had no idea the extent of her power.

"Sandra is absolutely amazing, Grayson. She has thoroughly convinced everyone – *everyone* – she was born and raised in Indianapolis, and we met last year in this incredibly obscure literature class. Is that part of your training? To know everything about everything?"

"To an extent, yes. We have to be convincing."

"Well, she is convincing. Even Mom and Dad are convinced." She sighed, only a slight weight to the sound. "I think they are glad I'm not alone. I'm not sure if it would be better or worse if they knew the truth."

"Regardless, the deception is necessary for now. I'm sorry to ask—"

"Nope," she said, cutting him off. "None of that. It is what it is, and whatever it takes is okay. I wish I could see you."

Before he could respond, Mac called out his name from the way he'd come. Grayson turned, seeing both Mac and Flannery heading toward him. "As do I," he said to Kipling, feeling the words even more as they approached. The lift arrived and the door opened, but based on the look on Mac's face as he jogged toward Grayson, he let the doors close again. "Is there a problem?" Grayson asked once they reached him.

"Do you need to go?" Kipling asked.

Grayson sighed, judging Mac's expression. "I fear so. I will try to call you in a few hours."

"It was good to hear your voice."

"I feel the same. Until later." He reluctantly closed the call and pocketed the phone, asking again, "Is there a problem?"

Mac crossed his arms over his chest, but it was Flannery who answered. "Yes and no. You want the good news first, or the bad?" Before Grayson could answer his ridiculous question, Flannery waved away whatever he might say. "Never mind. The bad news doesn't make any sense without the good. We found some video coverage that might help."

Grayson straightened, squaring his shoulders, a rush of anticipation pushing aside his fatigue. "What is the bad news?"

"Aye jist the hall ootside her uncle's place," Mac provided. Grayson waited for his further explanation, which he provided after a heavy sigh. "Nae sounds, jist pics."

"How then do we know it is of use?"

Mac looked to Flannery, his cheek crinkling in a wince. Grayson looked from Mac to Flannery, and back. "Well?"

"Because we've got Malcolm and..." Flannery paused, cleared his throat, squared his shoulders, and finished. "Burke DiMatto talking in the hallway."

Grayson's nerves sparked and he straightened, immediately understanding the ramifications of the discovery and Flannery's obvious discomfort. "Show me," Grayson ordered, already striding down the hall away from the lift banks. Flannery fell into step beside him, Mac one step behind them.

Flannery led him past their offices to a cluster of rooms at the far end and back of the building. They entered the audiovisual lab where three techs sat at massive Macintosh computers, high-definition headphones over their ears. When they entered one looked up, and nodded his chin to acknowledge them, taking off his headphones. He stood and walked toward them, meeting them halfway.

"Jerry, this is Grayson Holmes," Flannery said.

"Yeah, sure. I know who he is." He extended his hand to Grayson and Grayson took it, the handshake firm. "Welcome to America."

"Tell me about these recordings," Grayson said, ignoring the belated welcome.

"Yeah, sure," he repeated and motioned for them to follow him to his workstation.

He queued up a recording, and Grayson easily recognized the hallway outside the lecture hall where he had paced moments before the explosion, but this was not that night. The angle of the image implied the camera was likely tucked into a high corner designed to take in as much of the hallway as possible from the entrance from the lobby to the far end where the hall turned right. Standing across the way from the lecture hall door, Grayson identified Burke DiMatto. His back was to the traffic to the hall under the pretense of reading a bulletin board, but his body stance and agitated shifting of hand position and stance spoke to his state of mind. He glanced toward the lobby twice before turning, hands on his hips, clearly seeing whoever he looked for.

Into the frame stepped Charles Malcolm. The two spoke, and agent DiMatto tilted his head in the direction of the lecture hall.

"They already tell you there's no sound, right?" Jerry asked.

"Yes." Grayson crossed his arm over his body, bracing his other elbow against it so he could rub his thumb across his lips, thinking. "How long is this video section?"

"Maybe five minutes," Flannery answered. "Then DiMatto leaves in a huff, and Malcolm hangs out for a few minutes. He doesn't speak to anyone, then leaves. We're looking for anything after that, but nothing yet."

"This may be enough to hold Malcolm, correct?" Grayson asked, turning toward Flannery.

"We can try," Flannery said, raising one shoulder in a partial shrug. "But all this is right now is two men in a hallway. Nothing here says without a doubt they intended to meet, or that they planned anything together. It's circumstantial, at best. We're going to need something more concrete."

"For instance what they say to each other."

"Well, no shit, Sherlo–" Agent Flannery stumbled over the rest of the word, clearing his throat as bright color overtook his freckled complexion. "Yeah," he finished.

Grayson looked to Jerry, choosing to ignore Agent Flannery's bumble. "Can you edit the images to sharpen their faces?"

"Yeah, sure. The video quality is fairly good, just–"

"Please begin." Grayson turned to Flannery. "Do we have anyone trained in lip reading?"

Flannery set his hands at his waist and shook his head. "We're not idiots, Holmes. I already thought of that, and normally yeah. But Dan Jordan, our resident *expert* in lip reading, is on vacation in Florida. Lucky bastard."

"Is there no one else?" Grayson snapped out.

"We're working on it," Flannery ground out, his lips tight over his teeth. "There may be someone south of here in Connecticut, but in case you missed the weather outside, it's not that easy to get anyone into the city–"

"We hardly have time." Grayson turned to Jerry. "Work up as

many sections of video as you can with clear angles of their faces, specifically their lips. Do it as quickly as possible."

"You got it, chief."

Grayson took several steps back from the bank of computers to separate himself from the sound of the other stations. Flannery and Mac followed. "What are you doing, Holmes?" Flannery asked.

"Hopefully, solving our problem and keeping Malcolm in custody." He took his mobile from his pocket, pulling up his contacts. While a spark of curiosity showed in Mac's expression, Flannery's changed to full understanding and indignation, the spark of realization perfectly clear the moment Grayson's intent became evident to the agent.

When Kipling answered, the question in her voice came through quite clearly. "Grayson? I didn't expect to hear from you so soon."

"Unfortunately, my call is more business than pleasure."

She chuckled, and the simple sound soothed his haggard nerves. "Okay, then. What's going on?"

"Kipling, I hope you might be able to provide us with assistance in a manner no one else we are aware of can. Before I proceed with my explanation, I must ask a commitment from you that any information you may become aware of will remain confidential."

"Of course," she answered without hesitation. "What do you need, Grayson?"

"What the hell are you doing, Holmes?" Flannery demanded. "You can't just–"

Grayson held up a single finger to silence Flannery, then tipped the phone away from his mouth, only to dim his voice to Kipling, not silence it. "Kipling may be the only one at our disposal who can garner sufficient evidence to keep Charles Malcolm in custody." He brought the phone to his mouth again. "Kipling, we are in need of skills you possess. Would you be willing to come here and provide your assistance?"

"Of course," she answered again. "Sandra and I will be there as soon as possible."

"Please inform our receptionist in the entrance lobby you have arrived and she will notify me. I will explain further once you are here."

She laughed. "So formal." Then she paused and cleared her throat. "It's not my ideal way of seeing you, but I'm looking forward to it. Goodbye, Grayson."

"Goodbye, and thank you," he said and ended the call.

"What the hell?" Flannery said as soon as Grayson slid the mobile back into his pocket. "You can't just pull in civilians to work on an investigation! This is a murder investigation of a federal agent, and attempted murder–"

"I know exactly what this investigation entails."

"Geez, Stanton is going to have your hide!"

"What is the phrase?" Grayson said with a tilt of his head. "It is easier to request forgiveness than it is to obtain permission?"

Flannery cursed again and marched away several steps before turning back to face them. "Damn it, Holmes. Just…damn it."

Kip and Sandra waited less than five minutes in the lobby of the Federal Bureau of Investigation building, Kip's heart fluttering like a crazy bird hepped up on caffeine in anticipation of seeing Grayson. She caught Sandra's smirk as she eyed up Kip's nervous hand flutters, so she clenched her fingers together to keep from being too obvious. The action just made Sandra chuckle and Kip blush.

"Oh, hush," Kip muttered in Sandra's direction. "You'd be just as anxious if it were David coming down for you."

Sandra tilted her head and arched an eyebrow. "Quite possibly you're right. You're simply too adorable to let it go, though." Sandra giggled. "The best part is I'm willing to bet he's just as bad. And that is absolutely brill. Grayson Holmes deserves to have his foundation shaken a bit."

Before Kip could pursue the statement, a beep carried from the elevator bank beyond the reception desk, and Kip turned, forcing herself to merely smile and not run into Grayson's arms. She might admit to being lovesick, but not pathetic.

Grayson stepped out of the elevator and her heart did a funny jump, a pleasant tumble fluttering through Kip's stomach. He walked toward her, the fingers of his left hand toying with the button of his suit jacket as if he may have just buttoned it. A slow tick at the right corner of his lips turned into a smile the closer he came. He nodded to Sandra in acknowledgment but came straight to Kip.

"Thank you for coming," Grayson said to her, then turned to the receptionist. "Has Miss Branson been signed in properly?"

"Yes, Mr. Holmes. She and Ms. Sookoo. I've provided Ms. Sookoo with her permanent badge, as requested by Director Stanton. Miss Branson is all set as long as she has her visitor badge visible and is with authorized personnel."

Kip held up the badge and nodded. "Got it."

"Follow me, please," Grayson said, tilting his head in the direction of the elevators.

She moved past him and he turned to walk beside her, Sandra falling into step with him on his other side. Grayson's large hand a gentle, almost indiscernible touch at the small of her back through her heavy coat. Kip hoped her pulse wasn't as visible as it felt. When they reached the elevators he pushed the call button, but didn't look directly at her, his hand dropped from her back. Kip pressed her lips together, and linked her fingers palm-to-palm in front of her. The elevator couldn't have gone far because the doors opened almost immediately and he swept his arm in the direction of the car, allowing both to enter first.

The car was blissfully empty.

Sandra went in first, and moved to a corner, putting her back to it. Kip followed, and Grayson pressed a floor button. When he took his place standing between them, he slid his large hand over hers and laced their fingers together. Kip's heart pounded ridiculously hard, so hard she worried she'd keel over. She looked down at their hands, lost in the smooth stroke of his thumb over her knuckle, then managed to raise her chin and look at him. He smiled down at her, and her blood warmed so fast the heavy coat stifled her.

Sandra groaned. "God save us. You two are too much."

Grayson's smile spread, and his low, baritone laugh rumbled through his chest. "I survived your courtship with David, you can very well survive an elevator ride."

"There is a limit to what I should be asked to endure for crown and country, Grayson."

Kip couldn't see Sandra's face, but already knew the tone after three days living with the woman and it was pure affection that lilted her voice. Kip squeezed Grayson's hand, and he winked.

The elevator bumped to a stop and Grayson looked up at the floor indicator. "Not our floor yet," he said just as the doors opened and four people stepped into the car. To make room, they stepped together to the back of the car and all the new passengers gave them their backs. The added passengers forced Grayson to take a step closer to her, letting her cheek brush the smooth material of his suit jacket. She didn't realize until that moment how much she missed *everything* about him, right down to the clean, sandalwood that subtly clung to him. Kip indulged in tipping her head into his arm, just for a moment, and his fingers curled closer around hers in response.

Far too soon, the elevator reached their floor and everyone exited; first the recent additions, then Grayson led the way for Kip and Sandra. Lynne Connolly stood in the hall outside the elevator, waiting for them.

"Hello, love," she said to Sandra and tipped a nod to Kip. She looked down to their joined hands, since Grayson hadn't released her when the doors opened, and grinned wider. "Hello, Kipling. Lovely to see you again."

"Sandra, Lynne will take you and we'll be along once the situation has been outlined to Kipling," Grayson explained as he led her down the hall.

Both women nodded and walked ahead. Grayson took her halfway down the hall before he indicated with a motion of his hand she should precede him into a conference room with a long wooden table. In the room waited Agent Flannery and another man she didn't know. He was African American, middle-aged; a large man in height, and broad through the shoulders with salt-and-pepper hair.

The man turned when she entered, and although he smiled and extended his hand to her, the strain around his eyes told her he wasn't a happy man.

"Director," Grayson said, motioning between Kip and the man. "This is Kipling Branson. Kipling, Executive Assistant Director Stanton."

"Thank you for your offer to assist us," the director said, his accent indicating he was probably a Boston native. His eyes cut to Grayson briefly, but he focused on Kip again fairly quickly. "It's appreciated."

She took his hand and nodded, glancing toward Grayson. "As I told Grayson, anything I can do to help. What is it you need?"

Stanton canted his head toward Grayson. "Mr. Holmes will explain." Just like the pinch around his eyes, his underlying tone told Kip he wasn't the initiator of whatever plans Grayson proposed, and he wasn't pleased with the idea.

Grayson cleared his throat, touching his thumb to his lips. "Yes, quite. Kipling, it is my sincere hope you find no insult in this request for it is out of desperation we have sought your assistance." He stepped toward her, his hands held together in front of his chest. "Our primary investigation is no secret to you. We have come upon potential evidence, and because our time is running short for action, we are pressed to seek out whatever means available to confirm our findings."

"What our verbose British visitor is trying to say, Miss Branson," Agent Flannery interjected, "is we have a video we need you to–" He waved his hand in front of his mouth. "–tell us what they're saying because our tech guys can't get it done in time."

Kip looked from Agent Flannery to Grayson. "Lip read?"

Grayson shot a scowl at the other agent. "Yes, as my brusque American counterpart has blurted so effectively."

"Mr. Holmes has been hard at work for the last half hour

convincing me this is something you can do, Miss Branson. Is he correct?" Director Stanton said, breaking Kip's focus on Grayson.

She blinked and nodded, looking back to Grayson's superior. "I'm pretty good at it."

Director Stanton turned to the conference table and slid a single piece of paper toward Kip. "If you are willing to help, I'll need you to sign this non-disclosure agreement. In basic terms, it means you will not discuss with *anyone* outside formal channels anything you may learn today, under penalty of prosecution under the full extent of the law."

She entertained a glance toward Grayson, who nodded, a single dip of his chin. Kip crossed to the table, took the pen Director Stanton offered, and signed her full name at the bottom of the page.

"Please follow me," Grayson said, and Kip took a fortifying breath before she followed him out of the room.

Chapter Seventeen

"We've isolated and enhanced a total of five minutes, thirty-seven seconds of conversation in the hallway," the man Grayson had introduced as Jerry explained to Kip. "Unfortunately, most of the time you're only going to be able to see one guy talking. Not both. "

Kip nodded and sat in the desk chair Jerry had pulled out and shoved in her general direction. "Thank you. How will this work?"

"For the sake of time, we've set you up in here to record audio as you watch. Any time you catch what they say, just say it and we'll be recording both your translation and the time stamp on the video so they line up later."

Kip nodded again, feeling much like a Dustin Pedroia bobble head from Fenway Park. With Jerry on her right, Grayson came to her left and squatted beside her chair so he was below her eye level.

"I realize this may be a very difficult undertaking on a personal and emotional level, considering what you've experienced first-hand–"

"You, too," she said, the words out of her mouth before she considered whether she should say them or not.

The sincerity in his eyes made her heart ache. He raised his arm to set his hand on her shoulder. "Quite right. Your willingness means more than can be expressed."

"Anything I can do," she said with a nod to affirm again how much she wanted to help, not completely surprised by the catch in her throat.

Grayson stood and took a stance just behind her. Jerry reached past her to set up the video and the recording. As he adjusted the file, Kip looked past the top of the monitor to see Director Stanton and Agent Flannery on the other side of the room, talking.

"If she can't do this, and Suarez finds out, all our asses are on the line. Damn it, Flannery. Why'd you let him do this?"

"I didn't let him do anything," Flannery answered, hands set on his hips. "He had already called her and asked her to come by the time I knew what he was up to."

"It better work. I don't care who the hell he's supposed to be, and what the hell he's supposed to be able to do. Bringing in his damn girlfriend on a case?" Director Stanton shook his head. "He's got a damn legacy complex, and if it costs us this investigation, I'm sending his ass back to London on the next flight out of Logan."

"His ass is as much on the line as—"

"DiMatto is dead," Stanton said before Flannery could finish. His face darkened in anger and his lips straightened in a tight line. "I want his killer, and I want to know what the hell happened."

"And Grayson is in their crosshairs, sir."

Kip looked over her shoulder to Grayson, who still stood behind her, his hand resting on the back of her chair. "Who is Suarez?" she asked.

"Ronald Suarez?"

Kip shook her head and shrugged. "I only know Suarez."

Grayson's gaze shifted from her to the two men on the other side of the room. "Ronald Suarez is the FBI's chief of staff. He is, in essence, Executive Assistant Director Stanton's boss's boss."

"Oh…" She tried to smile. "No pressure, then."

He moved his hand from the chair back to her shoulder, his thumb stroking gently over her sweater. "Anything you provide will be helpful, Kipling. I know you will do your absolute best."

His use of her name soothed her, and she drew in a breath, releasing it with a nod. Jerry indicated he had everything set up. Before he hit play, she held up her hand for him to pause. Never able to completely shake her self-consciousness, Kip brushed back her hair and took her hearing aids from their nesting spots in her ears. She glanced at Grayson and nodded. "Probably seems strange, but it helps me focus more if there isn't an outside distraction."

"Makes perfect sense," she read on his lips, then he offered a reassuring smile.

Then she turned back to the computer, and Jerry hit play.

Kip immediately recognized the hallway outside Professor Crane's lecture hall, and her stomach tightened enough to make her feel ill. She clenched her hands in her lap beneath the edge of the desk and swallowed, determined to remain focused. If what she did kept Grayson safe, a little nausea was well worth it. Her skin prickled and she felt flushed, but she ignored it. There were a few people moving around in the hallway, and at first she wasn't sure where to look. Grayson stepped away from her left side, his movement in her peripheral, and came around to her right side to crouch again so she could see his face. This time, he put his finger to the screen to indicate a man facing a bulletin board, then looked at her.

"This is where you need to watch," he told her.

She focused on his lips for the explanation, then nodded, and watched where he indicated. When the man turned, she realized it was Agent DiMatto, the jerk who had come to her apartment. Kip wondered what a surveillance tape of an FBI agent would have to do with the attempts on Grayson's life.

She glanced at Grayson, but his grim expression didn't tell her much. Having Grayson, Jerry, Agent Flannery, and Director Stanton standing around in anticipation didn't help her anxiety. Kip clenched her jaw and focused. Agent DiMatto appeared to see someone approach.

"It's about f–," she faltered, darting her glance at Grayson, whose quick smile indicated they understood what was said, and what she left out."–time you got here," she finished.

A man approached from the lower edge of the recorded area,

his back to the camera. All Kip could identify was he had dark hair. The slight canting of his head indicated he probably spoke. "I can't see the other man's face." Rather than look up to confirm they understood, she kept watching. Grayson moved again to position himself crouched beside her, watching the screen with her.

"Why the hell did we have to meet here?" she recited, assuming they'd know she meant Agent DiMatto was the speaker. Each time he paused, she paused. He shook his head, his expression twisting into annoyance. "I don't give a damn about your damn literary references. It's my nuts–" She stumbled, heat permeating her cheeks. "–on the block here. I don't want to play your damn game."

The other man spoke, and Kip took the moment to swallow and blink. She was afraid to look away, her eyes burning for the strain.

Agent DiMatto tilted his head toward the lecture hall. "That room there. It's his uncle." Kip's chest tightened and she sniffed, her heart aching. "Great uncle. Whatever. He can get Holmes here. That's what you want, right? Something public."

Grayson's touch slid down her arm and he tugged her hand free of her own grip. She couldn't look at him, couldn't look away from the screen, but it was hard to take a breath.

The man Agent DiMatto spoke with took a step to his left, and turned so she saw more of his profile. She didn't recognize him at all. His mouth moved as he spoke, but she only had the profile, not his full face. Kip shook her head. "I can't read–I can't see his face enough. I'm sorry."

Grayson squeezed her hand, but she didn't look away.

"You're a real son of a bitch, you know that?" she read from DiMatto, fighting the tremor working through her insides. Kip had no idea this would be so hard. "You're demanding I let you kill an intelligence agent, British or not."

The other man spoke, turning away so she got nothing. He turned back for just a couple of seconds, pointing down the hall toward the lobby. "–or your family. Your choice," she caught, and sucked in a breath. "That was the second man." Kip stumbled over herself trying to relay it all. "Some f–," she stuttered. "–choice. That's Agent DiMatto."

She sensed the exchange of looks between Grayson and the others around him, but still couldn't look away. The second man was speaking again, but with his back to the camera, and it gave Kip a brief reprieve to catch her breath and try to steady her nerves before she continued. She quickly brushed the fingers of her free hand across her cheeks and huffed a deep breath.

"What the hell did Holmes do to you anyway?" DiMatto asked the question, then just as quickly waved off any answer provided. "Forget it. I don't want to know. I'm already balls-deep in this, and that's too much. Kill him, don't kill him, but I want out."

The other man shook his head. Whatever he said enraged Agent DiMatto, but it only played on his face. His expression twisted and he set his hands at his hips, shaking his head as he briefly looked away. "He's cursing out the other man," she ad-libed. "Um…D-don't tell me this sh–Why the hell would you plant a bomb if you don't want him dead?"

The answer to that question was lost. She couldn't provide it with the second man's back to her. Then her breath caught and Kip could only stare, wide-eyed until her eyes burned, when she saw herself come into the screen approaching from the other end of the hall. The unknown man purposefully nodded his head toward her, and Agent DiMatto turned his attention to acknowledge her approach. "That's her?" Kip's heart couldn't keep a beat and she felt dizzy. They were talking, but she couldn't see them clearly anymore. She pushed back, but Grayson stopped her chair, turning it so she had to face him. He motioned toward the computer and said something to Jerry, who immediately acted to pause the playback.

Then Grayson was right in front of her, his hands on her cheeks so she had to look at him, her name on his lips. Kip curled her hands over his wrists, both wanting to pull away and not break contact at the same moment.

"Stay on me," he said. There was a difference in the way a person's mouth and face moved when they spoke when they whispered, and when they just mouthed the words. At that moment, Grayson was silent to everyone else, only mouthing the words for her. "Kipling, stay on me."

She sucked in a deep breath, holding it a few pounding beats of her heart before she released it and nodded in his hold. "I'm sorry," she said, knowing she probably was not as silent.

He shook his head slowly, his gaze never breaking from hers. "You've done nothing wrong. This was my error. I should have viewed the video in its entirety before allowing you to see it."

"They were planning to kill you," she choked out. "How did they know me? Why did they know me?"

Grayson's attention shifted for a brief second past her, and his expression tensed. He jerked his head in a negative response to something, then came back to her again, his eyes softening. "I don't know," he answered, this time the tension around his lips indicating he did speak. Perhaps for the benefit of those around them. "We won't know until we know what they said."

The rest was unspoken but rang through her head like cloister bells and she felt sick again. They wouldn't know unless she finished the task they asked of her and completed reading the scene. She didn't make him ask, because it was clear he didn't want to. Kip swallowed, sucked in a hard breath, and nodded. "I'm sorry I lost it," she said, trying to force her voice low.

Grayson shook his head again. "We were both surprised by the revelation. Let's finish this and have it behind us."

Taking another deep breath, Kip turned the chair away from him and tucked herself to the desk again. Grayson stepped out of the way so Jerry could back up the video to where she entered the screen. With a glance toward her for confirmation, he began the playback.

"That's her?" she repeated from what she'd seen earlier. The unknown man nodded and turned his head to give his profile again. This time the angle was just enough that she could guess some of the words. She shook her head, squinting. "I can't be sure, but I think he said..." She nearly choked on the words. "She's the distraction."

Kip looked up, shaking her head. "I don't even know who he is, Grayson. I never met Agent DiMatto until he showed up after the explosion. How could I–"

Grayson spoke to Jerry again, and again they paused the playback. Before he could try to say anything to her, a wave of anger smothered the confusion and she waved him off, gritting her teeth. "No, just…play the tape. Play it."

Jerry complied, backing up the tape a few seconds. "She's the distraction," she repeated. Agent DiMatto looked confused but said nothing. The unknown man swirled his hands in the air, as if mimicking a dance, then tapped his finger against his cheek near his ear and said something else. "He's making a sign kind of like the one for the deaf like he doesn't know the real sign. Just sort of." She shook her head, focusing again on DiMatto. "How the hell is that going to–Yeah, I don't want to know," she repeated of DiMatto. "The less I know the better. Thursday, night class. Grayson Holmes will be here. I don't want to hear from you again."

Agent DiMatto tried to move away, but the man grabbed his arm and leaned in to say something close to DiMatto's face. Whatever it was, DiMatto didn't like it and jerked his arm away. Then he disappeared from the shot. The unknown man turned his back to the wall and set his shoulders against the bulletin board in a casual stance.

Grayson straightened and motioned for Jerry to stop the video, but Kip held her hand over the keyboard so he couldn't hit the command. "Wait," she said, not looking away from the screen.

It was a morbid fascination, like watching a train wreck. She couldn't remember the exact day but knew it was fairly recent. Maybe just a week or so before the explosion. Abbie Hastings stopped her in the hall to say hello, nothing special. They talked for a moment, Kip couldn't even remember about what now, and Abbie waved before she walked away. All the while, the unknown man stood on the other side of the hall, watching. A cold, sharp chill skittered up Kip's spine. She never looked his way, and watching, Kip was thankful she never paid the man any attention. After Abbie left, Kip continued down the hall, past the man, and out of the view.

Only then did she draw back her hand and let Jerry turn off the video. Kip refused to acknowledge the tremor in her hand when she reached for her hearing aids and avoided making eye contact with anyone until she slid them back into place and turned them on, waiting for the five-tone chime indicating they were on. When she looked up, the distant, calculating expression in Grayson's eyes made her stomach turn. His attention was on the computer, not her.

"We've got what we need," Flannery said, then punched the air.

Director Stanton didn't say a word but headed straight for the door, Agent Flannery on his heels. The lesser agent paused in the doorway, looked back at Kip and Grayson, and gave a thumbs-up before he left. Other than Jerry and the various agents not directly helping them, all of whom were still connected to their various machines, she was alone with Grayson and his team.

Kip looked up to Grayson. Moments before her heart had pounded so hard she thought she'd pass out; now, she felt cold. "Do you need me to do anything else?"

"No," he assured, his tone distant. He drew in a deep, quick breath through his nose then finally looked down to her. "Agent Flannery has successfully located an FBI employee in New Haven, Connecticut trained in lip reading who can assist in the absence of their usual technician. She is on her way here should any further files come to light." His gaze shifted momentarily past her to where Jerry was now hunched over the computer. Still seemingly distracted, Grayson turned her chair and offered his hand to bring her to her feet.

"Grayson—"

"You were amazing," he said, abruptly cutting off the question she hadn't yet been able to form. "I'm very proud of you." And yet, he didn't quite make eye contact.

"Well, I guess we're all set, Miss Branson," Jerry said. Jerry still looked at the computer screen and didn't look to her until he shut down the program. "Like Mr. Holmes said, we'll take it from here."

"Allow me to walk you to my office to retrieve your coat, and once I assure Director Stanton is satisfied, then I will see you out."

Kip nodded and picked up her bag, following Grayson into the hall. Grayson's team, now complete, all with unreadable expressions, fell into step behind them. He had taken her coat after she signed the non-disclosure agreement and had said it would be in his office until she left. They passed by the same conference room she'd been brought to upon arrival, and he motioned with a flip of his hand for the others to go inside, not following him to his office. By the time they reached his open door, she thought she might actually be able to navigate the hallways. Maybe.

"Have a sit-down," he said, pushing open the door so she saw the interior of the office. "I should be back shortly."

She smiled and nodded, but the smile he returned left her cold.

The space felt very temporary. Modern art hung on the walls, and the room was well furnished with a leather couch against the wall opposite the large wood desk. There was a desktop computer as well as a laptop, the laptop closed and set to the side of his desk blotter. The overhead fluorescent lights weren't turned on, but his blinds were open to let in the afternoon sun, and a single green-shaded banker's lamp illuminated the desk. What the office lacked was personality.

A single picture frame sat amongst the sparse accouterments on his desk – a pencil cup, stapler, a tape dispenser. Kip walked to the desk and stood opposite the leather chair behind in, deciding to walk behind the desk of an agent might be going too far, whether she knew him or not. She picked up the frame and smiled at the photo.

It was a family photo, or so she assumed, but not a posed portrait in a studio. The picture had been taken outside, most definitely in an English garden, and greenery and flowers surrounded them. Grayson sat on a white bench between two young women, maybe six to eight years younger than him, and his arms extended along the back of the bench on each side to circle the girls' shoulders. He wore the same navy blue sweater she'd seen him in when he came to the bookstore, but what struck her most was the genuine fullness of his smile.

The girl on his right had hair the color of honey, hanging in loose waves around her shoulders and arms, clipped back from her forehead. She was fair-skinned and bright-eyed, and her smile was no less bright than Grayson's. The girl on his left had hair a bit darker, closer to Grayson's brownish red, cut very short but the inherent Holmes curl had it waving around her ears like a retro-Flapper style. She smiled, but it was much more restrained than either Grayson or her twin.

Behind the children stood whom Kip had to assume was their parents. His mother was a robust woman probably in her mid-to-late sixties with white hair pulled back from her face in a bun at her crown, but wisps fell around her rosy cheeks. Smile lines marked her face and at the corners of her eyes, but based on the purity of her smile, Kip thought she probably didn't care. One hand rested on the shoulder of the honey-haired daughter, the other on Grayson's. Their father had equally white hair, but it was clear to see where the rebellious waves came from. While white, his hair was thick and wild, and she wondered if he hadn't given up trying to tame the curls. Mirroring his wife, one hand rested on the shoulder of the shorthaired daughter, the other on Grayson.

Kip remembered the way Grayson had described his sisters, one being her mother's daughter and the other their father's child. The photo provided a clear delineation, with Grayson the bridge between. He said he considered himself more like his father, and wished to be more like his mother, but if the smile was any indicator, Grayson was more like his mother than he believed.

The door swung open and Grayson stepped in, pausing when he saw the photo in her hand. With a warmer smile than when he left, but only by a small degree, he closed the door again, but not completely, leaving it open by about two inches. The desk was behind the door opening, so someone would need to open the door fully to see it.

"Can I guess?" she asked when he reached her.

"Please," he said, stepping behind her so his chest brushed her arm and he looked over her shoulder at the photo.

Her body was at war with itself. She'd missed him the last three days, and it would be so easy, so nice, to turn into him and press her cheek to his chest just to hear the rumble of his laughter, feel it. But, he had changed while watching the video. She was no fool. Kip swallowed, trying to force away the trepidation, the worry.

Kip tapped the image of the girl with honey hair. "This has to be Shirley." She tapped the other. "And this is Johanna."

"Quite right. And this is Emerson and Annalise Holmes," he added, swiping his finger across the glass from his father to his mother.

Kip tilted her head, looking again at his mother. "It's so odd. I swear she looks very familiar to me. But I can't imagine how I would know her."

"She would say she has that sort of face," he said with a chuckle. His laugh, whether loud and booming or low and subdued, was one of the most wonderful sounds she had ever heard.

Clutching the photo like an anchor to talk, Kip focused on his smiling face, the easy, happy gleam in the eyes of the man in the photo. "Grayson," she said, forcing the sound from her throat. "What do they think? Do they—" She shook her head and closed her eyes for a stabilizing moment before she gathered the courage to open them again and turn enough she could raise her chin and look him in the eyes. "Do *you* think—" The words caught and she pressed her lips together, furious with herself for once again letting stupid emotions she couldn't even understand, they were so foreign to her, control her. With a hard swallow, she looked him in the eyes. "Do you believe I had anything to do with what happened?"

His pause, had she not been looking him in the eyes, would have been enough to break her heart; but, his eyes kept her whole. He canted his head, only a couple of degrees, and drew in a slow breath as he studied her face. Kip forced herself to not look away, not move away, not run away. Grayson took the photo from her hands and set it on his desk, then wrapped his hand around her elbow and turned her so she fully faced him. When she'd finished the turn, he raised his hands to brush his fingertips across her cheeks and lay his palms against her jaw. A slow, warm smile tipped the corners of his mouth before he moved closer and pressed his lips to hers.

It began gentle and simple, but when Kip took in a breath and opened her lips, the pressure changed and he kissed her deeper, his tongue sliding alongside hers to make her heart race and her tummy tumble. But that was as intense as they allowed because even Kip realized the risk of indulging in this moment in this place. Grayson tipped his head so their chins touched, and their noses brushed each other, but their lips only hovered near each other, his breath mixing with hers.

"I have missed you, Kipling," he said softly. "And I have wanted to kiss you properly since the moment I saw you in the lobby downstairs."

"I've been wanting you to," she said, smiling when she felt his lips curve. "Does this mean you don't think–"

"No, I don't think you had any knowledge of DiMatto's involvement or Malcolm's plans. I don't have enough information to link the dots quite yet, but know I believe in you." He gave her one more cursory kiss then took a step back and lowered his hands, pushing them into his pockets. "I will be here for a few more hours," he said. "I would like to see you tonight. Take you to a proper dinner."

Kip arched her eyebrows and canted her head. "Will it be you and me? Or you, me, and Sandra make three?"

Grayson chuckled. "Most definitely just the two of us. The man on that video with Agent DiMatto is currently in custody, and the assistance you provided gave us the evidence we need to keep him."

Kip smiled, relief instantly easing the tension in her shoulders. "Is that the Malcolm you mentioned?" He nodded. "What about Agent DiMatto? Will he be arrested?"

Grayson's expression tightened. "Agent Burke DiMatto is dead. At the hands, we suspect, of Malcolm."

She knew it was probably the worst possible reaction, but a part of her was far from upset to hear the man involved in the plan to kill Grayson had fallen victim to his own cohort. Grayson stepped away from her and crossed the office to the couch where her coat had been laid out. To the left of the couch was a closed door leading to another room. He opened the coat and held it out to help her put it on and she turned to slip her arms into the sleeves. As she buttoned the front she turned to face him.

"I will call for reservations," he said. "Do you have a preference?"

"I'd eat a Big Mac and fries if it meant some time with you," she said with a wink.

"I will endeavor to do a bit better than that." Grayson lifted her hand to his lips and kissed her fingers. "May I come for you at eight?"

"I'll be waiting."

"Before we go downstairs, let me call ahead for a cab. I assume you and Sandra took one here?" He stepped around her to his desk and picked up his phone, dialing zero.

"There's no MBTA bus to the FBI building, funny enough."

Grayson chuckled, then adjusted the phone to speak into the mouthpiece, requesting the front lobby receptionist obtain a cab as quickly as possible.

After he hung up, he motioned toward his office door with one hand, the other sliding to the small of her back. "You didn't have issues with work, did you? I wouldn't have called had we not been desperate."

She shook her head as he opened the door and led her into the hall toward the elevators. "It's been painfully quiet this week at the shop. We were killing time dusting shelves and inventorying new stock." She tipped her head to the side, then back, with a shrug. "After last week, and this week, I'm not going to like my paycheck."

The walk to the elevators was short, and he pushed the call button, tucking his hands behind his back. "Your help was invaluable. We could not have garnered the information we needed in time without you."

"I would have done anything if it helped keep you safe again," she said as the elevator door opened.

Grayson's large, long fingers linked through hers, making her hand feel small. When the elevator reached the first floor, Grayson motioned for her to precede him once the doors opened. They crossed the lobby, hand in hand, and he went to the front desk.

"Has the cab arrived for Miss Branson?"

"Just now, Mr. Holmes."

"Thank you." He looked to Kip. "I'll walk with you."

A Green Cab sat at the curb waiting, and Grayson beat her to the door to open it for her. "I shall see you at eight," he said casually, offering his hand to help her into the cab.

Kip slid into the seat, the interior of the cab a bit too warm with her coat buttoned. She looked up at him, smiled, and puckered a kiss. He chuckled, a deep rumble in his chest, and shut the door.

As the taxi pulled away from the FBI building, she saw a light-haired man in a long coat and dark scarf, standing on the corner across the street, camera in hand. He took a picture of her passing, then tilted back his head and took a picture of one of the buildings beside the FBI building. She chuckled. Tourists took pictures of the weirdest things.

Chapter Eighteen

Grayson waited, despite the cold, until Kipling's cab was out of sight before returning to the interior of the FBI building. Though it had been warmer the last couple of days, without an overcoat, he felt the bite.

It was nothing compared to the cold lump in his chest.

He strode across the lobby, impatience clawing at his chest as he waited for the lift to return. Two people entered with him, and talked with each other, but he paid no attention, closing his senses to the intrusion. His mind churned around the data, shoving aside what appeared irrelevant, locking together the pieces that fit. The obvious had to be treated with prejudice, because the obvious was the most deceptive of facts. The truth, when in its full manifestation, rolled through his mind like a Bach fugue. But now truth was elusive, and without all the notes to play, the music was discordant and offensive.

Enough so to make him flinch against it.

The lift stopped, and he exited, walking with distracted determination toward his office where he knew his team had convened once he left with Kipling; by his orders. The door was partially open, and despite the complete trust he placed in the people beyond the barrier, Grayson could not – or did not – suppress his instinct to observe without detection.

For several moments, all he heard was the click of fingers on keyboards, no conversation. He wasn't surprised Lynne was the first to speak. Holding her opinion and her tongue was not her strong suit.

She led with a heavy sigh. "It's not bloody bad enough this bastard tried to kill Grayson but to use a woman to get in his head–"

"Fa' says she's in his heid?" Mac asked, his voice coming from a different angle. Grayson guessed he was the one seated at his desk, working on the computer there. "Fon has he ever lost the heid oer a bit o'skirt?"

"Oh, don't be thick, love." Her gentle condescension rang in her tone. "The Grayson Holmes I've seen since we got here is *not* the Grayson Holmes who left London last month."

"Is that a bad thing?" Sandra asked, then cleared her throat. "I haven't been with him this week, but I've been with her, and–"

Whatever she had to say was interrupted by the sound of the interior door between his office and Agent Flannery's opening and two heavy sets of steps coming into the office. If he had to assume, he would say Flannery and Director Stanton.

"Where the hell is Holmes?" the director demanded.

A squeak of leather and wheels implied Mac moved back from the desk. When he spoke, he was closer to the door. "Downstairs."

"He saw Kip to her cab," Sandra provided, and despite his clandestine surveillance, Grayson smiled. He was willing to bet Kipling had corrected her over the name. "He'll be back soon."

"Damn it," Director Stanton cursed. "If this woman has played him from the beginning, everything she just gave us is crap. We'll lose Malcolm."

"Grayson Holmes has never in his life been *played*," Lynne defended. Loyal to the end, even though she herself had moments before implied the same thing.

"Did you watch a different tape than I did?" Stanton asked. "Because on the one I saw, the killer of an FBI agent indicated Kipling Branson as a co-conspirator."

"Apparently we *were* watching different tapes," Lynne countered, and Grayson recognized the shuffle and slide of her standing from the couch. "What we saw was a man who, by all indications, has exceptional intelligence sufficient enough to evade Grayson for this long. What we also saw was how upset she was by the realization."

"You talk about him like he's infallible. Like he's some brainiac–"

"And you refuse to see what has been in front of you for weeks," Lynne snapped. "I told you in the alley three days ago, but you were too thick then and too thick now to see."

"And you're too prejudiced to see reality. If Kipling Branson is part of this, she clearly knows how to be convincing. Convincing enough to play the damsel in distress with your man. She's not the first woman to trick a man by seducing him," Director Stanton argued.

Grayson raised his hand to open the door, but Sandra's vehement tone stopped him. "No," Sandra said, the point of her voice having shifted as well. "You're too anxious to find someone to blame for the things your agent did, for his death, you don't want to consider all possibilities. If she were a part of this, why would she give us the interpretation? She could just as well have made up something. It's not like any of us can read lips."

"Yeah, but the tape implied–"

"The tape implied Kipling was isolated for manipulation," Grayson said, pushing open the door to enter the office. All attention turned on him, and at least Sandra had the good sense to look contrite. "As was I, apparently. She is not involved with Malcolm." He made sure his tone left no room for question.

"Sure, you're going to say that," Flannery said, tossing his hand out toward Grayson in dismissal. "You're thinking with your wrong head, Holmes. She did what she was supposed to do. She screwed with your head, screwed you–"

"Enough!"

Grayson's bark silenced Flannery's words. The agent scowled but stayed silent. Grayson pointed at Flannery, then Stanton, clenching his jaw to tamp his anger before he spoke. He drew a slow, deep breath through his nose before commanding the two men.

"Regardless of your opinions, you *will* speak of Kipling with respect. Am I clear?"

"Easy, chief," Flannery said, shaking his head. "Keep at it and you'll just prove our point."

"That's enough, Flannery," Stanton said, turning his head toward Flannery, but his attention stayed on Grayson. "Holmes is right. Let's keep things respectful—"

Grayson laughed, not because he found any humor in the conversation, but frustration. "Don't play me, Director. It won't work."

"I'm not—"

"Witness interrogation tactics week one, Director," Grayson said, cutting him off. He couldn't help the derisive tilt of his head or the grimace tugging his lips when he mocked the director. "Convince the witness you are on their side. Agree with them on small points, so they are willing to share or bend on the larger points. I think I might possibly be offended at the attempt."

Director Stanton's faux calm slipped and his features tightened, his eyes pinching at the outside corners. He huffed and shook his head, looking away. "Damn it, Holmes. We've got a hell of a mess here, and I need you to think with something other than your libido."

"There is a reason I do what I do, Director," Grayson said, taking a step further into the room. "Because I am very good at it. *Very* good. Call it pride, call it conceit, call it whatever you like, the fact still stands."

Director Stanton turned fully to face Grayson, hands at his thick waist, scowling. "Trust me, we've all heard of your magic mojo, but I've seen no proof of it yet. If you were so amazing, why has it taken this long to get this far?"

"I cannot—"

"He *did* narrow down our search parameters to the three names, and he did it faster than the computer," Flannery defended, cutting off Grayson's counterargument, much to Grayson's surprise. "Like he said to me, he can't build bricks without clay."

The glare Director Stanton shot to Agent Flannery was enough to make the man fall silent; he held no such power over Grayson. "I tell you now, Kipling Branson is not a willing player in this game. If proven wrong, I swear before all present, I will resign my commission and leave Six without further question. *That* is how confident I am."

"She's playing you, Holmes," Stanton argued again. "It's obvious."

Grayson pivoted away, turning his back on all of them, hands pressed palm to palm in front of his face so the side of his fingers touched his lips. He closed his eyes and drew in several slow, focused breaths to push out the anger he knew tainted his reactions; not his knowledge, but his reactions. He believed in what he knew, cerebral, amorous, or otherwise. No one spoke, waiting, he was sure, for his next words whatever they may be. Drawing in one more long, deep breath, Grayson raised his head, opened his eyes, and turned back.

"There is nothing more deceptive than an obvious fact," he said aloud, repeating the very thought he'd had in the lift on his way back. "The problem lies in what is considered obvious. It would be obvious to most, Director Stanton, that you are a man wholly dedicated to the FBI, having committed your life to the work. And while I would never venture to say you are not dedicated, this is far from the dream you held in your youth."

With each sentence, Director Stanton's scowl deepened and he lips pressed together into a thin, sharp line.

"In your youth, you dreamed of being a writer of fiction, a dream you carried into your early years as an agent; however, you joined the intelligence community at the urging of your father, who was in a similar profession though not likely the intelligence community. Either military, or a police officer, or possibly both. You have several manuscripts completed but are hesitant to pursue publication for fear of learning you are not a strong enough writer, and you do not want to face the ridicule of your father. You *are* a strong writer, and I suggest writing under a pseudonym."

Director Stanton's jaw fell open, and his eyes widened until white fully surrounded his irises. As he bustled in an attempt to speak, Grayson turned his skill on Patrick Flannery.

"You speak of your wife and children with great affection, mentioning often your weekend excursions and the artwork your children have created; however, you no longer live with your family, having separated from your wife approximately six months ago. Not so long that the sting has passed, but long enough you entertain the beauty and appeal of our own Sandra Sookoo." He offered only a cursory glance in Sandra's direction, enough to see her eyes widen and her cheeks color. "Your wife encourages your involvement, and allows amicable and freely given visitation with the children, but has told you she cannot continue with a marriage as it was." Grayson paused and pressed his lips together, tipping down his chin. "I'm sorry."

He continued, wagging an only moderately accusatory finger at Agent Flannery. "You are also far more educated and intelligent than you allow others to believe, likely so they are less on guard around you and willing to give up details they might not otherwise. You have understood every reference I've made since I arrived, but you choose instead to feign ignorance. It's a clever ploy and has likely garnered you information you might not have otherwise gleaned. Quite possibly, your performance led to Agent DiMatto's downfall as he has misjudged you for years. He grew sloppy around you, allowing you to see and hear details he might have guarded more closely had he believed you to be a more intelligent partner."

"Who told you that," Director Stanton demanded, his voice now strangled and tight.

Grayson looked at him, meeting the man's angry expression, and assumed he referred to Grayson's observations about him and not his agent. "You did," he answered with as much kindness as he felt warranted. "Perhaps not all at once, but over time each time we have interacted. I can tell you more, but it is my desire to make my point, not embarrass you."

"Do you get it yet?" Lynne said, walking toward them with slow, purposeful steps, her arms crossed over her body. "If he tells you this woman isn't involved, she isn't involved."

Grayson smiled when he looked at Lynne. "You had your own doubts not minutes ago."

"Yes, well, I'm afraid if I don't agree you'll start telling *our* secrets. No one wants that," she added with a smirk.

Grayson focused again on their FBI counterparts. "Tell me if I'm wrong," he ordered. Neither spoke, avoiding eye contact with both Grayson and each other. Flannery cleared his throat, but otherwise, remained silent. "If I am wrong in any substantial way, then I will submit to whatever investigation you deem appropriate. But you must tell me I am wrong, and I warn you…" This time, both men did look in his direction. "Both I and my team will know if you speak in deceit."

Director Stanton cursed under his breath, but Agent Flannery spoke first, preceding his words with a heavy sigh. "She filed for divorce three weeks ago. We're trying to keep the courts out of it," he confessed with resignation. "She said I'm a great father, but a lousy husband." Patrick shook his head. "I don't know how you knew, but you're right. On all accounts."

Grayson looked from him to Stanton, whose anger had dissipated from the deep lines around his eyes and mouth. "You're not wrong," was his only concession. "But if you think because you can say I write books and Flannery left his wife proves Branson's innocence, you're going to have to do better than that."

"I will not explain in detail the things which lead me to my conclusion about Kipling Branson any more than I will categorize every specific of how I came to my conclusions about the two of you. The fact I *did* correctly analyze you should be sufficient justification for my word."

"She's still connected to this. You can't deny that."

Grayson shook his head, a single, firm jerk. "No, I cannot deny it. But to proceed, we must not do so to prove her guilt but to protect her from the machinations set into play around her."

"What does that mean, exactly?" Sandra asked.

"We choose a beginning point. I am taking Kipling to dinner this evening. When her flat is unoccupied, Mac, you and Sandra will search it. I want to know about surveillance devices of any kind. Do not remove them. Rather I want means to interrupt them at our will without it appearing to be so."

Mac nodded. "I'll need some things."

Director Stanton tipped his head toward the door. "You know where to go." As Mac left, Stanton looked to Grayson again. "I don't like it, but I can't deny you've proven your point. We'll see where this goes."

"It is all I can ask, Director."

"Oh, that is absolutely awful," Kipling managed to get out between bursts of laughter and covering her mouth with her hand to muffle the sound in the otherwise relatively quiet restaurant. She squeezed her eyes shut and shook her head, her shoulders bouncing as she tried hard to smother her laugh.

Grayson chuckled, cutting a piece from his chicken scaloppini. "Mum had more to say than that when she learned of my deception. I was restricted from eating a single fresh donut for a year, only allowed one the day after she made them."

"Deception?" Kipling stared at him wide-eyed. "Perhaps I would see it differently if I had a brother who did it to me, but I think convincing your sisters the hole of the donut would make them sick is absolutely brilliant."

He grinned and swallowed his mouthful before speaking "I rather thought so."

"How old were they when they finally figured it out?"

"They were eight, so I was fifteen."

She giggled again, using the tines of her fork to work off a bite of her salmon. "Did your mother never suspect?"

"Oh, I was very good. I told them Mum had left me in charge of making sure they knew the rules, so they didn't need to worry her needlessly. She did, however, wonder why the girls always asked for a second donut each, and I was always satisfied with my one."

"You are awful," she said, shaking her head again, but her eyes sparkled in the candlelight. "I thought you said your mother raised you to behave."

"Oh, she did; however, my aunt was not quite as strict with my cousin Greg, and he in turn educated me." Grayson smiled but feared the squeeze of melancholy showed in his expression, so he kept his eyes cast down on the pretense of preparing his next piece of food.

"Greg…he's the one you went to Cambridge with, right? Is he also with MI6?"

"Yes," he answered because no one had yet convinced him otherwise.

Kipling sighed, setting her hands on the table on either side of her plate, a utensil in each. "That's great. Makes me wish I had a sibling or a cousin. But, Mina has been like a sister since we were kids, so I guess I'm still lucky," she finished with a single-shoulder shrug.

She took another forkful of her salmon and looked around the restaurant as she ate. It had taken a few special phone calls to get a table on such short notice, but the restaurant had come highly recommended by the concierge at the inn.

"I've heard about this place," she said, taking in the two walls of books around them. The restaurant was small, seating less than one hundred people, and decorated in beautiful woods, chromes, and cream colors. "I never figured I'd eat here." When she turned her smile on him, Grayson knew any cost or effort was worth it. "Thank you."

"The pleasure is utterly mine."

Kipling set down her utensils, and sat back, crossing her legs. She took his breath away and had captured his full attention the moment she opened her flat door. Wearing a deep red dress that wrapped around her body and accentuated everything that made her a beautiful woman, with her light brown hair bundled in a loose twist against her crown, she was enchanting.

Grayson took in her beauty. "Have I told you how absolutely stunning you are this evening?"

Kipling blushed, the appealing bloom of color creeping up her cheeks, and she smiled at him across the table, the candle between them softening her features. "You have, but I don't mind hearing it again."

Grayson reached across the intimate-sized table, palm up, and she took his hand. "You are altogether beautiful, my darling. Beautiful in every way."

"Song of Solomon," she said, smoothing her palm across his. "I think sometimes you throw out quotes just to see if I recognize them." She added a wink.

Grayson chuckled, something he found exceptionally easy to do when he was with her. "Not consciously, no; however, I do find it refreshing to be with someone other than my immediate family who is able to acknowledge my references."

He released her hand and sat back, returning to his meal. After a few moments, he realized she had not gone back to eating. Grayson paused, looking at her across the table, the candlelight accentuating the slight crease in her brow. "Is there something wrong?"

"I don't know."

Grayson set down his fork. "Then tell me."

Kipling sighed and looked away, to no specific spot, just across the room. She cleared her throat, and when she looked at him color had bloomed again in her cheeks. "Reading lips is as habitual to me as hearing. If I see someone speaking, I know what they say."

"A talent that served us well today," he said with a smile, hoping to ease whatever apprehension she obviously felt over what she needed to say.

"I hope so." She drew a breath and spoke as she released it. "Remember I asked you who Suarez was?" Grayson nodded his response. "Well, Agent Flannery and Director Stanton were discussing you, and bringing me in, and if it didn't work—"

"But it did, so there is no concern." He knew what the consequences would have likely been, but had never doubted her ability.

With her next statement, she looked him directly in the eyes. "Director Stanton said he didn't care who you were, or what you were supposed to be able to do, if I couldn't do what you said he'd send you packing. He said you had a legacy complex."

"I see," Grayson said.

"What did he mean?"

He cleared his throat. Despite the fact he had explained the reality more than once in thirty-four years, apprehension always stole into his thoughts and made him wonder where to begin. "Shortly after I met you, I wrote to Greg. In it, I explained the origin of your name and wondered if you would be amused by our own particular situation. Greg. Myself. Every male in the family for the last three generations since my great-grandfather." She didn't say anything, only canting her head slightly, listening, as was habit her focus on his lips. "My great-grandfather's name was William Sherlock Scott Holmes."

Her gaze immediately snapped up to look him in the eyes.

"At the age of sixty, my great-grandfather left London for Eastbourne in Sussex, where he met my great-grandmother Violet, who was a considerable number of years his junior. In 1918, they celebrated the birth of his only child Hamish Emery Sherlock Holmes. Hamish was the father of Emerson John Sherlock Holmes, who is my father." He picked up his napkin from his lap and set it on the table. "*My* name is Grayson Oliver Sherlock Holmes."

She blinked several times, her stare no longer on him. He practically saw the thoughts churning in her mind like cogs in a great and beautiful machine. He waited for the usual responses. Accusations of deceit. Delusions of grandeur. Possible insanity in his family DNA to perpetuate such a ridiculous story. The idea and popularity of the existence of Sherlock Holmes as a real man had only developed in the last few decades, growing in popularity until now he could barely turn on television without some film or television show or documentary discussing his lineage. Just as many believed Sherlock Holmes to be the fictional character Conan Doyle claimed him to be as believed he was a real, flesh-and-blood man.

Finally, she focused on him again, the slightest bow to her lips. "So, Sherlock Holmes was a real man after all."

The amazing thing was there was no lilt of question in her tone.

No derision. If anything, she stated fact. Grayson nodded and reached for his glass of red wine, taking a sip before answering. "Yes, he was."

She looked off again, then made a small "huh" sound, and grinned. Then she came back and leaned forward to set her elbow on the table, resting her chin on the heel of her hand. "Was Doctor John Watson real?"

Grayson nodded. "Yes."

"Why did Conan Doyle write him as fiction and say Sherlock was based on Professor Bell?"

"My great-grandfather wanted to maintain anonymity. He wasn't pleased Conan Doyle used his real name, but by the release of *A Study in Scarlet*, the deed was done. Conan Doyle created the story of Professor Bell to misdirect curious readers."

"Were they friends?"

"Conan Doyle and Sherlock?" Grayson shook his head. "No. Actually, John Watson and Conan Doyle were second cousins via their mothers, and Watson told Conan Doyle some of their adventures. The rest, as they say, is history."

"That is fascinating." She shook her head, a wide and honest grin bowing her perfect lips. "Absolutely brilliant."

Grayson took another sip of his wine before setting it down, and cleared his throat. "So, you believe me."

"Oh, don't tell me you made it up," she declared and slapped her hand on the table. "Please tell me you didn't make it up."

He chuckled, her sincerity and unexpected response throwing him completely off kilter. "No, I did not make it up." He held up his hand. "I do solemnly swear before you and God I speak the truth."

She returned to her previous position, chin in hand. "That must make you some kind of literary royalty."

Grayson laughed loud, drawing the attention of everyone at the tables around him. He raised a hand in apology, stifling his chuckle. "I hardly think so," he finally managed to say.

Kipling frowned and sat up, setting her hands in her lap. The waiter returned to take their plates and promised to return shortly with their desserts. Once he was out of earshot, Kipling crossed her arms. "So, Director Stanton thinks you've got some kind of complex because your great-grandfather was Sherlock Holmes?"

"It would seem other people have greater concerns over my lineage than I do. Consistently through my life, this fact has been brought into question – not the validity of it, as the reality of his existence was proven before I was born, but my mindset regarding it." He paused, considering the accusation by Director Stanton, and the lack of originality in it. "At a young age, I showed…promise," he said with a grin. "Mum would say my mind worked on a different plane than most, I could see patterns and inherent details others didn't. That inclination stayed with me through university and into MI6."

"The same kind of thing Sherlock Holmes was infamous for…"

Grayson nodded, answering simply, "Yes."

"So, because you can think like him, and he was who he was, they assume you think you're him or something?"

Grayson chuckled, wiping his lips. "I suppose so, yes."

"I've heard some Holmes *experts* speculate he was sociopathic. Others say he was possibly on the autism spectrum."

"If diagnosed by today's psychiatric standards, quite possibly, but it is only an assumption." He winked and grinned.

Kipling tilted her head and arched a single eyebrow. "You don't think it has an effect on you?"

"Of course it does," he answered, shaking his head slightly. "Just as any person would be affected by their lineage, whether you are the descendant of a war hero or an artist or a hard-working farmer. We are the sum of our past. Especially when ancestry and familial lines are honored, such as they are in the Holmes family, even before the popularity of Sherlock Holmes." Grayson sighed. "Perhaps I was raised being read *The Hound of the Baskervilles* as my bedtime story, but I also know my great-great-grandfather was a country squire, but he served in the Second Anglo-Sikh War, and my great-great-great–" He paused to grin as her eyes widened with each 'great' he added. "Grandmother was sister to the French artist Horace Vernet."

Kipling shook her head, her eyes wide and her lips parted. "So, *The Adventures of Sherlock Holmes* was more a biography than fiction."

"Once Conan Doyle began, he found it just as easy to tell the stories as they were, with a little embellishment, but the core is correct."

"Fascinating." Her grin was intoxicating. Then her eyes widened and she sat up straighter. "Grayson, you've dropped hints all along. I mean, I don't know if you meant to, or not, but you did. Am I right?"

"You are perfectly correct," he assured with a grin of his own. "Honestly, Kipling, I've never met anyone with the memory you possess."

"I get it from my grandmother. Her mind is like a steel trap." To illustrate her point, she held up her hand and closed her fingers together like the mouth of a trap. "A trait that skipped my mother. Unless it's a literary quote, she's not likely to remember."

The waiter returned with their dessert, which they'd opted to share: Indian pudding with chocolate bits and bourbon ice cream. With a cordial smile, the waiter set the dish between them and a spoon in front of each. Grayson waited until she dipped her spoon into the pudding and ice cream, and tasted. A satisfying, low hum set his blood to rushing. When she turned the spoon over and ran it again over her tongue, he wondered if she understood the torture she inflicted.

In evil irony, a jaw-snapping yawn grabbed him and he turned away covering his mouth. Kipling chuckled.

"Am I keeping you up, Mr. Holmes?"

Grayson finished the yawn with a snicker. "My apologies. I fear I have slept only sporadically in the last few days."

"Why did you want to go out, then? You should be catching up on your rest?"

"And I shall, but what I needed far more was some time with you."

Kipling smiled and laid her hand over his. Then suddenly she gasped, her eyes popping wide. "Oh, my God!"

"What?"

"I just realized why your mother looked familiar."

Grayson squinted. "Why?"

She swirled the spoon over the dessert, then dug in for another spoonful. "Eat up and take me home, and I'll show you."

"I have a general idea where I need to look," Kip said, pushing open the door to her apartment. "Shouldn't take too long."

"I will admit you have me quite curious," Grayson said, following her into the apartment. He unbuttoned his coat and shrugged it off, draping it on the back of the chair. "I'm very curious what it is you have to show me."

Kip looked back over her shoulder on her way to her bedroom to see Grayson taking off his suit jacket and loosening his tie. "Relax for a few minutes. I'll hurry."

His answer was a big yawn. Poor guy had practically fallen asleep in the cab on the way back from Cambridge.

She paused at the bedroom door. "Do you want a tea? Coffee?"

"No," he said, coming down off the yawn. "I'd rather not. As tired as I am, I'd rather avoid the caffeine."

Kip nodded and flipped on the light in her bedroom. She felt bad now for having him come back to the apartment, he looked so exhausted. Hopefully, she'd find the album quickly. His voice carried from the main room, but she only heard his deep baritone, none of the words were clear. She popped back to the doorway.

"Did you say something?"

He had taken a seat at her table, and sat hunched forward with his elbows on his knees. Grayson raised his head. "I said I'm very curious what it is you want to show me."

She grinned. "You said that already."

His smile was small, tired.

"Why don't you come in here with me? Sit while I look." Kip winked at him. "I trust you with my virtue."

Grayson pushed himself up from the chair with one hand on the table, the other on the chair back. He yawned again and rubbed the bridge of his nose as he walked. When he reached the door, she stepped out of the way and motioned for him to sit on the bed, glad she'd made it that morning, while she scanned her bookshelves for the album. Behind her, she heard the slight creak of the bed as he sank onto it.

"After all that praise from you about remembering things, I'm embarrassed it's taken me this long to remember why she looked familiar," Kip said, kneeling on the floor in front of her bookshelves. They sat edge-to-edge, perpendicular to each other in the corner of the bedroom, reaching from floor to ceiling. The photo albums and yearbooks were on the bottom shelves.

"But in my defense, it's been about twelve years and I was a teenager. Teenagers aren't exactly notorious for remembering the details. I'm kind of amazed I recalled as much as I have." She tilted her head so she could see the albums better, running her fingers along their spines. She came to one with a red, white, and blue cover, but it wasn't Old Glory. It was the British Union Flag. "Ahah! Got it."

She pulled the album free and turned to use the edge of the bed for leverage to stand.

And stopped.

"Grayson?"

Grayson had sat on the edge of the bed but had to have immediately reclined as soon as she turned her back. Now he rested his head on one of her pillows, hands linked together on his stomach. One leg was extended on the mattress, the other foot still rested on the floor. Eyes closed, he was sound asleep. Kip gained her feet and set the album on the foot of the bed, walking around to stand beside him.

His face was turned away from her, facing where she had been and the other empty side of the bed. Kip leaned over him and gently laid her hand on his chest. It rose and fell with his slow, even breathing.

"Grayson," she said barely above a whisper. "I'm going to go put on my pajamas, and if you're still asleep when I come out, I'm not waking you up. This is your only warning."

He didn't stir.

"Okay, mister," she said on her way to the adjoined bathroom.

She took her time changing out of the clingy red dress she'd chosen, and sighed in pleasure to get out of the shoes and tights. Her boring student life didn't call for much in the way of dressing for a night out, and while she loved the look on his face when she opened her apartment door, by the end of the night her feet had had it. She changed into flannels and a tee shirt and shook her hair out of the twist on top of her head. After brushing her teeth, instead of taking out her aids in the bathroom, she carried the case back to her bedroom.

Grayson hadn't moved.

Kip cleared her throat and set her hands at her waist. Sure, she'd threatened to leave him there if he didn't wake up, but did she dare? They'd known each other a couple of weeks and had only spent time together for less than half that. Wasn't it a bit soon to sleep with him?

"Well, I am *just* sleeping," she said to the quiet room.

With as much careful ease as she could, Kip eased off each of his shoes. The bigger challenge was loosening his tie fully and sliding it free of his collar, but even then he only hummed in his sleep and barely stirred. It took only the slightest nudge on his leg to encourage him to roll toward the middle of the bed and pull up the foot he'd rested on the floor. He was on top of the quilt, so she slipped out into the living room to retrieve the crocheted afghan on the back of the couch.

With the afghan draped over him, Kip went around to the other side of the bed and folded back the quilt. With one final look at him, she slipped out her hearing aids – turning off the sound of the world – and switched off the light. Once beneath the covers, she shifted toward him enough to press a kiss to his forehead.

"Good night, Grayson Oliver Sherlock Holmes."

Chapter Nineteen

The distant sound of his mother's ringtone played at the edge of Grayson's consciousness, dragging him toward being unwillingly awake. It poked at him, nudging him until he finally blinked open his eyes.

And found himself looking into Kipling's sleeping face.

Fully awake in a second, Grayson raised his head from the pillow nestled beside hers and glanced around her bedroom. The sun had come up, but barely, as the sunlight streaming through her blinds was still dim. She was curled under the quilt, her light hair fanning around her pillow and falling across her rosy cheek. One hand was beneath her cheek, and the other arm extended on top of the blanket so her hand rested on top of his. Trying to remember the night before, he looked down the length of the bed. An afghan covered him, his sock-clad feet sticking out of the bottom.

Kipling drew in a long breath, and released it on a shudder, but didn't stir and didn't wake, though her hold on his hand firmed a small degree. From the other room through the open bedroom door he heard the alert tone from his phone saying he had a voicemail message. Reluctant to slip away from the pleasant spot he'd woken in, Grayson eased his hand from beneath her, moved the afghan off his legs, and edged off the bed. One glance back as he stood let him know he hadn't woken her.

On the floor at the foot of the bed was a photo album with a Union flag cover, and Grayson's blurry memory cleared. She'd been trying to find something to show him. He'd only meant to close his eyes, to listen to her as she talked. He had to have been far more fatigued than he'd admitted to himself because he had no recollection of taking off his shoes or tie. His wrinkled clothing certainly stood as a testament that he hadn't thought about much before settling in for sleep. This was, quite possibly, the first time he had ever slept somewhere virtually unknown without waking repeatedly during the night. Sleeping too deeply could be dangerous.

He picked up the album as he walked by, heading to the kitchen and his phone, which should still be in his coat pocket. With the album on the table, he took her teapot to her sink and filled it, setting it back on her stove to heat before he sat. He ran a hand over his wrinkled shirt, and ultimately gave up on trying to smooth it out by yanking the tails free of his trousers. Digging his phone and Mac's interference device from his coat, he sat in one of the chairs and looked at the screen. One missed call, one voicemail.

He entered the security code to unlock the phone and brought it to his ear to listen.

"Hello, sweetheart. Nothing to worry about, just calling to say hello. Give your mum a call and let me know you're okay."

Grayson tapped her contact icon and flipped open the album as he waited for her to answer. The first few pages were of Heathrow, both interior and outside, and Kipling was in many of them surrounded by other people her age. She couldn't have been more than eighteen, maybe younger, the glow of youth shining in her face. She had matured since then, but only in a way that made her more beautiful. He flipped to the second page, with more shots either of students or typical tourist shots of Big Ben, Parliament, the Tower, and Windsor Castle.

"Hello, sweetheart. I didn't wake you, did I?"

Grayson glanced at the clock over Kipling's stove. It was after nine, and he usually would have been up two hours earlier. "It's fine, Mum. I should have been up anyway. Sorry I missed the call."

"Oh, like I said, nothing important. Just wanted to hear my boy's voice. Are you alright, sweetheart?"

"Tired," he answered, rubbing at the inner corner of his eye. "It's been a long week."

They chatted for a few minutes about nothing and everything, which was the usual way with him and his mum. As they talked, he flipped the pages of the album, smiling on occasion at some of the photos. In each one with Kipling, she always wore a wide, genuine smile. He remembered her story about taking a literary tour through the UK. He recognized the location of nearly every photo, and if he didn't, she had made notes and stuck in descriptions with the dates.

Three-quarters of the way through the album, he paused at an exceptionally familiar spot, and for a moment his pulse did a funny jerk. His family cottage, the photo taken from the road passing by it. It had been spring, and the wildflowers in the fields around the house were in full bloom in all their glory. The orchard behind the house was full of cherry, apple, and plum blossoms. For a moment, his heart squeezed with melancholy.

"Your sister has decided she wants the wedding in May."

"This May?" Grayson asked, trying to keep up with the conversation. "Can you plan a wedding in less than six months?"

"Sweetheart, your father and I married three months after he proposed. I certainly can."

"She's not pregnant, is she?"

His mother gasped, "Grayson Oliver! No, she is *not*. She simply doesn't want to wait longer than necessary."

He chuckled because he'd gotten the exact response he wanted. "Where will it be? Something at the cottage?"

"She'd like it, yes. She's talking about an outside ceremony in the orchard. You know how colorful it would be in May."

Grayson smiled, looking at the photos. "Vividly, yes."

He turned the page and knew immediately what photo Kipling had intended to show him. The photo was in the cottage parlor, which surprised him since his parents didn't open the home to visitors. There was another cottage in town that had long ago claimed to be Sherlock Holmes' final retirement home, and the Holmes family had chosen not to point out the reality. It let them live peacefully, and let someone else deal with the tourists. But there was Kipling, seated beside Mum on their floral tapestry couch that was still in the parlor, a teacup and saucer balanced in her hand. She was smiling, wide, bright, young, and sincere, as was his mother.

"Sweetheart, have I lost you?"

"No, sorry," he said, sucking in a breath. "Mum, about twelve years ago do you remember a young American girl being at the cottage? Might have been with a tour group?"

"Goodness, sweetheart, that's not much for me to go on. You know those groups go by here five or six times every spring. Wandering down the road, taking pictures."

"This girl was different. She came *in* the cottage. Had tea."

"How long ago?"

"Twelve years."

Annalise Holmes mumbled to herself, and Grayson could see in his mind her tapping her fingertips against her lips in thought. Then she gasped "Oh! Yes, I do recall a young girl. She had been walking with the tour group, but lagged behind, and the group was a good mile or more down the road before she realized she'd been off with the fairies and lost them. She was standing near the gate to the garden, staring down into the orchard with the most lovely look on her face." His mother sighed, a happy sound laced with her smile. "Why do you ask, sweetheart?"

"Do you remember anything else about her?"

"Well, yes. She was a very sweet girl, very well spoken and not nearly as rude as some of the lot we've seen traipse by. I remember offering your dad to drive her back to town once he got home since she'd lost her tour. She came in for tea. I do remember she wore hearing aids, the kind that tucked behind the ear. And she had an unusual name."

Grayson smiled. "Kipling."

"Yes! I remember when I said it was an unusual name, she said–"

"Better than Rudyard if I were a boy," Grayson finished.

"Yes. How did you know?"

Grayson chuckled and stood from the chair when the kettle whistled. "Because this is a very small world we live in, Mum, and life is infinitely stranger than anything the mind of man could invent."

"Strange, indeed, when you begin quoting your great-grandfather," she scoffed.

"In these last years, I've accepted the wisdom he shared. At least in part." Grayson touched the photo, his fingers crinkling the cellophane holding it in place.

"Have you met this young girl?" his mother asked.

"She's no longer a young girl, Mum. She's a lovely woman."

"Oooooh," his mother dragged out, the tone of "I see quite clearly now" in her voice. "I recall her being quite sweet and quite lovely, and I cannot imagine the years have lessened that. Will I possibly have the chance to decide for myself?"

"We are in early days, Mum," he said, not even attempting a game of denial with her. It had always been said the ability to see the truth was a Holmes trait, but Annalise Crane Holmes was truly gifted. "However, before you ask further, I would like nothing more than to one day bring her back to the cottage."

His mother's sigh was wistful. "Oh, sweetheart…" She added nothing further, but the simple words spoke volumes to Grayson.

"I've got to go," he said, leaving the tea to brew on the sideboard. "I'll call soon."

"I love you, my dear boy."

Grayson smiled. "I love you."

Then he disconnected and set the phone on the table. As he picked up the album and turned to return to the bedroom, Kipling wandered out, her hair mussed and her cheeks bright. She paused in the doorway to cross her arms and lean against the jamb.

"This is the second time this week I've found you in my kitchen in the morning, Mr. Holmes," she said with a smile. "I hope you intend to make a habit of it."

"Come and sit," he said, pulling out the chair adjacent to his. "I just made tea."

She padded barefoot across the lino and sank into the chair, pushing her fingers through her hair. "I suppose it's better this way. You already know I'm a rumpled mess in the morning."

Grayson set the cup of tea in front of her and kissed her hair. "You are a beautiful vision to wake to."

She grumbled and reached for a plastic bottle shaped like a bear on the table, pouring honey into the tea. "What is it you say? Perspective?" Grayson sat and put the album on the table between them, and she smiled. "Did you find what I wanted to show you last night?"

"I believe I did." He opened the album near the back and turned a few pages until he found the photos. "I don't think it's quite fair that you've been home to meet my mother before I could take you there myself."

Kipling drew one leg up into her chair, her bare toes curling around the edge of the seat, so she could rest her elbow on the raised knee. "So, I was right? That is your mum?"

"It is. And this is my family home." He rose and went to her fridge, retrieving a quart of milk to add a splash to his tea. "Before you ask, yes, it is the same cottage Sherlock retired to and kept bees, despite the one in the village claiming the same fame. We still have bees on the property, but I don't know if we qualify as beekeepers. Not officially, but the garden certainly attracts them."

"Wow," she said barely above a whisper and looked at him, her eyes bright. "You know, you're wrong."

"About what?" he asked, taking a sip of his tea.

"You are very much like your mother. I see her in you now. She was so wonderful." She sighed and sat back, holding the tea in both hands. "I was so lost in how beautiful it was there, I didn't realize my tour group had moved on. Your mom told me your dad would take me to town. He was so nice, too. Talked the whole drive."

"*My* father?" he asked, pressing his hand to his chest. "No, can't be. My father is a man of few words."

"Not that day he wasn't." She shook her head, chuckling.

"Must have been flustered by the beautiful young girl beside him."

"Maybe. I just remember them being so nice. Your mum told me she had a son at university, and her daughters were still in school. She spoke with such pride." Kipling shook her head again, releasing a sigh. "Wow, I can't wrap my brain around the coincidence. I'd meet you now in Boston, but met your parents over a decade ago in England."

"Coincidence is God's way of remaining anonymous."

"Einstein," she said, wagging a finger at him. "You haven't stumped me yet." Kipling smiled. "So you think God played a hand in this?"

"Perhaps. Or perhaps, I am just extremely lucky."

"Not yet," she said with a wink, then looked past him and gasped. "Oh, geez! I didn't realize how late it is!"

"You work today."

"Yes, and I need a shower." She popped up from her chair and took one step toward her bedroom before pivoting back so she stood right beside him. He raised his head, and she laid her palm against his cheek. Her smile warmed him to his bones. "Then you can take me to breakfast on the way."

"Perfect."

She leaned over him, and he indulged in the pleasure of curling his hand around her hip when she kissed him. The taste of sweet honey lingered on her lips. She purred a soft sound in her throat and straightened, but he wrapped his arm around her to pull her against his chest and his chin hovered near her breasts.

"I usually don't mind working on Saturday," she said with a pretty pout. "I'm really hating it today."

"We will have plenty more days." He squeezed her closer. "Days when there will be only us."

She smiled, one beautiful corner of her mouth tipping upward. "You tempt me sorely, Mr. Holmes."

"Go on," he said, patting her bottom before she stepped away. "Take your shower so I might indulge in a couple of moments to clean myself up before we go. I can't do much about the whiskers." He scratched at his rough jaw. "But I should try to look presentable."

Kipling blew him a kiss as she jogged toward her bedroom.

Once the door closed, he turned the album to look at it again. Coincidence or divine plan, he thanked whatever brought them together and past the first obstacle.

His mother adored her already.

Knocking at Grayson's door brought him jogging from his bedroom, and he tugged the hem of his jumper around his hips as he went, scuffing one foot to get his shoe properly in place. His face was still damp from shaving, but he'd managed to comb back his hair and hoped it would stay in place long enough to avoid comments. Watson bolted through the suite ahead of him, keen to be at the door first. He probably hoped the visitor was Kipling.

The knock came again as he opened the door. "Alright," he snapped. "No need to knock up the entire floor."

"Not the whole floor, just you," Lynne said as she strolled past him, glancing around the suite. "No Kippie?"

"Oh, don't call her that," Sandra said, the last to come in behind Mac. "She really, really doesn't like Kippie. It's worse than being called Kipling." She glanced at Grayson. "Which, I notice she doesn't correct *you*."

"We have a mutual agreement," he said, leaving them to go to his kitchen area, taking four cold bottles of water from the refrigerator. "She agrees I will call her Kipling, and I agree she won't correct me."

Mac barked a laugh and swiped one of the bottles off the counter before he crossed the space and dropped like a dead weight onto the couch. Immediately, Watson The Traitor was in his lap and on his chest. Lynne went past Grayson to the refrigerator and opened it, looking inside.

"You won't find much," he told her, twisting open his water. "I've not been here in four days, and I doubt I'd trust anything in there now." He grabbed the desk chair as he passed it and pivoted it so he could face the L-shaped furniture as each of his team took their seat. "Fill me in."

"There wis nae surveillance in the place, but I did get some background intereference. White noise kinda stuff, which mebbes does mean somebody has got an ear on her," Mac explained, petting Watson all the while. "Probably close, oer the street mebbe. I did find a wee tracker on her laptop, so anything she's getting or sending oot is bein' eye-balled somewhere. I put a wee pressie onto th elaptop, that'll test their sense I humour! Ifter they intercept anything else, they'll catch a nasty wee virus. Winna be immediate but every time they hae eyes in somethin' they shoulda, it'll gust get a wee bit worse." He grinned wide, then his eyes popped wide and he held up a hand. "Nae bother, Boss, it'll nae hurt her kit."

"Was her laptop examined otherwise?"

Grayson absolutely despised speaking of Kipling as if she were a suspect, but he hoped his willingness to listen would prove to the others the truth he believed with his whole heart and his mind. The sooner her innocence was confirmed, the sooner they could move on and have this behind them, confirming Malcolm's guilt.

"I went over it while Mac scanned," Sandra said, looking uncomfortable with the confession. "I felt like I was spying on a dear friend. Which…" She sighed heavily. "…I was. I'm sorry, but, I *really* like Kip."

"Why are you apologizing?" Grayson asked.

"Because we are supposed to be objective."

"Not always possible," Grayson said with a smile. "I admit, I'm far from objective, but I can still logically scrutinize the facts presented to me." Grayson canted his head, drawing down his brow. "Sandra, you have been with Kipling day and night. In truth, you have spent more time in her presence than I. Be objective. Tell us your observations."

Sandra nodded, her expression firm, and shifted forward to sit on the edge of the couch with her hands tucked between her knees. "Kip regularly left her laptop either in the television room where I slept or in the kitchen. She never made any attempt to hide it or keep it from me. She left it open, and it was not password-protected. So, I wasn't at all surprised when we found nothing unusual. The usual social media sites, email, and research files for her dissertation." Sandra's eyes lit up. "She's writing on time and space!"

Grayson chuckled. "Okay, so by what you observed she made no attempt to hide anything from you."

"None at all. Ever. She was very open and forthcoming. I will admit, I dug a little, at first. It was quite obvious to the three of us she was…" She cleared her throat and grinned at Grayson. "Something special seeing how clearly you had been affected by her. So, I gave a little, asked a little."

"She believes she has nothing to hide," Lynne interpreted, and Grayson was glad she said it, not he.

Sandra nodded. "Precisely. She asked some questions, but nothing too specific, about Six."

"Such as?" Grayson asked.

"One of her first questions was about David, honestly," Sandra said with a shrug of one shoulder. "How he feels about being with me when things can be dangerous."

Her question nights before echoed back to him, and he presumed she would have spoken to Sandra shortly after.

"Kipling," he had said on a sigh. "Don't think that for a moment. This is hardly the first time someone has wished to see me dead, and I rather doubt it will be the last. Your involvement is my guilt to bear."

Kipling's laugh resounded with more nervousness than humor. "You admit someone is trying to kill you with as much concern as hearing you're out of tea."

"Oh, no. Being out of tea would be much more serious."

Kipling laughed again, the sound lighter and more natural, but moments later the soft sound of a smothered sniffle preceded her question. "So, is this what it's like to-to be with you?"

The question had sat like a lead weight on the center of his chest. "Is it too much?"

"No," she said quickly. "I can't promise I'm not going to worry, though. Or ask too many questions. Is that okay?"

"I'd rather have your questions, than silence."

A thoughtful line dug in between Sandra's eyes and she pursed her lips, twisting them into something akin to a frown.

"What is it?" Grayson asked, shifting forward again.

"It's not anything condemning. I noticed…she doesn't sleep. I mean, she *does*, but not well. Not long. She's always restless. Up two or three times during the night, and when she actually is in bed, she doesn't sleep soundly."

Grayson shook his head, took a deep breath, and rubbed his palms together. "I suspect Kipling is experiencing post-traumatic stress, and am aware she has had difficulties sleeping since the bombing."

Lynne popped up an elegant eyebrow. "Has she?"

"Keep focused on the discussion at hand, Lynne," he said with a shake of his head. "What else…"

"Well, Watson, what do you make of it?

Holmes was sitting with his back to me, and I had given him no sign of my occupation.

"How did you know what I was doing? I believe you have eyes in the back of your head."

"I have, at least, a well-polished, silver-plated coffee-pot in front of me," said he. "But, tell me, Watson, what do you make of our visitor's stick? Since we have been so unfortunate as to miss him and have no notion of his errand, this accidental souvenir becomes of

importance. Let me hear you reconstruct the man by an examination of it."

"Are you a fan of Holmes?"

Kip looked up from the open book in her hands and smiled at the customer standing beside her, his decidedly British accent catching her attention. She seemed to be having a run on British men lately.

He was in his mid-thirties, perhaps late to possibly forty, with dirty blond hair and a mustache covering his upper lip, his skin fair and marred by some pock marks along his cheeks, but they all but disappeared when he smiled.

She closed the copy of *The Hound of the Baskervilles* and set it back on the display table. "Yes, I've always enjoyed Conan Doyle, but I've developed a greater appreciation for the Sherlock Holmes books as of late."

"Who hasn't? With all the movie and television adaptations."

Kip grinned in amusement, making a mental note to ask Grayson later how he and his family felt about all the retellings of the story since some seemed to go way off track from the originals while others paid decent homage.

"Oh, I have other reasons for my interest," she said.

The customer shifted his coat to drape it over one arm, the interior of the bookstore being warm, to put his hands in his pockets. "I've been a long-time appreciator. Who is your favorite villain?"

"Hmm, that's not a question I've been asked before. Usually it's just which story I prefer." Kip pursed up her lips and tapped her fingers on the book cover. "I think most people automatically say James Moriarty because he's the one popular media focuses on the most. And he was the villain notorious for supposedly killing Holmes."

The customer nodded, arching his eyebrows like he might appreciate her answer. "But..."

"But, he wasn't the one Holmes despised the most. That was Charles Augustus Milverton. Holmes thought he was far more insidious."

"Quite true. You know your literature well."

Kip chuckled. "I hope so. I'm earning my doctorate in literature in a few months."

"Well done..." He made an obvious point of looking at her name badge. "Kip. What an unusual name. Possibly short for Kipling?" Kip winced and nodded. "Ah. Your parents were fans?"

"*Un*fortunately. Was there anything I can help you find?"

"Actually, I've found it already." He stepped closer to her, invading her personal space more than she would prefer, and slid the copy of *The Hound of the Baskervilles* from beneath her hand. "You've inspired me to renew my interest."

Kip took a step back and moved around him. "Are you ready to check out, then?"

"I do believe I'd like to find something of Kipling's if you have anything."

He'd been pleasant enough when he'd first spoken to her, but now the hairs on the back of her neck bristled and an uneasy twist curled in her stomach. She didn't like the way he watched her, the way he blatantly appraised her, and there was something uncomfortably familiar about him, though she couldn't place it.

Looking away from him, Kip motioned toward one of the rows of books. "Right over here is our classics section. We have several editions of *The Jungle Book*, but we have a sizeable collection of his short stories, poetry, and one very rare copy of *The Second Jungle Book* if you're willing to pay the price." She smiled, or attempted to smile, over her shoulder as he followed her. "Since you're interested in that particular edition of *The Hound of the Baskervilles*, it seems price isn't your concern."

"The greatest treasures are always worth the price."

She didn't respond but showed him to the designated area. "I'll be out front when you're ready."

"Thank you ever so much, Kipling."

It was all she had not to wince or correct him. Why it was Grayson could say her name and it made her feel warm, like an endearment, and from anyone else it was a grate to her nerves, she didn't know. Her name had bugged her all her life, so the question was more why Grayson's use didn't bother her not while the use by others did. She stepped around the man again and headed back to the main section of the shop.

It was quiet for a Saturday, but more crowded than it had been all week. It had been so bitterly cold for weeks, people seemed more inclined to stay home and stay warm, but it had warmed in the last couple of days. Today it was nearly fifty out, and the ice-bound residents of Boston had stepped, blinking and wary, out into the sunlight again. Venturing out to shop, it seemed. As she rounded the end of the row, she gasped and pulled up short to keep from running into another customer. He stopped short himself with a "Whoa!"

"I'm so sorry," Kip gushed. "I need to pay better attention."

In his mid-thirties with dark brown hair, about six weeks past a decent haircut so it was ruffled and unkempt. It also looked like he hadn't shaved all winter, with a heavy beard and mustache in wiry threads covering his jaw. Kipling caught herself from staring. There was something strange about his eyes. Green, but an unnatural green. Almost too green.

He glanced past her. "You're definitely in a hurry to get somewhere. Or away from somewhere." He had no discernible New England accent, and reminded her more of a newscaster with his near-perfect diction.

She managed to avoid looking back at the creepy guy. "Busy day. Can I help you find something?"

"I heard you had a 1904 copy of *The Hound of the Baskervilles*."

Kip chuckled. "That title seems to be very popular today. Unfortunately, someone else has it in hand to purchase."

"Ah," he said and sighed. "I might wait around, and see if he changes his mind."

"Feel free."

Twenty minutes later, Creepy Customer paid for his purchase in cash, a substantial expense to be doled out in twenties, and said he hoped to see Kip again soon. It was all she could do not to shake off her unease as soon as he was out the door. She didn't see the other gentleman again. At six, they turned over the sign to "CLOSED", and by half-past, Kip was out the door and heading home. It was still warm, in the forties, so she could actually walk without her scarf wrapped around her neck and mouth. As soon as she stepped out of the shop, she took her phone from her pocket and dialed Grayson, putting it back in her pocket as soon as it connected with her aids. The Bluetooth option was the best upgrade she'd ever opted for.

Grayson picked up by the second ring. "Hello."

"Hey," she said, reaching the first intersection crosswalk. The heaviness of his tone immediately struck her. "Everything okay?"

"You are, as always, exceptionally perceptive," he said with a laugh that sounded flat. "No, I'm not entirely okay. Simply a taxing day. But that will be eased as soon as I see you. Are you on your way home?"

In the background, distant enough it was possibly the other side of the room or another room entirely, she heard Mac's booming laugh mingled with Sandra's familiar giggle. His team must have joined him at some point during the day.

"Yes, I'll be there in ten or fifteen minutes."

Kip paused at the corner, waiting for the crossing signal to change. She glanced left and right, and in her peripheral saw a man standing several feet behind her in a long, dark coat, tufts of light hair just visible between the hat he'd pulled down over his head and the scarf wrapping his neck. Unease and familiarity prickled at her simultaneously.

The customer from Dog-Eared Pages who'd made her uneasy. Creepy Guy.

"How do you feel about eating in tonight?" Grayson asked.

"Whatever you'd like. If you want to come over, I'll make dinner. I did promise I'm a decent cook."

The crossing signal changed, and she waited a beat before crossing. When she hit the other side, she glanced back again and saw the same man, closer this time, and her memory cleared. Someone in that same coat had been outside the FBI building the day before taking pictures.

Was he the same man? The ramifications made her skin prickle and she walked a fraction faster.

"I look forward to it. I will be there in an hour."

She couldn't help but look back again, and her breath caught to see he'd not only matched her pace but gained on her.

"Kipling, is something wrong?"

She wanted to say something about him being the perceptive one, but the bitter panic at the back of her throat kept her from joking. Kip hunched up her shoulders, hoping to disguise the fact she was talking, and perhaps her pursuer wouldn't realize she was on a cellphone call.

"Grayson, remember this for me. Dirty blond hair, mustache, late thirties or forty, maybe five-foot-ten. Damn, he paid in cash. I don't know his name—"

"Why am I remembering this?" he asked, his voice dropping low.

The man moved into a jog, and Kip bolted, nearly knocking over a couple walking. "He's following me," she gasped out as she ran. "Grayson, I saw him outside the Bureau yesterday and he was in the bookstore today."

"Go into a shop," he ordered. "A restaurant. Anything. Now, Kipling. Now!"

"There isn't one. Not for another block."

There was nowhere. The block she was on had apartments or empty spaces waiting for renovation. The next block had a pizza place and a thrift shop, but the thrift shop closed at five on Saturday. If she could get there—

"Run, Kipling. Run!"

Arms wrapped around her from behind, and Kip screamed, kicking and thrashing with every dirty trick she'd been taught.

"Kipling!" Grayson shouted in her ears.

"Let me go!" she shouted, fighting her way free of his gloved hand he kept attempting to put over her mouth. "Help me! Help me!"

"Do not let them find your phone," he told her, Grayson's tone level and far calmer than her pounding heart. "Stay with me as long as you can."

His voice was almost lost in her struggle. She saw two men

running toward them, hopefully her saviors. Then the man holding her raised his right arm, a pistol in his hand, and fired. One of the approaching men dropped and the other staggered to a stop, his hands in the air.

"No!"

Then pain shot through her head, and blackness overtook her.

Chapter Twenty

"Run, Kipling. Run!"

The sound of struggle made his heart freeze, and her scream tore it out. Grayson stood in the center of his suite, at a loss to do anything else. He pivoted toward the door.

"Kipling!" Grayson shouted.

"Let me go!" she screamed. Grayson couldn't breathe. "Help me! Help me!"

"Ye a'right, Boss?" Mac asked, the three of them immediately on their feet and crossing the suite.

Grayson shook his head and bolted to the door, and stopped, his hand pressed to the wood, eyes closed. He tamped down the rage and fear boiling in his chest like acid, and focused on the moment. On the need. On survival. For Kipling.

Think!

"Do not let them find your phone," he told her, trying with all his focus to keep his voice calm, level. "Stay with me as long as you can."

The sound of a gunshot ripped through the phone, and for a second he feared the worst until her scream echoed in the wake of the shot. "No!"

Her grunt and silence nearly killed him.

Dear God, no. Please. Don't let it be her that bullet was meant for.

Swallowing hard against the lump choking him, Grayson turned his back to the door to face his team. He focused on Mac first. "I need you locked on to this call *immediately*. I need it traced, to a fine point. Now!" he shouted and Mac turned away, heading for his laptop. Grayson recited Kipling's mobile phone number, knowing Mac would retain it even without paper and pen.

Sandra and Lynne stood side-by-side, Sandra wide-eyed. Grayson pointed toward his desk and the suite's landline. He rattled off Director Stanton's mobile number, and Lynne was dialing by the time he said the fourth digit. "Tell them Kipling has been abducted. Unknown identity. Berkeley Street."

"Help me get her inside before we attract any more of a crowd than we already have."

Grayson stilled. The accent was British. Received pronunciation accent – non-rhoticity with a trap-bath split and conservative vowel usage – which did nothing to narrow down even a region other than he was likely to be from a middle to upper-class family. The very same could be said for Grayson's own accent.

Another door opened, followed by the sound of struggle and effort "Go!" the male shouted, followed by the slam of both the cargo and side doors, then the rumble as they drove away.

He split his focus between the conversation Lynne had with Director Stanton, and listening for any small detail through the mobile connection that would be of help. All he heard was muffled movement and the rumble of a vehicle engine.

"He's sending Flannery–" Lynne began.

"We can't wait until Flannery reaches us. We will meet them on Berkeley. We can get there faster if we go directly."

Lynne nodded and relayed the information before hanging up.

For the moment, the only sound was of transportation, and if he listened closely, he registered the soft sound of Kipling's breathing. He moved around Lynne to the desk and yanked open the drawer, removing a Bluetooth-enabled earpiece. It took a few seconds for the device to synchronize to his mobile, and while it did he opened a

JIC-issued application designed to record any mobile communication for posterity. Once engaged, he locked the phone to ensure it would not inadvertently disconnect.

"Sandra, go to the vestibule and request a cab. Stress the urgency."

She was already out the door before he finished. Mac jumped up from where he'd sat on the couch with his laptop, looked to Grayson, and nodded. He was ready to move. As a unit, the three of them left the suite.

The sound of the engine lessened like perhaps they slowed at a light. He heard the distinct click-click of the vehicle's directional lights. Of course, they would be mindful of their driving; they'd just kidnapped a woman off the street. They wouldn't want to garner more attention than necessary. Grayson hadn't yet determined how many others, besides Kipling, were in the vehicle. No one spoke. The silence was more frightening than not.

When he reached the lobby, Sandra stood at the desk speaking with the attendant. By her hand movements and the tone of her voice, it had to be clear to anyone within view her discussion was aggressive. She turned when they stepped off the lift, a deep scowl around her eyes, and focused again on the hapless attendant. Grayson didn't slow his pace, catching sight of a cab pulling up in front of the hotel. He called Sandra's name as he passed, and she jogged after them as they pushed through the hotel doors. A man stepped free of the back seat, leaning forward to speak to the cabbie. Without pause, Grayson motioned for his team to get in the back.

"Excuse me. Sorry," he said to the shocked man, opening the door to sit beside the cabbie.

"Hey, chief," the cabbie said, scowling at him. "I ain't even got paid yet. Wait your turn."

"I'll pay his fare and mine." Grayson opened his dual ID, reflecting MI6 and his FBI clearance. "Get us to Berkeley Street in less than ten minutes, and I'll double it all."

The cabbie turned and settled behind the wheel. "You got it, chief."

With a jerk that pressed Grayson into the seat, the cabbie pulled away from the curb and into traffic. Grayson hunched forward and closed his eyes, focusing all his attention on every sound coming through the line. Other than the constant sound of the engine and traffic, nothing came over the call to tell him Kipling's condition. Every moment tore deeper at him.

It took eleven minutes, and they only got as close as a block away because of rescue vehicles and police blanketing the entire street. Grayson kept his word, paid the previous fare and his by double, and bolted from the car to run down the block toward the nearest police officer, not looking to see if his team followed because he knew they would. He scanned the area, looking for any sign of Stanton or Flannery.

"Hold up," demanded the officer as he approached, hand up.

"Let him through!" Director Stanton called from the other side of the barricade.

The officer glanced back, but already reached to lift the tape out of Grayson's way. As Grayson reached Stanton, he caught sight of Flannery parking at the corner.

"There are witnesses, but I believe our better luck will come from tracking the call," Stanton said as soon as Grayson was within earshot. "They're going to give us whatever they can before we head out."

Flannery reached them, hearing the end of Grayson's statement. "Tech is on it now. They should have it narrowed down in–"

"I'm hooked on tae her," Mac said, walking with his open laptop balanced on his left arm as he typed with his right. "North o here. Looks like doon at the watter."

"Nothing out there but warehouses and–"

Kipling's groan carried through the line, and Grayson shot up his hand, cupping the other over his earpiece to possibly hear better. The van stopped, the engine noise gone, and he heard the scrape of the side door being pulled open.

The scrape of metal on metal was the first sense to break through Kip's foggy state, then the thump of pain through her head. She groaned and pushed up from the cold metal floor, blinking to bring into focus the interior of a van. Her nose tingled with the mixed odors of grease, rubber, and old coffee and the taste of sheetrock dust coated the inside of her mouth. Sticky blood smeared the back of her hand where her head had rested, and she raised her fingers to touch the pounding spot.

"It's time to go, ma'am," came a deep male voice from behind her. Kip jumped and tried to look, but didn't have a chance before one hand wrapped around her ankle and another around her wrist, pulling her to the open van door. Not violently, but with force.

"Let me go!" she yelled, kicking out to the man holding her.

"We have to get inside soon before someone sees. The plan is for no one to see," he said, his strangely calm voice making Kip still. He gave her no time to find her balance before he forced her out into the frigid air. Kip stumbled, her vision tilted and blurred. She blinked, trying to focus, tears falling free.

A young man, probably just a few years younger than Kip, gripped Kip's elbow in his left hand, though he seemed to hold his own arm close to his side in a strange, compensating way, and pulled her several steps away from the van. She looked at his face, to see if there might be some compassion – some possibility of reprieve – but all she saw was a detached distance, a vacancy behind his dark, shifting eyes.

A chill, not from the cold, ran up her spine.

"Kipling…"

Grayson's whisper in her ear made her gasp and jump, and she glanced at her captor to see if he might have possibly heard. He showed no response, so she clenched her jaw and tried to will her heart to slow to a less frenetic beat. She closed her eyes, thinking a silent prayer of thanks for the miracle of the phone call staying live.

"Shhhh," Grayson said softly, and the strain in his voice sprung fresh tears to her eyes. She stared straight ahead, wide-eyed. "I'm still here. I'm still with you. Don't try to respond to me directly. Hum if you understand."

Kipling blinked hard and swallowed before she dared a small hum, accompanying it with a shift in stance, hoping maybe the young man holding her elbow in a painful grip would think it was a reaction to his vice on her elbow. He tipped up his chin and looked to the sky, but didn't look at her and didn't change his hold.

"Kipling, we are tracking this call and we are on our way to you, so we need to stay on it as long as possible. Listen to me carefully. I'm going to ask you questions. If the answer is yes, make some kind of sound again. A hum, clear your throat. Pretend you are hurt, anything that would make sense for you to make a noise. If the answer is no, don't make a sound. Do you understand?"

The man held her firm as he stretched back and slammed the vehicle door closed. His coat fell open and the handle of a gun protruded from the waist of his pants. Her heart jerked hard and violently against the back of her ribs and she caught her breath. Kip made a half-hearted attempt at pulling free, and when her holder yanked her back, she hummed in protest.

"Good, good, darling," Grayson assured.

"We have to hurry," the disturbingly calm man said as he pulled her along with him.

"What do you want from me?" she asked, trying to get him to look her in the eyes. His vacancy, or rather the way his eyes seemed to dance rather than focus on one thing, made her nerves prickle and her heart pound. The unknown variable of this man was more frightening than perhaps if he were angry or rough. Dark brown hair hung around his face in wild, busy waves, several months past the need for a haircut. The wind caught his hair, only then giving her a full look at his face. "Why are you doing this?"

He paused and turned his head to look at her, dark eyes jerking in a spastic dance. He tilted his head, neither smiling nor frowning. "You know…"

"No." Kip shook her head. "No, I don't."

The back of his hand across her cheek shot brutal pain through her jaw radiating up to her eye. She nearly fell, but his grip nearly pulled her arm from her shoulder to keep her standing. The metal tang of blood coated her tongue.

"You know!" he shouted at her, bearing down on her in intimidation. "Don't lie!"

Pain – hot and vicious – exploded across her cheekbone and radiated around the orbit of her eye. She laid her cold fingers against her hot skin, blood slicking her touch.

"I swear to you, Kipling…" Grayson's strained voice carried through her earbuds, and she hung on to every word for strength. "I am coming for you. You are going to be okay. I promise you. I swear on my life."

She hummed, but the sound was far too close to a whimper. The younger man dragged her forward and she found her stride to keep moving with him. They approached a large, clearly derelict warehouse, built of bright red bricks so typical of the region. Most of the windows were broken, some blocked with plywood, others on upper levels left simply broken. The building was four stories tall and built right on the water's edge, a rickety dock protruding out over the frozen river.

"We've narrowed it down to the bay area." The distant voice of Agent Flannery carried to her, so he was near Grayson. "Maybe warehouse district."

"Kipling, can you see where you are?"

She grunted, mimicking pain, which wasn't far from the truth.

"Are you near the water? Near warehouses?"

She did her best to respond, but now it was as much about fighting through the pain in her head and her arm than answering him and she hoped she could stay silent when and if she needed to. They reached a massive wood panel door, and her captor took a set of keys from his pocket to open a lock and then pulled free the chain holding the door closed. The clack and clatter of the chain cut through her head like an ice pick to her eardrums, and she flinched but tried not to make a sound. With a grunt, he grabbed the large handle on the door and yanked, the old and rusty door sliding on equally rusty runners to let them into the warehouse. The interior was massive, open to the four-story ceiling except for some rickety catwalks running the perimeter of the room. Heavy beams spanned the space, and the drip of water echoed through the hollowness, amplified by the emptiness. Boxes and crates were stacked against the walls. It was as cold inside the building as outside, except for the lack of snow. There were spots of ice from moisture that had penetrated the old walls and frozen in the frigid Massachusetts winter. Near some of the boxes were a couple of folded chairs and a table with some equipment piled on top.

They crossed the space, their footsteps echoing in the cavernous interior. When they reached the chairs, her captor kicked one away from the table and shoved her toward it. Kip dropped hard, wincing at the impact. Her head hurt viciously, and her stomach rolled with nausea. She took in several deep breaths while he went to the table, his back to her. He bowed his head, his hands resting on the cluttered surface, and he drew in a long, deep breath. Then he drew the gun from beneath his coat and laid it on the table. If she thought for half a second she had a chance of making it to the door and out of the building before he caught her, she would take it. But as frightened as she was, she wasn't a fool.

"We are coming for you, Kipling," Grayson said, his voice so clear it felt like he was right beside her. "We are nearly there."

She sighed, rubbing her forehead against the throbbing, and shook her head. "I don't understand what you want," she said, looking up again. "What do you want from me?"

He turned slowly to face her, the angry strain of minutes before replaced again by his still vacancy and dancing eyes. He canted his head to an uncomfortable-looking angle, studying her. Kip held her breath, waiting for him to either speak or hit her again.

"He said you played your part perfectly," he finally said. "You should be very proud, but you don't have to pretend anymore. Your part is done."

"My part?" Kip shook her head. "Who said I played my part? I don't know what you mean."

"Your part," he said like it was obvious. "He found you and showed you where to be so my gift could do its job. Everyone has their part. Now yours is done."

"Found me? Showed me?" Kip shook her head. Then the realization hit her, stealing her breath like a bucket of ice water dumped down her back. "Malcolm," she said softly. "Do you mean Malcolm?"

"Malcolm is cruel," this man snapped, his hands coming up again and Kip flinched, but no blow came. Instead, he waved his arms in frustration. "A barbarian. There is no beauty in what he does. No art. No magic." He snatched up the gun, waving it. "Anyone can shoot a gun. What I do is beautiful."

Kip nodded, fighting to calm her breath, terror bitter at the back of her throat. "Of course it is," she said softly, hoping to calm this man's ricocheting moods. "But, why is my part done?"

He bobbed the muzzle of the gun like the tip of a pointed finger, an exaggerated grin morphing his face into an insanity mask. "Your job was to keep the enemy distracted so he could play his game. I've heard you played it better than he ever imagined. But they figured you out, he told me. You shouldn't have let them do that."

The coldness of his voice brought tears, and a heavy dread hit her stomach. "I didn't mean to," she managed to say, choking on the words. Maybe playing along would stall the inevitable until Grayson arrived.

"I know," he said, sadness tingeing his voice. "He knows, too, but he said I need to take care of this for him."

Kip's heart jerked and she sucked in a sharp breath. "Please," she begged, knowing they would think she meant to beg for her life, but instead she begged for Grayson to hurry.

"We need to hurry," Grayson said to whomever he was with.

Kip closed her eyes, burning from the tears she tried to hold back.

"You know this is the way we have to do this, don't you?" he asked her. "This way, the enemy will believe they won. Malcolm will be gone soon, and then you. No more questions."

Before she could say anything, he lunged at her and grabbed her arm with his free hand, pulling her to her feet again. A cry lodged in Kip's chest. She sucked in several breaths, trying to stave off the sobs, but it was hard. So hard. She'd never been so terrified.

"Where are you taking me?" Kip asked, her words slurred

around the swelling in her lip. It had stopped bleeding but now swelled painfully. She looked up at the younger man, hoping – praying – to find some sign of hope. "Please. Don't do this," she begged.

"I am doing what must be done," he said with resignation, not looking at her as he shook his head.

"Please," she begged again, then glanced at the stack of boxes they passed as he dragged her along. She didn't know the exact details of what she saw, but the wires and digital screen made the hair on her arms stand on end and her heart jump. "Oh, God. Is that a bomb?"

"It's art…"

"Art?" she repeated.

They reached an open door, as rusted and decrepit as the rest of the building, and he kicked it open further with his foot, shoving her past it. Kip stumbled but kept her feet. "It will be beautiful. You'll see."

"No!" Kip cried, scrambling back toward the door, but he slammed it shut in her face. Moments later, she heard the clack and click of a bar being slapped across the doorjamb and a padlock being closed.

"They've set a bomb," Grayson said, confirming he'd understood.

"Fan out. Now!" came a different voice; Kip thought maybe the director she'd met. "We're looking for an older model van, probably American-made, dark green. No markings. Find the van, report. We need to move!"

Kip stood in the center of the small room, probably an office at one time. There was an old metal desk, light green wherever it wasn't covered with rust, a single chair with a split and peeling vinyl seat, and a metal file cabinet on its side, the drawers open and empty. A large window took up half the wall, the other walls covered with warped and peeling fake wood paneling. She could barely see except for the light coming through the dirty window. Beyond the mucky glass shone the lights of the city on the other side of the bay. The air smelled dank, and mold permeated the walls. She sniffed, no longer trying to stop the tears.

"Grayson?" Kip called out, hearing the tremble in her voice. "Are you still there?"

"I'm here, sweetheart," he said, his breath rapid like he might be running. "We're here at the waterfront, and we're looking for you."

"He put me in a room," she managed to say, sucking in her sob. "Like an office."

"Are there windows?"

"Yes, but they're filthy. Grayson, he set explosives outside the room. It's a huge building, but empty except for boxes and some machinery. It's old and doesn't look like it's been used in years. Maybe two hundred feet long, four stories high. Brick construction. There are no other buildings directly near it."

"Good girl. Go to the window. Tell me what you see. Anything."

She crossed to the window and tried to wipe away some of the grime, but much of it was on the outside from years of build-up. She rubbed and squinted, looking through the filth. "I'm right on the water. I don't see any docks. I see the naval shipyard on the other side of the water." She sniffed and swallowed hard. "Grayson, I'm so afraid."

"I'm coming for you. I–"

His voice stopped short and Kip gasped, fumbling with fingers numb from the cold to bring out the phone they'd never searched for, probably because they thought anything of importance would be in the purse she no longer had. She found the phone and stared at the screen.

Connection Lost. Call Over.

The screen said call dropped, and she had less than 18% power. The signal within the metal frame warehouse had to be weak, and holding the call so long had drained the battery. She sucked in a breath, wincing at the radiating pain from her temple and lip, and redialed.

After a few seconds, the line beeped indicating the call didn't go through. She tried again, her vision blurred by tears. A few seconds later, the same beep said the call had failed, and her battery power had dropped to 14%.

Desperate, she went to the door and tried the knob. It turned, but when she pushed she met resistance. She tried again until her shoulder throbbed with no gain. Kip grabbed the unsteady-looking chair and dragged it to the window, climbing onto it to reach the latch at the top. The metal was cold, but the latch gave way after she slammed the heel of her hand against it several times. It was hinged at the bottom, parallel to the floor, and opened outward leaving a gap of several inches at the top.

Distant sounds of the city reached her, but nothing distinct. Even if she could climb into the window, the gap wasn't big enough for her to get through. She leaned out as far as she could, the fresh, cool air outside stinging on her bruised and raw face. The temperature had dropped further since she left work, her breath now curling in front of her face.

He could still be in the warehouse. He could come back and kill her where she stood. But in a few minutes, she would be dead anyway.

"Help!" she shouted as loud as she could. "Help me! Grayson! I'm here! I'm here!"

"I'm coming for you. I swear."

Kipling's voice echoed off buildings, and every second pushed Grayson forward.

Silent and quick, agents came from around the van, weapons drawn. As soon as the agents reached the door, running into the space beyond, Grayson bolted past them and the vehicle into the cavern of the warehouse interior. He stopped short and looked left and right. Off to his right was an interior wall with a door, with a dark-haired man running away from them toward the far side of the space. He looked back at them, eyes wide, fumbling for a gun he'd tucked into his waist.

"Stop and get down! Now!" the agents shouted in unison.

The man pivoted, eyes wide, and Grayson immediately recognized him as Isaac Sheldon, one of the three men they'd listed as suspects. A man the FBI had dismissed upon Malcolm's capture. Instead of dropping his weapon, he lunged for the boxes beside the door.

"Get down! Now!"

Sheldon ran full force into the boxes, and a second too late Grayson realized his intent. The bomb. He'd manually activated the bomb. The other agents had to have realized the same because none fired at the risk of hitting the explosives. When he turned, a look of wide-eyed, insane, glee on his face, he raised his gun. Grayson stopped short, a sick dread slamming into his chest. He was weaponless, and without any protective gear, and he'd reprimand any agent in his charge for acting so recklessly. The agent to his right retargeted in an instant. His bullet found home straight through Sheldon's hand, the man screaming out in pain when his gun flew free and blood splattered the floor.

Grayson ran forward again, kicked the gun away from Sheldon's reach, and went to the locked door. Behind him, he heard the scuffle and drag of Sheldon being taken into custody, but Sheldon was no longer his concern.

"Kipling!" he shouted, slapping his palm against the door.

"Grayson!" Kipling's muffled voice came through the door. "I'm here! I'm here!"

"Damn it, it's live," said one of the men with Grayson, a fact he'd noted when he ran past. "Get a bomb expert—"

"There's no time," Grayson snapped, the digital timer indicating less than thirty seconds left before detonation. He thrust his hand toward the agent. "Give me your service pistol."

The agent squinted, looking from Grayson to the bomb.

"Give me your weapon and get out."

Understanding released the agent's jaw and his eyes widened.

He turned the Sig Sauer in his hand and held it out to Grayson, handle first. Grayson took it, checking the safety.

"I said get out now!" Grayson shouted and threw his shoulder into it to see if the lock at the top would give. "Kipling!"

"Go!" Kipling shouted through the warped wood. "Get out, Grayson. Please."

"Step away from the door as far as you can."

"Grayson—"

"Do it, Kipling!"

He leaned close to the door, listening, watching the seconds tick away on the timer. He motioned again to the two agents who had yet to leave him. "Get out!" They finally took his order and ran out the way they had come in, dragging Sheldon with them.

"Okay!" Kipling yelled.

Grayson took two steps back and targeted his weapon on the lock and bar holding the door closed. Two shots and the wood shattered where the lock was connected. Grayson stepped forward and kicked out, the door collapsing inward. His chest tightened when he saw Kipling, her face bruised and streaked with blood from her swollen lip and a contusion at her brow. He motioned for her to come to him, and as soon as she reached him he pushed her behind his back. Three shots in an arc across the window shattered most of the glass, and Kipling cried out behind him.

Stepping away from her, he engaged the weapon's safety and used the only option available, bracing it in the small of his back and grabbed the single chair near the window. Grayson drew it back and swung hard, crashing it through what remained of the window and framework, opening it enough they could get through. He set down the chair again, and stepped onto it, holding out both hands to her.

"Come on. We've only seconds."

She came to him without hesitation, taking his hand so he could assist her to the window edge.

"There's only water. Ice," she said, looking through the broken window.

"Better water than fire. Trust me."

"I do," she said, and he glanced at her for only a second.

Then he looked past her to the warehouse behind them, wrapped his arms around her, and hurled them both out the broken opening. The explosion came a second later, a blast from a furnace, propelling them into the air, and they hit the ice hard. It knocked all the air from his lungs before the ice gave way and the frigid water beneath enveloped them.

Chapter Twenty-One

Kip's heavy coat, saturated with icy river water, dragged her down and she flailed out, trying to force her way to the surface again. Her lungs burned, her consciousness wavering. It was so cold, so very cold. She lashed out, trying to see in the darkness. Then a strong hand gripped her shoulder and dragged her upward. She sucked in air hard as soon as her face broke the water line, gasping as the pain overwhelmed her.

The world was silent, not even the sound of her own breathing broke through the muted silence. An arm slipped around her chest and hauled her onto the ice, dragging her back away from the edge. Immediately, the frigid cold gripped her and her jaw chattered. The warehouse was a ball of flames shooting out over the water, licking at the sky; her gut clenched and she felt sick at the realization of how close they had been to death.

Then Grayson was in front of her, pulling her hands to bring her to her feet. On trembling legs, she followed, trying to walk under the weight of her waterlogged wool coat. They were twenty feet from the shore, the ice making a clear path, but her wet shoes slid out from beneath her and he caught her to keep her balance.

Her equilibrium was completely off, and the pressure in her ears was intense.

Just a few feet from the shore, her shaky legs gave out and she dropped to her knees, the weight and the cold and the pressure too much. Grayson knelt in front of her, pushing her shoulders until she sat back, but it was too dark and she couldn't see his face. Her entire body hurt, her jaw aching from the abuse and the vicious chattering of her teeth. She couldn't seem to take in enough air, her ribs felt like they'd crack under the pressure. Grayson reached for the buttons of her coat, pushing the stiffening material off her shoulders. Even though she was wet underneath, relief from the heavy chill helped. Beyond him, the rolling red flash of EMT lights momentarily lit his face for the second she needed to know he spoke, even though she couldn't read his lips or hear him.

She shook her head. "I c-can't hear."

The act of speaking shot pain straight from her jaw into her eardrums and she cried out, doubling forward. Her vision darkened, but she felt his urgent tug to gain her feet again and she drew from some unknown well deep in her soul to follow his lead. Standing again, he wrapped an arm around her to bring her flush to him, facing him, and he pulled at the aids until they released with a pop that both hurt and gave her relief. He pocketed the buds, and then by more his strength than hers they reached the shore and the waiting emergency response personnel.

They tried to take her away from Grayson, but something deep and instinctive lashed out in her and she hung on to his wet sweater. "N-No," she snapped, and looked up at him, finally able to see his face. "D-Don't leave m-me. N-not for a—" It physically hurt trying to speak, and she bit her tongue trying to get out the words.

"I won't," she read from his blue-tinged and shaking lips.

With an EMT on each side of them, one supporting her and the other helping Grayson while he held her to his side, they made it up the snowy embankment to the waiting rescue vehicles. The entire area was full of police, fire, rescue, and FBI, with more vehicles arriving. Red and blue lights strobed back and forth, making her head hurt even worse. Director Stanton and Agent Flannery approached them, but she caught Grayson's sharp headshake and they backed off, letting him proceed to the ambulance with her. Whether he had said something, she didn't know.

She had never been so cold in her life. Her feet prickled and burned, along with her hands. Her insides felt like they were in spasms in a desperate attempt to keep her warm and alive. Just feet from the ambulance her legs gave out again, but because of Grayson and the EMT she didn't hit the ground. Grayson swept her up, carrying her the last few feet and she wondered how he could find the strength. Or was she just so weak?

The EMTs opened the ambulance doors and Grayson stepped inside, ducking his head, seemingly without effort until she looked at his face. His jaw was clenched, his lips drawn tight. The interior of the ambulance was blissfully warm, and once inside, he set her down to sit on the edge of the gurney. Grayson crouched to look her in the eyes, already tugging at the back of his own sweater.

"You need to undress," he said, holding her gaze. "You can't stay in the wet clothes."

Kip nodded, heat infusing her cheeks, and she almost appreciated it considering the raw cold in her bones. Grayson nodded to the one woman EMT in the room who stepped up to help Kip as Grayson turned away and yanked his sweater and shirt over his head, tossing them in a pile on the floor.

Once down to the bare necessities, the EMT handed her some basic drawstring pants and a pullover cotton blouse; the same type of clothing they gave Grayson. The pain was vicious in her feet when she had to stand again to pull on the pants, and she clenched her jaw against the tears that fell anyway.

Finally, they draped a heavy, heated blanket over her shoulders. Kip bundled it close, her now thawed hair falling in curled strips over her face. She sank onto the gurney, and on the bench across from her Grayson had his own blanket, his hair in curly disarray from pulling his sweater off over his head. One of the EMTs looked at her momentarily, speaking, but he looked away again before she caught what he said. He was busy sliding a blood pressure cuff on her arm.

"G-Grayson," she forced through her still chattering teeth. "I c-can't c-catch what th-they're s-saying."

The EMT looked from her to Grayson, who tapped his index finger in front of his right ear. "She can't hear," he told the man. Then he made a V with his index and center finger, pointing beneath his own eyes, then toward her. "You need to look at her."

The female EMT shifted into Kip's view, raising her hands. "*Sign?*" she motioned with her hands in front of her.

Kip nodded. "Yes."

"*We are checking your vitals, and making sure you don't slip into hypothermia.*" She spelled out the last word, which Kip was glad for because she wasn't sure she herself knew the proper sign. "*We need to get you warm, but not too quickly. Once you are out of danger, we'll treat your injuries. Do you feel dizzy, nauseated? Do you have any pain?*"

Kip nodded. "Dizzy. My equilibrium is bad. My head hurts and my ears hurt."

Grayson said something, but she only caught the movement, not the words. When the EMT looked at him, Kipling focused on his lips. "She has had a recent head trauma. Just over a fortnight ago."

Grayson retrieved his jeans from the floor and dug into the pocket, holding out the hearing aids. She read on his lips his explanation to the woman that Kip had been wearing them when the building exploded, and when she'd gone underwater. With a nod, the woman opened a drawer and removed an otoscope, taking a moment to look into each of Kip's ears. She crouched again in front of Kip.

"*There is no excess fluid in your ears, so it's likely the aids prevented water from getting in, but it would have caused a lot of pressure. You should have your ears checked thoroughly at the hospital by a specialist. With a recent head injury, they're going to want to observe you for a bit just to make sure. Possibly a CT scan.*"

She nodded, finally beginning to feel human again and not like a Popsicle. The EMT spoke to Grayson, and he nodded. On his lips, Kip read, "I'm staying with her."

The EMT nodded. "*We're getting ready to go. I'll be right back.*"

She and the other EMT stepped out of the vehicle, presumably to possibly brief Grayson's director or do whatever notification they needed to do to leave. As soon as the door closed, Kip reached for Grayson and the blanket slipped away. He came off the bench and wrapped her in his arms, sitting beside her on the gurney. He felt incredibly warm in comparison to the chill and she bundled as close to him as possible, fighting the onslaught of tears she knew was coming.

But there was no winning the fight.

Grayson pulled the blanket around her again, wrapping them both in it, and held her tight, rocking her slowly. She felt the vibration in his chest and wished she knew what he said, but she didn't want to let go. Didn't want him to let go of her.

His lips pressed to her cheek, her jaw, and her chin until she tipped her head back at the touch of his hand and he kissed her mouth. It was no kiss of passion, but definitely of need. Need to feel him and know he was real, and they were alive. He kissed her gently, mindful of the swelling split on her lower lip, but thoroughly enough she finally felt a sliver of calm ease over her jagged nerves.

When Grayson drew back so she saw his face, the shine of tears in his eyes made her heart squeeze and her throat tighten. He released her enough to take her face in both his hands, his skin wonderfully warm, and stroked her damp cheeks with his thumbs.

"I was terrified I'd lose you," he said, a slight waver in his chin. "I don't think I've taken a breath in the last hour." His unique eyes shifted, and she knew they settled on the places that stung most – the throb at her temple where she'd been hit with the butt of a gun, the bruises on her cheeks and split at her lip from her captor's backhanded slap – and he pressed his lips together to swallow hard. "I will never be able to sufficiently beg for your forgiveness, nor will I ever be worthy of it. My words will never be enough."

"You came for me. You s-saved my life–"

He shook his head. "Were it not for me, your life would not have been at risk."

Kip smiled, even though it stung, and released more tears. "You f-forget how we m-met."

He closed his eyes, a tear releasing from one to slide down his cheek, and leaned in to press his lips long and firm to her forehead. The ambulance door opened again, and the EMTs returned. Past them, she saw Grayson's partner and his superior. Grayson drew the blanket around her again and stepped off the gurney to return to his spot on the bench while the EMT prepared them for the trip to the hospital. Once settled, he took her hand and held it all the way to the hospital.

Grayson sat hunched forward in the vinyl recliner chair beside Kipling's bed, the hospital room phone in his hand. His mobile phone still was not functioning after being soaked by the frigid Charles River waters. It was in a bag of rice, along with Kipling's hearing aids and her own phone, apparently a home remedy for wet electronics.

He raised his head enough to look to Kipling. She had been asleep since shortly after arriving at hospital. The doctor who examined her, and Grayson, said she would have no adverse effects from the cold water once she rested. She had a bruise and gash on the side of her head where her initial and still anonymous captor had knocked her unconscious with his weapon, and her cheeks were bruised, her lip split, from their abuse. They had done a scan to confirm she hadn't suffered a fractured skull, and although the bruising was bad and she'd so recently been similarly injured, she was okay. Various bruises and abrasions marred her from head to toe from the ordeal. She would likely be stiff and sore for several days, the trauma of hitting the ice and falling through as hard on the body as a vehicle accident. Doctor Scarborough said she was lucky, considering.

Grayson failed to see anything lucky about any part of the situation.

For himself, a few bruises and a couple scrapes, and he was none the worse for wear. So said Doctor Scarborough.

The man hadn't examined his heart. It took a greater beating than anything done to his body.

Finding the last of his courage, Grayson dialed in the number on the small piece of paper resting on his knee. He cleared his throat, waiting for the answer.

"Hello?" came the curious voice of Mrs. Branson.

Grayson rested his elbows on his knees, the phone in one hand, rubbing his forehead with the other. "Hello, Mrs. Branson. It's Grayson. Holmes," he added as an afterthought, thinking she might not remember his first name.

"Oh, Grayson," she declared. "I'm happy you called. Do you know where Kip might be? I've been watching all the excitement on the news and wanted to make sure she was doing okay. I worry it might upset her. But she isn't answering her phone."

"Kipling is the reason for my call, Mrs. Branson. Her phone is currently not functioning."

"Oh, that's too bad. I believe she just upgraded a few months ago. Technology just doesn't last like it used to."

"Mrs. Branson," he insisted, and she stopped talking. "I apologize for my abruptness, but it is necessary. Unfortunately, Kipling was involved in the events of this evening." Her mother gasped, and he immediately regretted his choice of words. "Again, I must apologize for my abruptness. I am…unaccustomed…to such conversations."

"Oh, goodness. Jack! Jack!" she shouted to some other part of their home. "Come quickly! I think Kip is hurt!" She seemed to come back to Grayson. "What happened? Where is she?"

"She has been admitted to hospital for the night, but I have been assured–" He cut himself off, knowing his words were too cold. "She will be fine, Mrs. Branson, but I know she would want to see you and your husband when she wakes."

"We're on our way. Which hospital?"

"Massachusetts General."

"Yes, yes, we'll be there soon."

Then the line went off, and Grayson returned the handset to its cradle. He drew in a deep breath through his nose and puffed it out his mouth. The borrowed clothing was stiff from washing and uncomfortable, but better than the wet jeans and shirt he'd removed in the ambulance. They'd given him clearance to leave, but he'd made a promise. He hunched further forward, his elbows on his thighs, his hands loosely linked in the space past his knees.

"Holmes."

Grayson snapped his head up and straightened, looking toward the door where Director Stanton stood. "Yes, sir." The director looked toward Kipling's sleeping form. "She's asleep," Grayson said, standing to move toward the foot of the bed. He'd concede some distance, but wouldn't leave the room. "Her hearing aids are drying still; she won't hear you."

"Sheldon has been treated and we're transporting him in fifteen. Guy's a real chowder head," Stanton said and sighed. "Mental. Wicked off his rocker. Needs a padded room."

"One might argue it takes a level of insanity to do what he has done. Has he provided anything on this third person he seemed to have referenced to Kipling?"

Director Stanton's right eye twitched and he looked past Grayson to the bed beyond. "No. Nothing other than the vague pronoun. He. Him. Like we should all know who he's talking about. We'll need to question her," he said with a jut of his chin toward Kipling. "We'll wait until she's up to it, but can't wait long. I'd kinda hoped she'd be awake. I need more information on the guy who grabbed her for Sheldon."

"She told me she'd seen him before; in the bookstore earlier today, in fact. Where she works."

"We don't have much—"

"Kipling described him as having dirty blond hair, a mustache, forties, Maybe five-foot-ten. Caucasian male based on the timbre and tone of his voice. He's British; unfortunately, his accent is one common to middle to upper-class Britons throughout England so I cannot pinpoint a region." Grayson dictated the details he knew, however limited, and finished with a tilt of his head. "He was in the shop, so Kipling should be able to confirm if he made a purchase. If so, we may have a name, though we must consider the fact he would have used either cash or an alias in hopes of avoiding detection." Grayson winced and shook his head. "Never mind. She said he paid cash."

"Still not much, but it's something. Maybe she can remember more, something she didn't say in the call." His scowl deepened. "My higher-ups are still questioning her possible involvement—"

"She is no more willingly a part of this than I am, sir," Grayson began, but stopped when Director Stanton raised his hand.

"I hear ya, I do. And I'm inclined to agree. Just know, that part of this investigation isn't closed. Not completely. Not yet."

"My team may have some information to provide."

"They aren't exactly without prejudice."

"I assure you, sir, they completed their investigation without prejudice. Kipling is significant to me, but not them."

Director Stanton chuckled, one eyebrow hitching upward. "You sure about that? Holmes, I don't think I've ever seen a more loyal team. Not here at the FBI, not anywhere. I get the impression they'd do what you said, no matter."

Grayson shook his head, crossing his arms over his chest. The strangely cut material of the borrowed clothing pulled across his shoulders, with no give in the cotton blend. "We rely on each other, absolutely and without hesitation; however, their judgment can be accepted without prejudice in this matter. I assure you. Either way, take what they have and interpret it as you will."

Stanton hitched his chin toward Kipling. "And if we interpret it to say she's involved?"

Grayson shook his head again. "You won't. I have faith in your deductive abilities, sir."

Stanton laughed, a booming sound that bounced off the walls of the sterile, stark room. "Coming from you, I'll take that as a compliment." Stanton huffed, his lips bunched in a frown. "You did a damn good job on this, Holmes. This has been a hell of a situation, beginning with Burke DiMatto." The frown twisted into an expression of contemplation. "I could use more agents like you."

"I'm pleased to have been of service."

Stanton shook his head and turned for the door. He paused before stepping into the hall and turned halfway back. "Would you consider it?"

"Consider what, sir?"

"Being here. Full time." He shrugged a shoulder. "I've got an empty spot in my ranks, and as much as you've pissed me off the last couple of weeks, you've impressed me too."

"Despite of who I am?" Grayson asked, with the smallest of grins. "You don't worry about my legacy complex?"

Stanton colored, jutting his head toward the bed. "Flannery tell you I said that? Or did she?"

"I told you, sir. She is very good."

"Yeah, I'm gonna keep that in mind next time I'm within a hundred feet of Miss Branson." He looked to Grayson again. "Consider it. Now. Later. Whenever. Just consider it."

"I will consider it, sir, though I am unfamiliar with the precedent for Six agents to transfer to an American agency, regardless of the designation. Thank you for the compliment, Director."

Director Stanton scowled again, mumbled a "yeah, okay", and left Grayson alone to wait for the arrival of Kipling's parents. He returned to the side of the bed and legged up to sit on the edge of the mattress beside her. He slid his hand beneath her still one, resting on the blankets.

Minutes later Kipling stirred, making a long sound between a hum and a moan as she rolled her head on the pillow. She opened her eyes and smiled, then hissed, bringing her free hand up to gingerly touch the healing split on her lower lip. When she spoke, her voice was low, rough, and slow; a result of the medications they had administered after her admission to help with the pain. "I could get very used to seeing you when I wake up, Grayson Holmes."

Grayson lifted her hand and kissed it, setting it again on his leg. He sat forward just enough to be sure she could see his face without having to move. "As could I, though I will never get used to anything marring your beautiful face."

"Let's not make a habit of that part." Kipling sighed, her eyes shifting to take in his face, her expression tense. She focused on his lips before asking, "Are you okay?"

"I'm fine," he assured, but when the scowl deepened a degree, he knew a simple answer would not appease her. "Like you, bruised and a bit sore. Might have singed my hair a bit." He fluffed the back of his chaotic curls, left so by the dip in the water and the brief shower he'd taken before changing into the hospital-provided clothing. She frowned, and he chuckled. "Nothing a trim won't clean up."

With a sudden jerk, she sucked in a breath and her amber eyes welled with tears. Her grip on his hand tightened, but she stayed silent. Grayson shifted forward to brace his hand on the other side of her hip and hovered over her to press a kiss to her forehead. He held it there for several beats of his heart, finding it painfully difficult to draw away. Even when he did, he kissed her again before sitting on the edge of the bed beside her.

"It's over now," he said softly, for once thankful she couldn't hear him, or the thick heaviness in his voice.

Grayson stroked his thumb across her damp cheek, then reached for the box of tissues left on her bedside table, handing her one so she could wipe her eyes. She laughed, but it was more self-deprecating than humored and smoothed away her tears. With a shaky breath, she huffed it out and sniffed. "Sorry," she said softly.

He waited until she looked at him. "Nothing to be sorry for, my darling."

She curled her lips together and tilted her head against the pillows. "You're really making me wish I could hear you say that."

Possibly more to comfort himself than her, Grayson set his hand on her leg on top of the woven blanket and rubbed gently up and down from above her knee to her hip, careful since he wasn't sure the location of every bruise and scrape. "I rang your parents–" She groaned theatrically, and rolled her head on the pillow, raising the hand he didn't hold to swipe at her cheeks. Grayson chuckled, enjoying the spark in her eyes. "They should be here soon. I rang about twenty minutes ago."

"What did you tell them?"

"They had seen the reports on the news, and I told them you had been hurt, but you would be fine in time."

"They won't believe anything until they see me."

"I'm quite sure I am one of her least favorite people right now. It seems we only speak when peril and you are bedfellows." He smiled to reassure, to attempt to lighten the mood. "Your way is easy. My mother and father already adore you. I fear I have a greater battle to win your parents."

"You intend to try?" she asked with a slight tilt of her head and mischief in her eyes.

"I am not easily deflected, and I am quite sure my parents, my sisters, even Greg would attest to my stubbornness."

"Good," she said, lifting her hand to touch his face, her smile slow and warm, but he saw the shadow of discomfort slide over her face. He took his hand from her thigh to brush his thumb across her forehead, near but not touching the bruise edging out from beneath her hair. "You'll have a nasty headache for a bit, I'm afraid."

"What happened? Did you catch him?"

Grayson nodded. "The man who held you is named Isaac Sheldon. He is in custody, and by what Director Stanton told me minutes ago, will be transported to a holding cell shortly."

"I still have a hard time believing you found me."

"I promised you I would," he assured.

She tried to smile again, but it was decidedly lopsided to cater to her injuries. "That was some pretty impressive 007 action, Mr. Holmes. Right out of an action film."

"Yes, well, I'm not exactly a field agent. It is quite infrequent when I am called upon to even carry a weapon."

"You could have fooled me." She tilted her head again, to the other side. "Grayson, if I ask you a question will you be honest with me?"

"Of course," he said, his brows pulling down. "Do you believe I would be anything but?"

"I think you are inclined to say only what you think will be enough to appease me, but it's not always the full truth."

Grayson shook his head, and glanced away, a sense of deep pride in her filling him, though he supposed some would wonder why he would be proud of being called to account for his actions. Many times in his life he had been complimented – and sometimes reprimanded – for his skills in observation, which he had worked to hone well. For Kipling, it seemed so natural.

"As I have said before, you are very perceptive," he said, looking to her again. "Ask me anything you like, and I will be completely honest."

"Is this over now?" Before he could answer, she pushed on, talking fast. "I've been on this emotional rollercoaster for days, wanting this to be done but dreading it because when it's over—" She finally did stop, her lips pressed together.

Grayson pulled in a breath through his nose, and looked down at their joined hands, contemplating an answer. "I almost said it was nothing for you to be concerned with, but I realize did it not matter to you, you wouldn't have asked."

"It does matter." She nodded and pressed her palm to her chest.

"I wish you wouldn't dwell on this right now, Kipling. You should focus on regaining your strength." She arched a single eyebrow, silently challenging him. Grayson sighed and answered, "Honestly, I don't know whether this investigation is yet considered complete, or at what point my participation and proximity are no longer required."

"Not very specific."

He shook his head. "I cannot be more specific."

Kip nodded and swallowed. "Okay."

Commotion echoed from the hallway, and he heard Kipling's name spoken in a mother's frantic tone. He licked his lips and smiled, squeezing her hand. "If I am not mistaken, your parents have arrived." He lowered his leg to slide off the bed, but she held tight to his hand.

He moved off the bed, but only so he could reach across her and set his hand on the bed on the other side of Kipling. He leaned over her, and as gingerly as possible, he carefully kissed the right corner of her lips free of Sheldon's bruises and abuse. When he pulled back her eyes were closed, but they opened to look at him. He withdrew only enough that he knew she could see his mouth.

"I am not leaving."

Kipling's gaze held on his words until he finished, and then her eyes shifted up to look at him directly. "Okay," was all she said.

Grayson nodded, tipping one corner of his mouth in a smile, repeating to her "Okay," a second before her parents burst into the room.

Chapter Twenty-Two

"When was the first time you believe you saw him?"

"The first time was last Friday, but I didn't realize it then," Kip explained, shifting in the conference room chair in an attempt to be comfortable. She still hurt in most of her joints, and the muscles in her back hadn't fully loosened from her submersion in the Charles.

"Where were you when you saw him?" the new agent asked. Kip thought his name was Brandt or Bryant, she wasn't sure. Director Stanton hadn't enunciated very well when he introduced her, so she wasn't positive, and the two names looked pretty similar on Director Stanton's lips. This agent looked younger than her, which had to put him in his mid to late twenties, maybe.

It irritated her a little bit that they were asking the questions again, especially since she'd already said it more than once. To Grayson. To his boss. But this was her "formal" debriefing following the abduction, so she had to rehash everything. She'd spent two days at Mass General, and had only gone home to her parent's house the night before under the watchful and overly attentive care of her parents *and* Mina. Unfortunately, that also meant she hadn't seen much of Grayson, though he'd made it a point to be there when she checked out of the hospital, and had called more than once.

This wasn't how she wanted to spend her day, even though she understood the necessity of it. What she *wanted* was to go home, with Grayson, and just *be*.

She swore she could hear a clock ticking, just like Captain Hook's crocodile pursuer, warning her of Grayson's soon departure, and no matter of running away would give her more time. She wanted to enjoy whatever they had until they had time again.

It made her feel ill to be so sure of someone – Grayson – and so unsure of something – their future – at the same time.

"I was here," she said, sighing. She sat back, trying to settle into a position that didn't pull at the muscles along her spine. "Technically, I was *leaving* here. I'd been assisting Grayson and Agent Flannery with a surveillance tape, and when I was done Grayson escorted me to a taxi. When the taxi pulled away from the building, I saw this man on the other side of the street. It looked like he took my photo, but then he turned and took another photo, so I figured he was a tourist."

Agent Brandt/Bryant nodded and made notes. "Understood. You identified him on Saturday as the same man. How did you know?"

Kip shrugged. "Same build. Same coat. Same hair. But I also recognized him at that point as a customer I'd spoken to in the bookstore that day. So, he was at the FBI building, he was in the shop, and he's the one who grabbed me." The last words caught in her throat, so she stopped and swallowed, hoping he'd give her a minute before asking another question.

The hardest part was to not look to her right and back to where she knew Grayson stood, observing in silence. He told her he'd be there since he had heard the events on Saturday, and this was directly involved; but by remaining out of her line of sight, he should be less of a distraction.

In theory, but not in reality.

"What did he say to you in the bookstore?"

Kip took a deep breath through her nose, releasing it. "He

approached me about a rare book we had in the store. Asked me a few literary questions."

"What was the book?" the agent asked.

This was all new information, even for Grayson. It hadn't seemed appropriate to bring up the details before now, but now she wished she had. Heat crawled into her cheeks. "*The Hound of the Baskervilles* by Sir Arthur Conan Doyle."

Agent Brandt/Bryant shifted his gaze toward Grayson for a split second before writing down the information. "He was interested in the book," he stated.

Kip nodded. "He asked some questions about it and my interest in the Sherlock Holmes novels. Wanted to know if I was a fan, and I told him literature was my field of study. He asked which villain in the books was my favorite."

"And who is it?"

Kip arched an eyebrow, wondering what relevance it had to anything. But like Grayson had once said, every detail is important. "I said Charles Augustus Milverton. Moriarty is overdone."

Agent B nodded, the pinched look between his eyes telling Kip he probably had no clue who Milverton was. "Is that all you spoke of?"

She shifted again, crossed her legs, and wrapped her arms over her body. "He made a comment about my name, and said he was in the mood for some Kipling," she said, lilting her voice to relay the uneasy way he had made her feel. "I took him to the classics section, and left him there."

"What else did you—" Agent B started.

"What are you not saying?" Grayson said from behind her.

She turned her head just enough to see him, and stilled at the dark intensity in his expression. Kip drew a slow breath, and answered on her exhale. "He started fine, but then he made me uncomfortable. Standing too close. Talking with innuendo, like he knew some inside joke I didn't or seeing if I'd take his bait. Making a point of touching my hand, that sort of thing. Like his Kipling remark."

Grayson's hands curled into slow fists. Kip caught the slow

action in her peripheral, but didn't look away from his face. She cleared her throat, and finished the details. "I think it was obvious he was being creepy, because another customer made a comment I looked like I was trying to get away from something, and looked right at him."

"Was there anything else specific about him you can recall?" Agent B asked, pulling her attention back to him.

She blinked and licked her lips, shifting again in the chair to face him across the table. Memory of the second customer niggled at her. "Just what he looked like, I gave you that. And he was British."

"British. English? Scottish? Welsh?"

Kip shook her head and shrugged. "English. Definitely not Scottish, but I'm not sure I would be able to differentiate English from Welsh."

"English," Grayson provided. "A common accent throughout England, so it offers no assistance in possibly pinpointing his origin other than likely one of the larger cities. London. Birmingham. Manchester. He's also likely from a middle or upper middle class, well-educated family."

"You know that from the little you heard?" Agent B asked.

Grayson arched a single eyebrow. "Would you not recognize the accent of someone from, say, Louisiana versus here in Massachusetts, or Texas versus Minnesota?"

The agent nodded, conceding. "Understood." He looked to Kip again. "Tell me what happened when you left the shop, please."

Kip drew in a long breath and exhaled, clenching her hands in her lap. "I left the shop and began walking home. As I stepped out onto the sidewalk, I called Grayson and put my phone back in my pocket. My phone connects to my hearing aids with Bluetooth, so I don't have to hold the phone. I think that's why they didn't know I was on a live call."

"What was your intent in calling Mr. Holmes?" He asked the question with his attention down, on his notes, but looked at her as he finished.

Kip held eye contact, hoping to make it very, very clear she had no problem answering his question. "We were making plans for dinner."

"Understood," Agent Brandt/Bryant said. He seemed to like the word. "At what point did you suspect you were being followed?"

"I'd reached a crosswalk, and glanced back and saw him. I recognized him, and it made me nervous, so I walked a little faster. It was about then I told Grayson I thought I was being followed and gave a quick description. He told me to run, to find somewhere more public, but there wasn't anywhere close."

The more she talked, the more she remembered the panic in her throat and the pounding of her heart. She stopped and swallowed, clenching her hands in her lap. "I looked back and he was closer, and coming fast, so I ran. But he caught me almost immediately. I fought against him. A van pulled up to the curb beside us, but I kept screaming for help. Two men came running at us to help me, but he…"

Her voice broke and her eyes burned, and she looked down. Grayson's hand appeared in front of her, holding a tissue, and she took it, sniffing. He drew back, the knuckles of his fingers skimming her damp cheek. Before stepping away, he set his hand on her shoulder and squeezed gently, stroking her tense muscle with his thumb through the knit of her sweater. She dabbed at her cheeks, then raised her head and looked at Agent B again.

"The man who grabbed me shot one of them. I screamed, and then I don't remember anything else until I woke up in the van and I had a pounding headache."

"Understood," he said, reading over his notes. "We have transcripts from the call from the time you were put into the van until the connection ended. Other than what we heard, do you know of anything else to add? Can you tell me what you saw?"

"Not much. The warehouse was nearly empty. I saw some boxes, some computer equipment, I think. I only thought the bomb was a bomb because I saw what looked like a timer." She shrugged and smiled. "I guess I watch too many action movies."

"Did you see any papers? Literature? Propaganda? Anything of the sort?"

"No, not that I recall. And the only thing I would say about the man was that he definitely came across as mentally unstable." She waved her fingers in front of her face. "His eyes *danced*. No focus. And his expression would go from distant and spacey to angry and frustrated, and back again. I didn't know what I'd get from one moment to the next."

Agent Brandt/Bryant set down his pen and pushed back from the table to stand. "Thank you, Miss Branson. Your assistance and willingness is greatly appreciated. May we contact you again if we have further questions?"

"Of course." She shifted and used her feet to push back the chair, but it moved without effort as Grayson pulled it back for her, then stood beside her, offering his hand. She took it, appreciating the help to stand when her body once again protested the movement. It would be a few more days before she'd be back to normal.

Agent Brandt/Bryant nodded to her, and to Grayson, his glance between them not going unnoticed, and headed for the door. He left the door open, but once he was out of sight, Grayson took her hand and smiled down at her. The tension coiled between her shoulders since she walked in eased a few degrees.

"You did wonderfully," Grayson told her. "I'm very proud."

Kip smiled, though she was fairly positive it looked strained. Her head hurt, her body ached, and she wanted all this mess done and over with; though, she knew it was far from over. There would be hearings and news coverage, and the city had not gone unscathed by the actions these men – Malcolm and Sheldon – had taken. People had died.

"Thank you," she managed to say.

Concern pinched at the corners of Grayson's eyes and worry lines marred his brow. "I wish they would have waited until you recovered more, but it was important to have you interviewed while the information was still fresh in your memory."

She nodded and sighed. "I know. I'm just tired and ready for a nap."

Grayson slid his arm around her, their hands still linked, in a loose embrace and drew her to him so he could press a kiss to her forehead. She leaned into the contact, eyes closed, enjoying his presence. Kip inhaled, letting his mix of sandalwood and shave cream mingle in her head.

"I have some minor things to see to this morning, but if you don't mind waiting we can have lunch before you return to Chelsea."

"You're still coming for dinner?" She tipped back her head to look at him, her fatigued mind focusing on the distinct dip of his upper lip.

"Of course," he said with a slow grin. "I have amends to make with your parents."

"Lunch first sounds nice. I haven't had any one-on-one time with you in days. Feels longer." Kip shifted her eyes to meet his gaze, her smile feeling more genuine this time. "I can wait if they don't mind me waiting."

"It shouldn't take long. You can have a kip in my office while I work if you like."

Kip grinned, letting the sauciness of her thoughts slide up the corners of her lips, and Grayson laughed – his wonderfully deep and rumbling sound that always made her feel something beyond just happy – and shook his head. Before he could speak whatever response made his eyes spark, a knock at the door interrupted him, followed by the clearing of a throat.

"Holmes…" Grayson turned enough to look, Kip still in his loose hold. Agent Flannery stood at the door, his knuckles still resting on the wood. "Stanton's looking for you. He's in your office."

"I'll be there shortly."

"Should I go, then?" Kipling asked.

Before Grayson could answer, Agent Flannery did. "He was actually hoping you were still here, so…"

Despite no solid reason for it, her nerves prickled. Grayson's grip on her hand firmed. Flannery nodded and smiled at Kip before moving down the hall. His fingers still laced with hers, Grayson led her to the door, where he then let go of her hand and walked beside her toward his office. She had a relatively solid feel for at least this floor, especially where she could and couldn't go, and where Grayson's office was in relation to the elevators and the ladies' room. The door to Grayson's office was open as they approached, and he led the way inside. Director Stanton stood in the center of the office, in front of Grayson's desk, his hands at his hips pushing his unbuttoned suit jacket over his wrists.

He looked toward them, a scowl – not so much of annoyance but of thought – digging in between his eyes. His greeting to Kip constituted a nod.

"Agent Flannery said you wanted to see Kipling as well," Grayson said, his hand at the small of her back to draw her into the office.

"Yeah." He jutted his chin toward Grayson's desk. "Holmes, bring up your computer and get into the image archives for…" His eyes darted toward Kip. "…Ms. Branson's abduction."

"Certainly."

"How can I help?" Kip asked, lacing her fingers together in front of her, annoyed at the scrape over her nerves at the mention of the abduction.

"Based on the description you provided, we isolated a face off some security camera footage around your bookstore on Saturday. It's from earlier in the day than your abduction, but he seems to be the only one we found that comes close to your description. It may or may not be him." Director Stanton explained and motioned for Kipling to approach Grayson's desk, and Grayson sat to engage his computer. "It's not a great image."

Grayson had the investigation file open, accessing the image database by the time she came around. Director Stanton gave the name of the file, and Grayson searched the folder list.

"Okay." A wary tinge tainted Kipling's voice and she laid her hand on Grayson's shoulder.

"Here we are," he said, clicking on the file. A preview program opened, nearly filling his screen with the grainy image.

The slight firming of her hand on his shoulder told him they had her abductor's face before she actually spoke. "Yes, that's him."

"You're sure?" Director Stanton asked. "It's a bad shot."

"I'm positive," she reiterated. "Director, I spoke to him face to face as close as you and I right now. As uncomfortable as he made me, I'm not likely to ever forget his face."

Cold recognition skittered across the back of Grayson's neck as he studied the man's face. The mustache was unfamiliar, and last Grayson had seen this face he had dark hair and was probably a stone heavier. But this man looked younger. How could that be?

Nelson Augustus Howell.

He was supposed to be dead.

Grayson was the one who killed him.

Dusk had long since settled by the time Grayson's cab pulled up in front of the quaint New Englander style home in Chelsea that matched the address Kipling had provided. The neighborhood was an older one, with most homes being no less than fifty to sixty years old, and constructed close but not so close they didn't afford work-able yards and privacy to the inhabitants. The Branson home was a light blue color with the common white trim seen on many homes surrounding it, with a gambrel roof wrapping over the second story and a bay window in the front facing the street. Interior lights glowed warm through the front facing windows on the first floor, the second floor window dark.

Grayson paid the cabbie, stepping free of the vehicle. The air was cooler here than in the city, but not raw. The sidewalk was cleared with a narrow strip for walking, and white beads of de-icer crunched under his shoes as he navigated the shoveled clear walkway and cement steps leading to the front door nestled in the left facing corner of the house. Christmas lights still hung to the edge of the slanted overhang shielding the front door and a sign painted on a square piece of slate read "Booklovers Welcome. All others enter at the risk of your illiteracy."

Grayson smiled and raised his hand, knocking three times on the door. A small window gave him a limited view of the foyer beyond and a wooden tread staircase leading to the upper floor hugged the outer wall. Though he couldn't see the images, copious amounts of photos hung on every wall of the foyer. The interior of the home, even the brief glance through the window, was warm and inviting.

Moments after knocking, Mrs. Branson appeared through a doorway at the back of the foyer, the glimpse of a counter beyond indicating it was likely the kitchen. She smiled when she saw Grayson looking through the window, wiping her hands on a dishtowel as she approached. She opened the door and ushered him inside. Tantalizing aromas permeated the air in the small house, making his mouth water immediately. Vegetables and potatoes and meat, fresh bread, and spices created a tantalizing combination.

"We started to think you were really stuck," Mrs. Branson said, shutting the door behind him. "You can hang your coat there." She indicated a row of pegs on the wall, and he recognized her brightly colored anorak and Kipling's new wool coat. She'd lost one coat at the university bombing, and her second coat had been ruined by the dunk in the Charles River, so Grayson had made sure she had a new one to wear leaving hospital. "Kip just went to wash up. She's had her hands in pie crust since she got home." She gasped, and attempted to look contrite. "Oh, I wasn't supposed to say she made the pie. Don't tell her I told."

"I won't," Grayson said, finding a moment to slip in a word while he hung his coat.

"She'll be right down." She motioned up the stairs and headed back the way she came. "I must check on the biscuits. Jack is in the front room if you'd like to take a seat."

"Thank you," he called after her retreating form.

Before he could take a step toward the room off the right side of the foyer, which he assumed to be the front room and where Jack Branson was likely to be based on the sound of the television, he heard the closing of a door at the top of the stairs and moved to the bottom step to see if it might be Kipling. A shaded light hanging from the ceiling at the top of the staircase cast a glow behind her as she bounded down the first few steps, her hand on the polished wood railing, her feet – covered in thick, pink stockings – thumped on the wood.

As her head cleared the edge of the ceiling leading into the stairwell, she raised her chin and looked down, seeing Grayson for the first time. Her steps stilled and her eyes widened, and Grayson smiled. He set one foot on the bottom step and rested his hand on the rounded top of the baluster.

"You looked surprised to see me."

She rushed down the stairs so quickly a rush of panic hit Grayson that she might fall, and fall she did – or leapt might be more appropriate – into his embrace, her arms wrapped around his shoulders. His arms around her, Grayson took a step back so her feet were on the foyer floor, but she didn't ease her hold and he had to bend a bit so she stood. Kipling kissed his cheek, and again, before she kissed his lips, her hands sliding around his neck to rest on his jaw.

Grayson hummed into the kiss, drawing his palms up her back to pull her closer, ever mindful they were in her parents' home and propriety of some kind had to be maintained. But barely.

When she drew back to look up at him, tears made her amber eyes shine. Her gaze shifted, studying him, the soft pads of her thumbs stroking his cheek.

"I've been going crazy," she finally said, her voice soft and rough. "My stomach has been in a knot since I left the Bureau."

Grayson brought an arm from around her so he could stroke the moisture away from her cheek with his fingertips. "Whatever for?"

"Everything changed when I identified the man in the photo." She shook her head, her eyes pinching slightly at the corners. "It just seemed to get tense, and the way you said I needed to go–"

"I'm so sorry for that," he interrupted, as gently as he could. "I was caught by surprise by the photo. It was nothing you did, and I regret my churlish behavior."

"I wouldn't go *that* far," she said, her smile edging back. "I'm concerned because I know Director Stanton and others – maybe even you–" Her gaze darted to him, then away just as quickly, and she focused somewhere around the knot of his tie. "–thought I might be–"

"No," he said sternly before she could finish the thought, and hooked his finger beneath her chin to encourage her to look at him. "Not for one moment did I believe you had any knowledge or involvement in what has happened. *Never*," he stressed.

"But your director did," she countered. "I even saw doubt in your team. Especially when that man, Malcolm, pointed me out in the video." A tremor shifted through her, and Grayson instinctively held her tighter, shaking his head against every word she said. "And then the man who–" She stumbled over the words, swallowing hard, her lips pressed together.

"Sheldon," he offered. Having a name to pin to her nightmare might help her push it aside. "Isaac Sheldon."

She nodded, but still avoided looking him in the eyes. "The way he talked like I knew everything, like I was part of it. I'm not a fool, and I may be deaf but I'm certainly not blind, Grayson. You've said yourself I'm observant, and I know full well what they believed." With every statement, she spoke faster, as if trying to get everything out before he stopped her. "Then to have them question me so many times about the video and the things the men said and did, I knew everyone doubted me."

"Not everyone," he said, even though he doubted she registered his words at all.

"As soon as I said I knew that man's face, you got so quiet. You closed off, and then next thing I knew I was on my way home. The longer the day went without hearing from you–"

He tipped up her chin and stopped her words with a kiss, holding his lips to hers until he felt the tension ease in her body and she released a breath through her nose, warming his cheek. He parted his lips enough to adjust the kiss, tilting his head in the other direction to taste her again. She raised her arms, wrapping them around his shoulders, a low, soft hum moving through her beneath his palms pressed to her back. Her kiss, the full surrender to it, filled him and demanded far more than he could give standing in the foyer of her parents' home. With near insurmountable reluctance, they eased from the kiss but he held her to him so she had no choice but to tip back her head and look him in the eyes.

"I am sorry," he said, repeating his apology. "Please forgive me for making you believe for a moment I doubted you. And for causing you worry. I was taken by surprise by what that image revealed, and I didn't handle it well."

"What did it reveal?"

"That is a conversation best kept for another day. I don't wish to spoil the evening."

Her dark eyes shifted and he waited for her assessment. He'd already learned to recognize that look of examination in her expression when she either observed something likely no one else saw, or she sought her observation. Her lips turned down in a small frown and she pressed her warm palm to his cheek. "No, I'm sorry," she said softer, her thumb stroking his skin. "I was caught up in what was going on in my head, I didn't pay attention. Grayson, who is he?"

"A ghost," he answered and turned into her touch to kiss her palm.

"Two minutes until dinner!" shouted Kipling's mother from the other side of the small house.

Grayson raised his head to look past Kipling to the kitchen door, and smiled. "I nearly forgot we were not alone."

"Probably why she keeps reminding us," she said absently, but the concern still pinched between her eyes and along her brow. "What does it mean? Please, just tell me," she requested.

Grayson sighed and relaxed his hold on her, taking her hand from his cheek to link their fingers in preparation for joining her mother in the kitchen. "Jeffrey Cooper is my direct superior in London. He is on his way here to discuss the situation in person. I will know more once we speak, likely some time tomorrow." He took a step down the hall, but she didn't move and he stopped, looking back to her.

"Will you be going back soon?"

Grayson drew in a long, deep breath through his nose and went back to her, squeezing her hand. "Yes. I do not yet know how soon, but the reality is much closer now." He leaned to her and kissed her tense brow, holding his lips there as he took in the scent of her hair. When he withdrew, she stared at him with wide, shining eyes. "It is inevitable, but it is not insurmountable. You *know* this, don't you, Kipling?"

She nodded, but didn't say anything.

Grayson wished for a few more minutes to quiet her concerns, even though he harbored his own concerns and dread for an event he'd known would come since the moment he decided he would rather be with her, and face the parting, than take the easy road of avoidance and never know her beyond a name.

From the other end of the hallway, Kipling's mother cleared her throat before saying, "Dinner is ready, you two. Come on. Jack!" she shouted toward the receiving room. "Dinner!"

With regret, Grayson took a step toward the kitchen.

"Wait, Grayson." She released his hand and he turned, only to catch her in his arms when she reached for him.

She stood on her toes, arms around his shoulders, her face pressed into his neck with such ferocity Grayson embraced her and crouched enough she stood flat on her feet again. Her heart pounded hard enough, and he held her close enough, he felt it thumping behind her ribcage.

"I want to say something," she said into the curve of his shoulder.

Grayson drew back to see her face, her eyes shining bright. "What is it? Kipling, you're trembling."

Her heart pounded harder and he firmed his hold, afraid to hold her any tighter. "I love you," she finally said, the words on an exhaled whisper.

For half a heartbeat, Grayson braced himself instinctively for the wave of guilt he'd always felt when Liz had said the same and he couldn't return the words – not with honesty – but the guilt didn't come. His smile slipped over his lips the same slow way warmth bloomed in his chest, spreading until he was full with it and his cheeks could yield no more. Grayson drew in three deep breaths, each one coming faster and harder than the one before it, inhaling again as he kissed her, feeling a release like chains falling away from his soul. Taking her face in his hands, Grayson punctuated the kiss with several short, firm kisses until she laughed, drawing a chuckle from him.

"And I love you, Kipling," he told her on the chuckle, knowing he smiled like a fool, but he didn't care.

"You do?" she asked, the surprise in her voice pitching it upward along with her brows. "You're not just saying it because I did? You don't have to feel—"

"No, I'm not just saying it," he scoffed, shaking his head. "Kipling, I've never spoken those words to anyone not related to me." He paused, waiting for her gaze to connect with his again. "Ever."

"Why didn't you say?" she asked, her voice a rough whisper.

Grayson laughed. "Fear. I feared that in saying it I might frighten you as much as the idea frightened me."

Her eyes widened. "Loving me frightened you?"

"No," he said, shaking his head. "Quite the contrary. We've known each other barely more than a fortnight, so the idea of telling you before you felt the same – if at all – frightened me, but as is true to your incredibly brave nature, you had no fear."

"Oh, I was afraid." She nodded. "I was terrified."

"And yet, you spoke the words regardless."

"Dinner is getting cold," came her mother's warning.

Grayson widened his grin and brought her hand to his lips, kissing the back. "We mustn't be rude. It will not help my campaign." Her mother glanced toward them, and down to their joined hands, as he led her toward the kitchen. Grayson kissed Kipling's temple before pulling out her chair for her to sit, and took the chair adjacent. "What's for dinner?" he asked. "It smells absolutely amazing."

Kipling's mother set a massive platter of food at the center of the table, with chunks of steaming meat, cubed potatoes, carrots, and cabbage. "Corned beef boiled dinnah," her mother answered, the thickness of her New England accent suddenly more strongly and affectionately profound. "I'll get the biscuits. Oh, and for dessert we have apple pie."

Grayson reached for Kipling's hand, holding it on the table at the corner between them. "Perfect."

Chapter Twenty-Three

Arms wrapped around her from behind, and Kip screamed, kicking and thrashing with every dirty trick she'd been taught.

"Kipling!" Grayson shouted in her ears.

"Let me go!" she shouted, fighting her way free of his gloved hand he kept attempting to put over her mouth. "Help me! Help me!"

"Do not let them find your phone," he told her, Grayson's tone level and far calmer than her pounding heart. "Stay with me as long as you can."

His voice was almost lost in her struggle. She saw two men running toward them, hopefully her saviors. Then the man holding her raised his right arm, a pistol in his hand, and fired. One of the approaching men dropped and the other staggered to a stop, his hands in the air.

"No!"

In the final second before pain shot through her head, and her vision blackened, she stared at the man who had stopped short, his hands high. It was him. The man from the shop! He shifted his wide gaze from the man holding her to look directly at her.

"I'm sorry, Kipling," she read on his lips. "I'm so sorry."

Blackness overtook her.

Kip gasped and sat up, tossing back her blankets to launch from her bed. Her heart pounded viciously against the back of her ribs, and she couldn't catch her breath. Clammy sweat made her flannels cling to her. She stumbled from the back bedroom of her parents' home to the single full bathroom in the hallway, gripping the side of the white pedestal sink to keep her feet.

She didn't dare look in the mirror, knowing she looked as haggard as she felt. She'd had maybe two decent nights' sleep in weeks – since the bombing at the university. Not counting the night and day she lost post-bombing, she'd slept the horrible night she'd convinced herself everything was just a nightmare only to wake in the morning to find Grayson in her kitchen. And she'd slept peacefully the night Grayson fell asleep out of pure exhaustion himself on her bed.

Kip was a literature major, but it wasn't difficult to do the math. Grayson was the common denominator. Suddenly, after thirty years, she didn't want to sleep alone. Couldn't sleep alone.

It wasn't until she'd showered and dressed, dried her hair, and made a cup of coffee in the empty kitchen did the broken details of her nightmare slip back to her. She thought she was once again reliving the abduction, but the bits of the dream finally cleared when she settled into the front room window seat with her cup of coffee and multicolored afghan.

"Holy crap," she mumbled, alone in the house.

Could the memory be real, or was she twisting up things in her head since Saturday? Ever since Tuesday, when she'd gone through the interview at the FBI building, the brown-haired customer who'd commented on her discomfort had niggled at her memory. She recalled a detail the day before, before creepy guy – who Grayson seemed to know, but wouldn't name – had cashed out, when she found him watching her and the blond man watching them both. The nameless man had smiled at her when he realized she'd caught him, and had winked. But his wink and smile felt nothing like creepy guy's skin-crawling leer when he spoke in veiled innuendo.

But, she'd remembered that while awake. Was this nightmare real? Was she really reliving it, or was her subconscious just jamming together things to warp her memories?

Kip shook her head and slumped into the stack of pillows in the window seat. She shifted and took her phone from her pocket, looking at the time. Not quite 9:30. Her parents were off to the market, Mina would be at work, and Grayson was already in the office. She should be home, working on her paper and preparing for work herself, but she was stuck in Chelsea until the next day when she'd gotten her parents to agree it'd be fine for her to return home. Just in time for the weekend.

If the memory was real, it was significant. Sure, the weird green-eyed customer might have read her name on her badge just like anyone else, but if the memory was real he'd looked sincere. Concern would have been expected, but his apology went further and he'd said it like he knew she'd read the words on his lips. How could he have known that?

Kip shook her head, contemplating her phone. With a huff, she slid aside the security bar and punched in her code, opening her phone program.

I DON'T KNOW HOW HE COULD BE ALIVE, GREG.

'I THINK THERE ARE CERTAIN CRIMES WHICH THE LAW CANNOT TOUCH, AND WHICH THEREFORE, TO SOME EXTENT, JUSTIFY PRIVATE REVENGE.'

THERE WAS A TIME WHEN I COVETED THIS STATEMENT AS VINDICATION FOR WHAT I DID, THAT SOMEHOW I WAS FULLY JUSTIFIED IN MY ACTIONS. BUT THE WEEKS AND MONTHS FOLLOWING HOWELL'S DEATH WERE SOME OF MY DARKEST, AND NO DOUBT WILL HAUNT ME UNTIL MY OWN DEATH. I HAD BEEN SO ENRAGED, SO DEVASTATED, I SAW NOTHING BUT MY OWN FORM OF JUSTICE. DEATH WAS HIS DESERVED FATE — THAT I BELIEVE — BUT I WAS NOT THE ONE TO DOLE OUT HIS PUNISHMENT.

To now see his face like some spectre rising from hell, I am forced to wonder if it had been a nightmare. I know it was not, but how…how can he be alive?

Perhaps this is some form of admonishment to me, reminding me of my sin. In over thirty years, I have not ever experienced the calm of my soul I have in the last fortnight. Were I one to believe in supernatural forces doling out rewards and punishment, I might believe Howell's rise from the dead is my punishment for finding unearned peace.

More than any one given moment in the last year or more, Greg, I wish you were here so I could talk to you face to face. More than talking out investigation details, more than venting frustrations and wishing for your advice, I wish I could tell you the greatest joy I've ever known. Mostly because typing it out makes me sound like a complete idiot.

For over a year, the cathartic act of writing to Greg had been automatic. He did it without thought, telling his cousin of all the puzzles he faced, the questions he asked, and the events in his life. He had told Greg of the end of his relationship with Liz before he told his parents or his sisters. He had worked on investigations remotely with the best Six agent he'd ever managed and had stopped half a dozen acts of terrorism before they ever happened. He had told Greg of his pending trip to Boston as a liaison and consultant between Six and the FBI, even before Mum and Dad.

He had told Greg of Kipling, realizing now his heart was committed to her long before his mind accepted it, and he had subconsciously admitted as much when he told his cousin of the way she intrigued him even before that, when he mentioned her in an email. Never before had he detailed a witness in an investigation, but she had been special from the start.

It wasn't a matter now of not knowing what to say, but the words to say it; a challenge Grayson had not often faced. Kipling had commented more than once, with a smile that warmed him, her captivation with his tendency to "go on". Despite the war of logic battling in his mind, he had been light of heart all day, so much so Flannery offered his backhanded commentary on Grayson's perpetual smile, and he wanted to share his lightness with Greg. The idea that his words would go unread stung.

His decision was made when his desk phone rang, and he reached to his left for it, bringing it to his ear. "Grayson Holmes," he said, closing his laptop.

"Hi," came Kipling's voice over the line. "I'm sorry to call you at work."

"No apology required," he assured, already smiling. "You are welcome to call whenever you like."

"Well, I'm actually calling for a reason."

It was then the unease in her voice registered with him, and he sat up straighter. "What's wrong?"

"I don't think it's anything *wrong*, but I think I should tell you. It's about the two guys I told you and the other agent about on Saturday."

"Did you recall something more?"

She sighed. "I'm not entirely sure. Well, I'll clarify and say I know I did recall one thing, but the rest I'm not sure if it's a memory or just my brain messing with me."

"Tell me," he said and opened his desk drawer to remove a writing table, snatching a pen from the container on his desk. "Even if you aren't sure."

"Okay, yesterday I remembered part of that day – Saturday – after I left creepy guy to look at the Kipling books. I told you I nearly ran into another customer, and he commented on my unease."

Grayson nodded, despite the fact she couldn't see him. "I recall. Do you remember something specific about the troublesome customer?" He refrained from saying Howell, still not ready to accept the probable reality.

"No, it's the other one. The man I almost ran into."

Grayson scowled, remembering her brief comment on the other

customer, but nothing more. "I wasn't under the impression he was significant."

"I wasn't either, until I really started thinking about it. Something struck me when he spoke to me in the shop. His accent was indiscernible."

"The same might be said for you," he pointed out.

"Yes, but *I* have a limited accent because I was in speech therapy for six years after I was fitted with aids." The admission seemed to come easy for her as she continued without pause. "I know everyone *has* an accent, but it's like he had one of those newscaster accents. They teach people in journalism to speak with as little accent as possible."

Grayson nodded. "We call it neutral speech. It can be useful in our profession to be able to change or suppress your speech patterns."

"Right," she agreed. "So, maybe he's a reporter, or something. I don't know. And he seemed to know the other customer bothered me, or at least made me uncomfortable. But, I remembered something from later. I had gone to the register, and was cashing out a customer. I looked up, and creepy guy was standing at the end of the classics aisle, watching me." He heard the unease crawl through her voice. "But I also saw *this* guy. He was further away, but he stood so he could see both creepy guy and me. When I caught him watching, he just smiled and winked. Not a creepy smile and wink. Friendly. Like…like maybe he wanted to assure me."

Grayson scratched out notes as she talked, taking down whatever struck him as possibly important, even if insignificant. "What did he look like, this other customer."

"He was probably mid-thirties or so. Dark hair, kind of shaggy, like he was way past getting a haircut. He was white. Tall, about your height, maybe a smidge shorter. I don't know about build because he had on a heavy coat, but he looked broad. Solid. Not heavy. That make sense?"

"Yes," he assured. "Anything else?"

"He had a full beard and mustache. Oh, and his eyes."

"What about his eyes?" Grayson asked, pausing in his writing.

"They were green. Like *really* green. Unnaturally green."

Grayson squinted, but wrote down the detail. "Did you interact with him at all after that?"

"No, but immediately after I cashed out creepy guy *this* guy left the shop. He'd told me he was interested in *The Hound of the Baskervilles*, which Creepy Guy bought. I figured at the time he realized he wasn't going to get the book so he left."

Grayson paused in his notes, tapping the tip of his pen on the writing table. "You don't believe that now?"

She sighed, speaking at the end of her breath. "Well, that's where things get fuzzy and I'm not sure if I'm remembering or if my sleep-deprived brain is making up stuff."

"You still aren't sleeping? Are you still in pain?" His concern shifted immediately from the investigation to her well being.

"Not sleeping, but nothing to do with physical reasons." She paused. "My brain seems to go into high gear when I try to sleep. The only time I've slept is when I'm with you."

Grayson glanced toward the office door, smiling. "I am happy to oblige," he said in a softer voice, but not so soft he worried she wouldn't hear him.

She laughed, a smooth and light sound. "I'll hold you to that, Mr. Holmes."

"See that you do," he said with a chuckle. "But for now, tell me the rest. What is it you are unsure of?"

"I woke up this morning from a nightmare. I was reliving Saturday, when they grabbed me on the street." The pitch and tone of her voice shifted, strained, and he wished he were there to ease her. "When he got hold of me, two men came running up to us to help. I told you that."

"Yes, and he shot one of them." He said it so she wouldn't have to.

"The other man, the one who stopped…I think he was the customer. The other one. The one who was watching creepy guy. And it gets stranger. I remember, just a split second before I was knocked out, I remember him mouthing 'I'm sorry, Kipling' to me."

The hairs on the back of Grayson's neck bristled. "He knew your name."

"Well, that wouldn't be unusual, since I wear a nametag. But my nametag says Kip, not Kipling. And in my recollection, he very clearly says *Kipling*. And he looked…devastated…that he couldn't help me. More than just someone on the street."

Grayson looked down again at the description he'd written. Mid-thirties. Brown hair, poor cut. Facial hair. Anglo. Tall. Solid build. Unusually green eyes. His nerves practically hummed.

"Do you think I really remember, or is my head making it up? But, why would it make up something like that?"

"I don't know," he said, staring at the notes. He sucked in a breath and raised his head. "But I will do what I can to help you figure it out. Do you think you might be up for dinner tonight?"

"Oh, lord, yes," she said on a groan. "Get me *out* of this house, Grayson, before I go crazy. I love my parents, but honestly, tomorrow cannot come fast enough."

He laughed and set down his pen. "I shall call for you around seven. We can eat close to Chelsea so your parents won't be overly concerned."

"Wonderful. I'll see you then." She paused only a moment before adding, "I love you."

He glanced toward the door again, not because it would be wrong for anyone to hear his response, but because his response was for her and not a general audience. "I adore you," he said. "I will see you tonight."

With a final parting, he set the phone down in its cradle and went back to the notes. His pulse jumped, and nervous energy vibrated through his fingers until he tapped them on the desk blotter. The general description of the second customer didn't raise any flags for him, not until she mentioned the unusually, unnaturally green eyes.

Three years before they had worked an investigation in Moscow, and as part of Greg's legend he'd worn a wig, facial hair, and green eye contacts. But like Grayson, Greg was born with sectoral hete-rochromia, a genetic defect in the Holmes bloodline that caused mild variations in the color of the iris. Grayson's eye color leaned more prominently to blue with variations of green, whereas Greg's variant was more prominently blue with gray variants. Enhancement tint contacts only exacerbated his variegation so he wore opaque tinted contacts to effect sufficient color change. Blue opaque worked well, but green did not.

If he didn't know better – no, that wasn't right. He knew better than the entire SIS – if it made any logical sense at all, this mystery man could be Greg. But why would Greg be here in Boston? Why would he be in disguise?

He shook his head. No, logic said it wasn't. Logic said this man was connected, but it couldn't – it wouldn't – be Gregory McQueen. If Greg were in Boston, why wouldn't he contact Grayson?

But what was more unlikely? Gregory McQueen in Boston, or Nelson Augustus Howell in Boston? Both were thought dead, so why would the coincidence end there?

"Holmes."

Grayson snapped up his head, looking to the now fully open door where Jeffrey Cooper stood, his hand on the knob and his face grim, two folders in his other hand. Grayson stood, coming around the desk. Once close enough, Grayson noted the tension lines around Jeffrey's eyes were a bit more pronounced, as were the frown lines bracketing his mouth.

"Have you learned anything?" Grayson said, pushing his hands into his trouser pockets.

"Yes." Jeffrey sighed and shook his head. "Bloody shock, truth be told."

Grayson's nerves prickled and dread settled in his gut, even though he as of yet had no indication what caused it. "What is it, Jeffrey?"

The slow, metered way Jeffrey turned and closed Grayson's office door made his blood go cold. He stood in the center of his office, waiting for his superior, mentor, and friend to cross to him. Jeffrey motioned toward the two chairs side by side on the office side of his desk. "You'll want to be sitting for this, Grayson."

His instinct was to remain on his feet, to face straight on whatever news Jeffrey had to impart, but respect propelled his feet to the farthest chair. As he passed the first, he pivoted it so they at least sat facing one another. Jeffrey sat with a groan, set the folder on the edge of the desk nearest him, and unbuttoned his jacket, his age showing in his movements.

"I don't much care for the question 'Do you want the good news first, or the bad news', so I'm choosing. Let's begin with the good news, shall we?"

"Whatever you prefer, Jeffrey," Grayson answered, biting back his desired reply to hurry it along one way or another.

"How is Miss Branson doing?"

The question felt like a switch in topics, but Grayson didn't let his confusion play on his features. "Physically, she's improving." He linked his hands and rested them in his lap, focusing on Jeffrey. "I am concerned the psychological injuries will stay with her much longer than the bruises and pains."

"The events she's gone through as of late are difficult enough to deal with when you're trained to do so. I can only imagine how challenging this has been for her." Jeffrey cleared his throat and shifted in his chair, his sudden discomfort evident. "Tell me truthfully, Grayson, what is your status with this relationship?"

"Are you asking my intentions?" Grayson asked, with a quirk of his lip at Jeffrey's panicked expression. Beyond assuring Liz, and Andrea before her, were vetted and cleared for a relationship status – both conversations that were far from charged with sentiment – Grayson and Jeffrey had very few discussions of a domestic sort between them. Grayson took in a breath, deciding to have mercy on his superior and friend. "I am fully committed to a future with Kipling Branson; does that sufficiently answer your question?"

"You've barely known this woman a fortnight, Grayson. Isn't this a bit hasty?"

"Complete, yes. Hasty, no. Jeffrey, have you ever known me to be a fool to my heart?"

"Absolutely not, which is why this entire situation has me completely gobsmacked."

"My previous lack of frivolous love affairs should speak in testament to the seriousness of my intent now." Grayson canted his head, studying his director. "You have dismissed your concerns Kipling may somehow be involved with Malcolm and Sheldon." It wasn't a question; he already saw the answer. Hearing Jeffrey say the words would be his justification.

Jeffrey took in a deep breath, letting it out as he reached for the folder, tapped his fingers on the closed file. "We've researched your lady friend by all standard vetting means, and a few non-standard means, considering the circumstances and her suspected link to the case."

Grayson bit back his retort, wanting to once again reiterate his unwavering belief Kipling was as much a pawn in the game as any of them. Through his mind rolled the quote from *Hamlet*, "The lady doth protest too much, methinks." He was no lady, but his protests were about a lady, and he feared his fixed resolve might shine doubt on his frame of mind rather than solidify a verdict of innocence for Kipling.

"Beyond the fact she failed her driving test the first time, she appears quite ordinary. No excessive debt beyond student loans, no arrests, no tickets, and above average academic standing throughout her schooling. An average American citizen with no ties or connections to anything questionable, no contacts with anyone affiliated in any way with questionable groups or organizations, nothing. Short of some civil disobedience in the 60s, even her parents are upstanding citizens."

Were Grayson a petty man, he might mock with "I told you so," but instead he kept his expression level. "Did you complete interviews with my team?"

Jeffrey nodded, lips pressed together. "Of course. If anyone would recognize a negative change in your behavior, it would be those who trust you the most. They agree she's clean in this, and by all accounts their judgments appeared unclouded. They are loyal to you, but not so loyal as to turn a blind eye just because you're–" He cleared his throat, and lifted the edge of several pages to read something. "–'getting your end away', to quote Ms. Connolly." He looked to Grayson, his head still down. "She's a bloody good agent, but one would never define her as a posh lady."

Grayson shook his head, unable to deny his grin. "Lynne has a colorful view of life."

"Yes, well, Sandra was a bit more subtle, though more direct ultimately. She confided they were all shocked by the relationship, surprised by your transformation, but ultimately pleased." Jeffrey grinned, a look of amusement pulling around his eyes. "That all being said, when spoken to individually they all had different things to say but with the same result. Every one of them is willing to state on the record they have every reason to believe Kipling Branson is as without guilt as you so adamantly stated from the beginning."

"And you, Jeffrey. What is your opinion?"

Jeffrey didn't answer immediately, instead studying Grayson. What he looked for, Grayson could only assume; something he preferred never to do. After what felt an eternity, Jeffrey huffed through his nostrils before speaking. "While all gathered evidence dictates this woman had no part in any of these events other than being used as a pawn, the very fact she was used so expertly causes me concern."

"In what way?" Grayson asked.

"Surely you have thought the same thing as I, Grayson. Or has this woman so befuddled your mind that you have lost your logical reasoning skills?"

Grayson looked away, his right leg bouncing in nervous energy despite his attempt at portraying level calm. He set his elbows on the arms of the chair and steepled his fingers together, his index fingers resting against his chin. Reluctantly, Grayson met his superior's gaze.

"I would be a liar if the thought had not crossed my mind – even if for the briefest of moments – that she was somehow a player in this chess game. The timing, the situation, seems almost too perfect to possibly be anything else."

"Yet, you have dismissed the idea."

"Utterly." At Jeffrey's immediate look of disdain, Grayson shook his head. "Jeffrey, I am not vain in saying I am a well-educated man.

My parents saw to it. But as much as I would very much like to set aside my lineage, it cannot be denied. My great-grandfather was infamous for many things. Was he not?"

"Of course," Jeffrey conceded.

"Amongst those skills was his ability to read a person within moments of meeting him. It was innate, natural. Will you deny one of the very reasons I was recruited by Six was because it is no secret I have the same innate ability?"

"Of course not, Holmes."

"If you are willing to admit that ability, you must do so without caveat. This is not selective. It is instinctual." Grayson chuckled and dropped his hands to his lap. "Kipling once told me reading lips is instinctual to her, as instinctual as it is for us to hear a noise when it occurs. She must make a concerted effort to *not* read lips. The same can be said for me."

"I understand the point you want to make, Grayson—"

"Do you, Jeffrey? More importantly, do you accept the point?"

"Your hubris will one day be your end."

"Hubris implies *excessive* self-confidence."

Jeffrey laughed, a booming sound that tipped back his head and made his expanded girth bounce. "Does this Miss Branson as easily accept your arrogance as we are expected to?"

"I've yet found necessity to prove anything to Kipling. She has simply accepted me at face value."

Jeffrey's smile slipped to a more serious expression. "Which forces me to bring up another point, Grayson. While this woman's record is impeccable, the same could be said for men such as Nelson Howell. Even until his death, no criminal activity appeared on any official record. Only the IC knew the extent of his sins."

Grayson squinted and leaned forward a few degrees. "Are you attempting to prove Kipling's guilt by bringing to question the evidence of her innocence?"

"No." Jeffrey huffed and cleared his throat. "Have you considered—"

"Probably."

"–Your immediate affection and dedication to this woman is precisely what your would-be assassin wanted?"

"Yes, I have considered it."

The upward jerk of Jeffrey's right eyebrow was his only means of requesting clarification.

"While I presume our chess master's intent was to create an absolute diversion in Kipling, I also suspect he assumed we would accept the conclusion drawn from the revelation of evidence. That she was part of the game. He hoped to either sufficiently distract me from the truth I wouldn't determine it, or cast the shadow of doubt on my judgment to distract Six from the true mastermind. He likely hoped we would end our investigation at Malcolm and Sheldon."

"It doesn't bother you to be with a woman hand selected for you by someone with nefarious intent?"

"My concern lies in the fact that whomever this is has such intimate knowledge of me, and has substantial enough an intellect, that he is able to choose a woman so perfectly matched to me. Which leads to my original and more pressing question: Who was in that video? Who abducted Kipling? We both know it isn't Nelson Howell."

"No, but that does not improve the situation." This time, it was Grayson who raised an eyebrow in inquiry. Jeffrey slid the bottom folder from beneath the top, and held it out to Grayson. "It would seem family vengeance would be the common denominator in this case."

Grayson held Jeffrey's accusatory glare as he took the folder and opened it. The image inside was a much sharper, clearer photo of the same man. He still looked remarkably like Nelson Howell, and yet, clearly not. Especially now that he had a proper visual. "Who is this?"

"Langdon Howell, younger brother to Nelson by four years. He apparently has continued Nelson's endeavors when you–when Nelson Howell died." Jeffrey cleared his throat and canted his head, still staring at Grayson. "He might very well be a more formidable challenge than Nelson, considering he has managed thus far to remain invisible to us."

"Which implies he has specifically chosen this time and place to make his existence known. He has been very calculated since the beginning, going so far as to taunt me with his clues." Grayson shook his head and closed the file. "Is this a bluff? Double bluff?"

"Either way, we have it on strong intelligence he has left Boston and is back in the UK. Which is where we now need to be."

Grayson pressed his lips together and closed his eyes, bowing his head. He drew in several metered, practiced breaths before he looked again to Jeffrey. "When do we leave?"

"I've purchased return flights for myself, you, and your team for later this afternoon."

Chapter Twenty-Four

Kip was in the kitchen unloading the dishwasher when she heard the knock at the door, four rapid thumps on the wood. She set the cups in her hand in the cupboard and reached for a dishtowel, but when Grayson's voice calling "Kipling" followed up the knock, she tossed aside the towel and headed for the foyer and front door. She glanced at the microwave as she passed, wondering if she'd lost several hours. It wasn't even two yet.

She caught his gaze through the small door window as she rushed through the foyer, and the strain she saw in that short glimpse made her gut clench and she almost caught her step. Kip opened the door, the gust of air pushing her hair back off her shoulders.

He stood on the top step, dressed in his dark suit but no overcoat, and the twist in his expression and pinch at his eyes immediately pressed down on her chest. "Grayson, what's wrong?"

Grayson looked toward the street as a city cab pulled away, then set his hand on her arm and guided her to step back into the foyer, following so he could close the door. She moved, but never looked away from him. His jaw was clenched with such strength, muscles jerked along his cheek and down his throat and his lips were a thin, tense line.

He glanced toward the kitchen, then into the front room through the wide archway. "Are your parents home?"

She shook her head. "No. They went shopping for the day. They're going on a cruise in a couple weeks. Grayson, what is wrong," she asked again, stressing each word.

He closed his eyes and bowed his head, his jaw working as he swallowed. His hand still rested on her arm, and the grip firmed just before he stepped to her and wrapped her in his embrace. Kip didn't resist, leaning into him when he pressed his face to her neck and drew in a long, rough breath; but tears burned her eyes for a revelation she hadn't heard yet. She didn't have to know the details to guess the outcome.

The day had come.

He pulled back, and laid his palms on each side of her face, and the torment shining in his eyes was nearly her breaking point. "I'm so sorry," was all he said.

Kip swallowed and shook her head, but not so hard to lose his touch. "When?"

He sniffed and dropped his hand to link his fingers through hers, drawing her toward the front room. "Let's sit. Please. My explanation is a difficult one, and I don't wish to do it standing in your foyer. It feels as though I am planning my escape, and nothing could be farther from the truth."

She let him lead her into the front room, and they sat on the thirty year old plaid upholstered couch sitting on the outside wall. Grayson never released her hand, and once seated, he sat so close their knees pressed to each other's and he sandwiched her hand between both his larger ones. Her heart pounded viciously, and she couldn't take a deep breath, staring at him afraid to blink that tears she had no cause for yet would fall.

It was foolish, since she'd known from the beginning the day would come that he would be required to leave Boston. Knowing the train was coming didn't lessen the impact.

"My time is short," he began with a heavy sigh. "Within the half hour, my director Jeffrey Cooper will be here to retrieve me. The man I told you of on Tuesday." The sadness in his eyes told her more than his words, but both tore at her.

"Half an hour?" she repeated, shaking her head. "Why only half an hour?"

He swallowed hard, but never looked away from her. "I must leave for Logan Airport and return to London."

Kip gasped, and his hold on her hand tightened so she wouldn't pull free. "Why so suddenly? I thought they'd give you a warning. Some time. The weekend, maybe. *Something*."

He was nodding before she finished, and brought her hand to his lips to kiss her skin before answering. "The details of our case have changed drastically, dictating my team and I return to London to continue the investigation." He sucked in a hard breath, releasing it to explain. "We have identified the man who orchestrated this entire chain of events, from the careful manipulation of your presence at the bombing to your abduction this Saturday past."

"Isn't he here in Boston?" she demanded again.

He shook his head. "No. He left the States a few days ago. I am not entirely convinced he fully intended for us to know of his departure, but regardless, he is no longer here. It is the opinion of my superiors that the threat is now within the UK."

"Who is he?" Kipling shook her head, not caring now the tears fell. "Grayson, seconds are ticking past and I don't want to spend the next twenty minutes guessing. Can you tell me who he is? Why he did this?"

He nodded, his gaze cast down at their joined hands. "I'm sorry, darling. You have complimented me on my eloquence, and yet right now, I don't know the words to explain." He raised his chin and met her stare. "His name is Langdon Howell, and everything he has done since the explosion at the university has been to exact revenge."

"Revenge? Why? On who?"

"On me." Grayson swallowed before looking her in the eyes. "I had every intention of one day sharing so much of this with you, but the short time we've been together has been far too valuable to me to spoil it with the sins of my past. Though, I realize you deserve to know the type of man you've fallen in love with, to determine whether I'm a man deserving of your love."

"Grayson, I can't imagine anything that would change—"

"I told you already, Kipling, I became a different man when I met you. You have no knowledge of who I was and what I am capable of."

"You're frightening me, Grayson," she whispered, the thought forming the words before her heart could tell her to keep them in.

His eyes saddened. "I hate I have done even that."

Kipling freed one hand from his hold only long enough to press her palm to his jaw, stroking his cheek. "Just tell me what you need to tell me, Grayson. I promise, I'm not going anywhere."

He turned into her touch to kiss the heel of her hand before she took it away to grip his fingers, waiting.

Grayson drew in a long, slow breath through his nostrils, seeming to firm his posture as he let it go. Then he began. "I have told you of my cousin Gregory. We grew up together, closer than brothers, and we went to Cambridge together and joined MI6 together." She nodded as he spoke to confirm she remembered everything. "Although we were recruited together, I became an officer within three years and Greg was part of my team, along with Lynne, Sandra, and Mac."

"Why are you speaking of him like he's gone?"

His hold tightened, but she didn't flinch. Grayson took three deep, hard breaths as if preparing himself, strengthening himself, to answer her questions. When he finally did, she couldn't breathe until he finished.

"Thirteen months, two weeks, and three days ago Gregory was trapped within a building in Edinburgh that had reportedly been wired by a militant faction out of North Ireland; a group using death and destruction to convince the Crown to release their country from British rule. They are so extreme the Real Irish Republican Army has disavowed them completely. I was on an open radio line with him when he told me he'd found the bomb." As he spoke, his voice grew quieter until she read the words on his tremulous lips more than she heard his deep voice. "It was on a timer, with fourteen seconds left when he found it."

"Oh, god…" Kipling whispered.

"He didn't tell me the time left. He provided to us the information needed from his visual inspection to shut down that cell, and then he said 'Goodbye, Ollie'. We were a mile away, and felt the ground shake when the building exploded."

Kip brought her free hand to her mouth, sucking back a sob. His face was a blur now, but there was no mistaking the tear that slid free down his cheek.

He smiled, but it was whimsical and melancholy. "He called me Ollie because Gregory and Grayson sounded too similar, he said. So, he used my second name, and shortened it because he knew I despised it."

"Greg is dead?" she choked out past the lump in her throat.

Grayson's chuckle was completely humorless. He bowed his head again, working his thumbs over her knuckles. "Therein lies a point of conflict between the Royal Majesty's Secret Service and I. I am of the opinion there is insufficient evidence to prove without a question, neither to myself nor our family, that Greg died that day. They found no remains, and my heart–" He chocked, and raised his head to look at her because when he spoke again his voice was almost non-existent and she read on his lips, "my heart cannot believe he is dead. My heart screams to me he is not dead, and I will not accept the alternative."

Kipling swiped at her cheeks. "I'm so sorry, Grayson."

Grayson cleared his throat and seemed to refocus. "We learned in the weeks following Greg's *death* that the entire course of events had been manipulated by a man named Nelson Howell, a man Six had been attempting to prosecute for years. He was an exceptionally brilliant criminal, forever able to divert guilt from himself and stay outside the arm of the law. Whenever we believed we had him, he would manage to slip away without punishment. Even in this, we had no way to prove his guilt within the confines of the law.

"I threw myself wholeheartedly into the search for Nelson Howell, determined to find a way to bring him to justice." He diverted his gaze, staring instead at their joined hand. "Eight months ago we found him, and my team moved in to apprehend him in a situation we believed would be his downfall. His ultimate trap." The tension in his body made him taut as a violin bow, and each word was spoken with eerie precision. "He was arrested and returned to London, where he was released within twenty-four hours' time."

Whether it was the cold levelness of his voice, or his obvious attempt to carefully school his features, she wasn't sure but she knew whatever he said next hurt him to his soul to say.

"I was enraged," he stated, unblinking. "Since Edinburgh, I had and have experienced vicious bouts of rage, so intense they have blinded me, fueled by sorrow like I'd never imagined could exist. That night, I was a man possessed. I found Nelson Howell and confronted him, man to man."

Kip's stomach clenched and her blood went cold. She fought to take in air, but her heart told her to not pull away from him. Now more than ever. His eyes shined when he looked at her, his lips turned down in a barely disguised frown that flinched with his words.

"He was arrogant, flaunting his ability to perpetually avoid consequences for his actions. He mocked Six, mocked me, mocked the name Holmes, and finally bragged with pride his responsibility in Greg's death. I–" Grayson closed his eyes, his lips, and bowed his head. "I attacked him. I killed–"

Kip sucked back a sob. She couldn't help it, no matter how she tried. Instantly, she felt his physical reaction and he pulled back, but instead of letting him withdraw when their hands separated, Kip scrambled forward and wrapped her arms around him, holding on as tight as she could.

"No," she ordered when she sensed his withdrawal. "Don't you dare, Grayson Oliver Sherlock Holmes."

His chuckle, though small and weak, was her reward and she held on tighter. Only because she needed to see his face did she draw away from him. Kip had only seen Grayson as this unwavering symbol of strength in the short time she'd known him, and to see the anguish he tried to hide squeezed her heart. It was more than anguish.

Shame.

Still more in his lap than on the couch, Kip took his face in her hands and held her breath until he tipped up his chin and looked at her, his unevenly-tinted eyes shifting slightly as he studied her face. "This changes nothing for me. Do you understand?" she asked. "I'm crying because my heart breaks for you, because I love you."

Grayson wrapped his arms over hers, mimicking her hold to thread his long fingers into her hair while his thumbs stroked her skin. "I am a better man because of you, Kipling."

Before she could reply, he met her in a kiss so different than any other they'd shared. They had kissed desperately, they had kissed with passion, with need, with reverence, and they had kissed with thankfulness to be alive. This kiss was possibly every one of them bundled together, and it stole her breath. His mouth moved slowly, meticulously over hers, his open lips drawing her into him. Against her parted lips, he paused and told her, "I love you, Kipling. Absolutely and completely."

She couldn't help her choked sob, and pushed her fingers into his short, waved hair to hold him as she kissed his words to silence. They hurt; they filled her to overflowing, but they hurt so deeply. Not the words, not the meaning, but the loss of them within minutes. Grayson leaned them both back into the cushions of the couch, a low rumbling moan playing across their lips.

The rude trill of his phone pierced the moment, a staccato and sharp tune, and his moan of pleasure changed to a groan of frustration. He sat away from her and reached into his trouser pocket to withdraw the phone, scowling at the screen.

"What is it?" she asked, struggling to steady her breathing

He swallowed and looked up before answering, turning the phone so she could see the text message as he told her. "My ten minute warning."

Kip bolted from the couch and ran for the foyer and the stairs, Grayson only a second behind. "Kipling! Where are you going?"

She paused half way up the stairs and looked back. He was at the bottom, his hand on the banister and one foot on the bottom step. "I'm going with you." When his eyes widened, her heart sank and she had to swallow before continuing. "I can't go with you to London. But I can go with you to Logan. I'm not having our last moments for who knows how long be at your director's discretion and on his timetable. He wants to take you away, he's going to have to put up with my dirty looks until you're out of sight."

Grayson smiled, despite the heaviness in his chest, because of her determination. She smiled back and finished her bolt up the stairs. He followed, not wanting to give up even a few minutes with her. The first floor was compact, much like the entry level, the gambrel roof wrapping down and around the two rooms he noted. Kipling had headed straight from the top of the stairs to an open bedroom door, the room seeming to take up the back one-third of the house. He glanced toward the front, and saw a matching closed door he guessed to be her parents' room, and parallel to the staircase banister was an open door to a bath.

He pushed his hands into his pockets and followed Kipling's lead to the open bedroom door. She sat on the end of a frameless double bed draped in a faded, but possibly handmade, quilt in yellows and pinks, tugging on and lacing a pair of trainers. The walls of the room were painted a pale yellow, and curtains of pink and white shaded the one window at the back of the room where the headboard of the bed rested.

The room fell somewhere between that of a child and of a young woman. Bookshelves lined the low walls before they angled into the ceiling angles, and the shelves were full, some stacked two deep with the spines of larger books extending beyond the edge of the shelf. A desk nestled against one wall, with her laptop on it, but also covered with figurines and framed photos. Stuffed animals sat in stacks on the opposite side of the room.

"I would have liked to have known the Kipling who lived in this room."

She looked up, grinned, then straightened and stood. "You know me, and you'll know me more." She crossed near him to a door and opened it, revealing a cramped closet beyond, retrieving a cream colored Irish cardigan she draped over her arm. It was a beautiful, mild day but her shirtsleeves wouldn't be enough.

When she crossed again to the bedroom door, Grayson turned sideways so they stood together, chest to chest, within the frame of the jamb. He touched her arm, his fingers wrapping above her wrist, and stopped her from moving past. Kip looked up at him and slower than before, with more intent and focus, he bent his neck and she raised her chin for his kiss.

He intended to remain the gentleman, to taste one more kiss alone with her, but the moment her lips parted and her tongue brushed along his own, propriety was all but lost. Desire flashed over him, like the heat of an explosion when he stood too close to the flame. The pitch and demand of the kiss changed, and there was no doubt she felt the same flame engulfing them. When her fingers slid open the buttons of his coat and she tugged at his lapel, drawing him away from the door, Grayson didn't entertain a single thought to stop, and willingly followed. The bed creaked, giving beneath their combined weight when he set his knee on the mattress and Kipling sat on the edge, tugging at the sleeves of his jacket. He shrugged free before kissing her open lips again and taking them both back onto the quilt.

Kipling's soft throaty sounds of encouragement, and her exploring hands over his sides and at his waist, were petrol to his need. Consuming. Blinding. Starving.

Everywhere Kipling touched begged for more, and he let himself be lost in her kiss and a desire for her he'd never felt for any other woman. He'd been attracted, he'd even wanted a woman, but this…this was so much more. This was his perfection.

It was that thought, and the scream of his blood that he neared the point of no return, that forced him to rake in a ragged breath and clench his fists in the bedding to keep from undoing her clothes any further. She already lay beneath him, breath rapid, lips glistening, wide irises looking at him, her breasts and stomach exposed where he'd unbuttoned her blouse in his frenzy. Kipling slid her hands over his abdomen and chest, holding her palm over his violently racing heart.

"What?" she asked on a heavy breath.

Grayson had to swallow to speak, and shifted his weight against her – an act of self-induced torture that sent shockwaves through him – so he could support himself on his left arm and hold her hand over his heart with his right. He opened his lips to speak, but instead had to first quench his thirst for another kiss. She gave into it fully, just as before, and it caused physical discomfort to pull away.

Still fighting to calm his chaotic heart and staggered breath, Grayson finally managed to speak. "Kipling, I've never been intimate with a woman I loved." Her eyes rounded briefly, then slipped into a confused pinch. He shook his head. "I've been with women I cared for, but never a woman I loved. Do you understand?"

The pinch relaxed, as did her body beneath him, and she let her head ease back onto the bed, never looking away from him.

"Nor have I ever wanted to be with a woman as much as I want to be with you. Trust me on this."

"I'm pretty aware," she said with a sexy bow of her lips into a smile.

He returned the smile. "I don't want this to be a rushed moment, with my impending departure looming over us," he said with a heavy heart. "I love you too much for that." When doubt flickered through her eyes, Grayson leaned in again and kissed her as chastely as his rebelling body allowed. "I would rather making love to you be a hello, not a goodbye. And…" He dragged out the word, winking, as he shifted again to look at his watch. "I'd rather have more than seven minutes."

At that she smiled, then drew in a long, deep breath and let it out. "I don't want to agree, but I do." Her eyes immediately saddened. "I wish we had more time. Not just more hours, more days."

"We will. I promise you."

Reluctantly, Grayson shifted his weight to his knees, then stood off the bed, offering Kipling his hand to bring her to her feet. With a level of control he would have thought impossible moments before, Grayson helped her re-button her blouse, committing to memory the feel of her warm, smooth skin against his knuckles and the pattern of freckles before they disappeared beneath the edge of her undergarments. He admired the delicate flush of her skin along her throat to the curve of her breasts until the final button was closed. Memories might be all he had for quite some time.

With their clothing back in place, Grayson reached for her and bundled her to him, holding her for a few precious moments before his phone interrupted again with a message from Jeffrey that they waited outside for him.

"Time's up?" Kipling said in a rasped whisper when he withdrew the phone from his pocket.

"Regrettably, yes." He looked from the screen to her, hating the shine in her eyes. "Are you sure you want to go?"

"I'm not ready to say goodbye yet."

Grayson slid his hand down her arm and linked their fingers, leading her to the bedroom door, across the small upstairs landing to lead her down to the foyer and front door again. Kip reached for her handbag where it hung by the door, but stopped short. When Grayson realized she'd paused, he took a step to her. "What is it?"

When she looked at him, an expression of either bewilderment or realization – he couldn't be sure – parted her lips and dug a furrow between her eyes. Grayson laid his hand on her shoulder.

"Kipling…"

"Howell," she said. "You said his name is Howell."

"Langdon Howell, yes."

When the furrow eased and her eyes widened, Grayson knew she'd fit together the pieces only someone who had taken time to study the Conan Doyle novels would be able to assemble. Grayson nodded, pressing his lips together before she asked the question, a question she likely already realized the answer to.

"Yes," he said.

"So, he *is* a descendant of Charles Augustus Howell, the man who supposedly inspired the villain Charles Augustus Milverton in the Conan Doyle books." So sure of her statement, the sentence held no lilt of a question.

Grayson nodded once. "Yes, he is. As much as the Holmes bloodline has inspired to continue the legacy of Sherlock, the Howell family has continued their own form of family business. Four generations of criminals, blackmailers, murderers, and heads of organized crime. As time has gone on, and technology has made the world a smaller place, the corrupted touch of the Howell family has expanded all over the globe. And they still carry a hatred and desire for vengeance against the Holmes name."

"So, Langdon Howell is playing this twisted game with you because you're a Holmes?"

Grayson reached for the forgotten handbag, slipping it over her arm to lay the strap on her shoulder as she continued to stare at him, her eyes flittered to the left and right in tiny degrees as she processed the information. "Yes," he finally answered. "Actually, I suspect he believes this new game is an act of justice for Nelson's death."

"But Nelson killed—" She faltered, pinched her eyes closed, and shook her head. "You attacked Nelson because of what he did to Greg."

His heart squeezed, hating the idea she knew his worst sin. Six had left the act as justifiable homicide, that Grayson's attack was one of defense and of necessity, but that had been to shield an officer. Grayson's soul knew the truth. He'd murdered Nelson for Greg's death, even though he didn't believe Greg was gone. Any justification he'd held was mute in his own argument.

"Vengeance is the act of turning anger in on yourself," he cited. "As Goldman said, it may appear to be directed at someone else, but ultimately it is an act of hatred on yourself. It would seem I am trapped in a loop of vengeance."

Kipling said nothing more, but slipped her arms beneath his and wrapped them around him until she pressed her cheek to his chest and closed her eyes, drawing in a deep breath. Grayson held her, resting his jaw against her soft hair. After too short an embrace, but quite longer than Grayson thought Jeffrey would appreciate, he released her; but not before pressing a kiss to her brow. Without speaking again, Grayson opened the front door. He stood on the walkway at the bottom of the three front steps while she shut and locked the front door.

"I'll text Mom to let her know I'll be back later, in case they come home before me," she said after a moment, her voice rough, and dropped her keys into her handbag.

Grayson held his hand out to her when she turned, and supported her down the steps before they walked toward the FBI-provided black sedan. The back passenger door opened and Jeffrey stepped out, leaving the door open.

"Holmes?" he asked, Grayson's name his only form of question.

Grayson drew Kipling closer to his side, so they stood arm to arm. "Jeffrey, this is by far the way I would have preferred you meet. This is Kipling. Kipling, Director Jeffrey Cooper of MI6."

Jeffrey had the good sense to at least look partially contrite as he cleared his throat and extended his hand to Kip. She took it, but Grayson knew her eyes well enough to know her politeness was a strain.

"Kipling is riding to the airport with us," Grayson provided.

Director Cooper's eyes widened and he looked hard at Grayson, who didn't waver. Then with a huff, he turned and opened the front passenger door of the car, taking the seat beside the driver. Grayson motioned for Kipling to slide into the backseat so he could follow.

"Push Watson aside. He's not the least bit pleased at the moment."

In apparent response, Watson wailed, his travel kennel shifting on the seat as he turned circles. Grayson had no doubt Jeffrey had faced a challenge managing to crate the feline, and a small part of him relished the thought. Kipling slid across the seat, pushing the kennel against the far door so she sat in the center, and Grayson beside her, pulling shut the door. Kipling hunched over the kennel, speaking softly to his vexed kitty, sticking her fingers in through the spaces in the door. In moments, Watson quieted. Grayson believed Watson had fallen in love with Kipling as deeply and completely as his owner. With the cat calm again, she buckled her seatbelt and settled against Grayson's side. He raised his arm across the back of the seat so she could be closer, and she laid her head on his chest with a long sigh. He understood the sentiment.

It wasn't until Jeffrey told the driver to go that she said anything, tipping back her head to look at him. "How long will it be before I see you again?"

"No longer than is required," he answered, touching a kiss to her forehead. "However, I know you are tied to Boston for at least a short while until you are finished this term. Am I correct?"

She frowned and nodded. "My passport is up to date, and I'm very tempted to just tag along."

Grayson caught the shift of Jeffrey's head and his glance in the rear view mirror to look at them. Grayson focused on her, and spoke softly, not so loud even she could hear but her eyes automatically shifted to his lips. "Even if you could, it is wisest I see to this situation alone. I hate it, despise it, but the sooner it is resolved the sooner we can work out everything else." He smiled and tapped the end of her nose, trying to find a few moments of normal before he was gone from her. "Besides, the next time I see you, I want to be able to call you Doctor Branson."

A wide smile slowly grew on her lips, and her eyes sparked until he had to ask, "What are you grinning about?"

"Don't you get it? Every Holmes needs a doctor sidekick. And you already have a Watson, you are just getting two for the price of one. Though, I'm not exactly the same kind of doctor—"

Grayson stopped her explanation with a kiss, her giggle vibrating against his lips. They spoke in hushed tones all the way to the airport, which sadly was less than a half hour even with the mid-afternoon traffic. "Give me your phone," he said as signs began to indicate the airport was eminent.

She shifted to draw her phone from her back jean pocket, holding it out to him. "Code zero five three zero."

He took the phone in his right hand, not wanting to move his left arm from around her, and typed in the code. "We must be serious if you're sharing your code. What is the significance?"

"My birthday."

Grayson winked at her. "Duly noted." He opened her contacts, searched his name and found his listing, what she had of it. His mobile number, office and suite contact numbers, and his email. He updated the listing, adding his London address, his parents Sussex address, and his contact numbers back at home. It wasn't easy doing all the typing with his thumb, but the alternative was to let her go and he refused. When finished, he saved and handed it to her. "There. You can reach me in all varieties of ways."

She held the phone, reading over the information, then looked up at him with wide eyes. He knew what part she had reached. "Are you serious?" Grayson nodded, humming an affirmative, and she smiled wide. "You're not serious."

"I just confirmed I am quite serious. Do you think I'd provide a false address? It's rubbish to get the post when you do that."

"Grayson, this address is on–"

"Baker Street, City of Westminster, London."

She shook her head, still grinning. With a clenching pain to his heart, Grayson noted the slowing of the car as they pulled up to the curb outside the international terminal of Logan airport. As soon as he stopped, the driver opened his door and exited, heading to the back of the car to open the boot. Jeffrey opened his door, and looked back at them before hefting himself from the car.

"The driver can't sit and wait," he said, then stood and shut the door.

Kipling turned into him, drawing up her knees so she curled into his side, her delicate fingers holding his jumper over his heart. She pressed her face to his chest and he wrapped her in his arms, pressing his lips to her hair. She sniffed and burrowed closer.

"I don't want to say goodbye," she said so soft and rough he almost didn't hear her.

"We'll not." He settled his cheek against her hair and inhaled the sweet scent of her shampoo and the mingle of fragrances he'd come to know as Kipling's own. "This is just until we–" He drew back and she tilted her chin to look up at him. "Until we can say hello again. No goodbye, just until our next hello."

She smiled, though not completely void of heartbreak. Then she shifted up and kissed him, probably the last proper kiss before he walked into the terminal, so he put his heart into it. He wanted her to have no questions.

The car door opened and the driver stood aside so Grayson could slide free. He stepped out of the car and offered Kipling his hand, leading her to stand beside the vehicle and on the curb while he retrieved Watson, who had begun his protests anew.

"I'll be inside," Jeffrey said from a few feet away. "We've not much time, Holmes. The others are likely waiting."

Grayson nodded and took a step onto the curb, setting down Watson beside his luggage. His entire Boston life was packed in two bags and a cat kennel. Grayson turned to Kipling, raising his hands to hold her face, his heart clenching at the shining tears in her amber eyes. She settled her hands at his waist, but he felt the tremble in her body.

"I will call when I've landed to let you know I've arrived." She nodded, her lips pressed tight together. "Please, sweetheart, believe me when I say this is only until we say hello again. Do you believe me?"

She nodded again, but a tear ran free, slipping into the crevice created between his hand and her cheek. Grayson kissed her again, and told her "I love you," before drawing all his strength to step away. Keeping his gaze on her, he raised the handle of his luggage to draw it behind him, with Watson in his other hand.

At the terminal door, he paused one last time whether for strength or torture. Kipling still stood outside the open car door, her hands clenched in front of her. As soon as he looked, she raised a hand to her lips and kissed her fingertips, turning the kiss out to him. She lowered the two center fingers, so only her pinky, index and thumb were extended. His understanding of manual language was limited, but that sign he knew. He mouthed back, again, so there was no doubt, "I love you."

Then stepped through the doors into the international terminal and his first step toward London.

"Ye a'right, Boss?"

Grayson inhaled a deep breath, the stale and recycled air in the Boeing 777 sticking in his nose, and looked toward Mac in the seat beside him. The interior of the jet was dark, lights dimmed for night travel except for those few who couldn't or didn't sleep and had their overhead lights glowing. In business class, the feel was even more subdued and many had extended their seats out to flat beds. Lynne and Sandra slept on the other side of the aisle, and Jeffrey sat separate from them two rows ahead at the very front of business class; whether by chance or design, Grayson didn't know.

"I'm quite far from okay," Grayson answered truthfully, then offered an unimpressive smile. "But I will be, in time. Right now, there are far more questions than answers, and far more uncertainties than assurances." He sighed and looked out the window into the darkness. "Had someone told me a month ago I would be so reluctant to leave Boston, and the reason for my reluctance, I would have called them a fool. Probably worse, since I believed myself incapable."

"Nae nae capable!" When he paused, Grayson looked to Mac again, who grinned. "Ya jist needed a wee honey tae hing aff yer airm."

Grayson chuckled, a single sound. "I know that's a compliment, but somehow it doesn't sound as such."

Mac bellowed a laugh, and several people stirred. Grayson caught the slight turn of Jeffrey's head to glance back at them, but he turned away just as quickly.

"For what it's worth, Boss, yer Kip'lin seems like a real fine lady."

Grayson smiled and looked back to the big man. "It's worth a great deal, Mac." In the dim light, Grayson still managed to observe the lines of tension and strain around Mac's eyes. "What else is on your mind?"

Mac scoffed and shook his head, but answered anyway. "I'm

worried aboot her, Boss. Yer Kip, that is. Seems Howell wis goin tae play her like a fiddle, but it didna pan oot quite like he wanted. Ye think she's oot o line fire now?"

"The thought has crossed my mind as well," Grayson admitted. The thought, rolling relentlessly through his mind, was what kept him awake now. "But Boston is outside my jurisdiction or power to protect her by any official means."

Mac winked. "Got it in one."

Grayson chuckled and turned away as Mac unfolded the complimentary blanket. Even out flat, the business class seat converted to a bed would be too short for his tall frame, but it was better than trying to squeeze Angus Hennessey in coach. With sleep far from him, Grayson stared out into the night sky over the Atlantic. Hours ago, he'd been anticipating an evening with Kipling, with the threat of returning home a somewhat distant event. How things had changed.

At a point, he'd even entertained the idea Greg was in Boston.

Perhaps Jeffrey and all his superiors at Six were right. Perhaps he was delusional.

But what if he wasn't?

Grayson reached inside the front of his jacket and took his smartphone from his breast pocket, tapping out his security code to unlock it. Now that they were in the air, he could use the in-flight wifi to connect to the Internet, and he opened his personal mail program.

There were a few unread messages, but nothing requiring immediate attention. There was an email from Shirl, the last in a chain of emails going back months. Neither ever bothered to create a new message, just tacking on to the last. Jo had sent an email with the subject line "Reading for Shirl's wedding…opinion?" There were few people he communicated with via email, at least on a personal level. Very little beyond family.

But it was for family he'd opened the program.

Grayson tapped open a new message, and began to type in the recipient field. He only needed to type "KingMc" before the field automatically populated.

To: KingMcQueen@freemail.uk.com2

From: SussexDownHolmes@freemail.uk.com2

Grayson stared at the screen, his thumb hovering over the keyboard. Would this be a final step into denial, or would it be the confirmation he needed? In early days, he'd sent emails to Greg, venting his frustration and confirming his belief Greg was not gone. But they went unanswered, of course. Eventually, he'd stopped the emails and began writing the long letters – though a therapist would more likely define them as journal entries – to Greg and saving them as encrypted and password protected files.

What had been the use?

Before he analyzed himself so extensively he convinced himself otherwise, Grayson took the phone in both hands and typed as rapidly as possible on the small touchscreen.

Subject: The most futile battle is the one never fought

Take care of her, Greg. Please.

Until we speak again,

Ollie

He didn't read it through. He didn't contemplate the ramifications of his choice. He hit send and stared at the screen as the message closed.

Chapter Twenty-Five

"Watson has been absolutely unbearable." Grayson's chuckle carried through her aids, sending a gentle chill up her neck. She closed her eyes to focus on the sound of his voice. "He spends his evenings pacing Baker Street, howling as if possessed by the spirit of some banshee, and I have come home this week to the coverlet tossed from my bed, three pots knocked down from my kitchen windowsill, and a missing slipper."

Kip laughed and shook her head, opening her eyes again. She sat alone in a booth tucked into the corner of the Dunkin' Donuts nearest the university. She had one of her few remaining lecture classes in half an hour, and intended to use as much of her time until then speaking to Grayson that his schedule would allow.

"Why is he being so miserable?" she asked.

"I suspect we suffer from the same heartache. We both miss you."

Kip smiled. "But you're not knocking over houseplants or stealing slippers."

"Ah, would that I could."

Kip laughed loud enough to draw the attention of several people in the coffee shop, and stifled her giggle by pressing her lips together. Five years before, someone speaking alone without a phone to their ear meant they were probably insane; now, most would assume you were on a wireless device. Didn't mean outbursts of laughter didn't seem odd.

Instead, her laugh turned into a yawn that threatened to pop her jaw and squeeze her hearing aids free of their nests. She tried to stifle it, but knew he'd heard.

"You still aren't sleeping," he stated, rather than asking a question.

"I sleep," she said, then added, "Just not well. I will. In time. And before you say you're sorry, don't." She smiled, hoping it carried through her voice. "I want you beside me as much as you want to be, trust me. And it'll happen. Right?"

"Absolutely." The weight of his voice soothed her nerves, which seemed to be on edge most of the time. "I long to say hello."

Heat flushed her skin from toes to nose, and she drew in a slow breath, her heart thumping hard at his not-so-subtle innuendo. "No fair," she said softer. "I'm in public and you're making me blush."

His deep, rumbling chuckle always made her smile. She wondered if she could just listen to him laugh on a continuous loop at night, if it would help her sleep.

"I'm sorry, my darling, but I must go. I have a meeting with the team in a few minutes."

"Oh, did the package arrive?" she asked quickly, wanting to find out before he had to hang up.

"Yes, it did, and Sandra loves it."

"Good." Two days after they left, Kip had been walking past the thrift shop near her apartment and caught sight of a vintage kitchen apron hanging on the window mannequin. Sandra had told her during her stay with Kip that she collected them. Sandra had an avid interest in 1950s Americana. She couldn't resist buying it for the woman she'd grown to consider a friend. She sighed and picked up her near-empty cup, swirling the lukewarm coffee inside. "Can we talk later?"

"Of course."

Kip smiled to herself. "What is my verse for the day?"

"I wondered if you would ring off without asking."

"Never."

"I carry your heart with me. I carry it in my heart. I am never without it. Anywhere I go, you go, my dear, and whatever is done only by me is your doing, my darling."

"E.E. Cummings. Lovely."

"As are you." He sighed. "I must go. All my love."

"I love you, too."

She waited until the line went silent and her aids re-engaged for ambient sound before bringing the cup to her lips and drinking half of what was left of the tepid coffee. The warmth wasn't what she needed; it was the double shot of caffeine to keep her going. She'd only fibbed when she said she slept, because less than an hour at a time hardly constituted sleep. Her doctor had prescribed sleep aids, but Kip balked against taking them. Rather than finding peaceful sleep, she feared sleeping pills would trap her in her nightmares rather than let her wake from them, even if sweaty and out of breath.

Checking the time on her phone, Kip stood and tossed her empty cup in the trash as she passed, contemplating the idea of another. But as much as she needed the caffeine, she knew another cup would leave her jittery and ready to climb the walls. She crossed the street and headed for campus, coming in from the opposite side from the lecture hall that had begun the rollercoaster ride that had been her life the last few weeks. Construction was nearly done, and the hall would reopen before the end of the semester, but she wasn't ready to see the progress. The class had been cancelled for the remainder of the semester, and the university had frozen everyone's grades from the time of the explosion, and no credit would be lost. Her date of graduation wouldn't be affected.

She couldn't say the same for her spirit.

The ramifications of that day were a strange juxtaposition.

Distracted by her need to distract herself, Kip ran into a solid force and gasped, stumbling backward. Two strong hands grabbed her arms, keeping her on her feet.

"Whoa! You okay?"

With her feet solidly under her again, Kip stepped away from whomever she'd nearly bowled over – or who had nearly bowled *her* over, she wasn't sure which – and nodded. "Yes. I'm so sorry. I guess I was off with the fairies."

He laughed, a deep rumble and Kip actually took a moment to see him. Probably mid-thirties, he was a relatively good-looking man with a prominent jawline and striking blue eyes, hazed with gray. Clean cut, his light brown hair hinted at a wave, but it was too short for Kipling to be sure. He was nearly as tall as Grayson, and broad through the chest and shoulders, and she had to take a step back to look him in the face or crane her neck trying.

He smiled, wide and sincere. "I have no idea what that means."

Kip smiled and laughed, waving a hand. "Sorry, it's just something my, um, the mother of a good friend says all the time. It means I was daydreaming."

He squinted and tilted his head. "Hey, you're Kip, right? We had a lecture together with Professor Kelton last semester."

Her post-graduate classes were small, and Kip usually was very good at remembering faces though not always names, but his completely escaped her.

"Yes," she said and made an apologetic face. "I'm sorry. I don't remember you."

"It's okay." He extended his hand. "My name is John."

CONTINUED IN BAKER STREET LEGACY BOOK TWO: THE EMPTY CHAIR

About the Author

Gail R. Delaney is a multi-published, award-winning author of romance in multiple sub-genres, including contemporary romance, romantic suspense, and epic science fiction romance. She always wrote stories as a kid through her teens, but didn't decide to write 'for publication' until her early twenties after the death of her mother. While helping her father go through her mother's papers, she found a box her mother kept with everything Gail had ever written—from book reports to short stories. It was then she realized her mother saw her as a writer, and it was time to live up to her mother's vision.

You can find out more about Gail R. Delaney's body of work at:

http://www.GailDelaney.com

Also by Gail R. Delaney

Contemporary Romance

Something Better

Precious Things

Feel My Love

Fools Rush In

THE FUTURE POSSIBLE SAGA

Book One: Revolution

Book Two: Outcasts

Book Three: Gaining Ground

Book Four: End Game

Book Five: Janus

Book Six: Triad

Book Seven: Stasis

Book Eight: Liber